KINDRED SPIRITS AT HARLING HALL

GHOSTS OF ROWAN VALE BOOK 1

SHARON BOOTH

B
Boldwood

First published in Great Britain in 2025 by Boldwood Books Ltd.

Copyright © Sharon Booth, 2025

Cover Design by Rachel Lawston

Cover Images: Rachel Lawston

The moral right of Sharon Booth to be identified as the author of this work has been asserted in accordance with the Copyright, Designs and Patents Act 1988.

All rights reserved. No part of this book may be reproduced in any form or by any electronic or mechanical means, including information storage and retrieval systems, without written permission from the author, except for the use of brief quotations in a book review. This book is a work of fiction and, except in the case of historical fact, any resemblance to actual persons, living or dead, is purely coincidental.

Every effort has been made to obtain the necessary permissions with reference to copyright material, both illustrative and quoted. We apologise for any omissions in this respect and will be pleased to make the appropriate acknowledgements in any future edition.

A CIP catalogue record for this book is available from the British Library.

Paperback ISBN 978-1-83656-747-9

Large Print ISBN 978-1-83656-748-6

Hardback ISBN 978-1-83656-746-2

Ebook ISBN 978-1-83656-749-3

Kindle ISBN 978-1-83656-750-9

Audio CD ISBN 978-1-83656-741-7

MP3 CD ISBN 978-1-83656-742-4

Digital audio download ISBN 978-1-83656-744-8

This book is printed on certified sustainable paper. Boldwood Books is dedicated to putting sustainability at the heart of our business. For more information please visit https://www.boldwoodbooks.com/about-us/sustainability/

Boldwood Books Ltd, 23 Bowerdean Street, London, SW6 3TN

www.boldwoodbooks.com

For all the ones we've loved and lost. Forever in our hearts.

1

As the train pulled slowly into the station, I felt a pang of regret that the journey had ended so soon. I'd been looking forward to my first ever ride on a steam train for weeks, and it had lived up to all my expectations.

Sitting here in this elegant compartment with its plush, burgundy seats, overhead luggage racks, and sliding door, my heart had soared, along with my imagination, as I'd gazed out of the window at the clouds of steam from the engine and seen myself in another age – one of smart clothes, well-mannered people, and schoolchildren who sat quietly and patiently as the teachers requested, instead of arguing, crunching noisily on boiled sweets, or making sarcastic comments about boring school trips.

The coach journey, from Lowerthorpe Primary School in Leicestershire to the Cotswolds town of Much Melton, where we'd caught the train, had seemed to last an awful lot longer than an hour and a half. I didn't envy the teachers who had to deal with some of these kids every day. I'd only volunteered to accompany the class on this school trip because it was an opportunity to spend time with my daughter, Immi. What with work and school, I hardly saw anything of her these days, so I was hoping this excursion would be a bonding exercise.

I glanced at my little girl, who wasn't so little any longer. Immi had taken no notice of the views from the window, nor had she shown much excitement about travelling on a steam train. She and her friend, Violet, were far too engrossed in the game they were playing on their mobile phones.

I hadn't wanted to get Immi a phone at all, but she'd begged and pleaded, telling me that everyone in her class owned one, and she was practically a social outcast because she wasn't on Snapchat. I'd finally given in and bought her a reconditioned phone last year for her tenth birthday. There's nothing so persuasive as a kid's emotional blackmail – especially when you already have a terrible feeling that, as a mother, you're just not cutting it.

The door slid open, and Immi's teacher, Mr Gaskill, quickly scanned the compartment. A short, balding man in his mid-fifties, he'd always struck me as an amiable sort of bloke, and Immi seemed to like him.

'Everything okay?' he asked. Whether he was addressing me or the six children who were with me, I wasn't sure. Either way, he hurried on without waiting for an answer. 'We're pulling into Harling's Halt now, so can you gather your coats and bags, please? We'll be getting off the train in a minute. When we do, I want you to form an orderly queue on the platform so I can do a head count. Miss Chase, can you see that they do, please?'

He gave me a brief smile as I nodded. 'The bus will leave for Rowan Vale from the station car park. You'll all have ten minutes to use the toilet facilities and ten minutes only, so no loitering, okay?'

He eyed them all sternly to emphasise his point then slid the door shut again, before making his way to the next compartment, presumably to deliver the same speech to its occupants.

There were twenty-four children on this trip, along with the teachers, Mr Gaskill and Mrs Ledbury, another volunteer mum called Diana Goodyear, and me. Each adult had taken responsibility for six children on the train. I could only hope that, between us, we'd manage to keep control of them all when they were let loose in an unsuspecting Rowan Vale.

'Okay, you heard Mr Gaskill,' I said cheerfully. 'Coats and bags, please.'

There were a few chaotic moments as the children grabbed their belongings and headed for the door. I collected a couple of sweet wrappers and an empty crisp packet from the floor, shoved them in my jacket pocket, and followed my charges into the corridor. They'd been joined by their classmates from the other compartments, as well as Diana and Mrs Ledbury, who were chatting animatedly about a new brand of lipstick they'd discovered which, apparently, had incredible staying power and didn't even leave a mark on a cup.

Mr Gaskill called for everyone to follow him. The children jostled and pushed each other a bit, vying to be the first off the train, but overall, they weren't too bad. I brought up the rear, automatically counting all the heads as we moved forward, even though I knew Mr Gaskill would do it again when we disembarked.

Finally, I stepped onto the platform at Harling's Halt and gazed around in delight. I hadn't realised that the station would be part of the Rowan Vale experience, although I should have. It was, after all, part of the Harling Estate which included the village, owned by a man called Sir Lawrence Davenport.

According to the website, when the line between Harling's Halt and the market town of Much Melton had closed in the

1960s, Sir Edward Davenport – Lawrence's father – had stepped in and purchased it, along with a couple of vintage steam trains. The Davenports had operated the private line between the two stations ever since.

Harling's Halt was where many visitors to Rowan Vale began their journey to the village. This was where they'd catch one of the vintage buses that would take them on a ten-minute ride to their destination – a privately owned village nestled on a large estate in the Cotswolds countryside, where modern vehicles were banned, staff dressed up in period costume from several eras, and many of the old buildings were used for their original purpose.

As Mr Gaskill counted the children for a second time, I looked around the little railway station, cheerfully decorated with bunting, hanging baskets, and flowerpots. Signs directed passengers to the Victory Tearooms, as well as a waiting room, ticket office, and toilets. But what really grabbed my attention were the people in period costume on the platform.

'Ooh,' Diana said, 'it's like *The Railway Children*!'

It was a bit, what with the Harling's Halt version of Mr Perks, the station porter, who was pacing up and down in his uniform, looking every inch as if he'd stepped out of the film.

However, despite that, there was no doubt that the station was dedicated to the First World War era. Union flag bunting was strung along the buildings, recruitment posters were pinned to the walls and stuck to the windows of the waiting room, and the faint chorus of 'It's a Long Way to Tipperary' could be heard as if from a distance.

Ladies in ankle-length skirts and dresses and wide-brimmed hats, and many men in First World War uniform, strolled along the platform, while others stood around in groups, chatting. Obviously, they were actors employed by the estate, but I could almost believe they were truly discussing the latest news from the front or preparing to say an emotional goodbye to their loved ones.

This place was already beginning to cast its spell on me. Maybe it would work its magic on the kids too. I glanced hopefully at Immi, but she was chatting to Violet and didn't seem too interested in her surroundings. I sighed inwardly. Well, I thought it was fascinating, even if not everyone appreciated it. Those uniforms looked so authentic.

I jumped as Mr Gaskill said my name loudly, and to my embarrassment, I realised everyone was staring at me.

'Sorry. Yes. No. I mean, what?'

Diana grinned. 'All the nice girls love a soldier,' she whispered, giving me a playful nudge.

'I asked if you or Mrs Goodyear would mind accompanying the girls to the toilets while I escort the boys,' Mr Gaskill explained patiently. 'Mrs Ledbury is going to the pick-up point to check on the travel arrangements to the village.'

'Of course. No problem.'

'I'll go with you,' Diana said. 'I'm getting that desperate, there'll be a puddle on the ground if we don't hurry up.'

'Oh, Mum!' Her daughter Katie's face turned scarlet as some of the boys howled with laughter at her embarrassment.

Mrs Ledbury – who could, apparently, retain water like a camel – headed through the archway to the coach and car park to check if the bus had arrived yet.

Diana, Mr Gaskill and I herded the children to the Ladies or Gents as appropriate. After using the facilities myself, I waited outside for the rest of the girls. Immi and Violet soon returned to the platform, followed by Mr Gaskill and most of the other children. Mrs Ledbury hurried back through the arch.

'The bus stop's at the entrance to the coach park,' she

informed us, 'and the bus is ready and waiting.' She glanced at her watch. 'Maybe we ought to head there now. Would one of you mums mind waiting for the stragglers while we settle the rest of the children on the bus?'

'I'll do that,' I said, glad of the opportunity to take a few more moments to soak up the atmosphere at Harling's Halt.

Immi looked at me uncertainly. 'Shall I wait with you?'

'No, it's okay,' I assured her. 'You go ahead with the others.'

As Diana and the two teachers herded the kids through the archway, I leaned against the wall, feeling genuine contentment. It really was like stepping back in time here, and this was just the station. What would the actual village be like?

It was a gorgeous, sunny day in early April. There were just a few more days until the spring term ended. As well as today, I'd booked next week off work so I could spend the first part of the Easter holidays with my daughter, and I couldn't wait.

Violet's mum, Mel, usually looked after Immi if my working hours clashed with school holidays. She had four children of her own and said one more was no bother. I'd been lucky as the agency that employed me as a carer was very accommodating around the hours I worked, but I certainly didn't get as many holidays as Immi did, and since I was a single parent with little cash to spare on childcare, Mel had been a godsend.

Immi would be going up to secondary school in September, which felt like a huge change in our lives. It was making me think about the future, and the direction I wanted it to go in. My options were limited, but my once dormant ambition was growing like Japanese knotweed. I wanted a job that would give me more time at home but would also pay enough to make life less of a financial struggle. And if I was being really greedy, I'd put a bigger flat for Immi and me on the wish list. Maybe even a house with a garden.

Yeah, right, Callie. Good luck with that.

I mentally shook my head. I was living in a dreamworld. Jobs like that didn't exist. Not for people like me anyway. I could imagine what Mum would have said: *Get your head out of the clouds and concentrate on the real world.*

It was just a shame that the real world wasn't much fun.

The sound of a kerfuffle to my right snapped me out of my daydreams. I pushed away from the wall and stared, open-mouthed, at the sight of two men – one dark haired and one fair – dressed as soldiers angrily pushing and shoving each other at the far end of the platform.

Was this part of their act? Funny sort of act if it was, especially when they must have realised there were children about.

I looked round at the other actors, but they were taking no notice. So it *was* part of the act then? Surely they'd at least look a bit alarmed if not? And 'Perks' was nowhere in sight, so I couldn't ask him.

The stragglers would come out of the toilets at any moment and the last thing I wanted them to see was two grown men in fancy dress having a punch-up. Since no one else seemed remotely interested, it was up to me. Great.

I rushed up to the soldiers, my heart thudding as I noticed the very real anger in the fair-haired man's eyes.

'Excuse me—'

'You're a liar, Ronnie Smith! She wouldn't have looked twice at you. Besides, she was loyal to me was my Lily.'

'Yeah, right. Loyal to all of us was Lily. One at a time, like.'

'You take that back or I'll kill you!' The fair-haired soldier aimed a punch at the dark-haired one. His fist landed on Ronnie Smith's cheek, confirming they weren't acting.

Fancy behaving like that when you worked with the public! What if Immi had waited with me and seen and heard all this?

'Oy! There are children about. What the hell do you think you're doing?'

The fair-haired soldier gave me a fleeting glance then, dropping his fist, he stepped back and stared at me. The one called Ronnie Smith rubbed his cheek and watched me through narrowed eyes.

'Are you talking to us?'

'No. I'm talking to that unicorn over there. *Seriously*?' I added as they both looked round in surprise. 'Look, there are children—'

I noticed the remaining pupils were now on the platform. Mrs Ledbury had returned and was clearly doing another head count. Her gaze fell on me, and she pointed to the arch which led to the car park.

'Bus is leaving in a minute!' she called.

I nodded. 'Be right there.'

As Mrs Ledbury turned back to the kids, I glared at the soldiers, who looked dazed.

'You see? Children. Well,' I said, nodding at the fair-haired man, 'I know he's called Ronnie Smith, but what's *your* name?'

For a moment, he gaped at me, then falteringly he replied, 'Bill. Bill Fairfax.'

'And who's your manager?'

'Our... our manager? You mean our superior officer?'

I rolled my eyes. 'Very funny. I mean who's in charge of you? Who employs you? You must have a supervisor of some sort? Or should I go straight to Sir Lawrence?'

The two men stared at each other, then at me. Were they really that gormless or were they having me on?

Exasperated I said, 'Oh for goodness' sake. Fine, I'll speak to Sir Lawrence then. I'm sure someone can tell me where to find him.'

Slowly, Bill Fairfax said, 'Are you really talking to us?'

'Well, who else...'

But my voice trailed off as I experienced the weirdest feeling. A chill ran up my spine and along my shoulder blades, making me shudder. A vague memory stirred, but I couldn't pin down what it was.

I swallowed, suddenly feeling a bit nauseated.

'Miss Chase, what are you *doing*? The bus will leave without us,' Mrs Ledbury called from further up the platform. She sounded impatient.

I shook my head, wondering what the heck was wrong with me.

'Coming!'

Without so much as another glance at the two actors, I hurried to join the class.

2

The little crimson and ivory vintage bus trundled along the country lanes, and I leaned back in my seat and stared out of the window in delight. My shoulders dropped and the muscles in my neck began to relax. Whatever that weird feeling had been at the station, I was fine now. How could I not be with views like these?

The glorious Cotswolds. Cornflower-blue skies over rolling, green hills, pastures where sheep, cows, and horses grazed, and verges bright with daffodils adding a splash of sunshine to the landscape.

'Are you all right, Callie?'

I turned to Diana, surprised. 'Of course. Why wouldn't I be?'

She shook her head. 'Just wondered. You seemed a bit tense when we left the station.'

Tense hadn't been the word. I wondered what word *would* do justice to the feeling I'd experienced as I'd stood on the platform with those two men. For a moment there, I'd felt real fear, and a weird sensation of familiarity as something stirred within me. Something I used to know. But what?

Then again, I'd always had an overactive imagination. One of my clearest memories of Mum had been her telling me off for it.

'Stop daydreaming, love,' she'd told me repeatedly. 'Start living in the real world. Be *normal*.'

Mr Gaskill leaned towards us from his seat across the aisle. 'What do you think to this bus then? Fantastic, isn't it? A 1946 Leyland Tiger. I checked up on it when I came here to do a site visit.'

Diana rolled her eyes and nudged me.

'Very cute,' I agreed, ignoring Diana. Mr Gaskill was right. This vintage bus was like something you'd see on a period drama. I could imagine it trundling through the Dales on *All Creatures Great and Small*. There was even a conductor wandering up and down the aisle with his ticket machine, having a friendly chat with the kids.

'And wasn't the station great? Those characters in their First World War outfits, and the vintage tea shop! There's another one in the village, you know, with a World War Two theme. It's right by the—' He broke off as, unaccountably, I shivered again. 'Are you all right?'

'To be honest,' I said, 'I was just wondering whether to report those two actors who were fighting on the platform to their boss.'

Mr Gaskill's eyes widened. 'What two actors? Are you sure they were fighting? Maybe it was part of a performance.'

'It wasn't,' I assured him. 'I don't want to get them into trouble but it's not right. They must have seen the kids arrive on the platform and they should have shown more restraint, don't you think?'

'Certainly. Is that what you were doing then? We wondered what was keeping you.'

'Yes. What do you think? Should I report them?'

'I suppose we ought to. It could have got out of hand. You know how fights can escalate, and it would have been a disaster if the children had seen it or been hurt by one of them. Imagine if they went home and told their parents!' He shuddered at the horror of it all. 'Good grief, that would be all we needed. No, there's no question about it, Callie. You should definitely report them.'

'Who to, though?'

'I suppose Sir Lawrence Davenport himself has overall control. After all, it's his estate.' He frowned. 'The booking was made through his office at Harling Hall, so there must be a secretary or a manager or someone. I'll email them when we get back.'

I wasn't so sure that was a good idea. What if Sir Lawrence sacked the actors? I'd hate to have that on my conscience. I knew all too well what it was like to be broke. Of course, they needed to understand that their behaviour was unacceptable, but I didn't want them to end up in the job centre because of me.

'It's okay,' I said, deciding it would be better if I spoke to someone in Sir Lawrence's office in person so I could stress I wasn't looking for him to fire them. 'I'll do it. I'll go to Harling Hall today. I was the one who saw them fighting, after all.'

'Ooh, are we here, sir?'

There was a chorus of excited cries as the bus turned right off the main road and we spotted a large sign at the roadside which read:

Historic Woodland, Heritage Site, Rowan Vale Living History Village

I suspected the excitement was because the kids were dying

to stretch their legs and run around a bit, rather than because they were thrilled to be visiting what was, essentially, a huge museum.

'Settle down, please,' Mr Gaskill said loudly. 'We're nearly there, so I'm sure you can sit quietly for a little longer.'

The bus trundled along a long, straight road, edged on both sides by woodland, which Mr Gaskill told us, rather pompously, was called Quicken Tree Avenue and ran for almost two miles. 'Quicken Tree,' he added, 'is an old name for the rowan. We'll be turning off for Rowan Vale village about halfway down, though.'

'How come there are cars on this road?' Diana asked suddenly. 'Thought they were banned?'

Mr Gaskill gave the patient sigh of one who'd already explained all this to us. 'It's the actual village of Rowan Vale where cars aren't permitted, and there are no coaches allowed on the estate at all – hence the coach park at the railway station. There's a large car park just past the turn-off to the village for visitors who haven't travelled by train.'

'Oh,' Diana said. 'I get it.'

Shaking his head slightly, Mr Gaskill leaned towards me again. 'If you want to visit the estate office first, it's fine by me, but I'll still put a complaint in an email,' he said in a low voice, before settling back in his seat.

The bus turned down a lane on the left-hand side of the road, and I spotted a sign which read:

Rowan Vale Village. Permitted Vehicles Only.

After a few moments, the woodland gave way to open fields and farmland, then some buildings came into sight, and I spotted a church steeple in the distance.

The murmuring from the children grew louder and I noticed Mrs Ledbury shrugging on her jacket in preparation.

'Look, we're passing Harling Hall now.' Mr Gaskill nodded at the window. 'You can pop by later, when the rest of us have our lunch. That okay?'

'Will do,' I said. Who needed to eat anyway?

I peered out of the window, trying to see Harling Hall. I'd skimmed over its description on the estate website but knew it had been built in the late sixteenth century by the Harling family, who owned the village at the time.

The house was surrounded by a stone wall, and the bus passed the gates far too quickly for me to catch more than a brief glimpse of multiple chimneys before it was lost to my sight. I supposed I'd see it up close soon enough.

When I went to cause trouble for two young lads.

And got them fired.

Possibly.

Oh heck, I was a horrible person. Maybe I should have kept my mouth shut after all.

* * *

We'd been in Rowan Vale for just over two hours, and I'd already fallen in love with the village, which was breathtakingly beautiful with its honey stone cottages, thirteenth-century church, and stunning surroundings.

A golden wall of daffodils graced the banks of the River Faran – a shallow body of water, more like a wide stream than a river – which ran through the centre of Rowan Vale, crisscrossed at regular intervals by little stone footbridges. I only wished I could have explored the whole village in depth, but we had a schedule and there was to be no deviation.

The school excursion was focused on two places: Rowan Farm, a real working farm on the outskirts of the village, run as it would have been during the Second World War, and Ashcroft Mill, a former working mill which had now been turned into a museum of life in Rowan Vale over the centuries. It had a whole section devoted to the 1940s, as well as a vintage wartime teashop and a bakery in the building attached to it. Both places, it was felt, would aid the class with their project on home life during the war.

If there was enough time after their tour of the museum, the children would be able to visit some of the shops in the village, which were replicas of ones that used to serve the villagers in bygone eras.

Rowan Farm consisted of a beautiful old farmhouse set in acres of prime Cotswold land. It was, as one of the 'land girls' who worked there explained to the children, a mixed farm, growing crops as well as raising animals.

It had been fun to find two young women dressed in dungarees, sturdy shoes, and dark-green jerseys, playing the role of land girls with obvious relish. The one who spoke to the kids introduced herself as Erin and seemed more than happy to explain about life on a farm in the 1940s. It was good to see Immi listening avidly to her stories.

As well as being shown around the farm, we were taken into the farmhouse itself, which had been decorated exactly as it would have been during the Second World War. There was even a radio playing old music, with the occasional news broadcast interrupting the songs.

The farmer's wife, who introduced herself as Betty, was busy baking bread, and told us all how lucky she felt that, unlike the poor unfortunates in the cities and towns, they were never short of food at Rowan Farm. She made the children laugh as she told them about the day the two land girls had arrived at the farm from the city, 'dolled up to the nines with their fancy nail polishes and their hair all done up, and not a clue about life in the country.'

I noticed the rapt expression on Immi's face as both Erin and Betty told them about the two German prisoners of war who worked there too. She was fascinated by this, and she wasn't the only one. The boys clearly perked up at the thought of German prisoners. I had to admit, Erin and Betty were very convincing. I almost believed the stories were true myself.

We wandered round the farmhouse, noting the old-fashioned decor and furniture, examining the ration books and exclaiming at how little people had to eat in those days. We were then escorted to the adjoining dairy, where the other 'land girl', Rissa, was busy churning butter. After that, the class headed outside again.

We led the children to one of the old barns, which had been turned into a sort of dining room. Union flag bunting had been strung from the beams, and there appeared to be a sort of stage at one end of the building. Picnic tables had been set up for visitors to sit and eat their packed lunches, and we quickly settled the children into their seats. Mr Gaskill and Mrs Ledbury seemed pleased that the class were far more engaged with the visit now than they had been when we arrived.

Just as I was about to dip into my backpack for my lunchbox, Mr Gaskill suggested I might like to slip away to Harling Hall and report his two badly behaved employees at the station to the estate office.

Despite my rumbling stomach, I agreed. Far better that I explained what had happened to the manager, rather than Mr Gaskill sending him an official email. At least I could try to ensure that the two young men were reprimanded but didn't lose their jobs.

'Could you tell Immi where I am if she asks? Although don't mention the fighting soldiers. Just say I've gone to have a quick look around the grounds of the manor house. I doubt she'll ask too many questions.'

'Of course, no problem. Let me know the outcome, though I'm sure a strongly worded email from the school will ensure they take this seriously if appropriate action isn't taken. I'm quite certain Sir Lawrence wouldn't want the reputation of his business damaged.'

Feeling thoroughly uncomfortable, I headed through the farm gates and wandered along the lane back towards the village, the distinctive red-brick chimney of the eighteenth-century mill and the spire of the church my points of reference.

The more I thought about it, the worse I felt. I hated the idea of getting anyone into trouble, especially two young men who couldn't have been more than twenty, if that. I'd have to be very diplomatic with whoever dealt with staffing issues and, while I realised that Ronnie and Bill – if those were their real names – needed to be reprimanded, I really hoped the punishment wouldn't be too harsh. I wouldn't have thought employment was that easy to come by around here.

Lost in thought, I barely noticed I was being followed at first. I gradually became aware of a hum of voices and some giggles, and as the sound permeated my thoughts, I turned to see who was following me.

Two young boys and a girl – probably between six and ten – were creeping behind me and judging by their expressions, they were plotting mischief. As I frowned at them, the girl stuck her tongue out.

I decided to ignore them and carried on walking, but within

seconds, the children had run past and began walking backwards in front of me, pulling faces and mocking me.

I stopped and put my hands on my hips. 'Okay, that's enough of that, don't you think?'

The children straightened, a look of shock on their faces. The boys glanced around as if checking for someone, then turned back to me, open-mouthed. One of them, the eldest, nudged the girl.

'She's talking to us, Florrie.'

'Don't be daft.' The girl sounded dubious. 'Are you?'

'I don't see any other children being rude to me.' I glanced at my watch. Ten past twelve. 'Why aren't you in school?' I asked, noting at the same time that they were all in costume. The boys were in grubby, white shirts that looked far too big for them. They wore equally shabby, buff-coloured trousers but my biggest concern was that only the older boy was wearing shoes – heavy, brown ones with a low heel that appeared slightly too large for him. The younger boy was barefoot. Both had matted, light-brown hair that fell almost to their shoulders.

The little girl looked very different. She had long, black hair in two plaits, and was wearing a cotton print dress, a clearly hand-knitted cardigan, and – of all things – a pair of black wellies. She was clearly supposed to be from the 1940s or 1950s.

Okay, so maybe their parents worked for Sir Lawrence and had dressed their children in costume for the fun of it, but this was surely taking things too far? The little boy shouldn't have been running around without shoes on. And why *weren't* they at school? Unless their Easter holidays started earlier than the ones in our area.

'Don't go to school,' the girl said, tilting her chin defiantly at me.

The boys stared dumbly at me, their eyes wide. They looked as if they needed a good bath.

'What do you mean, you "don't go to school"?' I asked suspiciously. 'Are you home taught?'

'We just don't go. Don't 'ave to. You can't make us.' She grinned widely, revealing a gap between her two front teeth, her eyes flashing a challenge. 'Besides, there'd be no point. These two can't even read, so they wouldn't learn much, would they?'

'They can't...' I frowned. 'Are you having me on? Where do you live?'

'Mind your beeswax,' the girl said. 'Got nuffink to do with you.'

'If you're not at school, and these boys can't read or write, not to mention one of them hasn't even got any shoes on, then it's got everything to do with me. Whether you realise it or not, you need protecting.'

The younger boy's face crumpled, and I crouched down, feeling guilty that I'd obviously scared him. 'Don't look so worried. You're not in any trouble. But I would like to speak to your mum and dad.'

Looking into his big, brown eyes, my heart thumped, and, for some reason, I shuddered. The prickling sensation I'd experienced earlier at the station was back again, along with something else. Something I couldn't quite catch hold of and wasn't sure I wanted to.

The girl yanked the little boy away and said fiercely, 'Clear off and leave us alone. I'm going to tell Lawrie about you. He'll sort you out good and proper.'

With that, the children ran away, leaving me bewildered and not a little worried.

Lawrie? Could that, by any chance, be Sir Lawrence? Well, that had made up my mind once and for all. Things were very wrong in Rowan Vale, and I was going to have strong words with the manager about his staff, not to mention the welfare of their children.

As I carried on towards the Hall, I wondered, with a sudden shiver, why I couldn't get one name out of my mind. The boys had called the girl Florrie, but no one had mentioned what they were called. So why was *David* echoing through my head?

3

FLORRIE

'He is, you know. He's going to kiss her.' John wrinkled his nose. 'If they do, I'm out of here.'

Florrie's eyes narrowed as she watched the man and woman just a few feet away from them, utterly oblivious to the fact that they were under observation by a trio of amused children, who were sitting cross-legged on the grass listening to every word the couple were saying.

Neither Bram nor Rissa had been blessed with the gift, which was a very good thing as far as Florrie was concerned. And luckily, she, John, and Robert had no living descendants or close relatives who might be able to see them either. They were pretty much free to come and go as they pleased, and spying on unsuspecting courting couples was one of the few perks of an afterlife that could, in Florrie's opinion, be way too boring for her liking.

Of course, if all that kissing business started, the trio would always make a hasty retreat. Who wanted to see all that yucky stuff? In her opinion, though, they were safe with Bram and Rissa. Whatever John thought, she was convinced that Dutchman Bram –

who masqueraded as a German prisoner of war – had no interest in the 'land girl' from the farm. He had far more sense than that. After all, he must know she was still sweet on Brodie. Everyone did.

'Is he 'eck,' she said scornfully. 'He don't like her very much at all, and who can blame 'im? Done up like a dog's dinner to work on a farm...'

Her voice trailed off as she recalled her mother's voice suddenly. It had been such a long time since she'd heard it, but just then, her words came back to her with painful clarity. *That Elsie Jones at number four, all dressed up like a dog's dinner. Does she think we're daft? We all know who she's orf to see.*

'Why isn't she at work, anyway?' she finished dully. 'Skiving, no doubt. Someone should warn 'em at the farm about her.'

'I think she's pretty,' Robert said softly. 'All that yellow hair. It's like a cloud of butter.'

'Bleach,' Florrie said dismissively. 'And 'ow can you 'ave a cloud of butter? Are you soft in the 'ead? Anyway, what do you know about it?' She nodded towards Bram and Rissa. 'Look at 'er, staring at 'im, all daft and soppy. Pouting 'er lips like that. Looks like a goldfish.'

She mimed a goldfish opening and closing its mouth, which made Robert laugh.

'Well, I think they'll get married,' John persisted. 'I'm glad. I like it when people are happy.'

'Sometimes,' Florrie said darkly, 'I wonder why I bovver with you.'

'Bet he kisses her in the next couple of minutes,' John said, as if determined to wind her up.

'Ten bob says 'e won't,' Florrie retorted. She wasn't sure how much ten bob was but the way her mum used to go on about the cost of everything, she suspected it was a lot.

'You haven't got ten bob,' John pointed out, which infuriated her so much that she was tempted to slap him.

A moment later, she forgot her anger and gave a triumphant whoop, as Bram got to his feet, bid a casual farewell to Rissa – who gave a heavy sigh before tucking into her packed lunch – and headed off across the field, taking a shortcut back to the farmhouse.

'Ha! Told you! Well, that's twenty minutes we'll never get back,' Florrie said, even though she had no real idea how long they'd been watching the couple. She jumped up, deciding to find something more interesting to do with her time.

'Where are you going?' Robert was soon at her side, as expected.

'Finding something better to do,' Florrie told him, walking directly through the closed gate of the field into the lane. She jerked her thumb behind her. 'Your brother can stay there and moon over 'is girlfriend all he likes.'

'She's not my girlfriend!' John had rushed up behind her, as she well knew, and she thought with some satisfaction that, if he'd been able to blush, his face would be bright red now. He was very easy to embarrass. 'Just cos I said she looked nice once doesn't mean—'

Florrie, however, had lost interest. She'd spotted someone new walking down the lane just ahead of them, and her eyes gleamed with curiosity.

'Tourist,' she said.

The three of them grinned at each other and Florrie began to prance behind the young woman, swinging her arms in an exaggerated fashion and wiggling her hips.

Robert laughed and Florrie responded by flicking her plaits back. She could always rely on Robert's devotion. John was sometimes more difficult to keep in check, but she had ways of dealing with him if he got too independent.

She was momentarily distracted from her thoughts when the young woman stopped and turned round. For a second, Florrie could have sworn she was looking directly at them, but of course, she couldn't be. Just to be certain, she stuck her tongue out at the visitor, who didn't respond but turned and continued walking.

Knowing she was safe, Florrie winked at Robert and John and the three of them ran past the woman, then turned to face her. Walking backwards, they pulled faces and hurled insults at her, mocking her dark-auburn hair, her clothing – she was wearing a black jacket and a pair of jeans, which Florrie knew would make Agnes shudder – and even the way she walked.

Suddenly, the woman stopped and put her hands on her hips.

'Okay, that's enough of that, don't you think?'

Florrie wasn't quite sure what to make of that. Momentarily stunned, she was annoyed when John nudged her and informed her the woman was talking to them.

'Don't be daft.' For once, though, Florrie wasn't so sure of herself. She eyed the woman nervously. 'Are you?'

'I don't see any other children being rude to me. Why aren't you in school?'

Florrie could feel Robert trembling beside her. John murmured, 'Uh-oh.'

Who did this woman think she was, frightening them like that? And anyway, how could she see them? It didn't make sense. Florrie decided the best form of defence was attack.

'Don't go to school,' she said defiantly.

'What do you mean, you don't go to school? Are you home taught?'

Florrie wasn't entirely sure what that meant. 'We just don't go. Don't have to. You can't make us. Besides, there'd be no point. These two can't even read, so they wouldn't learn much, would they?'

'They can't... Are you having me on? Where do you live?'

'Mind your beeswax,' Florrie snapped. 'Got nuffink to do with you.'

'If you're not at school, and these boys can't read or write, not to mention one of them hasn't even got any shoes on, then it's got everything to do with me. Whether you realise it or not, you need protecting.'

Florrie watched, feeling increasingly annoyed as the woman crouched down and spoke to Robert. 'Don't look so worried. You're not in any trouble. But I would like to speak to your mum and dad.'

John swallowed hard and Florrie saw the tears well up in Robert's eyes. How dare this woman mention the boys' mum and dad? What did she want to go and upset them for? Who did she think she was, anyway?

Grabbing Robert's arm she yelled, 'Clear off and leave us alone. I'm going to tell Lawrie about you. He'll sort you out good and proper.'

She almost dragged the boys away, and together, they ran down the lane and through the village before finally huddling together behind the ancient wishing well on the green. Even if the woman came this way, she wouldn't spot them from the path.

Florrie wasn't used to feeling alarmed and she didn't like it.

'How could she see us, Florrie?' John whispered, clearly as scared as she was. 'I thought only Lawrie could see us among the living ones?'

Florrie had assumed the same, and it deeply unnerved her that this stranger had proved her wrong. 'I don't know,' she admitted, hating having no answer for them. She straightened suddenly, determined they weren't going to see any weakness in her. 'But I'm off to tell Lawrie about 'er. He needs to know. Come on, let's go to the big 'ouse.'

Robert and John shrank away. 'We don't go there. You know that.'

'I don't see why not,' she grumbled. 'You're such babies.'

'No, we're not,' John snapped. 'You're just mean. You know why we don't go near the big house. *He* might be there.'

'I've told you loads of times; 'e never comes to the 'ouse. It's not my fault if you don't believe me.' Florrie felt increasingly flustered. Today was not going according to plan. First, some weird woman who could see them, and now John and Robert refusing to do as she said. She wasn't sure what to do about any of it.

Robert sniffed and rubbed his nose and John put a protective arm around his little brother.

Florrie's mouth tightened.

'Oh no!' she cried.

John and Robert jumped in fright.

'What is it? Is it that woman?' John looked wildly around him.

'It's 'im!' Florrie gasped, clutching her chest dramatically. 'It's Pillory Pete!'

'No!' Robert wailed. 'Florrie, make him go away.'

'You'd better run and 'ide,' she said. 'I'll try to distract 'im.'

The boys didn't need telling twice. They took to their heels and fled, leaving a grinning Florrie behind. That, she thought, would teach them. They were too soft for their own good, and she was doing them a favour, really. They'd have to toughen up one day. It wasn't like they were all alone in the world either. Not like her. They had each other, just like Henry and Francis. She had no one.

Watching the boys disappear into the distance, Florrie sighed, then turned towards the house. Time to tell Lawrie about the interloper, and she'd spice the story up a bit just to rile everyone up. Agnes would be furious by the time she'd finished, she thought with some satisfaction.

Feeling a bit better, she fairly sped along the path – a thin, running figure with bobbing plaits and ridiculously out-of-place black wellies.

4

I'd half expected to find the gates to Harling Hall locked, but they weren't. In fact, there was nothing to stop me heading up the drive to the house, and I had to admit, I'd sort of hoped there would be.

I'd taken a long, slow walk there, unable to shake the feeling of dread as I made my way through the village. Now as I approached the imposing Elizabethan manor house, I was half tempted to forget the whole thing, even though I knew I had no choice. It wasn't so much about the actors any longer. I was seriously worried about the welfare of those kids, even if they *had* creeped me out.

Harling Hall was a beautiful, three-storey, E-shaped building, built of golden Cotswold stone, with a multitude of stone mullioned windows, chimneys, gables, and a large, solid, wooden door which loomed up before me all too soon.

I couldn't see any signs directing me to an office, so could only presume it was inside the house. Steadying my nerves, I lifted the heavy brass door knocker and banged it loudly three times against the wood.

After a few moments, the door opened, and I got another surprise. The man who stood there was probably around my age – thirtyish – tall and broad-shouldered, with very dark, curly, close-cropped hair and piercing blue eyes. Wow!

'Er, I'm here to—'

'You'd better come in,' he said curtly, opening the door wide.

Not what I'd expected and, quite frankly, rather rude. Nevertheless, I stepped inside the house, finding myself in an impressive hallway with a flagstone floor and a sweeping, L-shaped staircase to the right.

The man closed the door behind me. Didn't he even want to know who I was or what I wanted? Come to that, who was *he*? Dressed in faded jeans and a white T-shirt, he clearly wasn't the butler. I assumed he must work in the office.

'Come with me,' he said, and led me to one of the doors on the left of the hall.

Wondering if he thought I was here to do some cleaning or something, I followed him into a room that appeared to be a study. The walls were lined with bookcases filled with ledgers and files, and there was a large, oak desk at one end of the room. An elderly man with surprisingly thick, white hair was sitting on a Chesterfield sofa which faced the desk, his mouth curved into a welcoming smile.

'Please, take a seat,' he said, patting the space on the sofa next to him. The younger man said nothing but headed round the desk and plonked himself in the chair, where he faced us both, unsmiling and as far from welcoming as it was possible to be. Wow again, but in an entirely different way. He might be hot as hell, but he was a miserable so-and-so.

I sat down, thoroughly confused by now. 'I'm not here to clean,' I said, in case that's what they were thinking.

The elderly man laughed. 'I'm well aware of that. I should imagine you're here to complain. Am I right?'

I thought that assumption said it all. 'Do you get a lot of complaints?'

'Few, if any,' he said with a shrug. 'But you've had quite a time of it today, what with one thing and another.'

'Is this the estate office then?' I asked hesitantly.

'I suppose it is. I'm Sir Lawrence Davenport,' he said. 'Although, please call me Lawrie. Everyone does. And you are?'

I swallowed. I really hadn't expected to meet the big boss, and it had quite thrown me. 'Callie,' I said. 'Callie Chase.'

'I'm delighted to meet you, Callie. And this jolly chap here is my grandson, Brodie.'

I glanced at Prince Charming, who glowered back.

'Why do I get the feeling you were expecting me?' I asked suspiciously.

'Because we were.' Sir Lawrence's eyes, almost as blue as his grandson's, twinkled with amusement. 'Bill and Ronnie came to see me earlier in rather a state with themselves. I understand you really tore a strip off them. Gave them quite a fright.'

'Yes, well...' I couldn't help feeling a bit annoyed that the two young men had got to Sir Lawrence first, though I couldn't really blame them. They'd have wanted to put their side of the story to their boss before he heard my version of events. 'Look, I don't want to get anyone sacked or anything like that, but they were openly fighting on the station platform. I was with a group of schoolchildren who could have walked out of the toilets at any moment and witnessed the whole thing. Imagine if they had!'

Sir Lawrence nodded gravely. 'Imagine if they had indeed.' He glanced at his grandson. 'Wouldn't that have been something?' When Brodie didn't reply, he sighed. 'Bill and Ronnie are always fighting, I'm afraid. It's what they do best.'

I'd assumed it was a one-off, and I didn't like the casual way Sir Lawrence seemed to accept their behaviour. 'And you think that's okay, do you?'

He didn't answer the question. 'Would you like some tea, Callie?'

'No,' I said, feeling crosser by the minute. He clearly wasn't taking me seriously. In fact, he seemed to find the whole situation amusing. And to think I'd been worried he'd be too hard on his staff! Remembering my manners, I added quickly, 'But thank you. I'll have to get back to the others soon, so can we get on with discussing what happened at the station?'

'Certainly.' He leaned back on the sofa, suddenly more serious. 'Where are you from, Callie?'

What on earth did that have to do with it?

'East Yorkshire, originally,' I said reluctantly. 'But I don't see—'

'Interesting. Have you any connection to the Cotswolds at all? To this area in particular?'

I glanced at Brodie, who was leaning forward, listening intently. 'No. Look, Sir Lawrence—'

'Lawrie, please.'

'Lawrie,' I said uncertainly, 'I really must get back to the kids, but speaking of kids, were you aware that there are at least three school-age children running around this village in period costume? One of them didn't have any shoes on and, quite honestly, both boys were filthy. The girl who was with them told me they didn't go to school, and said the boys can't even read or write. Surely that can't be true?'

'I've already heard about your encounter with the children from Agnes,' he admitted. 'She's not impressed, but then – she only heard Florence's side of the story and the dear child can be a little, er, economical with the truth. Looks like an angel, but

John and Robert don't stand a chance, do they? All the same, I wouldn't worry too much about them.'

I gathered Florence was Florrie, but who the heck was Agnes? And why was Sir Lawrence telling me not to worry? How could I not? At the very least, those children were being neglected, and he didn't seem at all concerned. Neither did Brodie, who sat there, silent and stony-faced, and as much use as a chocolate fireguard.

Sir Lawrence got up, opened the study door, and called into the hallway, 'Agnes, Aubrey, could you spare me a moment please?'

He left the door open and sat down again.

'Forgive me, Callie, but I really do need to see this for myself,' he said kindly.

'See what?' I had no idea what was going on any more. This meeting wasn't going at all as I'd expected. Maybe I should have let Mr Gaskill deal with the matter, as he'd suggested. Sir Lawrence clearly had no intention of sacking Bill and Ronnie so my worries had been for nothing, and now I was stuck here when I could have been eating lunch with Immi. Curse my conscientious nature.

My eyes widened as two middle-aged people entered the study – presumably, Agnes and Aubrey.

The man had dark, grey-streaked hair, almost white at the temples, with a rather impressive beard, moustache and side-burns. He was dressed like a Victorian gentleman in a black frock coat and grey trousers, with a stiffly starched white collar and a wide, blue necktie tied in a loopy bow.

As if that wasn't surreal enough, the woman appeared to have been called from her bed, dressed in a way I could only imagine Mrs Bennet in *Pride and Prejudice* would have been, in a white, cotton nightdress, woollen stockings, and a flannel bed-jacket, brown ringlets peeping out from beneath a white linen night cap.

I almost laughed at how ridiculous this whole thing was, but my amusement quickly died when the woman, who I presumed was Agnes, glared at me with such contempt that I reared away from her in shock.

'Is this her?' she demanded.

'Come now, Agnes.' The man – presumably, Aubrey – patted her arm. 'Let's not overreact. We should hear what she has to say for herself.'

'Should we indeed?' The woman fairly bristled with indignation. 'And I suppose you think it's all right for a perfect stranger to accost our daughter in the street?'

Oh heck, this was all I needed. 'So let me guess. You're that little girl's mother – Florence, did you call her?' I asked, turning to Sir Lawrence. I simply couldn't think of him as Lawrie no matter how much he insisted. He was looking far too pleased with himself, which only annoyed me further. 'I think her friends called her Florrie anyway.'

Agnes tutted. 'Friends indeed! And her name is Florence.'

Sir Lawrence raised his eyebrows at her. 'Why don't you formally introduce yourself to our guest?' he suggested to her. 'This is Callie Chase. She is, indeed, the lady who spoke with Florence earlier.'

'Spoke with her! Is that what she calls it? Downright rude I call it. To speak in such an offensive manner to a child. Have you no manners, girl?' Agnes clearly wasn't in awe of Sir Lawrence. I wondered if she was a relative of his, rather than an employee as I'd first assumed.

'I don't think it's *my* manners you should be concerned with,' I said indignantly. 'If you'd seen and heard the way—'

I swallowed nervously as the man moved to my side, staring down at me with obvious curiosity.

'Well, well,' he said, glancing at Sir Lawrence. 'So, she's the one, eh?'

'It would seem so,' Sir Lawrence told him. 'Not only did she encounter the children, but Bill and Ronnie fighting at the station.'

The man tutted. 'Typical of those two. Shockingly bad behaviour. A disgrace to the uniform.' He studied me for a moment, as if mentally examining me for faults, then gave a little bow. 'Aubrey Wyndham. Very pleased to meet you, Miss Chase. We've been rather anxious of late. Time ticking on and all that. Splendid news that you've been found at last.'

'What do you mean, found?' Quite honestly, I was beginning to wonder if everyone in this village was insane.

'This can't be happening. It's too much.' Agnes groaned. 'It can't be. Not *her*.' She stared down at me with distaste. 'After the way she spoke to Florence?'

'The point is, my dear,' said Aubrey gently, 'she *did* speak to Florence. And to Bill and Ronnie. And we all know what that means.'

'And to you,' Sir Lawrence added. 'I really don't see what more proof we need.' He turned to me, understanding in his eyes. 'You must be thoroughly confused by all this, but I'm so very grateful you came here today. You really are the answer to our prayers.'

Over by the desk, I heard a grunt from Brodie, then he got up and strode out of the study without saying a word. He might have been gorgeous, but he was the surliest man I'd ever met – and that was saying something, given the childhood I'd had.

'Bad form, that,' Aubrey said, shaking his head.

Kindred Spirits at Harling Hall

Agnes sniffed. 'Can you blame him? Answer to our prayers indeed. There must be someone more suitable than her, surely, Lawrie, dear? Mr Wyndham, tell him.'

Aubrey shook his head regretfully. 'Lawrie's quite right. With all due respect, time is running out.' He gave Sir Lawrence an apologetic look.

'Absolutely. I'm eighty-four and I may not have long left to carry this out. Callie fits all the criteria. I must do this, Agnes, I'm sorry.'

By now, confusion had started to give way to genuine fear. Either this lot were putting on one heck of a show for me or they all needed serious psychiatric help. I decided that whatever was going on in this village, I was leaving. Maybe I'd judged Brodie too harshly. Maybe he felt the same way and that was why he'd left so abruptly.

I got to my feet. 'I can't stay here any longer. The school will email you, but right now, I need to get back to the kids.'

'Good,' said Agnes.

'But you can't,' Aubrey protested.

'Callie, could you please spare a few more minutes?' Sir Lawrence pleaded. 'I wouldn't ask but this is so important.'

As I shook my head and moved forward, intent on getting out of there fast, Agnes stepped in front of me, her arms folded. 'Rude! Sir Lawrence is speaking to you, girl!'

I was now in no doubt that everyone in Rowan Vale was bonkers.

'Sorry,' I told Agnes, 'but I'm a busy woman.'

I put my hand on her arm to gently but firmly manoeuvre her out of the way, but my hand grasped only air.

I was clearly hallucinating.

I tried again with the same result, and suddenly, that awful feeling returned. The prickling sensation. Icy fingers running down my spine and across my shoulders, making me shudder.

David!

5
———

I barely had time to register the name or give any thought to what it meant as Agnes gave me a smug look and said, 'You won't budge me. Just try it.'

Overwhelmed by a feeling I couldn't put a name to, I dropped back onto the sofa.

Aubrey tutted. 'Really, Agnes, you could have been gentler with her.'

'After the way she spoke to Florence? I think not, Mr Wyndham, and I would thank you to put your daughter first for once!'

Aubrey cleared his throat but said nothing. Tentatively, I reached out to touch his sleeve. When my fingers passed through it, I gasped and covered my face with my hands.

'Oh, God! I've lost the plot!'

'Not at all,' Sir Lawrence said kindly. 'You have nothing to be afraid of, I promise you.'

Slowly I spread my fingers and peered out at him. 'Are you a ghost?' I asked him fearfully.

In reply, he patted my arm. He was solid. Real.

As for the other two...

I reluctantly lowered my hands. 'But these two are,' I whispered. 'Aren't they?'

'Let me introduce you to Aubrey Wyndham and his wife, Agnes Ashcroft.'

'His wife?' I thought that a bit odd. She appeared to be dressed in Regency or Georgian style, whereas he was almost certainly from the Victorian era. So how did that work? And how could Florrie be their daughter when she was obviously from the 1940s or 1950s?

They must have recognised the doubt in my voice because Agnes scowled and Aubrey shuffled awkwardly as Sir Lawrence said hastily, 'That's right. Look, Callie, what about that cup of tea now?'

I couldn't reply. Fear and confusion seemed to have robbed me of all ability to speak.

Sir Lawrence seemed to take that as a yes. He went to his desk and pressed a button. Within minutes, a young woman with long, dark hair entered the room. She glanced at me, obviously curious, but said nothing other than, 'Yes, Lawrie?'

'Two cups of tea, please, Mia. And some of those biscuits we had yesterday if there are any left.'

'You'll be lucky, but I'll see what I can do.'

As Mia left the room, he smiled at me. 'Brodie's very partial to them. Hopefully, he's left us one or two.'

'Is Mia – I mean, is she...' Nope, I couldn't finish that sentence. It would sound crazy. Maybe I *was* crazy? None of this could be real, after all. 'There's no such thing as ghosts,' I said firmly, blushing as I realised I'd said that out loud. I couldn't even look at Agnes and Aubrey. If I didn't see them, they weren't there.

'Really?' Sir Lawrence asked, suddenly serious. 'You're sure you believe that? You've honestly never encountered this sort of thing before? Think carefully, Callie.'

There it was again – that weird feeling that I was missing something. A memory that I couldn't quite grasp...

'David,' I said slowly.

'David?' he asked eagerly. 'Who's David?'

'Nothing. No one. A dream.' I shook my head frantically as a sudden memory flashed through my mind, released from somewhere I'd imprisoned it long, long ago.

'A dream? Tell me about your dream.'

I bit my lip. Talking about it would make it real, and it wasn't real. He was just an imaginary friend at best. Someone I'd made up when I was a little girl, perhaps three or four years old. A young boy who waited for me every night at the bottom of the stairs. A tousled-haired boy of around my age, wearing a blue dressing gown and stripy pyjamas.

'All kids have imaginary friends,' my mum had said desperately.

'I never did,' Dad had replied, giving me a disgusted look. 'It's weird, that's what it is.'

How had I forgotten David?

'The girl will never fit in.' Agnes's tone was dismissive. 'She's not right.'

And just like that, another memory unlocked. Dad queueing at the cafe in a department store while Mum browsed the school uniform section. Me, five years old, sitting at a table, happily chatting to a kindly, elderly woman who'd joined me. Dad almost dropping the tray when he returned to find me deep in conversation with a person he couldn't see, even though he was standing right next to her.

'She's not right in the head,' he'd told my mum furiously as we drove home.

'She's just got an overactive imagination,' Mum had said anxiously. 'She can't help it.'

'It's not her imagination,' Dad snapped. 'She's weird. She's not bloody normal! The apple doesn't fall far from the tree, does it?'

'Please, love,' Mum had begged me that night, as she tucked me up in bed. 'Please, just try to fit in. Just be normal. For me.'

And I had tried, I really had. I'd ignored anyone who gave me that strange, icy feeling. I stopped going to the top of the stairs each night, and I never saw David again. And after Mum died, when I was six years old, the ghosts stopped bothering me. So successfully had I suppressed this strange ability that it had deserted me. I'd literally given up the ghost, and eventually I'd forgotten I'd ever been able to see them.

'She has no breeding. Tell her, Mr Wyndham,' Agnes continued. I forced myself to look at her. To acknowledge her existence.

'Well, er...' Aubrey cleared his throat again. 'Look here, Agnes, I know this isn't what we expected—'

'She's just a chit of a girl!' Agnes shook her head decisively. 'This is a job for a man! Oh, if only Brodie had the gift. Such a nice young man. So personable. I would have enjoyed conversing with him, of that I am quite certain.'

Aubrey patted her arm. 'Now, don't upset yourself. We must make the best of things. Brodie cannot help us and that's all there is to it. Sad business, but there it is.'

'What can't Brodie help you with?' I asked, drawn into the conversation despite myself.

'With all this of course!' Agnes cried. 'With the house – our beautiful house. And the entire estate. It's too much, Mr Wyndham. I'm going to my room to lie down. I have one of my headaches coming on.'

'Quite right, my dear. Best thing to do in the circumstances,' Aubrey assured her.

'Ghosts get headaches?' I asked, genuinely confused.

Agnes hurled one last look of disgust at me and swept out of the room.

Aubrey shook his head. 'She's a woman of fine feeling, I'm afraid, and this has come as quite a shock to her.'

'*She's* shocked?' I muttered. 'Have you any idea how *I'm* feeling right now?'

Bloody hell, I was really doing this, wasn't I? I was actually making conversation with a ghost.

'Well, yes, quite,' Aubrey said. 'I can imagine. I well recall the day I—'

'Aubrey, perhaps you'd be kind enough to let Callie and me have a little talk,' Sir Lawrence suggested tactfully.

Aubrey straightened. 'Of course, Lawrie. I'll leave you to explain.' He nodded at me. 'Very pleased to have met you. I'm sure I'll be seeing a lot more of you. Good afternoon.'

With that, he strode purposefully from the room, leaving me to question Sir Lawrence over just what he'd meant by that remark.

'Why would he be seeing a lot more of me?'

He was saved from answering as Mia returned, carrying a tray with two cups of tea, a jug of milk, a bowl of sugar, and a plate with three chunky, chocolate-covered biscuits on it and a few custard creams. Evidently, then, she was as real as Sir Lawrence.

'I've had to improvise as I'm afraid that's all we have left,' she said, giving him a knowing look. 'It was a full packet yesterday. If I were you, I wouldn't buy them again. They only get eaten.'

'That's what they're there for,' Sir Lawrence said, sounding amused. 'Thank you, Mia.'

She nodded but paused as she looked directly at me through black-fringed, grey eyes.

'So, you're the one then?' she asked, in a voice that sounded posh enough for her to be related to Sir Lawrence.

'The one?'

'I'm very much hoping so.' Sir Lawrence confirmed. 'We're about to have a little chat so I can explain everything.'

Mia took the hint. She gave me a sympathetic smile and said, 'Good luck with it all,' then left the room, closing the door behind her.

'Mia is my housekeeper,' Sir Lawrence explained, reaching for a custard cream. 'She's also a splendid cook, and does some secretarial work for the estate too. We'd be lost without her.'

I sank back in the sofa and groaned. 'Why is she wishing me good luck? And what did she mean, *the one*? Am I dreaming?'

'I'm afraid it's all too real,' Sir Lawrence said cheerfully. 'Do help yourself to milk and sugar, although I find it's best taken just as it comes.'

It occurred to me that maybe low blood sugar was causing hallucinations. I hadn't eaten lunch yet and I'd skipped breakfast entirely. Maybe I ought to have a biscuit, just to be on the safe side.

'I think perhaps I should start at the beginning.' Sir Lawrence gave me an approving look as I stirred sugar into my tea.

'That would be useful,' I agreed, adding a splash of milk for good measure.

'How to explain?' He sipped his tea – black without sugar – thoughtfully. 'No one ever had to explain it to *me*, you see. I grew up here, knowing all about it, as did my son and grandson. If things had worked out as we'd hoped, I wouldn't be in this position, but unfortunately, fate had other ideas. I now realise I haven't prepared for this day at all. I really don't know where to start.'

I tried to focus on the chocolate biscuit I was frantically crunching. Sugar was supposed to be good for shock, and God knows, I'd had a few of those today. I wished he'd hurry up and get this over with so I could get out of here.

When he didn't speak, I said, 'I can't stay here all day, so what is it you want to explain? About how, somehow, I've met two ghosts today? That might be a good place to begin.'

'Two?' Sir Lawrence put down his cup. 'But surely you realise, my dear, that you've met at least seven ghosts today to my knowledge.'

I yelped as I bit my tongue instead of the biscuit.

'Thorry, wha'?'

He held up his hand, counting on his fingers as he reeled off the names. 'Agnes, Aubrey, John, Robert, Florence, and, of course, Ronnie and Bill. They were the ones who tipped me off about you. They couldn't get over the fact that you spoke to them. It's not often they agree on anything, but they certainly agreed you could see and hear them both, and they ran all the way here to tell me the news.'

I stared at him, my stomach swishing around nervously. 'Just how many ghosts are there in this place?'

He shrugged. 'Hard to say. Not all of them come into the village itself and some like to keep themselves to themselves, making their homes on the fringes of the estate. It's hard to keep track.' He leaned towards me. 'We think it might have something to do with the ley lines, you know.'

'Ley lines? But that's just airy-fairy stuff. It's not real,' I said scornfully.

'Really? You mean, like ghosts?'

Point taken.

'Rowan Vale and Harling's Halt are on a ley line. And a little further south of the village, in the centre of the estate, where four ley lines criss-cross each other, is the Rowan Vale Barrow and, nearby, the Wyrd Stones.'

'Oh well, that explains everything.'

He laughed. 'Have you heard of the barrow and the stones, Callie?'

'Nope. Oh, hang on. I saw a mention of them on your website, but to be honest, I didn't click the links, so I only skimmed what was on the home page.'

The barrow, I recalled, was where a bunch of skeletons had been found, dating from thousands of years ago, marked by four stones known as The Guardians. The Wyrd Stones were a large circle of Neolithic stones, and a separate, huge monolith standing in a different field. I should have paid more attention.

'I just quickly looked at the things I knew we'd be visiting, like the farm and the mill museum.'

'Ah yes, with the children. Are you a teacher?'

'No.' I blushed. 'Actually, I'm a carer. I go into people's homes and make sure they're okay. You know – clean and fed, and that they have any medications they need. That sort of thing. I'm here as a volunteer because it's my daughter's class who are having the school trip.'

His eyes lit up. 'You have children? Is your husband here, too?'

'Just Immi. She's ten,' I said. 'And there's no husband.'

'I see. And does Immi share your remarkable gift?'

I could feel my blood pressure rising, indignant on Immi's behalf that he'd assume such a thing.

'No,' I said crossly. 'She's perfectly normal, thanks very much.'

'And you're not?'

'There's nothing normal about being able to see ghosts, is there? Talk about bad luck.'

'Well, I suppose that depends how you look at it. Personally, I've always felt very fortunate that I've been blessed with this gift, and extremely sad for my son and grandson, who weren't.'

'I'm not feeling very fortunate,' I told him. 'And to be honest, I'm still half convinced I'm dreaming this entire thing. Or maybe there's something in the water around here.' I eyed the cups dubiously. 'Are you sure that's just tea?'

'Darjeeling,' he said, sounding amused.

I wrinkled my nose in disgust. Not even Yorkshire Tea? Could things get any worse?

'I can see this is a lot to take in,' he admitted.

'A lot to take in? You haven't told me anything yet! What have Aubrey and Agnes and the rest of them got to do with ley lines?'

'We're not really sure,' he admitted. 'But we believe they're connected. Our ancient ancestors were far more in touch with death than we are today. Why did they construct the barrow in that spot? Why erect a stone circle and an enormous monolith there? We don't know but there must have been a reason.'

I managed a feeble laugh. 'Can't you ask them? Are they not still hanging around?'

'Unfortunately, we have no prehistoric ghosts,' he said, sounding regretful. 'Or, if we have, they haven't made themselves known to us.'

'Shame,' I said sarcastically.

'Indeed. Our oldest ghost, as far as we're aware, is Quintus Severus. Charming chap, if a little reclusive. A Roman centurion who died in the second century. Of course, the barrow and the stones were here long before then so he's as clueless as we are.'

I gaped at him. 'A Roman centurion?'

'Anyway, the point is, we think the barrow and the stones

were placed there because our ancestors knew of the power of the ley lines, and that, somehow, they were connected to death and the afterlife. How else to explain this estate? Of course, most of the residents move on after death, but there's an extraordinary number who remain. And that's where we come in. The owners of this village. First the Harlings, then the Ashcrofts, the Wyndhams, and the Davenports. Naturally, there may have been others before the Harlings, but they are the first family to be recorded – in the Domesday Book, actually. Built this house in 1588. Then, of course, it all went wrong.'

'What did?' Despite asking myself if I really wanted to know, the fact was, I did. I couldn't deny I was intrigued.

'The gift was lost. You see, Callie, the veil between the worlds seems to be thinner here. Many of our living residents are able to see the ghosts of their own blood relatives, but their gift is limited to that. Unfortunately, not every ghost has surviving family members. Those poor souls would be unable to communicate with any living person, making things very difficult and frustrating for them, if not for the fact that every owner of this estate has had the ability to see and communicate with *all* the ghosts here. No one knows when that started, but the gift seems to be passed on through the generations.' He sighed. 'Until it isn't.'

I guessed he was thinking of his son and grandson.

'And what happens then?'

'For hundreds of years, the Harling heirs had the gift and life went on smoothly in the village. Then Joshua Harling was born and, as he grew, it became obvious that, for some unknown reason, he didn't possess the abilities of his forefathers. Worse, when his children were born, not one of them could see the ghosts either.'

I realised I was sitting on the edge of the sofa, gripping the handle of my cup as I listened intently to his story. How had that happened?

'So, what did they do?'

'What they had to. There was no choice. There was a farm labourer in the village. A chap called Benjamin Ashcroft. Word reached the Harlings that he had the gift, so Joshua Harling did the only honourable thing. He sold the village to him for ten pounds.'

'What? But why?'

'It's said that the owner of Rowan Vale must possess the gift. If it skips two generations then the village must be sold to a person who *does* possess it, in case it never returns to the family.'

'But how could a farm labourer afford ten pounds?' I asked incredulously. 'It would have been a fortune to him.'

'The entire village chipped in. Rich and poor alike gave him money – whatever they could spare.'

'Why would they do that?'

'Because they all knew how important it was. The owner of Rowan Vale *must* be able to communicate with the ghosts. You see, they are as much in our care as our regular tenants. If we can't see or hear them, how do we make sure they're happy? And an unhappy ghost – well, can you imagine? How would you like to be miserable for eternity? They have rights, too, you know. Life isn't only for the living.'

'Fair point.' I could hardly argue. 'Even so, I'm guessing this Ashcroft man's family also lost the gift at some point. Oh! Ashcroft? Is he related to that old— I mean, to Agnes?'

Sir Lawrence gave me a knowing smile. 'He's related to Agnes's husband.'

'Aubrey? But I thought—'

'Her first husband.' He gave a little cough. 'We'll discuss that another time.'

'So, after the Ashcrofts, it went to the Wyndhams – Aubrey's family?'

'That's right. After them, my great-grandfather purchased the estate.'

'How much did he pay?' I asked, taking a sip of tea. 'I mean, if you don't mind telling me.'

'Not at all. Ten pounds.'

'Ten quid?' I spluttered. 'Have you never heard of inflation here?'

'Ten pounds is what the Harling Estate sells for. That's the way it is and the way it will always be,' he said firmly. His expression softened. 'I presume, Callie, that you can raise the sum of ten pounds?'

I laughed. 'I think I can just about manage it. Why? Are you going to sell it all to me?'

He didn't reply but the way he raised an eyebrow and met my gaze steadily was enough to give me my answer. I put my drink on the floor, my hands shaking so much that the cup clattered hard on the saucer.

'You're having me on,' I murmured.

'Callie, this isn't easy for me, but with neither my son nor my grandson having the gift, I've had to accept that the time of the Davenports is over. The estate must be sold to someone who has the gift. I'm eighty-four and—'

'Oh no. No!' Panic rose up in me. 'I'm not the person you're looking for. You've got this all wrong.'

'I admit, I'm perplexed. The successor has always come from the village. But no such person has been found and I was beginning to despair. Today, when Bill and Ronnie came to me and told me about you, I knew my prayers had been answered.'

'No,' I repeated, my heart thudding. 'I'm really not. I mean, I can't. I just can't. I'm... I'm *normal*!'

'Callie,' he said gently, 'if you don't do this, I honestly don't know what will happen to Rowan Vale, or to my tenants. The ghosts need to be able to communicate with the living. They need a voice. They need someone to hear them. All of them. This village is their home, and they should have a say in how it's run, as well as the security of knowing there'll always be a place for them here. Please, think about it. For just ten pounds, all this can be yours, and you can bring peace of mind to so many souls.'

'You're serious, aren't you?' I stared at him in dismay. 'My God, you really mean it.'

'Callie Chase, I'm making you a formal offer. You can purchase my entire estate for ten pounds and start a new life here at Harling Hall, as well as ensuring the security of Rowan Vale and its tenants for the foreseeable future, or you can walk away and leave us to face whatever happens next. What's your answer?'

6

FLORRIE

Florrie was sitting at the kitchen table, her chin propped in her hands as she surveyed Brodie and Mia, who were having a serious discussion.

Florrie quite liked Mia, despite her having a posh accent. She didn't think Agnes was so keen, but since Mia had practically taken over the running of Harling Hall since she'd arrived here a few years ago, maybe Agnes was just jealous.

Florrie had obviously never tasted any of Mia's cooking, but she'd smelled it every day and, if she'd been able to produce saliva, she had no doubt that her mouth would have watered frequently. She'd caught the scent of the sauce as she'd walked down the stairs a few minutes ago, and it had led her to the kitchen as surely as if she'd been led by the Pied Piper's music.

Skipping through the door, she'd plonked herself on a chair and watched Mia at work, wishing with all her heart that she could taste the food for herself, and daydreaming about what she'd most like Mia to cook for her if that impossible dream was ever realised.

Brodie had entered the room not long after, jerking Florrie

out of her pleasant thoughts of juicy roast beef, crispy roast potatoes, warm bread straight from the oven, and – oh, imagine the *bliss* – jam roly poly and custard!

'He's in a real state,' Brodie had announced without preamble. 'Honestly, I could throttle that woman. What was she playing at, turning down an offer like that? Who does she think she is?'

Florrie nodded in agreement. She'd asked herself the same question after Lawrie had announced to the household yesterday that the stupid woman had said no. Not that she wanted her to take over Rowan Vale, and she certainly didn't fancy sharing a house with her of all things, but even so, she'd had no right to refuse Lawrie's request, and him being so generous an' all. Some people didn't know which side their bread was buttered.

'I suppose she had her reasons,' Mia said mildly. She tasted the sauce she'd been stirring and nodded in satisfaction. 'Perfect.'

Florrie sighed enviously. She'd just bet it was!

'What reasons could she possibly have to turn down an offer like that? It's like turning down the winning lottery ticket. I mean, how else are you going to get your hands on an entire estate, complete with country manor house to live in, all for a tenner? She must be insane.'

Mia turned and smiled at him. 'I thought you'd be glad about it.'

'I am. I was. I mean...' Brodie shook his head impatiently then sat down in the chair opposite Florrie. He rubbed his chin and sighed. 'Honestly, Mia? I don't know what to think.'

'Clearly, you think she made a mistake and that Lawrie needs her. And you're right. We all need her.'

'Well, you don't sound very rattled about it.'

'Why should I?' Mia shrugged. 'She said no. What would be the point of stewing over it?'

A distant memory of her mother's stew and dumplings popped into Florrie's mind, distracting her for a moment. She forced herself to pay attention as Mia continued.

'You know, from what Lawrie told me, you were hardly welcoming to her, which can't have helped. She'd just had a heck of a shock with all that stuff sprung on her. The very least you could have done was be polite, instead of storming out of the room.'

He gave her a stricken look. 'Is Grandpa blaming me? It's not my fault she doesn't know a bargain when she sees one.'

'You tell 'er, Brodes,' Florrie muttered. 'None of us wants that woman 'ere, anyway.'

'Whether you want her here or not...' Mia paused and seemed to steady herself. 'Look, we *need* her. Lawrie needs her. The villagers need her. The ghosts need her.'

'No, we don't,' Florrie said with feeling. 'We can manage just fine without her.'

'Because at some point,' Mia continued, 'and I hate to say this, believe me – but at some point, Lawrie isn't going to be here any longer, and then what will happen? You might have helped persuade her. It's a lot to ask of her – uprooting her and her daughter's lives to move here. If you'd been a bit gentler, she might not have wanted to escape as quickly as possible.'

'So, this *is* my fault?'

'No, but... you didn't exactly help, did you?'

Brodie sighed. 'You're right. I was an idiot. But how do you expect me to feel, Mia? This is my home. My life! Do you really think I can just act as if nothing has happened? As if the fact that I'm about to be turfed out of the place I love means nothing?'

'Look,' Mia said kindly, 'I get it, really I do. Giving up the estate means you'll both have to leave it completely. It sucks, and it makes no sense to me or to you. But...'

'But that's what always happens when the estate changes hands, and we all know Grandpa is a stickler for the traditions.'

'Florence, there you are, dear.'

Florrie looked round, irritated, as Aubrey entered the room and headed straight to her. 'Your mother was looking for you. You're supposed to be having elocution lessons, remember?'

'Elocution lessons!' Florrie gave a dismissive snort. She'd been learning to speak "proper" since she'd first found herself in Agnes and Aubrey's care, and much good it had done her. Who wanted to sound like Agnes? Besides, she was trying to listen to Brodie's reply and Aubrey was making that very difficult. 'And she's not my mother,' she added for good measure, her annoyance getting in the way of her compassion.

Aubrey looked deeply wounded and Florrie felt a pang of guilt.

'Sorry,' she said. 'I didn't mean that.'

Aubrey sat next to her and his hand folded over hers. 'As far as Agnes and I are concerned, you're our child. I know you had a real mother and father once upon a time, but we've done our best to take care of you ever since... that dark day. We think of you very much as ours, and I'm sorry if you don't see it the same way.'

'I do! Honest, I do. It's just...' Florrie sighed. 'I don't know. Sometimes, just sometimes, I remember...'

Aubrey squeezed her hand. 'I know, my dear. I know.' He glanced over at Mia and frowned. 'What are you doing here anyway?'

Florrie shrugged. 'I like to smell her cooking. It's ever so nice. And then 'e came in,' she added, nodding at Brodie, 'and I wanted to know what they were talking about.'

'It's terribly bad manners to eavesdrop,' Aubrey told her sternly.

'Oh, codswallop! Not like they know about it, is it?' Florrie said, thinking it was perfectly reasonable to listen in on people's conversations providing they weren't aware of the fact.

Aubrey looked nervous. 'I still think—'

He broke off as Brodie pushed back his chair and thumped his fist on the table.

'Good lord,' Aubrey said, startled.

'It's that Callie woman,' Florrie confided. 'He's in a proper tizz cos of her turning down Lawrie's offer.'

'Yes, well. Even so...'

'Oh, do calm yourself,' Mia said, sounding perfectly calm herself. 'It's no use getting worked up about things, is it? What will that solve?'

'I've really messed this up! Grandpa's aged ten years, and he could hardly afford to do that. This is an impossible situation. I don't want her here, Mia. I just don't.'

'Callie? Or anyone?' she asked shrewdly.

'Good question,' Aubrey said, nodding.

Brodie slumped. 'I don't suppose it would make any difference who it was,' he admitted grudgingly. 'The fact is...'

Mia nodded, understanding in her eyes. 'The fact is, you want it to be you.'

'Is that so wrong?' he pleaded.

'Of course not. It's perfectly natural. I'm quite sure everyone here would want that, too, if it were only possible. Unfortunately, Brodie, it *isn't* possible, so now we must look at the bigger picture and think what's best for the Harling Estate. And what do you think that is?'

'Getting Callie back,' he said dully.

'Oh no, Brodes! Don't give in that easily!' Florrie cried, as Mia and Aubrey chorused, 'That's right.'

'So, what are you going to do about it?' Mia continued.

Brodie glanced around helplessly. 'No idea.'

'Really?'

'Okay. Find her. Talk to her. Persuade her that her taking over the estate is what we all want, and that it will be the best thing she'll ever do.'

'Good answer,' Mia said, giving the sauce one final stir before turning off the heat. 'So how are you going to do that?'

'Don't listen to 'er, Brodes,' Florrie advised. 'We don't need no living soul to boss us about. We can manage fine without one.'

'Hush, dear,' Aubrey said gently. 'I'm afraid that's just not true.'

'The booking!' Brodie said suddenly. 'They booked a school visit, didn't they? If we can find out which school it was, we might be able to trace a Callie Chase in that area. I'll go to the study and—'

'No need.'

Mia fished in her apron pocket and brought out a mobile phone. Florrie craned her neck, eager to see it in action. How she wished she'd had a mobile phone when she was alive. She'd have been able to keep in touch with her mum, and then maybe she wouldn't have felt so isolated when they packed her off to this place.

Then again, she thought bitterly, her mum had no doubt been far too busy with Janet, so wouldn't have had time to talk to Florrie anyway.

'We received a rather stroppy email this morning from a teacher called Mr Gaskill at Lowerthorpe Primary School in Leicestershire,' Mia was saying. 'He complained that one of the parents accompanying pupils on a school trip to the village yesterday had witnessed an altercation between two actors playing First World War soldiers at the station. The parent was a Miss Callie Chase.'

Brodie grinned. 'And did you reply?'

'Naturally. I assured him that the two men in question would be disciplined and that we'd take care that nothing like this would ever happen again. I also asked if it would be possible to have Callie's home address so the estate can send her some flowers as an apology.'

'He'll never fall for that!'

'Do you want to bet? To my utter horror, he gave me her address immediately. I think we should tip her off about that. The man's an idiot.'

'Wow. That was easy! I thought we'd have to spend days trawling social media or something,' Brodie said.

'Perhaps we should give her a few days to calm down and think about Lawrie's proposal,' Mia mused. 'Give her the chance to think what's on offer rationally before you go round there putting more pressure on her.'

'Excellent plan,' Aubrey said approvingly.

'What's social media?' Florrie asked.

'I'm not entirely sure,' he admitted. 'But from what I can gather, it's not something that you or I should be part of. Now,' he said, gently pushing her plaits back over her shoulders, 'are you going to come upstairs and see your— Agnes? I will try my best to get you out of elocution lessons. Perhaps we can do something else instead? Maybe you and I can go for a walk around the grounds?'

Florrie thought he had the kindest eyes she'd ever seen, and knew he was doing his best, even if she wasn't always appreciative of the fact.

She smiled up at him. 'Okay. Thanks.'

As she dropped a kiss on his cheek, the light in his eyes and the delight in his face was enough to convince her to head upstairs, even if he couldn't manage to get her excused from Agnes's interminable lessons.

It really didn't take much to keep them both happy, she reflected, heading out into the hall with her hand in Aubrey's, and really, it was always worth keeping them onside.

Bless 'em, they were old and needed some sunshine in their afterlives. She just felt sorry for 'em.

That was all.

7

'Is it okay if Violet stays for tea, Mum?'

'Of course, if that's okay with her mum.'

'Yeah, she said it's fine.'

I pulled a box of fish fingers out of the freezer drawer and shut the door, then turned to my daughter a little worriedly. 'Will fish fingers, chips and peas be okay?'

'Cool.' She beamed at me and ran back to her room, where she and Violet were avidly watching some American children unboxing the latest must-have toys on YouTube.

I really should stop worrying so much, I thought, as I spread the fish fingers on a baking tray. Immi never acted as if I wasn't good enough, so maybe she genuinely thought I was.

Just because she'd never had a dad in her life didn't mean I'd failed her, or that I was weird or abnormal. Just because Violet's mum had to take care of her so much while I was at work. Just because we didn't have much money to spare for luxuries, or even some basics. Just because I saw ghosts...

I closed my eyes, wondering for the thousandth time if I'd made the right choice. Things could have been so different. We could have swapped this two-bedroomed flat for a manor house in the beautiful Cotswolds. I could have left my job as a carer to be – what? The owner of a living history village? How could that possibly be true?

Sometimes, I wondered if I'd dreamed the whole thing. Our visit to Rowan Vale last week had already taken on an unreal quality. And yet I knew it wasn't a dream. If it was, I was still dreaming, because these last few days I'd seen… things. People. People I knew couldn't possibly be there because no one else around me saw them. It seemed whatever had happened to me in the Cotswolds had reawakened something, and I had no idea how to put it back to sleep.

I'd barely slept for the last few nights, lying awake worrying. Worrying about a future where I saw dead people. Worrying about how to keep that terrible burden from Immi. Worrying that I'd slip up and scare her; that she'd tell Violet or her mum what was going on.

And worrying, most of all, that I'd just turned down the one and only chance I'd ever get to make a better life for myself and my daughter. She'd loved it in Rowan Vale. How could she not? All that fresh air and glorious countryside. All those beautiful honey stone buildings. Had I been mad to walk away from such an opportunity?

While the tea cooked, I made myself a coffee and sat down at the tiny kitchen table, looking around the small and basic kitchen in my rented flat and wondering what it would be like to live somewhere as grand as Harling Hall, with all those rooms, all those grounds, and my very own housekeeper.

I felt a twinge of guilt at the thought of Sir Lawrence. His stricken expression when I'd politely but firmly turned down his offer was enough to keep me awake at night, even if I hadn't had all the other stuff to worry about.

Would he find someone else able to represent the interests of the ghosts? Surely, I couldn't be the only person who could see them all? Of course he'd find someone else. He had all the residents of Rowan Vale keeping an eye out for a suitable candidate, after all. And his grandson Brodie.

Brodie. Hmm. I couldn't deny that, in those long sleepless nights, his gorgeous face had flashed through my mind a few times. Honestly, he was the first man I'd fancied in years and wasn't it just typical that I'd choose someone like him! It wasn't as if he was a nice person. I was, I told myself firmly, very lucky that I wouldn't have to see his sullen expression again.

Besides, I'd done what was right for Immi. That should and would be my consolation. I couldn't have her growing up in a place where the presence of ghosts was normal and acceptable. Where her mother was – what? A glorified ghost wrangler? How would she explain that to her friends at school?

And that was another thing. She'd have to leave the school she was at and leave Violet behind. It wouldn't be fair.

No. I sipped my coffee with sudden relief. I'd made the right choice.

Collecting two plates, I called to Immi that the meal was almost ready, then began to dish up.

Hearing the girls' laughter from Immi's bedroom, I sighed, realising they hadn't heard me calling or they'd chosen to ignore it. I put the plates and cutlery on the table then hurried down the hallway to Immi's room, where the door was half open.

I was just about to walk in when I heard her say, 'Don't be stupid! I couldn't tell Mum. She'd have a fit.'

I froze. What couldn't she tell me? What had she been up to? My mind immediately conjured up the most horrific and terrifying scenarios, and I gripped the door handle so tightly, I was amazed it didn't come off in my hand.

I should have walked into her room and demanded to know, of course, but I couldn't make myself do it. What if she refused to tell me? What if she made up some story to cover her tracks? I had to know the truth.

Instead, I did the only thing a concerned and responsible mother could possibly do.

I eavesdropped.

'So, what did she say?' Violet asked eagerly.

'She asked me not to tell anyone I'd seen her because it would attract reporters to the village,' Immi said. 'And I told her no one would believe me if I did anyway, cos no one ever does. I said most people I've ever told have called me a liar, so she needn't worry about that.'

'And what did she say to that?'

There was a loud sigh. 'She looked really sad. She said, "People can be very cruel," and then, guess what?'

'What?' Violet asked eagerly.

'She turned to black and white! You know, like the photos they had in the olden days, like when your nanna was little? *And*,' she added smugly, 'she was American.'

'*American*?' Violet sounded awestruck. 'But what was an American doing in Rowan Vale?'

There was a long silence, and it occurred to me that the fish fingers, chips, and peas would be growing colder by the second.

I was about to knock on the door and breeze in, all innocent, when Immi said something that stopped me in my tracks.

'I don't know what she was doing there. But I do know how she died, cos she told me.'

I forced myself to throw open the door and say cheerily, 'Hey, girls, didn't you hear me? Your tea's ready and it'll be getting cold.'

Not as cold as the blood in my veins, though, which I was pretty sure had turned to ice at Immi's words.

'Sorry, Mum.' Immi jumped off the bed and, giving Violet a warning look, she filed past me to the kitchen, her friend trailing behind her.

That evening, with Violet safely back home, Immi and I curled up on the sofa in our pyjamas, drinking hot chocolate while watching one of her favourite films on the television. And all the while, the question I longed to ask her gnawed away at the pit of my stomach, yet I said nothing.

Eventually, she kissed me on the cheek and said goodnight, then went to bed, while I sat, staring unseeingly at an old episode of *Vera*, wondering how the heck I fixed this mess.

If I'd heard her conversation innocently rather than earwigging at the door, it would have been easier, I thought crossly. But then, would it? Would there ever be an easy way to ask my precious, innocent, *normal* ten-year-old daughter if she'd inherited this curse? And if she had, why hadn't I known about it? Why hadn't she told me? It didn't make sense.

I tried to tell myself I'd misheard her, or that I'd got it wrong, or that she'd been telling stories to impress Violet. But I knew, deep down, that she hadn't been. And I hadn't misheard her.

My daughter had seen a ghost, and I hadn't the foggiest idea how to deal with that.

8

I didn't get much sleep *that* night either.

After breakfast the following day, we trudged around the supermarket, Immi putting things in the trolley that normally I would have taken straight back out again. She was clearly taking advantage of my distracted manner, as I only realised when the woman at the checkout announced the total price, which was a good fifteen pounds more than usual.

Mind you, a bit later in the day, I was quite glad she'd tricked me, as I sat at the table drinking endless mugs of coffee and munching my way through a multipack of salt and vinegar crisps.

Comfort food. That was my excuse anyway, and lord knows I needed comfort. I had to say something. I couldn't stand the not knowing any longer.

'Is it okay if I go round to Violet's?'

I blinked, realising Immi had entered the kitchen without me even noticing. Her gaze fell on the empty crisp packets, and she gave me a hard stare worthy of Paddington Bear.

'You've eaten all those?'

'I was hungry,' I said, embarrassed. Bloody hell, I'd eaten six bags of crisps! How had that happened?

'They were supposed to be for both of us,' she said accusingly.

'I'm sure you won't starve,' I reassured her. 'Especially given the number of biscuits and bars of chocolate you must have added to the trolley when I wasn't looking, though how they came to fifteen pounds, I don't know.'

'Check your receipt,' she said.

'I would, but funnily enough, it's gone missing. And don't think I didn't notice the comic you sneaked in that added another four quid to the bill.'

'I didn't sneak it in,' she said indignantly. 'I asked you and you said it was okay.'

'I'm sure I didn't.'

'You said, "Whatever",' she told me. 'If that doesn't mean it's okay, I don't know what does.'

'Immi,' I said tentatively, 'we need to talk.'

'Uh-oh.' She plopped onto the chair opposite me and folded her arms. 'What have I done now? If it's the sticker book—'

'What sticker book?'

She puffed out her cheeks. 'Nothing.'

Even when she was fibbing to me, she was adorable. A little cherub with two auburn pigtails, rosy cheeks, and big, hazel eyes which everyone said were just like mine. I knew she was the double of me when I was little because I had a photo of myself, aged five, with my mum that proved it. I'd always been secretly relieved that Immi had taken after me, rather than her feckless so-called father. Now, though, I wondered if it would have been better if she'd inherited more of his genes. She might have been spared this curse.

'Is there – is there anything you want to tell me?' I asked

hopefully, thinking how marvellous it would be if she just admitted it all, meaning I wouldn't have to make my own confession that I was nothing more than a despicable spy.

She frowned. 'Like what?'

'Like – I don't know.' I shrugged. 'You just seem a bit odd lately. Ever since we got back from Rowan Vale, in fact. Did something happen there?' I hesitated. 'Something – unusual?'

'Nope.' She gave me an innocent look.

'Are you sure?' I asked. 'Really sure? You know you can tell me anything, don't you? I mean, you can trust me. You do know that?'

'I think,' she said shrewdly, 'that it's you who's got something to say, so why don't you just say it?'

If only it were that easy! How did I put this to her calmly, gently, in a non-judgemental way, without scaring her to death or making her feel abnormal?

'Did you see a ghost at Rowan Vale?'

Oh, well done, Callie! You couldn't have been more tactful, could you?

Immi gaped at me. 'Why would you ask me that?'

'Lucky guess?' I ventured hopefully. 'Okay, okay. I heard you and Violet talking yesterday. I heard what you said about the American woman who turned black and white, and that you knew how she'd died.'

'You were spying on me?' she gasped.

'Not really,' I began, but the protest died on my lips. 'Yes. Yes, I was. I'm shameless. But that's not the point.'

'Mum, that's so wrong!' she cried. 'You just said I could trust you, but you listen to my private conversations. You'd kill me if I did that to you.'

'You *do* do that to me,' I reminded her wryly. How many

times had Mel and I caught her and Violet trying to listen in on our talks? I couldn't even count them.

'When I was a kid,' she said dismissively.

'You're still a kid,' I said.

'I'm eleven!'

'You're ten.'

'Eleven in June! I'm going up to high school in September. You have to start treating me like an adult.'

'Okay,' I said, humouring her. 'If that's the case then you should start acting like one, and that means being honest with me. Did you or did you not see a ghost at Rowan Vale? Just tell me.'

'I'm not sure you could handle it if I did,' she said. 'Violet reckons you'd lose the plot if you found out that—'

'Never mind what Violet says,' I told her firmly. 'She doesn't know me anyway, and you can't keep something as huge as this from your own mother. It's – it's mental cruelty.'

Immi considered the matter, her teeth nipping at her lower lip as she obviously tried to decide if it was safe to confide in me.

'Okay,' she said at last. 'But don't go off on one, okay? Yes, I did see a ghost at Rowan Vale. She spoke to me.' Her eyes shone with sudden excitement. 'She's the first American I've ever met! She was well cool.'

I noticed that she hadn't said the American was the first *ghost* she'd ever met.

'Have you – I mean, is that the first time...' My voice trailed off. I couldn't bring myself to ask her.

'The first time I've seen a ghost?' Immi looked at me with some concern. 'You're not going to be weird about this, are you, Mum? I know it must be scary for you, but the truth is, I've seen quite a few. Always have done, ever since I can remember. But it's okay,' she added hastily as she grabbed my hand and squeezed it reassuringly. 'They never hurt me. They just want to talk, that's all. It's not like you'd see on a horror film.'

'How would you know what you'd see on a horror film?' I asked automatically. My mind was reeling, not only from the fact that my little girl had been seeing ghosts all these years without me even knowing, but that she was so matter-of-fact about it. She wasn't worried at all. In fact, judging by the gleam in her eye she was quite proud of it.

'Oh pur-lease.' Immi rolled her eyes. 'Anyway, at least you're not freaking out, which is something. Violet's mum said you would.'

'Violet's *mum?*' I squeaked. I couldn't deny that hurt. 'Why did you tell *her* and not me?'

And just who had Violet's mum told? Did this entire town think my daughter was insane?

Immi held up her hands. 'I didn't! It happened by accident. I think I was about six at the time, though I can't really remember. I saw one at the park. A ghost, I mean. An old man with holes in his boots and a dirty old coat. I felt sorry for him, and I asked Violet's mum if we could give him some of the sandwiches we'd brought for our picnic, but she gave me a proper funny look and said it was time to go home. She said I was a weird little thing.'

'Did she indeed?' I said tightly. 'Nice of her to tell you that.'

'*Well.*' Immi fidgeted a little. 'She said it to Violet's dad really, but I heard her.'

'You heard her?' I eyed her suspiciously. 'Were you spying on them?'

Her rosy cheeks turned a darker shade of pink. 'I wanted to know what had bothered her so much, but as it turned out she was laughing. She wasn't horrible or anything. She just didn't believe me. *He* said it was like something from a Netflix film and was she going to tell you about it, but Violet's mum said no because it might freak you out and why do that to you? I obviously just had a vivid imagination.'

'Are you sure?' I felt weak with relief.

'Positive. She told Violet's dad I had my head in the clouds, and he said not to worry, and that I'd grow out of it. Most weird little kids did. Mum, I'm not weird,' she added urgently. 'Honest, I'm not. And I don't usually tell people about it because they only say I'm lying when I do, but I did tell Violet, and she believes me. She thinks it's great that I can see ghosts. She wishes she could see them too. Sometimes,' she added, 'we go looking for them, just for something to do. Violet wanted us to go to the graveyard, but I told her that's just daft. There aren't any ghosts there. People don't usually die in graveyards, do they, and everyone knows ghosts are stuck where they died.'

I could barely see for tears. 'Not *everyone* knows that, sweetheart, but I know you're not weird. The truth is—' I swallowed, aware that she might look at me very differently from now on, but that I couldn't leave her thinking she was the only one this had ever happened to. 'The truth is, when I was a little girl, I saw ghosts, too, and your grandparents couldn't deal with that. They made me stay quiet about it, and over time, I stopped seeing them...'

Until I'd gone to Rowan Vale, and something had reawakened the ability in me.

'You saw ghosts?' she asked incredulously. 'Really?'

'Really.' I smiled, seeing the amazement in her eyes. 'The first one I ever remember was a little boy called David.'

For the next half hour, we sat together, munching on Jammie Dodgers and telling each other about some of the ghosts we'd seen over the years.

'It's so sad,' she said, shaking her head. 'Why did you stop seeing them? *I* won't stop seeing them, will I?'

'Don't you want to?' I asked, surprised.

She raised her eyebrows. 'Why would I want to? It's great! Not many people get to talk to ghosts, do they? I love it.'

'But some people wouldn't...' I paused, not sure how to phrase it.

'I know. I get it. They're just jealous, you know.'

I almost laughed. 'Jealous?'

'Of course! They'd love to see ghosts and they can't. It must suck.' She put a hand to her mouth and stared at me in horror. 'Sorry, Mum! I totes forgot that you can't see them any more. Oh, I *hope* that doesn't happen to me!'

Unfortunately, I didn't think it would. Immi had embraced her ability to see the ghosts, not pushed it away and pretended it wasn't real. I'd crushed my 'gift', whereas she'd allowed hers to flourish. She wouldn't go the way I had. Not unless she felt forced to.

'Rowan Vale,' I said slowly.

'Isn't it a great place?' She sighed. 'Honest, Mum, the place is full of ghosts! I mean, I only spoke to the American lady, but I could see others. There were even some mingling with the staff on the station platform. I knew as soon as I got off the train that I was in for a treat.'

'You knew even then?' I asked, amazed. 'But you looked so – so...' I'd been about to say normal, but how would that sound?

Luckily, she understood what I meant. 'I've learned to put on an act,' she confessed. 'How else was I going to keep it from you? I'm good at it. Violet says it's called a poker face. It's something her dad's always wishing he had, apparently.'

'You *are* good at it,' I told her. 'Worryingly so. But how can you tell which ones are ghosts?'

She shrugged. 'I just can. There's a feeling you get when you look at them. Don't you remember?'

'Like ice running up your arms and along your shoulders and neck,' I said.

She grinned. 'Yes, exactly!'

'And you get that feeling straight away?'

'Pretty much. Oh, Mum, I'm so sad you can't see them any more!'

I wasn't sure what to do. Should I admit that my so-called gift seemed to have returned? Or was it better to stay quiet? But then, would it be fair to leave Immi feeling so isolated in all this? She needed a friend and ally. However I felt about the ghosts, I didn't want my daughter to feel she couldn't talk to anyone about them, and having someone in the same position she was in must surely help her.

I took a steadying breath. 'Thing is, Immi – thing is, I seem to have got the sight back.'

She gave a squeal of joy. 'When? How? Tell me!'

Reluctantly, I told her what had happened to me when we'd visited Rowan Vale, and when it came to the part about Sir Lawrence and his offer, she nearly fell off her chair in excitement.

'We can move to Rowan Vale? To live in that big house? When? OMG, this is *brilliant*! I can't wait!'

I felt a pang of guilt, seeing the shine in her hazel eyes and the wide smile on her face, knowing that we wouldn't be moving anywhere.

I did it for the best. She deserves a normal life.

'You'd have to leave your school,' I reminded her hopefully. Maybe that would put her off.

She didn't miss a beat. 'So what? I'm leaving anyway in July, aren't I? There'll be loads of people at my secondary school that I won't know, so what's the difference if I start a new one somewhere else?'

'But you wouldn't see Violet,' I pointed out. 'She's your best friend.'

'Mum, there's Snapchat,' she said, with all the patience of a young person talking to someone in their dotage. 'I'll message her every day. And she can visit, can't she? She'd love it there. And it's not like there won't be room!' She gave a yelp of excitement. 'Harling Hall! It's massive, isn't it? We saw it on the website at school. Oh, it's going to be awesome! When are we going?'

I stared at her in dread. How on earth did I break the news to her that I'd turned down the opportunity, and that we wouldn't be moving anywhere?

There was a knock on the door, and I was so relieved to have some extra time to think of a way to break it to her gently that I leapt up and practically ran down the hall.

All thoughts of Immi flew from my mind, though, as I opened the door and saw who was standing on the outside landing.

Brodie gave me what, in his mind, probably passed for a smile.

'Miss Chase.'

I stepped back in shock. 'Bro— I mean, Mr Davenport.'

'May I come in?'

I looked wildly round, wondering if Immi had followed me. The last thing I needed was for her to hear about me declining the job from him. I needed to find a way to tell her gently.

'It's not convenient,' I said. 'And how did you know where I lived anyway?' I added, as the thought suddenly occurred to me.

'With surprisingly little effort,' he said ruefully. 'You really need to have a word with that teacher, Mr Gaskill. But – look, are you sure I can't come in? Just for ten minutes.'

I closed my eyes as I heard Immi say, 'Who is it, Mum?'

Slowly, I turned around and saw her standing behind me,

her gaze fixed on Brodie. I turned to him, hoping to give him some sort of signal to push off as now really wasn't the time, but he wasn't looking at me. To my amazement, he smiled at Immi. A proper, warm smile that made his blue eyes twinkle. Not the forced rictus grin he'd given me.

'Hello,' Immi said.

'Hello.' Brodie gave me an enquiring look and I cleared my throat.

'Mr Davenport, this is my daughter, Imogen. Immi, this is Mr Davenport.'

'From Rowan Vale?' Immi cried, clearly excited. 'Are you here about the job? When are we moving there?'

Brodie, unsurprisingly, looked baffled.

I sighed. 'You'd better come in then,' I said, realising the jig was up. I stepped aside and let him in, blushing fiercely as Immi led him through to the kitchen, instead of the living room, which meant the first thing he saw was six crumpled crisp bags and an empty Jammie Dodgers packet lying on the table.

'Take a seat,' I said, hastily gathering up the evidence and dumping it in the bin.

'Are we really moving into Harling Hall?' Immi asked, before the poor man had even settled himself. She plonked herself into the chair next to his, her eyes shining.

Brodie glanced up at me. 'You've changed your mind? You've decided to take up Grandpa's offer after all?'

Immi stared at me. 'You turned it down?'

'I was coming to that bit,' I said weakly. 'I just hadn't had the chance before Mr Davenport knocked on the door.'

'Mum, why would you do that?' she demanded, the anguish in her face almost too much to bear.

'Because of the ghosts,' I mumbled. 'Because I wanted you to live a normal life. Because I didn't want you to know I was... strange.'

'You think *I'm* strange?' she asked, sounding hurt.

'Of course not! That's different.'

'I don't see how,' she said, and to be honest, she had a point.

I turned to Brodie, eager to halt that line of conversation. 'What are you doing here, Mr Davenport?'

'Well, what do you think? I came here to ask you if there was any possibility of you changing your mind.' He looked doubtfully from me to Immi. 'Is there?'

'Yes!' she squealed, then turned to me. 'Mum, *please. Please* say yes.'

'It's out of the question,' I said wearily. 'We'd have to find you a new school for starters, and what would we tell everyone?'

'You wouldn't have to tell them anything,' Immi said.

'I think people would notice if we moved to the Cotswolds,' I pointed out. 'What am I supposed to say to Violet's mum for a start? "You won't have to look after Immi any more because I'm giving up my flat and my job and dragging her to the countryside so I can talk to ghosts for a living." You must be joking.'

'Tell her you've got a different job then,' Immi pleaded. She turned to Brodie. 'Tell her, Mr Davenport!'

'Well...' Brodie seemed nonplussed by the situation, and clearly wasn't sure how to handle it. 'The thing is, Miss Chase—'

'Callie,' I said. 'Just call me Callie.'

'Okay, Callie it is. Well, the thing is, you're very much needed at Rowan Vale.'

'You've changed your tune,' I said suspiciously. 'You couldn't have made it more obvious last week that you didn't want me there.'

'No, well.' He looked embarrassed. 'Look, I'm not going to pretend I'm thrilled about the situation, but can you blame me?

Rowan Vale is my home, and my inheritance, but thanks to a twist of fate, it's all going to be taken away from me and given to a perfect stranger.'

I couldn't deny he had good reason to want me gone. 'So why are you here then?'

'I love my grandpa,' he said heavily. 'He's everything to me, and it's awful to see him so worried and stressed about the future of the village. I'd do anything to put his mind at rest, including tracking you down to beg you to change your mind, even though it sticks in my throat.'

'Wow,' I said. 'Charming. How could I refuse an offer like that?'

'I'm sorry. It's nothing personal.'

'Mum, how would you feel if it happened to you?' Immi demanded. 'Give the guy a break.'

I made a mental note to stop her watching so many precocious children on YouTube.

'That might be true,' I said, 'but he ought to bear in mind that if it wasn't for a similar twist of fate, the Davenports wouldn't have owned the estate in the first place.'

Brodie hesitated. 'You're right,' he said at last. 'I never thought of it that way before.'

'Yes, well.' I folded my arms, not sure how to react to his almost instant capitulation. 'Now you have, so think on.'

'The fact is,' he continued, 'you were the only person we'd found who could see *all* the ghosts, and believe me, we've been looking for long enough.'

Immi waved her hand in the air as if he were her teacher and she knew the answer to a particularly difficult question. '*I* can see them!' she whooped. 'I'll buy the estate if Mum doesn't want it. It's my birthday in June and I'm bound to get a tenner off Violet's mum. I always do.'

Brodie laughed, and I marvelled at how much nicer he looked when he wasn't being all sullen and miserable. The change didn't last long, though, as he looked at me through narrowed eyes.

'I thought you told Grandpa she didn't have the gift,' he said, a note of accusation in his voice.

'She didn't know,' Immi told him immediately. 'We only found out about each other just before you arrived.'

'Seriously?' He looked from one to the other of us as if he wasn't quite sure whether to believe her or not. 'Well, er... I can see why you said now wasn't convenient.'

'It *is* convenient,' Immi told him. 'It means Mum can say yes with me as a witness.' She folded her arms and gave me a smug look. 'Doesn't it, Mum?'

'You're supposed to be back at school in a week,' I said faintly. 'And I'd have to give notice on the flat, and at my job.'

'All perfectly simple, I'd have thought,' Brodie said. 'There are schools near Rowan Vale, you know. In fact, there's a primary school in a nearby village called Kingsford Wold, and a secondary school just a few miles away in Chipping Royston.'

'I haven't got a car. How am I supposed to get her there?'

'Can you drive?'

'Well, yes, but—'

'Then we'll get you a car,' Brodie promised.

'I thought cars were banned?'

'Not for locals. I'll explain how it works if you say yes.'

'Wow, you're not making this easy, are you?'

'It's meant to be,' Immi said. 'Please, please say yes!'

'I must say,' Brodie admitted, 'I'm amazed you haven't jumped at the chance.' He glanced around my little kitchen and my hackles rose.

'You mean because I obviously live in such squalor?'

'I never said that,' he replied mildly. 'I just know from experience that Harling Hall's an amazing place to grow up. There isn't a garden here, is there? At the Hall, she'd have acres of space to run around in.'

'And all those ghosts to talk to,' I said sharply.

'Oh, not this again. I thought we'd got past all that,' Immi said, talking to me like I was the child and she the parent. 'They need us. How can we turn our backs on them? Besides, I like talking to ghosts. Didn't you used to like it once? What about David?'

'I can barely remember him,' I said, but it wasn't quite true. Now that I'd started to think about him again, I could remember him a bit more clearly. Not that I could recall any of the conversations we'd had, but I knew we'd had some, and I remembered how happy I used to be to see him. I'd never once felt scared of him. He was my friend. Is that how Immi saw all ghosts?

'What if it doesn't work out?' I asked desperately. 'What if I mess it all up and then you find someone else who'd be much better at the job? I don't want to turn our lives upside down then get the sack. Where would we go? I've my daughter's security to think of.'

'Miss Chase – Callie.' Brodie rubbed his forehead. 'This isn't a job you're being offered. My grandfather made it very clear. You would own the estate, lock, stock and barrel. No one could kick you out. And with Immi here having the gift, it seems your daughter's future would be secure, too, as it would pass directly to her.'

'You mean I'd own the estate and village one day?' Immi's eyes widened in excitement.

'Don't sound too pleased. I'd have to die first,' I reminded her.

'I don't want that to happen,' she said solemnly, 'but it does mean I could help the ghosts too. They'd have someone to talk to for a long time with the two of us there, wouldn't they? That's the important thing.'

She put me to shame. I had to admit, if only to myself, that I hadn't given the plight of the ghosts much thought. If – when – Lawrie's time came, they'd have no one who could communicate with them. No anchor in the living world. No one to make sure there was a place for them where they could be comfortable and make their voices heard. It had all been about me and Immi. Maybe, at a push, I'd considered Sir Lawrence, but the ghosts themselves... They must be worried, too, even if Agnes had a funny way of showing it. Agnes!

'Lord, I'd have to share a house with Agnes,' I said, thinking aloud.

Brodie laughed again. 'She can't be that bad,' he said. 'Grandpa adores her. Anyway, she's got a soft spot for children, so I think Immi might be your way to her heart.'

'And she's got a daughter,' I remembered in dismay. 'I don't want Immi talking to Florrie. She's a little minx.'

'Oh, Mum!' Immi said scornfully.

'Are you thinking about it?' Brodie asked hopefully.

Was I? The thought of committing myself to Rowan Vale terrified me. This would be for the rest of my life, and what did I know about running an estate? Let alone a living history village complete with ghosts. Funnily enough, there hadn't been a course on that sort of thing at the local college.

'Mum?' Immi asked hopefully.

'Your life will all be about... *them*,' I murmured. 'It's not fair on you. I just want you to have a—'

'Don't say normal again,' she begged. 'I *am* normal. This is normal. For us anyway.'

'I don't think you appreciate what you've got,' Brodie said

roughly. 'I'd give anything to be able to see the ghosts. Anything.' He shook his head, as if dismissing that clearly painful train of thought. 'Look, do you really think I'd be here begging you to take my inheritance for a measly ten pounds if I wasn't seriously worried? Rowan Vale needs you, Callie. I hate to admit it, but it's true.'

I had no idea what to say to such a heartfelt plea.

'And—' Brodie took a deep breath. 'If it helps, I'm sorry. Really sorry for the way I behaved when you were at the house. I was petulant and childish, and I truly apologise.'

Oh crikey! Don't look at me like that. How am I supposed to think straight with you looking at me with those puppy-dog eyes?

But he sounded genuine, and as Immi held her breath waiting for my answer, I simply didn't have any more ammunition.

'Well...' I ran a hand through my hair and gave a half-laugh, born as much from panic as joy. 'Then I guess I'll transfer that ten pounds to Sir Lawrence.'

Immi squealed with joy and Brodie got to his feet and held out his hand.

'Thank you, Callie,' he said as I shook it. 'I'm sure you won't regret it.'

Yet his expression told me he was already half regretting it himself. He was smiling at an ecstatic Immi, but I could tell he was feeling pretty low about having to say goodbye to the family estate, and how could I blame him for that? I just hoped he was right that *I* wouldn't regret it. For all our sakes.

9

Sir Lawrence did everything he could to make the transition as easy as possible for us. The day after Brodie's visit, I spoke to him on the phone to confirm that I was happy to go ahead with purchasing the Harling Estate, and he'd been so obviously relieved and delighted and humbly *grateful,* he'd nearly made me cry.

All I had to worry about, he said, was moving here, and he would do all he could to help. He and Brodie would remain at the Hall for a month to help me settle in and to show me how things worked at the estate. After that, they would leave, and I'd be on my own. I tried very hard to believe that a month would be ample time for me to learn all the things I'd need to know, but I can't deny panic was already setting in even as I transferred the ten pounds into his account.

All those warnings about scams had obviously gone over my head, as I'd paid him before signing anything. I realised none of this was usual for the sale of property, but I didn't have a lot of experience in the matter. I mean, he could have been a conman, but if he was, he aimed low. Even I could afford to lose ten pounds. Just. Part of me hoped it *was* a scam, and I could forget all about it.

Sir Lawrence, however, kept his word. Ten days after our conversation, an enormous brown package arrived from Eldridge and Smales, Solicitors.

There was an introductory letter inside from a Mr Harold Eldridge, who explained that Eldridge and Smales had been the solicitors for the Harling Estate ever since the Wyndhams bought the place in 1820, and that the business was still in the hands of the same families, so they were fully aware of the "special circumstances" pertaining to the village.

The letter went on to explain that the package contained various documents relating to the rights and responsibilities of the new owner, as well as a contract for the sale of the estate. Mr Eldridge urged me to read all documents thoroughly before I signed anything, adding that I was welcome to seek advice from my own solicitor (what solicitor?) and that the contract would also require the signature of a witness.

This was what I'd dreaded. All my life, I'd struggled with reading and writing, but it was only when I admitted as much to one of Immi's teachers that I was finally tested for dyslexia. It was a relief to find out I wasn't stupid, but that didn't help me when it came to reading this mammoth document from the solicitor.

I tried reading it all but honestly, I couldn't make head nor tail of it, and had a blinding headache before I'd finished the contract, never mind started on all the 'rights and responsibilities' stuff. Besides, it was a bloody long contract written in legalese, and who understands that unless they're Mark Darcy?

What was I supposed to do? I'd paid Sir Lawrence ten pounds. Once the contract was signed and witnessed, I'd be the new owner and get to live in that massive country house in the

Cotswolds with Immi. And ghosts. But at least my daughter's future would be secure, and I'd get to spend more time with her at last.

Happy ever after.

After everything we'd been through, didn't we deserve that?

And I couldn't afford to consult a solicitor anyway so...

As I sat chewing my pen wondering what to do for the best, Mel knocked on the door.

'Did our Violet leave her jacket here this afternoon?' she asked without preamble. Her mouth dropped open as I practically dragged her into the flat.

'Just in time. Would you be my witness?'

She looked thrilled to be asked. 'Ooh. A witness to what?'

I could hardly tell her I was about to buy an entire estate in the Cotswolds for a tenner, so I simply explained that I'd been offered a new job complete with accommodation, working in the office of a country house.

'You never have! That's amazing! I'm so happy for you,' she said warmly. 'Mind, I'll miss your Immi. And Violet will miss her too. She's going to be gutted when I tell her.'

'I promise Immi will keep in touch with her,' I said. 'Maybe she can come and stay with us when we're settled?'

It was just something to say but I realised immediately I'd made a huge mistake. Her eyes lit up, and I could almost read her thoughts. *About time* you *looked after* my *kid for a change!* I'm sure she wasn't really thinking that, but I couldn't blame her if she was.

'That'd be great. Violet would love that. Give me a pen, love, and I'll sign. Oh, I'd better read through it all before I do, though.' She laughed. 'I could be signing my life away for all I know!'

'Of course,' I said. I handed her the huge package and beamed at her. 'There you go.'

Her laughter died immediately. 'Really? All that? Maybe I'll just sign it, eh? I know I can trust you.'

'Of course you can. Thanks so much,' I told her.

Violet's mum scarpered as soon as the deed was done, and the very next day, I sent the papers back by recorded delivery, which cost me an absolute fortune because I'd completely missed the bit that said I was supposed to keep the 'rights and responsibilities' stuff and only return the contract. I had to admit, it didn't bode well for my future as a businesswoman.

A few days later, Mia got in touch, and she became the go-between for Sir Lawrence and me. She seemed to be doing a lot of the organisation, from what I could make out.

Having decided that the best time to move to Rowan Vale would be during the May half term holidays, I gave my month's notice to the agency in late April. Mia, meanwhile, contacted the primary school in Kingsford Wold on my behalf and made an appointment for Immi and me to speak with the headmistress on the second of June, which was the first day back after half term.

I hadn't seen or heard from Brodie since the day he'd come to my flat over a month ago, but I guessed the situation was still proving difficult for him. Even though he'd wanted to help his grandfather and the ghosts, handing over his inheritance and his home couldn't be an easy prospect. He might have done the honourable thing by persuading me to take up Sir Lawrence's offer but that didn't mean he had to like it.

It didn't ease my anxiety, though. As if moving to a new home and taking on a new job wasn't enough to deal with, the thought of sharing a house – even one as large as the Hall – with someone who didn't really want me there was daunting. It was going to be a long month. And that was before I even thought about what it would be like living with Agnes.

But moving day was drawing ever closer and there was nothing else to do but wait. Our new life was about to begin, and I could only keep everything crossed that I hadn't made a huge mistake.

10

We'd said our goodbyes to Violet and her family and had exchanged cards and gifts – a thank you from Immi and me and a good luck present from them. Immi had promised Violet she'd keep in touch via Snapchat, they'd solemnly sworn to stay friends forever, and it had been agreed that Violet would spend two weeks with us during the summer holidays when, hopefully, we'd have settled in.

Mia had booked a removal van for us, and on the last Friday in May, we watched as all our worldly goods were loaded onto it. Sir Lawrence had assured me there was plenty of space for our own furniture, which he hoped would make us feel more at home, even though the furniture at the Hall was apparently part of the sale and now belonged to me.

A man called Jack arrived just as the removal men were setting off. Probably in his early forties, he had dark hair and a cheery smile. He was driving a roomy, pale-blue hatchback that looked almost new, and informed me that this would be my car in future, but for today, he was acting as my chauffeur on Sir

Lawrence's orders, and he was here to take Immi and me to our new home.

'It's a pleasure to meet you,' he told me, shaking my hand. 'I live in the village with my wife Clara and our boys. You'll love it there. Lawrie made a big announcement in church last week about you taking over, and it's all people have been talking about. Everyone's dying to meet you.' He laughed. 'Well, some of our residents have already had that experience, but you know what I mean.'

So, Sir Lawrence had told everyone about me? I hoped they were all as friendly and welcoming as Jack.

'Do all the villagers know about the ghosts?' I asked, curious at his casual mention of them.

He looked surprised that I'd even asked.

'Of course!'

'And it doesn't bother you?'

He laughed. 'Bother us? Why would it? They were here long before us, and they don't cause us any trouble. Anyway, most of us can't see them. Unless you're special, like you and Lawrie, only the people who are related to a ghost can see them, and even then, only that particular ghost. Luckily for me and Clara, we've never bumped into any ancestors so it's very peaceful at our place.'

A whole village full of people who didn't find the idea of ghosts freaky! I couldn't even imagine what it must be like to grow up somewhere like that.

I swallowed down the lump in my throat as I locked up the flat for the last time. It may not have been up to much, but it had been home, although you'd never know it from Immi, who barely gave it a backward glance before jumping into the back seat of the car.

Resigned to our fate, I got into the passenger seat. Jack drove us to the rental agency for the flat, where I dropped off the keys, then we set off to the Cotswolds.

Before I knew it, we were heading down the drive to Harling Hall, where I could see the removal van had already arrived.

This was really happening. It had all moved so fast that I'd barely had time to catch my breath. I glanced over my shoulder at Immi, and the delight and excitement on her face was almost enough to chase away my nerves. Almost.

Look, I told myself, it's still May – just – and May is my favourite month. The hawthorn and the cherry trees are in bloom, and the rowan trees we passed on the way in are flowering. There are still patches of yellow rapeseed in the fields, and Immi and I are starting a whole new life.

I allowed myself a smile. It was going to be all right. I could feel it.

I glanced up at the house as a movement caught my eye. On the first floor, a woman's face stared down at me. Lips pursed. Arms folded. I could feel the disapproval radiating from her.

Agnes was obviously still not happy that I was about to move into her home, and if I was expecting a warm welcome from her, I was going to be disappointed.

'Okay,' I murmured as the car pulled up outside the front door and Jack jumped out. 'You can sulk all you like, Agnes Ashcroft, but I'm here now, and you and I are going to have to learn to get along. Whether we like it or not.'

At least I couldn't fault Sir Lawrence's behaviour towards us. He was in the sitting room when we arrived and greeted us with undisguised joy when we popped in to say hello, telling us to make ourselves right at home, and that Mia had already brewed up for the removal men and had them eating out of her hand.

I'd expected that Immi and I would have a bedroom each and maybe a bathroom, too, but you could have knocked me down with a feather when he informed us that we had an entire wing to ourselves.

It meant we had a home for all our furniture and belongings, which I was sure would make us feel less intimidated and might help Immi settle in better. Not that she needed any help really. She was clearly in her element, so maybe it was me who needed the help.

It still all seemed like a dream to me. How had I gone from a tiny, two-bedroomed flat in Leicestershire to a stately home in the Cotswolds?

And how had I gone from being a carer on little more than minimum wage to the owner of an entire country estate? It was completely bonkers, and I couldn't help but think that the bubble was about to burst at any moment, and I'd be told it was all some cruel joke, and I'd actually donated that tenner to a home for the terminally gullible.

Mia was brilliant. She was quite happy to roll up her sleeves and help me shift the furniture around. She made mugs of tea and bacon sandwiches for us, as well as the removal men, who'd clearly taken a shine to her as Sir Lawrence had observed, and cheerfully helped Immi make up her bed and set out her belongings the way she wanted them.

When the removal men finally left, Mia and I sat on the sofa, drinking tea and eating chocolate biscuits, while Immi headed to her bedroom to set her books out on the white Ikea bookcase she'd brought with her.

'So, you're here then,' Mia said with a grin. 'How does it feel to be the new lady of the manor?'

'Crazy,' I admitted. 'It's all happened so fast, I haven't had time to take it all in.'

'I'm really glad you changed your mind,' she said, cradling

her mug of tea. 'I was worried for a while, you know. And I know Lawrie was too. You've made him so happy.'

'More than I've made Agnes,' I said with a sigh. 'I saw her earlier, glaring at me from the window. She's not happy about me moving here, is she?'

'Agnes is, from what I can gather, not backwards in coming forwards,' she acknowledged. 'But Lawrie's firmly of the opinion that her bark's worse than her bite, and seems terribly fond of her, so don't be too discouraged. Although, whatever you do, don't let her think she can bully you or she'll show no mercy.'

I watched her as she sipped her tea, a thoughtful expression on her face. She was an attractive woman with an inner calmness about her that was reassuring. I had a feeling I'd be turning to Mia for support quite a lot in the future.

'It must be weird for you,' I said. 'Living here, working here, and knowing the place is haunted by—'

'Don't!' she said quickly.

I looked at her in surprise. 'Don't what?'

'Never,' she whispered, leaning towards me, 'use that word. We don't say the H word.'

I frowned. 'H word? You mean haunted?'

'Shh!' She placed her mug on the coffee table and shook her head. 'It's considered terribly bad manners. They have as much right to be here as anyone. After all, it's not their fault they got left behind, is it? The H word implies that they shouldn't be here, and that they're unwelcome. They're not. You must make that very clear to them from the off if you don't want to stir up trouble or hurt their feelings.'

'Crikey,' I said. 'I never even thought about that. This is going to be a minefield, isn't it?' I crunched my biscuit, considering. 'Why *were* some of them left behind? Does anyone know?'

'Not a clue. I know in films and books they go on about the

ghosts having unfinished business or something, but according to Lawrie, most of our ghosts were quite contented and ready to go when they died. And even the ones who died unexpectedly don't feel they have anything to hang around for. It's all a bit baffling.'

'And worrying,' I said with a shiver. 'It means it could happen to any of us. We could end up living in Rowan Vale for eternity.'

'Don't think it hasn't occurred to us,' she said. 'Believe me, we all live with that possibility.'

I really wasn't sure what to think about that. What was so special about Rowan Vale that this sort of thing happened so often?

'Do you think it *is* something to do with ley lines and the Wyrd Stones?' I asked her.

'Honestly? I have no idea. There's no point going down that road, Callie, believe me. We've all tied ourselves up in knots coming up with theories, and it's got us nowhere. Best to just get on with it and deal with things as they are, without worrying why this place is the way it is.'

I leaned back on the sofa and sighed. 'Such a lot to take in. I noticed Brodie didn't hang around to greet us. I hope he's not going to be too grumpy about this, especially with Immi being in the house.'

She hesitated. 'Don't be too hard on Brodie, will you? It's a lot for him to deal with. He genuinely loves this estate. It's hard for him, knowing he'll have to leave it all behind.'

I frowned. 'You know, he doesn't have to go if he doesn't want to. I wouldn't mind.'

'Oh, he'll want to stay with Lawrie, and Lawrie will never agree to staying on. I should imagine Brodie has the option to join his parents but I doubt he will. Anyway, wherever they go, it's going to be a wrench for them both. Rowan Vale means everything to them.'

I wasn't following. 'Sorry, maybe I'm being a bit dense here, but why wouldn't Lawrie agree to stay on? If they both love it here, there's no reason to leave, is there? The house is certainly big enough and we're not likely to get in each other's way.'

And I haven't a clue what I'm supposed to be doing and there's no chance I'll take it all in in a month...

She looked surprised. 'It's what happens. When there's a new owner of the estate, the old one moves away. I suppose it's to give the incomer free rein to deal with their responsibilities their own way. Find their own way of doing things without interference from the previous owners. It's always been that way. You won't find any living descendants of the Harlings, the Ashcrofts, or the Wyndhams here. Once their time is over it's really over. They leave.'

'And what happens to them?' I asked. 'Where do they go? How do they manage without their home and land?'

She shrugged. 'No idea. It's sort of an unspoken thing that they stay away from the estate and no one in the village goes looking for them.'

'But why?'

'It's the way it is,' she said. 'Kind of like the ten-pound purchase price. It's always been that way, so it stays that way.'

'That's ridiculous,' I protested. 'There's no need for Sir Lawrence or Brodie to move away. Why should they have to? This house is more than big enough for us all, and I wouldn't dream of turfing them out of their home.'

'But it's not their home any longer, Callie,' she said gently. 'It's yours.'

I gazed around the living room. *My* living room. At the polished, wooden floorboards and the large rug in the centre of the floor; at the stone fireplace which dominated one end of the room; at the latticed windows and the ancient oak door. My furniture looked ridiculous in here. Lost. Out of place.

Like me.

What on earth was I doing here? And how was I going to learn all that I needed to know in such a short space of time, especially given my dyslexia?

'Where's Sir Lawrence now?' I asked.

She glanced at her watch. 'Having his afternoon nap, I expect,' she told me.

'And Brodie?'

'Oh, he'll be out and about on the estate. He's a very busy man.'

'Doing what?'

'Just about everything. You'll learn more about how the estate works in time. I know Lawrie's planning to go over some stuff with you tomorrow, and hopefully, things will start to become clearer.'

'I can't imagine it,' I said gloomily. 'Oh, Mia, what have I done?'

'Saved Rowan Vale,' she told me, a warm smile on her face. 'And we'll be forever grateful to you for it.'

11

AGNES AND AUBREY

'You should see what she's done to those rooms!'

Agnes barged into the drawing room, startling Aubrey, who'd been standing by the window, watching the comings and goings of the removal men as they slowly emptied the van of Callie's belongings.

He closed his eyes for a moment then, steeling himself, he turned to Agnes with a smile.

'Well, my dear, they *are* her rooms, and what she chooses to do with them is up to her.'

Agnes sank onto the sofa, shaking her head in dismay.

'Why on earth did he give her the west wing? A whole wing, Mr Wyndham! And here we are, forced to share the east wing with Sir Lawrence and Brodie.'

'Hardly forced, dear.' Aubrey sat beside her and took her hand, ever the comforter. 'Lawrie's rooms have always been in this wing and you've been very glad about that until now. Besides,' he reminded her gently, 'the Davenports won't be here much longer. You know what happens when new blood takes over at the Hall.'

'Oh, don't remind me.' Agnes sighed. 'I shall miss him so much, you know. I shall miss them both, of course, but Lawrie...'

'I know. As shall I. Maybe they'll stay in the village? We might see them around. If we ever venture out of the grounds, of course,' he added, with a hint of hope in his voice.

'But they never do, do they?' Agnes said sadly, seeming not to notice. 'Stay, I mean. As soon as they hand the estate over to the next owner, they leave. Why should it be different this time?'

'I stayed,' he reminded her with a nudge.

She gave him a reproachful look. 'Now is not the time for frivolity, Mr Wyndham. Of course you stayed! You hardly had a choice. Those who were alive and able to leave the estate boundaries did so. Not that one can blame them, I suppose. Seeing the home you've loved handed over to strangers can't be easy or pleasant, as you should know.'

'Hardly strangers, my dear. Benjamin Ashcroft was well known to the Harlings, and my father was, after all, the Ashcrofts' gamekeeper.'

Agnes sniffed. 'Yes, well, the less said about that, the better. We hardly need reminding—'

'Of my family's humble beginnings?' he asked wryly.

Agnes gave him a stricken look. 'I wasn't going to say that! I was going to say, we hardly need reminding of your father. Nor your mother, come to that. Loathsome creatures.'

'Agnes!'

'I know what I know,' she said, nodding furiously. 'Anyway, we digress. The point is, that woman and her offspring now have the run of the west wing, and they're seemingly intent on turning it into a circus sideshow.'

'A circus sideshow?' Aubrey struggled to hide a smile and failed. 'And what do you know of circus sideshows, my dear?'

Agnes huffed, clearly put out that he wasn't taking her seriously. 'You know perfectly well what I mean. The furniture! They are the ugliest pieces I've ever seen. And she had the nerve to tell that child of hers that she's glad Sir Lawrence cleared the rooms before they got here because she thinks our furniture would give her "the creeps". I'm not entirely sure what that means, but it's perfectly obvious it's not complimentary. Lawrie should show her the door. He's far too kind.'

'Agnes, you know that won't happen,' Aubrey said firmly. 'Miss Chase and her daughter are here now. They're the new owners and there's an end to it. We must make the best we can of the situation. We've been here before, after all. New blood and all that. I daresay we'll be here again one day.'

Agnes got to her feet and walked slowly over to the window, taking up the position he'd just surrendered. Staring down at the van, she shuddered as the sound of the removal men's voices floated upwards.

'So common!' she muttered. Turning round to view Aubrey, she found him sitting with his head down, lost in thought, and her heart melted. Such a handsome man. She hated it when he looked sad or wistful.

'Do you ever wish it could be different, Agnes?' he asked softly.

'Different? In what way?'

He threw up his hands and looked around the drawing room. 'You know. Us. This. This house. This village. Why are we still here? What did we do wrong?'

Forgetting to be cross about the interloper and her shocking lack of manners, Agnes rushed to his side and took his hands in hers. 'My dear Mr Wyndham, you did nothing wrong! Nothing! Why the very idea...'

'But we're stuck here. We've been stuck here for so long. One always accepted the possibility, of course. You can't live in Rowan

Vale and not know there's a chance you'll end up marooned here forever. Even so... Why us? Why didn't we pass on like so many others?'

'I don't know,' she said firmly, 'but I for one am very glad we didn't.'

'You can't mean it?'

'I do.' She nodded vehemently. 'If we'd moved on, you and I would never have discovered each other. And what about Florence? Oh, Mr Wyndham, imagine if we'd never become the little family we are today. Why, it hardly bears thinking about!'

'You're quite right, my dear. We have much to be grateful for.' He hesitated then bravely went for it. 'Agnes, about Florence. We really must— oh!'

His gaze transferred from Agnes to the door, where he saw a young girl with auburn pigtails watching them, a look of delight on her face.

'Hello,' she said.

Aubrey and Agnes exchanged shocked glances.

'You can see us?' Agnes murmured.

'Of course I can.' The girl ran into the room and sat beside them on the sofa, a wide smile on her face. 'I'm Imogen, but most people call me Immi. Who are you?'

'I'm Aubrey—'

'Mr Wyndham to you, child,' Agnes said sharply. 'And I'm Mrs... Wyndham.'

Aubrey cleared his throat. 'Ahem. I suppose you must be Miss Chase's daughter.'

'Indeed she is. I saw *Miss* Chase and this child conversing with Mia in the west wing,' Agnes said pointedly.

Immi (and really, what sort of name was that? Almost as bad as Callie!) laughed. 'Yes, I know. I saw you snooping around, trying to stay out of Mum's sight.'

'Snooping!' Agnes spluttered, outraged. 'I'm quite sure I was doing no such thing.'

'We were given to understand that you didn't have your mother's – er – talent,' Aubrey said, puzzled.

'Oh, that was a misunderstanding,' the little girl said airily. 'She didn't know I could see ghosts, but she does now. It's all sorted. Isn't it great?' she added eagerly. 'I'm so happy to be here. Isn't it a gorgeous house?'

Agnes felt slightly mollified. 'It is indeed,' she agreed.

'Ever so big, though,' the child continued. 'I'll probably get lost loads. I might have to leave a trail of breadcrumbs, like Hansel and Gretel.'

'You will not!' Agnes told her indignantly. 'And attract mice?'

'Perhaps a ball of wool,' Aubrey suggested, a twinkle in his eye.

Agnes smiled at him. She loved that twinkle and his kind voice. It was that twinkle and his kind voice that had...

Embarrassed by where her mind was going, she pulled herself together. Now wasn't the time for such inappropriate thoughts. Especially when they had company.

Adjusting her bed-jacket, she said briskly, 'I'm sure you'll find your way around quickly enough.'

'Perhaps Florence could show her?' Aubrey suggested.

'Who's Florence?' The girl's eyes lit up. 'Oh, you mean Florrie, right?'

Agnes decided that twinkle or no twinkle, Aubrey was pushing his luck.

'I mean Florence,' she said stiffly, 'and I hardly think so, Mr Wyndham.'

'Florence is our, er, daughter,' Aubrey explained, as if Agnes hadn't spoken. 'She's ten years old. How old are you?'

'I'm eleven next month,' the girl said.

'Splendid!' Aubrey beamed at her then turned to Agnes. 'There you are, my dear. A new friend for Florence at last.'

'Florence has friends,' she said abruptly.

Aubrey frowned. 'But you keep saying you'd prefer it if she didn't associate with Robert and John. And, after all, Immi is a little girl. Much more suitable I'd have thought?'

Agnes eyed Immi with suspicion. 'What on earth are you wearing?' she demanded.

The child glanced down. 'Jeans,' she said puzzled. 'Have you never seen jeans before?'

'I've seen them,' Agnes said with a sniff. 'Usually on tradespeople. Never on people with breeding.'

'Brodie was wearing them when he came to our flat the other week,' Immi said slyly. 'Doesn't *he* have breeding?'

Agnes could have sworn Aubrey smothered a smile.

'That's different,' she said. 'You're a little girl. You should be in pretty dresses. Anyway, the point is, I don't think you'd be suitable company for our daughter. You're too – modern.'

'Oh.' Immi got to her feet. 'Well, I'll soon be making friends at my new school anyway. Never mind. I'd better go and help Mum unpack now the removal men have finished. It's going to take us *ages*. Catch you later.'

She ran lightly to the door and Aubrey called, 'It was very nice to meet you, Immi.' He waited until she'd run down the landing then said, 'Now Agnes, about Florence—'

He turned to find Agnes had gone.

'Oh, my dear,' he murmured mournfully. Had there ever been a more stubborn woman than Agnes Ashcroft?

12

Mia left Immi and me to finish unpacking while she headed downstairs to prepare dinner, which would be served at six o'clock sharp.

Immi still couldn't get over how large her new room was. 'I could fit a double bed in there easily, you know,' she informed me, a gleam in her eyes. 'Also, I was thinking, if we do get a bigger telly for the living room, can I have our old one in my room?'

'What, so you can watch YouTube until all hours? I don't think so,' I said, smiling. 'Besides, I'm not getting a bigger telly. How would I pay for it?'

My smile faded. I'd been such an idiot. I'd been so preoccupied with how I was going to feel being surrounded by ghosts, that I hadn't given much thought to how I was going to afford to live here. A big house might sound amazing, but it would cost a lot of money to keep it going. And what about the rest of the village? There would be repairs and maintenance. How was I supposed to fund that?

I felt a sudden panic as it dawned on me that neither Brodie nor Sir Lawrence had mentioned any of that stuff, and I'd been too stupid to ask. Naturally, there'd be rent coming in from the village's tenants, and there was an entrance fee to the estate, plus parking fees, but would that be enough to cover all the costs? Had I been taken in? Had this all been one giant con? What if they were struggling to cope and had offloaded the whole problem onto my shoulders, and now they were planning to scarper and leave their worries behind?

I should have read the epic 'rights and responsibilities' document! There could be anything in there. How did I know I hadn't agreed to take on a mountain of debt? I could be in court before the end of the year.

'What are you thinking?' Immi asked suspiciously. 'You've got that look on your face again.'

'What look?' I asked warily.

'The look that means you're worrying about something and you're trying really hard not to show it because you don't want me to worry about it too.'

'Nothing,' I said. 'I was just wondering how much those big tellies are, that's all.'

She beamed at me. 'I knew you'd come round to the idea!'

'Hmm.' I glanced at my watch. 'Okay, we'd better go down to dinner. We don't want to make a bad impression on our first day, do we?'

She slipped her arm through mine, and we headed out of our room, along the landing, and down the staircase.

'Oh no,' I murmured, seeing Agnes and Aubrey in the hall. That was all I needed. I'd hoped to spare Immi the pleasure of Agnes's acquaintance for at least the first day.

Aubrey glanced up and saw us descending the stairs. He nudged Agnes then beamed at us. 'Good evening, Miss Chase. Immi.'

'Hello, Mr Wyndham!' Immi said cheerfully. She nodded politely at Agnes. 'Hello, Mrs Wyndham.'

Mrs Wyndham? Hmm. I thought she was called Ashcroft.

'You've met?' I asked Immi. 'When did that happen?' I gave her a stern look. 'Did you sneak out of your room when I thought you were sorting out your bookcase?'

She looked guilty. 'I just wanted to have a quick look around, that's all. I can't help it if I bumped into Mr and Mrs Wyndham, can I?'

The casual way she talked about meeting up with ghosts blew my mind. I wasn't sure whether to be proud of her or terrified for her. How would she ever have a normal life and be accepted by other children with this curse hanging over her? Not every kid was like Violet.

We stepped into the hall and Agnes pursed her lips as she looked me up and down in obvious disapproval. Was I supposed to change for dinner or something? I had a sudden horrible feeling that Sir Lawrence and Brodie would be in evening dress. And there was I, still in my leggings and T-shirt! Then again, Agnes was in a nightgown and bed-jacket, so she could hardly talk.

'Your daughter took it upon herself to visit us earlier,' she told me. 'Barged into our room without so much as a knock on the door. Quite appalling manners.'

'Immi, you didn't,' I said in dismay.

'No, I didn't,' she said, eyeing Agnes with some reproach. 'The door was open. I waited outside until they noticed me and then I went in. They never said I couldn't,' she added.

'It really doesn't matter,' Aubrey said hastily. 'It was a pleasure to meet you, Immi, as I've already said.'

'Are you going to dinner?' I asked, wondering what they were doing in the hall.

If I hadn't known better, I'd have sworn there was a sharp intake of breath from Agnes, although given that she'd been dead for goodness knows how many years and hadn't taken a breath in all that time, it was hardly likely. She certainly did a good impression of it, though.

'Dinner?' she said bitterly. 'What would be the point of that?'

I could feel my face burning as I realised my faux pas. 'I'm so sorry,' I said, meaning it. 'I never thought...'

'Clearly,' she said.

'No harm done,' Aubrey told me. 'As a matter of fact, we're on the lookout for Florence. She should be home by now. We've told her time and time again not to stay out past five.'

'They never listen, do they?' I said, in a desperate attempt to worm my way into their good books. 'Kids, eh?'

'Quite,' Aubrey said.

'Florence is a free spirit,' Agnes said with a sniff. 'One cannot entirely blame her for choosing to ignore instructions on occasion.'

Her expression didn't match her words, though. I could see she was torn between concern and annoyance, and I knew that feeling all too well. I suppose most parents do.

'She can tell the time, right?' Immi asked.

'Of course!' Agnes spluttered.

'Well,' Aubrey amended, 'she can tell when it's five o'clock. We've taught her that much and told her to stay where she can see the church clock, so she won't be late. She tends to get rather confused with watches and clocks. Not to worry. She'll be with John and Robert, no doubt. Up to all sorts of mischief.'

'I can go and look for her if you like?' Immi offered.

'I – I wouldn't put you to any trouble,' Agnes said hesitantly.

'It's no trouble. I'm happy to help.'

I swear Agnes visibly softened as she stared at my daughter.

That harsh gleam in her eyes vanished, and it was like she was finally seeing Immi for the little girl she was and realised that all she was trying to do was make friends.

'That's kind of you,' Agnes murmured. 'Thank you, Imogen. Perhaps—'

She broke off as Aubrey said, 'Ah, here she is! Young scamp.'

Florrie, or Florence as Agnes obviously preferred, came skipping through the front door. Literally. It was a bit of a shock seeing her pass lightly through the solid wood, but I supposed it was just one more thing I'd have to get used to.

She looked completely unconcerned about being late, plaits flying, little wellies looking incongruous with her cotton dress and knitted cardigan. She stopped skipping when she saw me and Immi, though.

'Oh,' she said. 'You're here then.'

'Manners, dear child,' Agnes said gently. 'Florence, this is Imogen. She's Miss Chase's daughter, and she's ten years old, just like you.'

'I'm eleven next week,' Immi said.

'Lucky you,' Florrie said coldly. 'I'll never be eleven.'

'Oh, I'm so sorry!' Immi said immediately.

'I'm sure Immi didn't mean anything by that,' Aubrey told his daughter.

Immi looked stricken. 'I promise I didn't.'

'Don't care if you did,' Florrie said. She pushed past Agnes and ran up the stairs. 'You can go boil your 'ead for all I care!'

'*Head*, Florence! Boil your *head*!' Agnes called after her.

'I say,' Aubrey said with a tut, 'we really must have words with that child about her manners. I'm so sorry, Immi.'

'Yes, well...' Agnes looked deeply uncomfortable. 'I expect she's had a trying day, keeping an eye on those two young rogues. We'll leave you to your meal, Miss Chase. Imogen.'

She headed up the stairs and Aubrey went to follow her. 'It's lamb,' he whispered in my ear as he passed me. 'It smells utterly delicious. It's a cruel trick of fate that one's sense of smell is only heightened after death. I can't touch or taste anything, but oh the scents on the air...' There was a yearning tone to his voice that told me he'd give anything to be eating dinner with us that evening. Bless him.

'That went well,' I said to Immi, who wrinkled her nose uncertainly.

'I didn't mean to hurt Florrie's feelings,' she promised me.

I ruffled her hair. 'I know you didn't. Florrie isn't exactly the most genial of children. If I were you, I'd keep well out of her way.'

'Mrs Wyndham doesn't want me to play with her anyway,' she confided, as we headed to the dining room. 'She says I'm too modern for her.'

I never thought I'd agree with Agnes on anything, but I was on her side about this. The less Immi had to do with Florrie, the better.

13

It felt rude, somehow, to enter the dining room without knocking, so I tentatively rapped on the door before leading Immi in.

We'd seen the room earlier, as Mia had given us a whistlestop tour of the main rooms we'd be using, but even so, I couldn't get over how large and grand it was. Nor could I get over how ridiculous Sir Lawrence and Brodie looked, sitting next to each other at the far end of a long table that could have seated twenty people at least.

Both men got to their feet as we entered the room, and I was relieved to see they were dressed casually.

'Sit down, Callie,' said Sir Lawrence. 'You too, Immi. How are you managing up there? Settling in all right?'

The table had been set for four and, thankfully, we'd all been seated at the same end of it. It would have been pointless for Immi and me to sit at the opposite end, especially as we'd all probably have had to use loudspeakers to communicate if we did.

'The head of the table is vacant now,' Sir Lawrence pointed out. 'It's your seat, my dear.'

I reddened. 'Oh no! Please. That's your seat, if anyone's, not mine.'

'You're the owner of Harling Hall now, Callie,' he reminded me.

Brodie rubbed his temples, and I felt a sudden compassion for him. For both of them.

'I really don't want to sit at the head of the table,' I said. 'I wouldn't feel comfortable. Can we swap?'

He nodded. 'Very well. Maybe when we've moved out, you'll feel differently.'

'Actually,' I said, moving into his recently vacated seat, 'I want to talk to you about that.'

'Oh?' He raised an eyebrow, but at that moment, Mia pushed open the door and walked in carrying a tray of dishes.

'Let me help you,' I said, jumping to my feet.

'There's no need,' she assured me. 'I can manage.'

I watched, feeling increasingly uncomfortable as she set out dishes of various vegetables and a jug of gravy then tucked the tray under one arm and left the room again.

It seemed to take forever before she'd finally delivered all the plates and dishes she'd prepared for us. I wondered if it was always like this – Mia fetching and carrying for the Davenports while they sat and watched her.

'Is she not eating with us?' I whispered as Mia wished us all bon appétit and left, closing the door behind her.

Brodie shifted in his chair but said nothing, while Sir Lawrence gave me a surprised look and confirmed that Mia ate in the kitchen.

I mean, don't get me wrong, the kitchen was a lovely room and, if I'm being honest, I'd have preferred to eat in there myself, but even so. I wasn't sure I liked this set-up. Clearly, I wasn't cut out to be lady of the manor. I'd never had staff before, and I didn't care for it.

I had to admit, though, that Mia had done a cracking job with the evening meal. I'd never seen so many different vegetables served at once, not to mention the fluffy mashed potatoes and golden roasties, the mint sauce (which Sir Lawrence assured me was homemade with mint that grew in the herb garden at the back of the house), the roast lamb that made my mouth water just looking at it, and gravy that I was soon to discover was better than any I'd ever tasted before. She'd even made Yorkshire puddings – apparently in my honour. Not the frozen ones either. These were huge and very impressive.

Immi immediately began tucking in to her food, so it was a good job the Davenports showed no signs of wanting to say grace or anything like that.

Brodie ate quietly, making little eye contact with anyone. The only time he spoke was to offer his grandfather the mint sauce.

'I hope you have room for pudding,' Sir Lawrence said, winking at Immi, whose eyes positively lit up at the prospect of dessert. I, meanwhile, was busy wondering how much the Davenports spent on food, and whether I should have a chat with Mia about cutting the grocery bill.

My stomach turned over in dread at the thought. Not just of having to talk to Mia about such matters, but at the prospect of facing up to what this little venture was going to cost me, and how the heck I was going to pay for any of it.

I'd been so irresponsible and reckless to sign the contract without reading it properly. I should have asked for help from someone, but I'd always been sensitive about my inability to read as well and as quickly as other people. Now I was paying the price for my pride. There was no way I could afford this place, and now I was stuck with it until I found someone else who could see all the ghosts. How long would that take? I'd be bankrupt long before then. The council tax alone must be eye-watering.

Maybe Immi and I would die of starvation and then we'd become ghosts ourselves and live here forever at Harling Hall. At least it would be rent free.

'Callie?'

I blinked, realising I'd gone off into my own little world again, and that Sir Lawrence had been talking to me. I caught Brodie's eye, but he looked away. Miserable swine. He must be fed up with the situation, but he wasn't the only one with worries, and after all, it had been a different story when he'd tracked me down to beg me to take up his grandfather's offer. He ought to make up his mind what he wanted.

'Sorry, what did you say?' I asked, spearing a roast potato with my fork before shoving it in my mouth.

'I was asking how you'd settled in. Is everything all right for you?'

'More than all right,' I said, then blushed as I realised I'd spoken with my mouth full. He'd think I was a peasant. I chewed frantically then swallowed the potato, feeling a moment's panic as it seemed to sit somewhere in my throat before finally sliding down where it belonged. 'I really wasn't expecting the whole west wing,' I said, after taking a sip of water. 'Honestly, we didn't want to put you to any trouble.'

'Callie,' he said kindly, 'you're going to have to get used to the idea that Harling Hall is now yours, and although I suggested the west wing for you and Immi, the fact is, you can use whichever rooms you like. This is your home. The only thing I would say is that Agnes and Aubrey, along with young Florence, of course, stay in rooms close to ours in the East Wing, and I do think you'd be unwise to ask them to move.'

'Believe me, I wouldn't risk that,' I said, imagining Agnes's face if I so much as suggested it. 'This is as much their home as mine, and I wouldn't dream of asking them to change rooms.'

He nodded. 'I knew you were the right woman for the job as soon as I met you,' he said, leaning back in his chair with a contented smile. 'I can leave here now knowing that the estate is in good hands. It's such a relief.'

'That's what I wanted to talk to you about,' I said, grasping the opportunity while I had the nerve.

'I'm sorry?'

'About you leaving Harling Hall,' I continued.

Brodie made proper eye contact with me for the first time that evening.

'Wow, you really can't wait, can you? We'll leave as soon as possible, believe me, but first there are things you need to know about this place. Or do you think you're so amazingly capable that you don't need our help?'

'Brodie,' Sir Lawrence said sharply, 'I'm quite sure Callie didn't mean it the way it sounded.'

'For your information, *Mr Davenport*,' I said coldly, 'I was going to ask if you'd consider staying on here permanently, but if you're so eager to leave...'

Brodie's face turned pink, which would have been quite endearing if he hadn't proved himself to be such an arse.

'Permanently?' he asked, somewhat sheepishly.

Sir Lawrence shook his head regretfully. 'I'm sorry, Callie, but that won't be possible. It's very generous of you to offer, though, and I do appreciate your kindness.'

'But why?' I asked, genuinely perplexed. 'The Hall's more than big enough.'

'It simply isn't done that way,' he said.

'Rules were meant to be broken. Especially rules that make no sense. Who made these rules anyway?'

He shrugged. 'Who knows? It's just the way it's always been. When the estate is passed to a new family, the old one leaves.'

'Well, if you don't mind me saying so, it's a stupid rule,' I said. I glanced at Brodie, who was listening intently. It was obvious he didn't want to leave here, and why should he have to? 'Look,' I said, 'I'm the owner, right? So surely, it's up to me whether you stay or not?'

'I don't think it is.' Sir Lawrence laid his cutlery on his plate, pushed it away, and steepled his fingers, considering the matter.

'Is anything written down about this?' I asked. 'Is there some sort of guidebook dating back to the Norman Conquest or something?'

He laughed. 'I wish! I'm afraid not. These things are passed on verbally, and we've always continued the traditions.'

'But why?' Brodie asked, clearly frustrated. 'Just because something's been done a certain way in the past doesn't mean it has to be that way in the future.'

There was a plea in his voice that was unmistakable, and I thought maybe I could forgive him for being such an arse. Maybe.

'*I* think,' said Immi, carving up a Yorkshire pudding with relish, 'that it would be much better for the ghosts if we were all here to help them. Mum's scared stiff of messing this up, so she needs you here, Sir Lawrence. It would be a bit mean of you to go away and leave her to it, wouldn't it?'

Sir Lawrence smiled. 'Call me Lawrie, dear,' he told her.

'Okay.' Immi shrugged. 'What do you say then, Lawrie? Is it a deal?'

I couldn't help but admire her. Maybe Sir Lawrence had

chosen the wrong person for the job after all. I had no doubt, at that moment, that my daughter would be a far more capable ghost wrangler than I ever would.

'Are we going to stay here or not?' Brodie asked, his eyes boring into his grandfather's.

Sir Lawrence frowned. 'Is that what you'd like, Brodie? Really?'

'Of course. Why wouldn't I?'

'And how, dear boy, do you think that would help Callie?'

'Me?' I asked, startled. 'Well, from my point of view it would help a lot. What do I know about running this place?'

'And how would you learn if we were still here to do it all for you?' he asked reasonably.

'Probably a lot faster,' I said without hesitation.

He shook his head. 'You don't understand the mindset of the people in this village. Some of them have been here for generations, and they're fixed in their ways. As for the ghosts... The thing is, Callie, I fear if Brodie and I were still around, our residents – both living and otherwise – would always look to me for help and guidance. They'd struggle to accept you as the new owner, and it would take you far longer to settle in.'

'Is that a problem?' I asked slowly. 'Really? I mean, I don't mind if they look to you—'

'But you *should* mind,' he said. 'You must put your own stamp on this place, Callie. You must let everyone know in no uncertain terms that the Harling Estate is now in your hands, and if there are any problems or issues, it's you they should come to. Think about it,' he added gently. 'You haven't met many of our people yet, alive or not, and yet you must already be aware that Agnes and Florence are both determined to ignore you and will expect me to overrule you in various matters. If you were to implement some change –

however small – they'd be issuing demands for me to stop you.'

That much had become obvious. Neither had said so outright, but their attitudes towards me had made it clear they considered me an interloper, with no right to change anything. They would always think of Sir Lawrence as the true owner.

'Well...' I said.

'Mum!'

I flinched at the shocked expression on Immi's face.

'I know, but he's right,' I said reluctantly. 'It's going to be hard enough to win everyone over. If they've always got Sir Lawrence to turn to, it's going to be ten times worse.' I wouldn't admit it out loud, but the thought of him watching and judging me wasn't a great one either. It would be embarrassing enough when I kept messing up without having him and his grandson there to witness the terrible job I was doing as new owner.

Even so...

'What if I do something wrong?' I asked glumly. 'What if they *never* accept me?'

'You'll find your way,' he promised. 'Every new owner has faced the same dilemma, but they've all made it work somehow. However,' he turned to Brodie, 'having said all that, I suppose it's different for you. The ghosts can't communicate with you, so you being here wouldn't help them. They'd still have to rely on Callie.' He gave me a rueful look. 'I shouldn't ask for favours, but I will ask for this one. If you would allow Brodie to stay on after I leave, I'm sure you wouldn't regret it.'

'Grandpa!' Brodie sounded horrified.

'What? It seems the perfect solution to me. Brodie is very useful around the estate,' Sir Lawrence told me, 'and our living residents trust him. I'm sure he would be an asset to you.'

'Well...' I eyed Brodie doubtfully, all too aware that he wasn't particularly keen on me and wondering what he'd be like to live with if Sir Lawrence wasn't around to remind him about manners. I didn't want to take away his home, obviously, and I was sure he'd be a help with the tenants, but sharing a house with someone who doesn't like you and resents you for being there isn't the best recipe for a happy life. Besides, how would Sir Lawrence cope without him? I imagined he'd miss his grandson terribly. I'd much prefer it if they both stayed.

Brodie cleared his throat. 'Out of the question,' he said. 'Grandpa's right. Our time here is done. It's all on you now.'

I gaped at him. Wow! That was quite a turnaround. Five minutes ago, he'd been desperate to stay. He must really hate me for taking over his home. I felt sorry for him, naturally, but I didn't think it was fair of him to hold it against me. I hadn't asked for any of this, and he'd been the one to hunt me down and beg me to agree to the sale.

'Brodie—' said Sir Lawrence anxiously.

'If that's what you want.' I shrugged. He needn't do me any favours. If he felt that way about me, the sooner he was gone the better, as far as I was concerned.

'It is,' he said.

I was aware that Immi was giving me one of her hard stares, but I deliberately avoided looking at her.

'Well,' said Sir Lawrence dazedly, 'in that case, we'll leave together at the end of next month as arranged and make a new life for ourselves.'

'Do you have somewhere to go?' I asked worriedly, imagining the two of them turning up at some hostel or something.

'We'll be fine,' he promised. 'I do have one request, though, if you'd be so kind, Callie.'

'Go ahead,' I said, suddenly desperately sad and not a little scared that I hadn't managed to persuade Sir Lawrence to stay. I couldn't bring myself to look at Brodie.

'Will you please take a leaf out of your daughter's book and start calling me Lawrie? I really don't like being addressed so formally.'

How could I refuse?

'Done,' I said.

Immi glanced round at us all and I followed her gaze, noting the shuttered look in Brodie's eyes as he pushed away his plate. My stomach churned with nerves.

Oh lord, this was really happening, wasn't it? Lawrie and Brodie would be leaving this place at the end of June, which would leave me in sole charge. And I knew nothing about running a living history village, let alone how to deal with the two communities who lived here.

Suddenly, I'd completely lost my appetite.

14

It was agreed over pudding (which, like Brodie, I barely touched, even though it turned out to be the yummiest Eton mess) that Sir Lawrence – or rather, Lawrie – would show me the entire estate tomorrow and explain more to me about the ghosts. When I asked him how long it would take us to view the whole estate, he merely smiled and told me I'd find out soon enough.

Immi asked if she could come too, but I wasn't too sure what I was about to see, so I said she could maybe come the next time, hoping that would fob her off.

'But Mum! This is my home, too, and I need to meet the ghosts,' she begged.

That was exactly what I didn't want. The less Immi had to do with them, the better – at least until she was an adult. One day, she'd possibly have complete control of this village, but until then, I was determined to shelter her as much as possible and give her the most normal life I could manage.

'Not now,' I said firmly.

She pouted sulkily. 'Great. You can't keep me a prisoner here forever,' she said darkly.

I can try.

Mia agreed to keep an eye on her while I was gone, and I thought I'd really have to see what I could do to ease her load. She appeared to be doing everything in this house, and it didn't seem fair. It was something else I wanted to talk to Lawrie about.

My main concern, though, was broaching the subject of finances. I couldn't put it off any longer. It occurred to me that night, as I lay in bed, that I might now be responsible for feeding and supporting the Davenports for the next month, as well as Immi and me.

Brodie wasn't at breakfast the following morning and Mia said he'd eaten early and headed out to deal with some problem at the museum.

'Sounds ominous,' I said.

'Oh, Brodie will handle it,' she said. 'He always does. Er, what are you doing?'

I was filling a bowl with hot water, so I'd have thought it was obvious. 'Helping you with the washing up,' I said. 'Oh, don't tell me. The lady of the manor isn't allowed to put her delicate hands in soapy water.'

She laughed. 'It's not that, but why bother? We have a dishwasher.'

'Oh!' I hadn't expected that. 'Where?'

I turned the tap off and Mia gave me a more thorough tour of the kitchen, which had been fitted out beautifully with ivory cabinets and solid oak worktops. There was a large, pastel-blue range taking pride of place in what had once clearly been an inglenook fireplace, and a surprising number of modern appliances, hidden behind doors that I'd presumed belonged to cupboards.

'There's also a utility room that used to be the scullery,' she explained.

'Do you do the washing for everyone in this house?' I asked.

She nodded. 'I do. Do you have anything that needs washing today?'

'I'm not being funny,' I said, 'but I'd rather do my own washing if it's all the same to you. And Immi's. And while we're on the subject, I don't feel comfortable with you doing all the cooking either.'

She stared at me. 'Didn't you enjoy last night's dinner?'

'Oh, God, no! I mean, yes! Of course,' I said hastily. 'That's not what I meant. I just don't think it's right that you're cooking for us and then eating your own dinner in the kitchen. Not to mention all the other stuff you do. It's not fair. I think we should talk about your terms of employment.'

And maybe she could tell me exactly how much I'd be expected to pay her. Quite frankly, I had a strong suspicion that I'd be making her redundant before the week was up.

'But it's my job, Callie,' she said patiently. 'And I enjoy it.'

'You do?' I couldn't imagine why. 'How do you fit everything in and keep this place so spotless?'

She laughed. 'You surely don't think I look after Harling Hall all by myself?'

I frowned. 'You don't?'

'Of course not! Good grief, if it was all down to me, this place would be filthy. There's no way I could keep on top of it. Lawrie has staff. I mean, er, *you* have staff.'

'Staff?' My heart sank. More money. This just got worse and worse.

'Yes, staff.' She opened the dishwasher and began loading the breakfast dishes into it. 'There's Douglas, Mac and Andrea, who work in the gardens. Then Angela, Bonnie, and Monica do the cleaning. I do the cooking, the laundry, and various admin tasks.

Of course, we have various people who come in now and then to do extra stuff when needed.'

'How often do these gardeners and cleaners come in?' I asked faintly.

She looked puzzled. 'Every day, obviously.' She eyed me with sudden suspicion. 'You did *read* the papers Mr Eldridge sent you, didn't you? It wasn't just a deed of sale, you know. Everything to do with the running of the house was explained in there.'

'I may have skimmed,' I admitted.

'As in...'

'As in I barely glanced at it.'

She sighed. 'Well, why don't you read it now before Lawrie calls you?'

'Because,' I said, 'I don't have it. I accidentally sent it all back to Lawrie's solicitor.'

'Not Lawrie's solicitor,' she reminded me. 'Mr Eldridge works for the estate, which means you.' She slammed the dishwasher door shut. 'So haven't you asked him to return your copy?'

'Not yet.'

'Have you told them you've moved?'

I blushed. 'Er, no.'

'Callie!' She shook her head, exasperated. 'I'll get onto them straightaway. I'll ask them to send the documents here instead of the flat. We wouldn't want those to get into the wrong hands, would we?'

My face was burning. 'I told you I'd be rubbish at all this,' I muttered.

She put her arm around me. 'You're not rubbish at it. Well, maybe a bit. But look what's happened to you over the last few weeks! No wonder you're all at sixes and sevens. Hey, don't look so down. That's what we're here for, remember? To help you.

You'll get the hang of it, believe me. If I can settle in this village, anyone can.'

'You're not from round here?' I'd assumed she was Rowan Vale born and bred.

She hurried over to the sink and poured the water away. 'Er, no. London. I only arrived here five years ago.'

'Really? What brought you here?'

Mia gave me a bright smile. 'Came for a visit and fell in love with the place. Luckily for me, Lawrie was looking for a housekeeper stroke admin assistant, and I fitted the bill. He offered me the job and I accepted.'

'Just like that?' I asked, curious.

She laughed. 'Unbelievable, right? Who in their right minds would accept an offer from a total stranger and move to a new place without checking it all out first?'

'Okay, you've got me,' I said. Even so, I wasn't convinced it had been as simple as she was making out. There was something distinctly edgy about her tone of voice.

I decided, though, that would wait for another day. I had enough to worry about for now, knowing I was going to be left alone to manage this entire estate very soon, and not having the faintest idea what that involved and, more to the point, how to finance it.

Brodie was out of the house all morning, and there was no sign of Lawrie, though I'd met the cleaners who were cheery enough. They clearly thought I was far too young and inexperienced to issue orders, however, and before I could even say anything other than my name, they informed me in no uncertain times that they had a routine which had always suited Lawrie and they intended to stick to it.

Not that I'd had any intention of changing it, but it didn't bode well for the future, and I couldn't help thinking that Lawrie had been right. If he was around, I was never going to be accepted, even though it grieved me to admit it.

Immi and I spent the morning finishing up the unpacking and getting the rooms we were occupying just as we wanted them. I'd given all my kitchen appliances to a charity shop before we left home because I clearly wasn't going to have my own kitchen, but at Harling Hall, we had a bedroom each, a living room, and a bathroom, and I wanted them to feel as familiar and comfortable as possible. Everything in our lives had changed so much, it was important that Immi and I had some continuity in our living quarters.

'What are you going to do this afternoon while I'm out?' I asked her, feeling a bit pensive about leaving her alone with Agnes on the rampage. Although, I did think she'd maybe softened towards my daughter a little, and I supposed Aubrey was likely to be on hand to make sure she behaved herself.

'Explore the house,' Immi said immediately. 'I want to know as much about the history of this place as possible. I'm going to ask Mr Wyndham to show me round.'

I felt sick at the thought, particularly as I'd deliberately kept her from joining Lawrie and me on our tour of the village. I had to accept that my daughter could see ghosts, but the last thing I wanted was for her to voluntarily mix with them. She should be outside, making new friends. There must surely be some children other than Florrie, John and Robert living in Rowan Vale? Preferably children who were alive.

'Okay,' I said reluctantly, 'but tomorrow, we'll walk round the village together, okay? I should know a bit more about the place after today's tour with Lawrie, so I'll be able to show you round too. We need to spend our time with people who are – well...'

'Breathing?' she suggested, a knowing look on her face.

'Mum, I'll probably be starting school on Tuesday, though I don't know why I'm bothering when term finishes in July.'

'You know why,' I said. 'You need to settle in and make new friends. It will help you when you move to secondary school in September.'

'Yeah, yeah.' She dismissed this argument with a wave of her hand. 'Anyway, the point is, I'll be spending every day with people who are alive. It won't hurt me to mix with a few dead ones until then, will it?'

I couldn't imagine how she could be so blasé. I remembered my attitude when I was even younger than she was now. The knowledge that I'd spoken to ghosts had left me feeling so isolated, so different. I'd spent all the years since trying to be as normal as everyone else, that feeling of abnormality never leaving me, long after I'd forgotten about my paranormal experiences. Given the position I was now in, I couldn't help reflecting it all seemed like a gigantic waste of time and angst.

Immi's future lay in Rowan Vale, and that meant accepting she was always going to talk to ghosts, even though I was determined to limit her time with them as much as I possibly could.

It also meant accepting that ghosts were *my* future. I had to find a way to deal with it and learn how to stop feeling like a freak because of it.

At five to one, I kissed Immi goodbye, after first extracting a promise that if Mr Wyndham said no to showing her around the Hall, she wouldn't badger him or make a nuisance of herself. The last thing I wanted was for her to give Agnes any ammunition.

Lawrie was waiting for me downstairs, and he beamed at me as I stepped into the hall. I noticed he had a walking stick with him, and immediately asked if we were going to do the rounds in the car, as that seemed a more sensible idea given his obvious age and difficulty walking. After all, surely as the owners past and present of the village, we were entitled to drive? Come to think of it, hadn't Brodie said something about villagers being able to have cars? That had probably been in the paperwork too...

'Oh no,' Lawrie said, leading me out of the house with evident determination. 'There are far easier ways to see Rowan Vale. Are you looking forward to this?'

I swallowed. 'I suppose so.'

'Oh, come now, Callie! That's not the attitude, is it? This is the first real day of your new life, and I want you to embrace it. To understand how blessed you are to have this incredibly good fortune. What we have is a privilege, do you see? Well,' he added with a nod, 'you will do after today. I'm sure of that.'

'Sorry,' I said, ashamed. 'It's not that I'm ungrateful, although I must seem that way. There's just so much to get my head around, and I really do have to talk to you, Lawrie. There's something worrying me, and I can't focus on anything else until I get my answers to that particular problem.'

'We'll deal with all your questions later today,' he promised me. 'For now, let's just enjoy our adventure. Time to view your domain, Callie. You're going to be amazed.'

15

It took a fair old amount of time just to get to the bottom of the drive. I hadn't noticed how infirm Lawrie was, but then I realised I'd only really seen him sitting down. It dawned on me that he wasn't the powerhouse of energy I'd presumed him to be. No wonder everyone had been so anxious to find a replacement for him. They'd clearly understood that, before too long, running the estate was going to be far too much for him.

I was beginning to worry about how long this tour of my 'domain' was going to take, but to my surprise, we stopped just outside the gates of Harling Hall, and Lawrie leaned against the wall with some relief.

'Are you okay?' I asked. 'Maybe we should go back? I can get the car.'

'No need, Callie,' he said with a smile, and I turned my head to see the old Leyland bus trundling down the road towards us.

Lawrie waved his walking stick in the air, and the bus drew to a halt outside the gate.

'Wow,' I said, impressed, as we settled into our seats,

surrounded by excited tourists. 'I didn't know there was a bus stop here.'

'No stop,' he admitted, as the bus set off again, 'but if anyone wants to get on or off at the Hall, they only have to ask the conductor or wave the bus down.'

'Good to know,' I said. 'I should have brought a notebook or something to make notes, shouldn't I?'

'You won't need one,' he assured me. 'You can't learn all you need to know about the village from notes. You have to see it. You have to *feel* it. And you will.'

It was good to be back on the old bus again. It felt like a lifetime ago since I'd travelled on it in April.

'There are four buses working in the estate,' Lawrie murmured. 'Two cover the inner circle and two the outer circle. This route runs from the train station to the village centre. The other runs from the garage to the outer boundaries on the other side of the estate, via the woodland. It takes you as close to the barrow and stones as it's possible to get by vehicle. After that, it's a short walk through the woods to where they're situated.'

I wasn't certain he'd be up to that, but I was momentarily distracted by the snatches of conversation I could hear from the other passengers. They were clearly already enchanted by the views of the village, and there were lots of appreciative murmurings about the pretty buildings and stunning scenery.

I felt a sudden and unexpected rush of pride as the realisation hit me that they were talking about *my* village. My home. I had to swallow down tears as the emotion threatened to overwhelm me.

I turned to find Lawrie smiling knowingly at me. I blushed but he kindly didn't say anything. He really didn't have to.

We all got off the bus at the central stop, opposite the church. The tourists quickly divided into two groups. One group rushed to explore the grounds and interior of the Church of All Souls, while the others headed straight to the riverside where they cooed over the clear water and the little stone bridges that crossed the Faran.

They were soon taking photos of The Quicken Tree on the other side of the river. Its golden stone walls could be glimpsed through a boundary of rowan trees, and I mused that if they thought those views were pretty, they were going to be in for a treat when they walked a little further along, rounded the corner and discovered the entrance to the pub.

'Shall we?' Lawrie asked. For a moment, I'd entirely forgotten he was there.

'Sorry,' I said, but he chuckled.

'It's a marvellous feeling,' he said, as we began to walk, 'when you realise how much other people appreciate the beauty of your home. It was different for me. I was born and brought up here. I always knew it was my home, but for you it's all new.'

'I still can't believe it's real,' I admitted. 'Sometimes, I think I'm dreaming. Oh!'

I stopped as an old man with grey hair and a dog collar came rushing through the lych gate of the church, waving his hands as if trying to shoo the tourists away. They took no notice of him whatsoever.

'Who on earth is that?' I asked. As the icy tingles began in my shoulders, I said, 'Or who *was* he anyway?'

'Now, Callie, we never talk about our residents as if they no longer exist. They're as real as you or I. The fact they're not actually breathing is neither here nor there. That splendid chap is Silas Alexander. Died in 1927, aged seventy-five. Used to be the vicar of All Souls. Sadly for him, he's witnessed a lot of change over the last century that he finds, er, difficult.'

At that moment, Silas spotted us and shook his fist at us

alarmingly. 'I blame you for this, Davenport. You and your family! Turned the place into a wretched circus!'

Lawrie smiled and waved at him and Silas gave a snort of rage and stomped back into the church.

'Good grief,' I said. 'Who's rattled his cage?'

'Silas doesn't approve of the tourists,' Lawrie explained. 'More than that,' he added with a twinkle in his eye, 'he definitely doesn't approve of Amelia Davies. Our current vicar.'

'Oh? *Oh*.' I nodded. 'I see. No doubt Silas doesn't approve of women vicars in general, right?'

'To put it mildly.' Lawrie chuckled. 'He's quite a forceful character, as you can probably see.'

'Are they all this bolshy?' I asked worriedly, as we passed The Quicken Tree and walked along the picturesque Faran Lane. 'Apart from Aubrey, who seems lovely, I've had nothing but grief. Agnes is a real tyrant, and Florrie seems to be heading the same way. Then there's Bill and Ronnie, fighting on the station platform. I mean, I get that it must be quite traumatic to find yourself dead, but even so.'

'Oh, their bark is worse than their bite,' he said cheerfully. 'Bill and Ronnie wouldn't know what to do with themselves if they didn't have their feud to keep them going. Florence is just a child, after all. As for Agnes – you might find this hard to believe, but deep down, she has a heart of gold. Life wasn't easy for her, you know, and her afterlife is her opportunity to assert herself for once. I daresay Silas has a gentler side, although it must be said he hasn't so far shown it.'

He laughed. I took comfort from the fact he obviously wasn't intimidated by any of the ghosts, however badly they behaved. And really, if I'd found myself trapped forever as a spirit, unable to touch or taste anything, or make myself seen or heard to almost every other person, I'd probably have got quite bolshy too. I supposed I should be a bit more generous and understanding towards my ghostly tenants.

We passed a couple more little stone bridges where several people were holding up their mobile phones to film the scenery, exclaiming loudly as a family of ducks paddled towards them. On the opposite side of the river was the village green, surrounded by more beautiful buildings – a variety of Victorian-themed shops and cottages.

There was an old well in the centre of the green, dating from the fourteenth century, and lots of tourists were gathered round it, snapping away with their cameras. Others were excitedly photographing the staff who, dressed in Victorian finery, were parading outside the shops.

'Is it always this busy?' I asked, noting how many people were crowding the pavements and both sides of the riverside, peering through the shop windows, or just sitting on the grass – many of them eating and drinking.

'In late spring and summer, yes,' Lawrie said. 'It quietens down in autumn and winter. After Christmas, it's almost like a ghost town.' He gave a whoop of laughter, and I thought it would be quite nice to see Rowan Vale out of season.

I noticed we were walking more slowly now, and I eyed Lawrie with some concern. 'You really don't have to do this,' I said. 'I'm sure Mia could give me a tour of the village.'

He looked surprised. 'Why on earth would you want that? Mia can't introduce you to any passing ghosts and— oh, good afternoon, Walter.'

He nodded courteously as an elderly man wearing an embroidered jacket with a broad linen collar and ribbon ties, and a pair of breeches, walked towards us.

'Sir Lawrence.' The man gave a theatrical bow. 'How are you this fine day?'

'Very well, thank you. Walter, allow me to introduce you to Miss Callie Chase. She is the new owner of the Harling Estate. I expect you've been waiting to meet her.'

Walter's eyes gleamed and the icy feeling in my shoulders returned.

'Indeed I have!' He bowed a second time. 'It is an honour to meet you, Mistress Chase. I expect Sir Lawrence has already told you a good deal about me.'

'Not yet, Walter,' said Lawrie hastily. 'I'm just showing Callie the village and explaining a few things to her. There's a lot for her to take on board, as I'm sure you can imagine, so I'm taking my time.'

'Of course,' Walter said gravely. '"Wisely and slow; they stumble that run fast."' He beamed at me. 'That was one of mine, you know.'

I had no idea what he was talking about, so I just nodded and smiled.

'If I can be of any assistance, do let me know,' Walter told Lawrie. 'I am more than happy to help, and I have a great deal of knowledge and experience, so—'

'You certainly do,' Lawrie said, 'and I will bear that in mind. Thank you, Walter. Now, we really must get on.'

'Of course, of course. "Let every man be master of his time",' Walter said, nodding furiously. 'That was one of mine too,' he added. 'I well remember the day I said it to him. I was—'

'We must go,' Lawrie interjected. 'I'm sure we'll be seeing you again very soon. Good day to you.'

'Good day, Sir Lawrence. Mistress Chase.'

Lawrie took my arm, and I swear he walked away from Walter at twice his usual speed, stick or no stick.

'Who on earth was that?' I asked, hardly able to suppress a giggle.

Lawrie rolled his eyes. 'That was Walter Tasker,' he said. 'Don't get me wrong – he's a decent man, but an insufferable bore, with delusions of grandeur. He died in 1612, aged seventy-one, and if I told you he once taught at The King's New School, would that give you a clue?'

I shrugged. 'Nope. Sorry.'

'The King's New School in Stratford-upon-Avon?'

I gasped. 'Shakespeare?'

'That's right.' Lawrie sighed. 'Walter was one of Shakespeare's schoolmasters, and he's convinced that he taught "Young Will" everything he ever knew about great writing. Not only that but he takes credit for many of his quotes.'

'So that's what he meant.' I grinned. 'Completely wasted on me. I know very little about Shakespeare.'

'I'm sure Walter will love to educate you,' he said wryly. 'We're going down here now, Callie,' he added, nudging me slightly so I turned left off Faran Lane and we walked down Honeywell Way, a narrow, winding road edged on one side by a tall hedge, but with a few scattered dwellings on the other.

Lawrie led me to the second of those. It was another gorgeous stone house, larger than the cottages I was more familiar with in Rowan Vale and set back from the roadside with a five-barred gate leading into a big courtyard.

'Posh,' I observed. 'Who lives here then?'

'Oh, the house may be big,' Lawrie remarked, 'but don't worry. Clara and Jack aren't posh. They're lovely people. Jack's most probably at work. He's a train driver,' he explained. 'Drives one of our steam engines. Clara's expecting us, though.'

'Jack? The chauffeur?'

'That's right! I'd forgotten you'd met him. Lovely chap.' He pushed open the gate and ushered me into the courtyard.

What, I wondered, was I about to see now?

16

Clara must have seen us coming, as she'd thrown open the back door before we'd even knocked. She was probably fortyish, with untidy, red hair and a wide smile. I liked her immediately.

'You must be Callie. You made it then! Come in, and I'll put the kettle on.'

I glanced at Lawrie who nodded and motioned to me to follow her. We were led through a large, though slightly chaotic kitchen, into a comfortable living room with squashy sofas and a rather hairy carpet, due no doubt to the most gorgeous dog I'd ever seen who was lying in front of the fireplace, eyeing us with interest.

As I gazed at him appreciatively, he got to his feet and came over to investigate.

'Oh,' I said, ruffling his ears with pleasure, 'aren't you beautiful?'

Clara beamed at me. 'He is, isn't he? That's Toby. He's a Bernese Mountain Dog.'

'He's very friendly,' I observed with some relief. He was quite a hefty dog, after all. 'How old is he?'

'Four.' Clara waved a hand round the room. 'Apologies for the dog hair everywhere but he sheds terribly, especially at this time of year. I've practically got my Dyson glued to my hand. You're Callie Chase, I take it? I'm Clara Milsom. Sit yourselves down. Tea? Coffee?'

'We can't stay long,' Lawrie said gently. 'We're here to look at the village.'

I nodded at the framed photos on the walls, showing three lively looking, red-haired, freckle-faced boys. 'You have three sons?'

Clara beamed at me. 'We do. God knows where they are at the moment. I can't keep them indoors when the sun's shining. That's Freddie, the youngest. He's six. And Declan, nine. And then there's Ashton, our eldest, who's eleven. He starts big school in September. How old's your daughter?'

'Nearly eleven,' I said, realising that Immi's birthday was next week and I hadn't even bought her a card, let alone a present. I'd have to do something about that. 'She starts at the local primary school on Tuesday all being well. We're seeing the headmistress on Monday.'

'Oh, she's lovely. You won't have any problems there. Your girl might be in Ashton's class. I'll ask him to keep an eye on her, bless her. Well, I won't keep you waiting any longer. You're here to see the village and see the village you will.'

I frowned, not entirely sure what she meant, but Lawrie indicated I should once again follow her, so I did. Clara led us back into the courtyard and through one of the outhouses, which contained some bikes and a few tools. We went through another door and stepped out into an amazing new world.

'Oh, my goodness!'

Whatever I'd been expecting, it certainly hadn't been this. The entire village of Rowan Vale in miniature lay before me –

knee-high buildings complete with the distinctive red-brick mill and its water wheel, the Church of All Souls, and the village green with the old well. A few moments later and I realised even the model village itself was represented, which struck me as incredible.

'Isn't it wonderful?' asked Lawrie with obvious pride. 'Built in the 1930s to one-ninth scale, out of real Cotswold stone, and by genuine local craftsmen. You'll find everything here, Callie. Not just the village, but the entire estate – even the Wyrd Stones and the railway station. Come with me and I'll show you its secrets.'

Now I understood why we hadn't needed a car. Lawrie could show me around the whole estate from this very spot. I linked my arm through his when he offered it, and together, we strolled through the little streets and lanes, as he pointed out various buildings.

'Wait a minute,' I said, as we paused beside an impressive model of All Souls, 'is that – no way! Is that *Silas*?'

I peered down at the little figure in the dog collar, shaking his fist at unwitting parishioners. 'Bloody hell,' I said, unable to suppress my laughter. 'It is!'

'I'm afraid some of the craftsmen weren't entirely respectful of our residents,' Lawrie said dryly.

'Are any of the other ghosts represented?' I asked eagerly.

'I'll leave you to it,' Clara said. 'Nice to meet you, Callie.'

'And you,' I told her warmly. 'Thank you for making us so welcome.'

When she'd returned to the house, Lawrie squeezed my arm. 'You see, although I do object to the way some of the ghosts have been depicted here, it's nevertheless useful to see them all in one place. My legs aren't what they were so being able to show you around the estate from here is a blessing.'

'Are you saying all the ghosts are here?'

'The ones we know about, and the ones who'd arrived when this model was made in the thirties. Unfortunately, there are others on the outskirts of the estate who keep themselves to themselves, as I told you before. I expect they have their reasons. Maybe the modern world is just too much for them. Who knows? However, there are plenty of others who dwell in the village, and they're depicted here. For instance, do you recognise this one?'

He bent forward slightly and pointed to a figure who was bowing deeply to a bemused looking woman. I squinted at it, realising he had a book under his arm.

I bit my lip as I met Lawrie's gaze. I knew he didn't approve of how the ghosts had been depicted but I had to admit to finding it very funny.

'That's Walter Tasker,' I said. 'I believe he's carrying a book of Shakespearean quotes.'

'I know. Isn't it awful?' To my relief, Lawrie suddenly chortled with glee. 'I really shouldn't laugh. It's so disrespectful. Goodness knows what Walter makes of it.'

'He's seen this?'

'Oh, they've all seen it. We can hardly keep them out, can we?'

'I don't get it, though,' I said. 'After you made me that offer, I'll admit I googled the heck out of this place, and there was no mention whatsoever of a model village.'

'Because it's not open to the public,' Lawrie explained.

'Seems like a waste to me,' I said. 'I think the tourists would love it.'

'This belongs to Jack, not me. Or rather, you. His great-grandfather was one of the craftsmen who built it. I shouldn't think he and Clara would want tourists tramping around their back garden, especially as they have three young children to consider.'

'It's amazing,' I said, gazing around in wonder. Deep in the woodland at the centre of the model estate, I spotted something through the trees. 'Are those the Wyrd Stones?'

'Indeed. Let's take a closer look.'

We carefully picked our way over to where an incredibly realistic replica of the stones was laid out. I imagined it was a lot easier to find them from our viewpoint than it would be on the ground.

'I googled these, too,' I admitted. 'It's all very odd, isn't it? No wonder they're called the Wyrd Stones.'

He laughed. 'It's not Wyrd as in weird, Callie. In this context, it comes from the Anglo-Saxon word for fate. Controlling human destiny.'

I stared down at the barrow in one clearing, where human bones had been discovered. In the corner of an opposite clearing stood a ring of fourteen Neolithic stones, with three separate stones in the middle – a fairly big one with two smaller ones leaning towards it. Hidden between a dense group of rowan trees was a monolith. Looking down on them now, I could see that the three sites were positioned in a perfect triangle.

'The King's Court,' Lawrie said, pointing to the ring of stones, 'with the Queen Stone and her children in the centre, and there, all on his own, The Penitent King.' He gazed down at the monolith and sighed.

'It's just a story,' I said, seeing how depressed he looked suddenly.

I'd read all about it online. The stones were the subject of a local myth. Long, long ago in the mists of time, a witch had apparently seduced a king. Despite his wife's anguish and the pleas of the courtiers, he was besotted, and all set to have the Queen murdered so he could marry the witch.

Then at the last moment, his youngest child, the apple of his eye, brought him to his senses. The King realised what he'd been about to do, declared he'd been enchanted, and instead, ordered the death of the witch.

In a fury, the witch turned first the Queen and her two children to stone, before doing the same to the courtiers who'd surrounded them in a vain bid to protect them. The King was forced to watch, his heart allegedly broken. Finally, he met the same fate, and the witch left him all alone so he could never be with his wife and children again. She'd reputedly sworn that the villagers and all their descendants would be doomed to stay on the King's estate forever, effectively as trapped as he was. Maybe that was one explanation for there being so many ghosts round here?

'Who knows?' Lawrie murmured when I asked the question. 'It's a sad story all round, isn't it? No one really wins. Maybe even the witch only acted so cruelly because her heart was broken.'

'All because of one man and his lust. He sounds a bit like Henry the Eighth to me. Pity someone didn't turn *him* to stone before he started divorcing and beheading his wives. It's the same old story,' I added bitterly. 'Married man fancies a fling, then when his wife finds out, the woman's branded a witch and the blame lands on her. Nothing changes.'

'He behaved badly,' Lawrie agreed, giving me a curious look. 'Perhaps some things can never be forgiven.'

I wasn't sure if he was referring to Henry the Eighth or the mythological king, but he was right. Some things never could.

'Who's that?' I'd noticed a figure standing to attention between two trees, not far from the monolith. 'One of the King's guards?'

'Oh no!' Lawrie cheered up immediately. 'That's Quintus Severus, our second-century Roman centurion. Isn't he splendid? He was one of the army's North African soldiers, you know. Came to Britain and had a very distinguished career. Quite remarkable what he achieved. Started as an auxiliary, became a Roman citizen and a legionary, rose through the ranks to become a centurion. Served forty years, can you believe?'

'Forty years? Wow!'

'After he retired, he was well rewarded. He ended up a wealthy man, living in the colonia, Glevum – the place we now know as Gloucester. His common-law wife was originally from a village a few miles from here.'

'What's he doing on the estate then?' I asked.

'He was on his way to visit her family. Sadly, he never made it. He died here in Rowan Vale.'

'How did he die?'

Lawrie hesitated. 'One rule, Callie. We never reveal the manner of the ghosts' deaths. Those are their stories to tell, and when they trust you enough to tell you – well, that's when you'll know you've won them over.'

'Right,' I said, suitably chastened. 'Duly noted.'

'What I can tell you is that, after a period of mourning with her family, his wife and children returned to Gloucester. Quintus says he never saw them again.' He sighed. 'I think perhaps that's why he stands guard near the King. He can relate to his plight. He's a most interesting chap. I'm sure you'll like him, once you can get him to actually talk to you.'

'So many people to meet,' I murmured. 'So much to remember. How am I ever going to do it?'

'Oh, you'll manage,' he assured me. 'It will take time, but you'll do it. Believe me, if you forget anything, they'll be sure to remind you.'

We turned away from the stones and back to the village. I could see the models of Harling Hall, complete with Agnes and Aubrey. There was no sign of Florrie, though.

'Of course not,' Lawrie said when I mentioned it. 'As I told you, this was created in the 1930s. Florence didn't move here until 1941, bless her. The year I was born, as a matter of fact. Agnes always says she was blessed with two children that year.' He laughed. 'There's the farm, look, and the mill. It was a proper, working mill back in those days, of course. Rather dingy and grubby compared with how it looks today, and no teashop or bakery back then. The teashop started up in 1938, and the bakery not until the late 1950s.'

He continued to show me around, pointing out various sites of interest and filling me in on the ghosts that were depicted, while admitting that several newer arrivals were absent, and that I'd have to be introduced to them personally.

'That's the garage,' he told me, pointing to a building down a lane I'd missed as I'd arrived in the village. It was just before we passed Harling Hall. 'It's where the buses live at night, and you'll see a few vintage cars on the forecourt, too, to give it some atmosphere. There are proper working petrol pumps – no self-service, of course. We have mechanics who fill up your car for you. Sadly, the petrol is charged at today's prices, whatever the signs say.' He chuckled.

'Brodie did mention some cars were allowed in the village,' I said.

'It would be impossible and unfair to ban them for locals, particularly as some of our tenants work in other villages or towns,' he said. 'However, the cars must be parked on the tenants' car park here.' He jabbed his finger towards a patch of land just beyond the garage. 'See that building there? That's where visitors can hire mobility scooters or wheelchairs to tour the village. And we provide taxis with disabled access that can be booked at the railway station, as unfortunately our vintages buses can't take wheelchairs.'

'I was going to ask you about that,' I said, relieved. 'Good to know.'

I also learned that the station porter who I'd nicknamed 'Perks' was yet another ghost. His name was Percy Swain, and he'd died in 1905. Apparently, he still took his role very seriously and was extremely peeved by Ronnie's and Bill's behaviour. I'd have been, too, if I'd had to deal with them every day. Even in miniature the two of them were engaged in fisticuffs on the station platform.

'And here,' Lawrie said proudly, 'is the cinema.'

'There's a cinema?' How had I missed that? Visions of cosy, popcorn and nacho-filled evenings watching the latest blockbuster with Immi filled my mind. Something normal for us to do!

'Of course.' He indicated a stone building tucked away in a small cul-de-sac almost directly opposite the mill complex. 'There. It's marvellous. We have a wonderful collection of 1940s movies, and usherettes serving orange squash and those little tubs of ice cream in the intermission.'

'Great,' I said, my heart sinking. I could well imagine Immi's reaction if I invited her to watch a 1940s film with me, with orange squash as an incentive.

'Did Clara and Jack both grow up in the village?' I asked, as we finally prepared to leave Honeywell.

'Jack did, but oddly, he met Clara when they were both on holiday in Scotland. What are the chances? Love at first sight. Very romantic. Clara – well, she's a good sort. I was delighted when she and Jack married. She fitted in beautifully, and it's good to see Honeywell House full of children again.'

'Was Jack brought up at the house?'

'He was. His family have been tenants here for as long as anyone can remember.'

'And does it have any other occupants?' I asked.

He smiled. 'There doesn't appear to be a ghost at Honeywell House at all.'

'Lucky Jack and Clara then,' I said. 'Can either of them see any of the ghosts in the village? Well, Jack at least.'

I wasn't sure, but I thought Lawrie hesitated before answering. 'Er, no. They can't.'

There was one thing I still wanted to know as we headed back to the church where we'd be able to hail the bus.

'I know this sounds crazy,' I said, 'but you don't happen to know of an American ghost around here, do you?'

He stared at me. 'How did you know that?'

'Well,' I confessed, 'Immi saw her, back when we were on the school trip. I'm not sure where she was but they talked a bit and she told Immi how she died and – hey, didn't you say that meant a ghost trusted you? If they tell you how they died, I mean.'

'Yes, that's right.' Lawrie looked amazed. 'And she confided in Immi? How very odd. That's Harmony. Harmony Hill. You may have heard of her?'

I frowned. The name was ringing a bell, but I couldn't think where from. 'Not really,' I admitted, 'but she told Immi she'd drowned.'

'So she did, bless her. She was a Hollywood actress,' he explained as we sat down on a bench in front of the church.

'Hollywood? What on earth was she doing here?'

'It's a very sad story,' he murmured, glancing round as if to check she wasn't there listening. 'Harmony was over here filming in 1946.'

'In this village?'

He shook his head. 'No, about twenty miles away, but for some reason, she'd taken herself off and spent the entire day drinking at The Quicken Tree. No one wanted to refuse her, what with her being a Hollywood star, so sadly she got very drunk indeed. They found her body in the Faran the next morning. It caused a furore in the papers at the time. Apparently, she had quite a reputation in Hollywood, and some of the reporters seemed to believe her fate was inevitable.'

'Poor thing,' I said. 'What a way to end up. I do vaguely remember hearing about her. Why were you so surprised that I mentioned her?'

'Harmony is one of those ghosts who keeps herself very much to herself,' he explained. 'She's been seen in the village occasionally, but we have no idea where she stays. If any of the ghosts know, they're saying nothing. As for conversation – she simply doesn't talk. Not to those of us who are living anyway. Not to anyone, as far as I know. It's a shame but it's her decision. It's extraordinary that she talked to Immi. But,' he added, brightening, 'perhaps it's a good sign. Perhaps she's finally beginning to accept that being around people isn't as bad as she thinks. Maybe she'll be seen more frequently from now on. Oh, I do hope so. She must be terribly lonely.'

I had a feeling that loneliness was one of Lawrie's biggest fears, and I was suddenly grateful that Brodie had decided to leave with him. I wouldn't want him to be alone, and he was far too stubborn to stay on. I also realised I was going to miss him. I hadn't known him long, but I was already growing fond of him. I wished things could have been different.

'Lawrie,' I said slowly, 'I really do need to talk to you.'

'Oh yes, so you said.' He got to his feet, waving his stick in the air, as the bus trundled up the road towards us. 'When we get back to the Hall, Callie. We'll talk then.'

Inwardly sighing as I got on the bus behind him, I thought determinedly that we certainly would. I couldn't put this off any longer.

17

As we walked slowly back up the drive towards the Hall, Lawrie assured me there was still a lot for me to learn and see, and that I should go to the Wyrd Stones myself to experience the extraordinary feeling of power there. I wasn't so sure I wanted to, but promised him I'd venture there before too long.

'Lawrie,' I said, 'about that talk.'

'Ah, yes. What is it you wanted to talk about, Callie? Because if it's to ask me to stay on after the month is up, I'm afraid I've already told you—'

'It's not that,' I said, 'although I do wish you'd reconsider. No, it's – well, it's a bit awkward really.'

'You can ask me anything,' he assured me. 'My job now is to settle you in here and make sure the handover goes smoothly, so don't be afraid to say what's on your mind.'

'Well,' I said reluctantly, 'I hate to bring it up, but it's about money.'

'Ah.' Lawrie nodded wisely. 'That's always a tricky subject, isn't it? What about it?'

'The truth is,' I said, deciding there was no more time to

dodge the questions, however difficult they were, 'I don't have any. And I'm a bit scared to be honest. How am I going to pay Mia's wages? Not to mention feeding us all and keeping the lights on at the Hall, and paying for all the staff Mia reckons we employ...'

'*You* employ,' he pointed out, which I didn't think was at all helpful.

Seeing my face, he smiled. 'Don't worry, Callie. Things aren't as bleak as you seem to imagine. But surely you should know all this? Our solicitor—'

'I didn't read it,' I blurted. 'I know I should have, but I didn't. And now I haven't a clue how I'm supposed to pay for anything, and I can't sleep for worrying, and—'

'Good grief,' he said, patting my shoulder, 'you really have got yourself into a tizz, haven't you? Well, the truth is, I don't deal with that side of things. I always found facts and figures so tedious and left it to others to handle. Then Brodie took over once he was old enough, thank goodness.' He pushed open the front door and ushered me inside. 'No, it's him you need to speak to.'

'Brodie?' I hoped I'd managed to keep the dismay from my voice.

'Yes. I'll have a word with him. Arrange a meeting for you both. Perhaps this evening after dinner would be best? That way he'll be able to put your mind at rest, and you should get a good night's sleep at last.'

Mia came into the hall and took Lawrie's coat.

'How was it?' she asked. 'Did you enjoy your tour of the village?'

The amusement in her eyes told me she was perfectly aware that it was the model village I'd toured. I wondered if there was anything Mia didn't know. She seemed to be very important to the Davenports. I wondered if, when they left, she might want to go with them. I wasn't sure how I felt about that. There was something reassuring about Mia, and I liked having her around, though I still wasn't convinced I could afford her.

'Fantastic,' I told her. 'What an amazing model village that is. And Clara's lovely.'

She nodded. 'She is, isn't she? Shepherd's pie all right for dinner? Immi tells me it's her favourite.'

'Ooh,' Lawrie said, 'that sounds good. I haven't had shepherd's pie for a while now. Mia, have you seen Brodie?'

'He's at Appleseed Cottage, mowing Mrs Smithson's lawn. She rang up this morning and said it's looking very untidy.'

'Mowing her lawn?' I asked, astonished. 'Who's this Mrs Smithson?'

'One of our tenants,' Lawrie explained. 'She's even older than I am, and can't manage her garden, but she doesn't want to leave her cottage even though it's on the very edge of the village, so Brodie does the garden for her, and other odd jobs. It's a large cottage, you see, but I can't bring myself to move her to a smaller one.'

'But surely...' I was confused. 'Aren't there any proper gardeners around here? One of ours maybe? I mean, Brodie...'

I didn't know how to put it. It just seemed so unlikely. Besides, Brodie was Lawrie's grandson, and the idea of him being at the beck and call of villagers to mow their lawns seemed absurd.

'Brodie is a very helpful boy,' Lawrie said proudly. 'You should have seen him last autumn. How many gutters did he clear in one day, Mia?'

Mia raised an eyebrow. 'A world record, I'm sure. Go and sit down, Lawrie, and I'll bring you a cup of tea.'

'Thank you. I'll be in the sitting room, watching that afternoon quiz I like.' He turned to me. 'Don't worry, I won't forget. I'll have a word with Brodie as soon as he returns.'

'Thank you,' I said. 'I appreciate that.'

As Lawrie made his way slowly to the sitting room, Immi came skipping down the stairs.

'I've had the most fab time,' she announced, her eyes shining, her sulk evidently forgotten.

Mia grinned. 'I'll put that kettle on,' she said.

I put my arm around my daughter's shoulders. 'Go on then. What was so fabulous?'

'Mr Wyndham showed me all around the house,' she explained, as I tried to keep a smile on my face. 'There's so much history here! It's amazing there aren't loads more ghosts hanging around, but there's only Mr and Mrs Wyndham. Oh, and Florrie, of course.' She wrinkled her nose. 'She's a right one, you know. She followed us around, scowling and pulling her tongue out at me when her dad wasn't looking. She doesn't like me at all. I don't know why. Anyway,' she said, brightening, 'her mum wanted to teach her how to speak properly, so we got rid of her, and Mr Wyndham showed me the attics and—'

'The attics?' I said nervously. 'Are they safe?'

'Oh yes, perfectly. Do you know, the servants used to sleep there back in the day? Poor things. I said to Mr Wyndham what a horrible time it must have been for them, having to go up and down all those stairs, fetching and carrying all sorts – even hot water – and he admitted he'd never thought about that before and felt quite sorry he hadn't. He's ever so nice, you know, Mum.'

'I know,' I said, wondering again what on earth he was doing with Agnes, of all people.

We wandered into the kitchen, Immi still chattering away, and found Mia preparing a tray for Lawrie.

'A mug of tea and a plate of biscuits,' she said. 'Then, no

doubt, he'll have a nap. He usually does at this time. Never makes it to the end of that quiz, you know.'

'You know him very well,' I said. 'How do you feel about him moving out?'

She poured boiling water into a teapot. 'It makes me sad, if you must know,' she admitted. 'He's a lovely man, and I'm worried what will happen to him without me to take care of him. I know I'm being silly. He's got Brodie, and anyway, they'll probably hire someone else to care for them.'

'You won't go with them then?' I asked.

She looked at me doubtfully. 'Did you want me to?'

'Oh, no! No, that's not what I'm saying,' I said hastily. 'I just thought that, with you obviously caring about him a great deal, you might want to continue working for him after he's left here.'

Mia shrugged. 'Not especially. Would either of you like some of these biscuits with your tea?'

I got the distinct impression she was changing the subject.

'So, you'd prefer to stay at the Hall, even after Lawrie leaves?' I pushed.

She sighed. 'Yes, I would. If that's okay with you, of course. This place – it's where I belong. I wish Lawrie and Brodie were staying, but if they're set on leaving, there's nothing I can do about it. I'm sure they'll find someone just as capable to look after them.'

I couldn't help thinking that there was something Mia wasn't telling me. I had enough to worry about for now, though. Not least the prospect of an evening in the charming Brodie's company...

18

After a dinner of shepherd's pie and chocolate cheesecake, Mia offered to keep Immi company while I had my meeting with Brodie.

I was ridiculously nervous, which made me quite cross with myself. After all, I was the boss here, right? This was my estate now. I shouldn't have to feel anxious about asking Brodie for help, although he hadn't exactly reassured me over dinner. He'd barely said a word, and when Lawrie had told me the meeting was on, I'd thanked Brodie, and he'd merely grunted in response.

I couldn't fathom him out. Was he the misery who let his disappointment over his life not turning out the way he'd hoped turn him into a sullen jerk, or was he the kind-hearted man who was nice to Immi and mowed old ladies' lawns for them? Maybe, I thought philosophically, he was both.

Most of us are, after all.

Finding myself alone with him in the study was enough to make my palms sweat. Mia had kindly brought us coffee and left us to it, and Brodie indicated that I should take the seat behind the desk.

'I think you should sit there,' I said. 'You're the one explaining things to me, after all.'

'It's your study,' he said mildly. 'Your desk. Your chair. You should sit in it.'

'I'd really rather not,' I began, but I saw his eyebrows knit together in a frown and changed my mind. 'Okay.'

Brodie sat on the other side of the desk and surveyed me with cool blue eyes. Brilliant blue eyes. Gosh, they were so blue. I'd never seen anything like them. And those black eyelashes...

'Right,' he said. 'Where do you want to start?'

'As far back as you can go,' I said glumly. 'I don't understand much at all.'

He nodded. 'Right. Well—'

'But the main thing that's worrying me,' I said, considering, 'is money. How am I supposed to finance this house? It's huge. And then there's all the staff popping in and out, and the food bills – because, let's face it, Mia hardly skimps on the cooking, does she?' I held up my hand as he opened his mouth to speak. 'I know, I know. Everyone in this village is a tenant, and we get rent from them all. But is that enough, really? I'd have thought the rent would go towards maintaining their properties. They're not exactly newbuilds, are they? When I think of the upkeep, it makes me shudder. And anyway, what about—'

Brodie cleared his throat. 'Am I allowed to speak?'

'Oops,' I said. 'Sorry. Go ahead.'

Brodie opened his mouth again.

'The council tax must be astronomical on this house,' I considered. 'You *can* see why I'm worried?' I didn't, after all, want him to think I was making a fuss about nothing.

Brodie remained silent.

'Well? Aren't you going to explain?'

'I've been trying to!' He shook his head. 'Good God, you'd try the patience of a saint. Will you let me get a word in edgeways or not?'

My face burned with embarrassment. 'Sorry. Again. Go ahead.'

'The Harling Trust,' he said simply.

There was nothing else. I waited then gave an impatient shrug. 'And?'

'Oh, sorry, I assumed you'd be butting in, so I was waiting for you to get it over with.'

'Very funny. What's the Harling Trust?'

'It's a fund that was set up back in the days of the Harlings, hundreds of years ago. It's only to be used to fund the upkeep and repair of the estate. Nothing else. No personal gain whatsoever.'

'Does that include keeping this house going? Doesn't Eton mess and chocolate cheesecake count as personal gain? Personal weight gain at the very least.'

'Callie!'

'Sorry. Go on.'

'The estate includes Harling Hall, naturally. The upkeep of the house is covered by the fund, and that includes the cost of staff to keep it maintained and clean. Personal items are not covered, and that includes replacing original furniture with new, and any food or clothing. The fuel bills are covered, though, as is the council tax, you'll be relieved to know.'

'But if the fund doesn't cover food or clothing,' I said frowning, 'that means I'm already in debt.'

He shook his head. 'Grandpa's covered all that for now, until your allowance kicks in.'

I gave him a hopeful look. 'My allowance?'

'Naturally, you're not expected to live on fresh air. The Harling Trust pays for the estate. The money from the entrance fees and parking charges goes into a separate account for emergencies, along with the rents. Apart, that is, from your monthly allowance. It's not an astronomical sum so don't get your hopes up, but I've no doubt it will be more than you were earning at the agency, and you'll have no rent or bills to pay, obviously. It should be in your account by the end of next week.'

I felt weak with relief. 'But where did all this money come from?' I asked.

'The Harlings were close friends with William.'

'William who?'

Brodie sighed. 'Who do you think? The King of England after 1066 and all that. Basically, they saw what was happening and wormed their way into his good books. He awarded them this estate, although rumour has it that it belonged to them before he seized it after the Conquest anyway. Seems they did whatever it took to win it back. We have no details of what that entailed and it's probably a good thing.

'Grandpa's of the opinion that they wouldn't have tolerated him if not for the ghosts. He believes they were already guardians of the place and were determined to claw it back by whatever means necessary, to continue their duty. Anyway, whether that's true or not, they managed it and made a huge success of it. Their fortune grew and they hid money away for centuries. Masses of gold and possessions, stashed away safely. They even managed to keep it safe from the Parliamentarians in the Civil War, which can't have been easy.'

'Ooh,' I said, entranced. 'I'd forgotten about the Civil War! What happened to the Harlings then? And this house?'

'It was seized, of course, and sold to another family who weren't Royalists. But the Harlings were determined people.

Even before the monarchy was restored, they'd paid land agents to buy the estate back for them and continued as before. It was only when the gift of the sight wasn't passed on that they gave it up.' He shook his head. 'It must have been so traumatic for them. They were here centuries – far longer than any other owners managed. Everything they did was to protect this place, invest in it, guard the ghosts. They must have been an incredible family.'

'What happened to them after they left here?'

Brodie shrugged. 'There's no record. I guess they made a new life for themselves somewhere and tried to put this place out of their minds. What else could they do? They could have driven themselves mad pining for it otherwise.'

The set of his mouth told me he was expecting much the same fate, and I felt another pang of sadness for him.

'Anyway,' he said brusquely, 'the Ashcrofts took over and, although they started as lowly peasants, they soon changed their fortune and managed to add to the Trust, as did the Wyndhams and, actually, the Davenports.' He gave a modest shrug. 'So, you have no need to worry about funding this place.'

'Thanks so much,' I said, incredibly relieved. 'Honestly, if you knew how scared I've been!'

'I don't get it. Why didn't you just read the documents that came with the contract? They explained everything.'

I hesitated, not wanting to admit my dyslexia to someone I was sure would never understand it. 'It looked so complicated and, well, boring. Just skimming the first paragraph told me I'd never grasp it.'

I waited for his scornful retort, but to my amazement, he burst out laughing. 'You sound just like Grandpa! He leaves all that sort of thing to me.'

'So I heard,' I said, amazed that he found my incompetence funny rather than another source of irritation.

'You should see his face go pale when I start talking about finances. "You deal with that, Brodie; you're so good at this sort of thing."'

It was my turn to laugh at his surprisingly accurate impersonation of his grandfather.

'Tell you what,' he said, 'I'll do you an *Idiot's Guide to the Harling Estate*, so you won't have to read the real thing, and you'll know how everything works. How does that sound?'

'You will?' I couldn't believe it. 'That would be amazing! Do you understand all this financial stuff then?'

'I should do,' he said. 'I trained as an accountant.'

'You did?' I wrinkled my nose at the thought. 'Why?'

'Probably the same reason most people do any job. To earn money.'

'But you don't have a job,' I said puzzled.

'Of course I do. I'm the estate's accountant,' he explained patiently. 'The trust pays me a salary. It was Grandpa's idea. I was happy to go along with it.'

'Oh.' Did that made him staff? Awkward. 'Then what will you do when you leave here?'

'Get another job or set up my own business. That was always the plan. We knew the day was coming when we'd have to leave, so Grandpa figured I'd better get a decent career for when that happened. In the meantime, I took care of all the financial matters for him, which he hates.'

'But,' I said dismayed, 'who'll do the accounts when you go?'

'You'll employ another accountant,' he said. 'Don't worry. Mr Eldridge will help you find someone suitable. He's probably already on the case, knowing him. He's very capable.'

'He'll have to find someone exceptional then,' I said worriedly. 'I mean, you're obviously doing a fantastic job, and you understand the estate. You know the people. I mean, you mow some old lady's lawn, for goodness' sake!'

He sighed. 'Gets me out of the office. But you're right, I do understand the estate. I always loved it here, and Grandpa was more than happy to nurture my interest. I think it upset him a lot that Dad was never keen.'

'Wasn't he?' I leaned forward, interested to know more about him and his family. 'Where is your dad anyway?'

'Sydney,' he said.

'Blimey, he couldn't have got much further away, could he? What's he doing there?'

'Living a very happy and fulfilling life with my mum,' he said with a shrug. 'He's got several business interests in Australia, and he loves the place, so...'

'How old were you when they moved there?' I asked curiously.

'Twelve.'

'Twelve! And you didn't go with them?'

He shook his head. 'I was supposed to, naturally, but I played up so much about it that they were seriously worried. When Grandpa offered to look after me, it was all sorted.'

'They just let you stay here?' I couldn't imagine letting Immi go so easily. The thought of leaving my daughter to move to the other side of the world filled me with horror.

'They knew I wouldn't settle and that I much preferred the Cotswolds, but they had to be in Oz for business. What could they do?'

Sod the business and stay with their child I thought but said nothing. I supposed people were all different, and besides, it had clearly been a good decision as far as Brodie and Lawrie were concerned.

'I'm in touch with them regularly,' Brodie said hastily, as if worried I was judging them too harshly. 'We have a great relationship, and I don't have any regrets about not going to Australia. I belong here. I mean, I *belonged* here...'

He looked away, clearly embarrassed.

I said gently, 'I'm so sorry the way things have turned out, Brodie.'

For a moment he was still, as if considering how to respond, then he turned back to face me. 'Thank you,' he said simply and smiled.

I smiled back and for a moment, I felt a real connection with and empathy for him. Then my hand flew to my chest, and I shrieked before I could stop myself.

Brodie jumped. 'What is it?'

'Florrie!' I said, leaping up.

I glared at a grinning Florrie, who'd stuck her head through one of the portraits on the wall, crossed her eyes and waggled her fingers at me, momentarily frightening the life out of me.

She wasn't grinning for long, though. Agnes's head appeared next to hers, and she glared at her.

'Behave yourself, young lady! Can't you see Callie and Brodie are in a meeting?'

'Ooh, a meeting,' Florrie said, pretending to swoon. 'Is that what it is? Callie and Brodie sitting in a tree, K-I-S-S-I-N-G!'

'Do you mind?' I said, my embarrassment temporarily making me forget that Brodie couldn't hear her.

'What on earth are you babbling about?' Agnes asked, clearly bewildered. With obvious reluctance, she said, 'I'm sorry about this, Callie. I'll take her back upstairs.'

They disappeared and I landed back in my chair with a thud.

'That girl!' I said crossly. 'Honestly, you have no bloody idea how lucky you are not to be able to see ghosts!'

Brodie's expression darkened and I realised my mistake.

What a stupid thing to say to someone who was about to lose everything for that very reason.

He got to his feet. 'Well, I'll be going,' he said, and the old, sharp tone was back in his voice. It felt as if all the closeness we'd just achieved had been washed away by my one careless remark.

'I'm sorry,' I said. 'I didn't mean—'

'Don't worry about it,' he replied. 'I do have to go, though. I'm meeting someone. I'll get onto the simplified version of the contract tomorrow. Have a good night.'

With that, he left me sitting alone in the big, empty study, and I sank back in the chair with a sigh. Just for a moment there, I'd really thought we'd connected. There was such a nice side to Brodie, and I couldn't help wishing I could see it more often.

Then my thoughts turned back to Florrie, and I frowned. What was I going to do about that little madam?

19

A couple of days later, having turned the page on the calendar to June, Immi and I had a meeting with her headmistress at the primary school in nearby Kingsford Wold. It was a much larger village than Rowan Vale, but like our own village, it was a magnet for tourists. I could see how beautiful it was, but I gave thanks that someone had had the foresight to make Rowan Vale practically car free. The traffic here was horrendous. I could only imagine the frustration of the locals as they dodged the endless stream of vehicles and fought for parking space every day.

Luckily, the school had a car park, and Immi and I made it to our appointment in time. The school was surprisingly large, but then it served a few local villages. The headmistress, Mrs Parker, was a tall woman, probably in her fifties, who greeted us with a friendly smile. I took to her immediately and was relieved to see Immi clearly liked her as well.

We chatted for a while about the school's impressive record and the sort of things they focused on, but Mrs Parker acknowledged that Immi's stay there would be brief. She was pleased that I'd already applied to get her a place at the local academy in

Chipping Royston and was just waiting to hear if she'd been accepted. I didn't mention that it was Mia who'd arranged all that for me.

'The Year Six pupils will be making a second visit to the academy in a few weeks. Hopefully, Immi will know if she's been accepted by then and she'll get the opportunity to tour the school with the other children,' she said.

She very kindly informed me that, as there were only seven weeks left in the term, she didn't expect me to buy Immi the uniform.

'The children wear navy-blue jumpers and grey skirts or trousers. If you could dress Immi in something similar, that would be sufficient,' she said. 'After all, you'll have a whole new uniform to purchase for her soon enough.'

We had a brief visit to Immi's new class, where the pupils eyed us both with undisguised curiosity, and the teacher was forced to firmly tell them to settle down and get on with their work. She told Immi that the class was currently doing a project on the Second World War and was delighted when Immi wearily explained that she'd done the same project at her old school last term.

'You'll know all about it then,' she said enthusiastically. 'You'll catch up in no time.'

After agreeing that Immi would start the following morning, the two of us left and had a wander around Kingsford Wold, while Immi moaned about having to do her project all over again and I tried to cheer her up by pointing out that she'd be ahead of the rest of the class as she'd already covered the subject thoroughly.

We both agreed Kingsford Wold was stunning, with teashops and pubs galore, and lots of trendy-looking independent shops.

'It's not as nice as our village, though, is it, Mum?' Immi said with some satisfaction.

I smiled at her. 'You're settling in okay then?'

She nodded enthusiastically. 'Love it there. Mia took me to the Swinging Sixties street again. Have you been back there since our school trip?'

I had to admit I hadn't. I thought I really ought to go and make myself known to everyone there, as well as the Victorian shops on the village green.

Amelia Davies, the vicar, had visited me at the Hall. She was a smiley sort of woman who reminded me a bit of Clara, being friendly and informal. She had gently reminded me that Immi and I would be very welcome at the services at All Souls, and she hoped to see us there.

I couldn't resist asking her if she'd ever seen a photograph of Silas Alexander. She'd chuckled at that. 'I have, in the church archives. Angry-looking chap. You've met him then? Luckily for me, I can't see or hear him, which I think is a blessing going by what Lawrie's told me. Apparently, I'm hardly flavour of the month with our old vicar. Bless him, he must be apoplectic having a female vicar not only in the church but in his old home too.'

'Doesn't it bother you?' I'd asked. 'Him sharing your home when you can't even see him?'

She'd shrugged. 'From everything I've heard about him, the pious Reverend Alexander wouldn't do anything he shouldn't. I'm sure he avoids the bathroom and my bedroom and that's all I can ask really, so why should it bother me?'

I thought that if she'd actually seen Silas ranting and raving, she might think differently, but I decided she didn't need that mental picture.

As new owner of the estate (I still couldn't believe that!) I knew it was my duty to make myself known to my tenants, so vowed to spend the next few days doing just that.

It occurred to me, however, that it was Immi's birthday at the end of the week, and I still hadn't got her a present. While she was buying some sweets in the newsagents, I managed to sneakily pop next door into the gift shop to buy her a birthday card, but though I looked around quickly, I didn't spot a suitable present and returned to Harling Hall feeling increasingly worried about the situation.

It was Brodie, funnily enough, who solved the problem.

I was sitting at the kitchen table later that afternoon, telling Mia what a terrible mother I was, and wondering if I could fit a shopping trip to Chipping Royston or Much Melton into my day, when he wandered in and, though ostensibly minding his own business as he put the kettle on, was clearly listening to our conversation – intentionally or not.

'Does Immi like cats?' he asked suddenly.

I turned to him. 'Cats?'

'Yeah. Little furry things with whiskers and pointy ears.' He grinned. 'Say miaow a lot.'

'Funny. What have cats got to do with anything?'

'It's just, Nick and Betty have some kittens at the farm they're looking to rehome. Immi might like one, don't you think?'

'A kitten?' I asked doubtfully.

'She doesn't like cats?' he asked.

'It's not that...' Immi had often said how much she'd love a pet, but I'd always envisioned a dog. Thinking about it, though, I thought a cat might be a better option. Immi would be back at school from tomorrow, and I'd be busy getting to know the villagers and being a full-time ghost wrangler, not to mention ploughing through the *Idiot's Guide to Running a Special Living History Village*, which Brodie had kindly presented me with earlier that morning, just an hour before Mia had given me my enormous copy of the official documents, which had arrived in the post at last.

'What's the problem then?' Mia asked. 'Is she allergic?'

'No... It's just – these kittens, they're not feral, are they? I mean, their mum's not some wild cat that lives out in the barns?'

Brodie shook his head. 'Far from it. Mitzi's Betty's pride and joy, and lives with them in the farmhouse. The kittens are really cute and very tame. They've been fussed over by Betty and Nick, not to mention everyone else who works at the farm.'

'You've seen them?' I asked.

'Last night, when I went to see Nick about his tractor needing repairs.'

So that's where he'd been going.

'His tractor? Do we pay for those then?' I asked worriedly.

'It's all in the *Idiot's Guide*, but spoiler alert, yes, we do. Well, sort of. Why don't you go over to the farm and see the kittens for yourself?' he asked. 'It can't do any harm, can it?'

I hesitated but then figured I had nothing to lose. It would solve everything if I could pick a kitten for Immi's birthday, and I was fairly sure my daughter would fall in love immediately.

'Okay,' I said cheering up. 'Thanks, Brodie. I'll do that.'

* * *

With Immi starting school the following morning, we spent the evening making sure she had everything she needed in her school bag. I could only be grateful that ghosts are unable to touch anything. Florrie kept popping in and eyeing up the stationery supplies and everything else that I'd got ready for Immi's first day, and I had a feeling that if she could have hidden something just to make things difficult, she would have done.

I hadn't seen Agnes since she'd dragged Florrie out of the study, and I suspected she was rather embarrassed by the whole thing, and probably seething that she'd had to take my side over her daughter's for once. Manners mattered to Agnes and even she hadn't been able to turn a blind eye to the youngster rudely interrupting my meeting with Brodie.

Aubrey had popped by the previous evening, just before Immi's bedtime. We were just finishing mugs of hot chocolate as we watched the final five minutes of one of Immi's favourite films as a treat when we heard a cough and a male voice saying loudly, 'Knock, knock.'

We looked at each other and grinned.

'Come in, Aubrey,' I called.

He walked straight through the door looking surprised. 'How did you know it was me?'

'Wild guess,' I said. 'How can I help you?'

'Oh, I don't want anything,' he assured me. He smiled at Immi. 'Just came to wish you good luck for your first day at school. I'm sure you'll do splendidly.'

'Aw, thanks, Mr Wyndham!' Immi beamed. 'That's really nice of you.'

'Not at all. Agnes said to send you her best wishes too.'

I wondered if that was true. 'And Florrie?' As he shuffled a bit, I felt sorry for putting him in such an awkward position. 'Thank you,' I said quickly. 'We appreciate that.'

He looked relieved as he turned back to the door. 'Well, I'll be getting off then. Er, enjoy *Back to the Future*.' He glanced at the television over his shoulder before frowning. 'Oh. *Two*. Ahem.'

As he vanished from our sight, Immi and I stared at each other. 'How did he know we were watching *Back to the Future Part II*?' I asked in amazement.

She laughed. 'He's cool. I really like him. Florrie's lucky to have him as her dad.'

My amusement died and I ruffled her hair. 'Pity she doesn't realise it, eh?'

I waited for her to ask me about her own dad, but again, the question didn't come. It never did. It was as if Immi had no interest in him whatsoever, and I wondered if I should be glad or sorry about that.

'Right,' I said as the final credits rolled. 'Time for bed, young lady. Early start tomorrow.'

'Okay, okay. I'm going.'

She put down her empty mug and got to her feet.

'Are you nervous?' I asked, sympathetically.

'Bit,' she admitted.

I gave her a hug. 'You'll be okay,' I said. 'I know it's a hard thing to do, but they'll love you. How can they not? *I* love you.'

'I know you do,' she said, 'but you have to really, don't you? It's your job.'

'You're right. I remember signing the contract.' I kissed her cheek. 'Want me to tuck you in?'

'Mum! I'm nearly eleven, not five. See you in the morning.'

'I'll set my alarm,' I promised her. 'Sweet dreams.'

* * *

I have no idea what time I'd set my alarm for, but it was supposed to be seven o'clock. By the time I heard the knocking on my bedroom door the following morning, it was almost seven forty-five. I stared at the clock in horrified disbelief and tumbled out of bed, before rushing to the door.

I'd expected to find Mia standing there, but it was Brodie who greeted me by looking me up and down in surprise, blushing to his hair roots, and mumbling something about Mia sending him up to check we were awake and to tell us breakfast was ready.

'Er, thanks. I'll wake Immi up,' I said.

He hurried away and I glanced down, realising I was wearing a tatty old Betty Boop nightshirt that finished well above my knees, that I was in bare feet, and – going by every other day since I could remember – my hair looked like a bird's nest. Drat.

'Immi! Immi! You're going to be late!'

I ran into my daughter's bedroom and stopped in surprise. She was sitting at her desk carefully checking through her bag once more. She was fully dressed in the clothes I'd hung up on her bedroom door for her, and her hair was neatly tied back in a ponytail.

'Oh.' I didn't know what to say. 'Why didn't you wake me?'

'I was just about to,' she informed me. 'I thought you were setting your alarm?'

'I did! Well, I thought I did.'

'I have to be in registration in an hour,' she reminded me.

'I know. I'm so sorry. Mia's done breakfast.' Hopefully, that would appease her.

'You'd better get dressed.' She picked up her bag. 'I'll go downstairs and eat.'

'You do that. Phew, good job you were awake, right?'

'You mean, good job Mrs Wyndham woke me,' she said primly.

'*What?*' I couldn't believe it. 'Agnes did? Are you sure?'

'I think I know who woke me up, Mum,' she said patiently. 'She was standing by my bed saying my name and telling me it was time to get up. Seven o'clock on the dot.'

'Oh, right.' I wasn't sure what to make of that. Agnes had

done me a favour and it felt weird. 'Well, she could have woken me up too.'

Immi gave me one of her stares and I said feebly, 'I'll get dressed.'

By the time I was ready to go, Immi had eaten her breakfast, been fussed over by Lawrie, Brodie and Mia, and was waiting patiently in the hallway with her school bag over her shoulder.

'I haven't even had coffee yet,' I grumbled.

'Mum, it's ten past eight and I have to be in registration by quarter to nine,' she chided me.

'I know, I know.' I grabbed the car keys just as Brodie entered the hallway.

'I can take her if you like,' he offered.

My eyebrows shot up in surprise. 'Why?'

'Well,' he said with a shrug, 'you're obviously running late, and you haven't even had breakfast, so—'

'That doesn't matter. It's her first day. I'll take her,' I said, wondering what they must all be thinking of me. 'But... thanks,' I added, as an afterthought. 'It was nice of you to offer.'

'No problem. Good luck, Immi.'

'Thanks, Brodie.'

As we walked towards the front door, she called up the stairs without looking in that direction, 'See you later, Florrie.'

I whipped round just in time to see a scowling Florrie pull back out of sight behind the bannister.

Grinning, I followed my daughter to the car.

20

After dropping Immi at the school gates – thankfully in plenty of time – and wishing her all the luck in the world for her first day, I headed back towards the car park.

'Callie!'

I looked around, surprised to hear my name being called here of all places. A smiling Clara waved at me, and I relaxed.

'Hi! I forgot your son goes to this school, doesn't he?' I said, as she walked up to me, looking, I was pleased to note, as untidy and harassed as I no doubt did, though her face was perhaps more flushed than mine.

'They all do. Is it Immi's first day?' she asked, pulling her red hair back into a ponytail as we walked.

'Yes. I'm quite nervous for her.'

'Don't worry. I'm guessing she's in Miss Brooke's class? Ashton said a new girl was shown around his classroom yesterday and I thought it might be her. I told him to make sure she was okay, and he will. He's a good kid if I do say so myself.'

'Oh, thanks so much.' I couldn't deny it was a relief to know Immi would have at least one friendly child to talk to.

'No worries. Fancy following me back to Honeywell for a coffee?' she asked, as we halted beside the hatchback I still couldn't quite believe was mine. 'I've got a stack of housework to do so I'm looking for an excuse to get out of it.'

I laughed. 'I'd love to, but I've got to go to Rowan Farm, and then I need to do a tour of the village and introduce myself properly.'

'Fair enough. I'd come with you, but I really do have to get on with the washing and cleaning. How are you getting on at Howling Hall?'

'*Howling* Hall?'

'Oops! That's what we call it round here,' she admitted, blushing an even darker pink. 'What with the ghosts and everything. Same as Howling's Halt. And the Howling Estate. You can't deny it lends itself to the nickname, can you?'

'I suppose not,' I said, amused. 'To be honest, it's a bit tricky, learning to live with the Wyndhams – especially Florrie. She's a pain in the backside.' I sighed. 'Still, she's only a kid, so I'm trying to cut her some slack. You're lucky you can't see any ghosts, that's all I can say.'

She gave me a wistful look. 'If you say so. Hey,' she added, brightening suddenly, 'if you like, I'll pick Immi up and take her to school. Seems daft us both doing the school run every day. I'd suggest alternating but it hardly seems fair when I've got three of them.'

'That wouldn't bother me,' I said. 'I'd be happy to take them if you're all okay with that. Thanks so much. I'll pick Immi up alone this evening, with it being her first day. I'd like to know how she got on. But we can start tomorrow? Shall I take the first turn?'

'Seriously? Ooh, brilliant. I'll drop the kids outside the gates of the Hall. Well, I'll let you get off. Good luck with your introductions. Oh, what am I like!' She turned back to me and rolled her eyes. 'Totally forgot to mention. Blame my perimenopause brain. The pub quiz!'

'Pub quiz?'

'Yes, at The Quicken Tree. Every Thursday. We have a proper laugh, though some people take it very seriously. Why don't you join us next week? Seven o'clock. It's not on this week because they're painting the room, but it's back on the twelfth. You can be on our team. I mean, it's not really my team, it's Jack's, but they could always use someone with brains cos we haven't got a functional brain cell between us.' She laughed. 'Fancy it?'

I hesitated then smiled. 'Actually, yes, I do. That sounds great. Something *normal*.'

'Excellent! Anyway, I'd better get home. Probably left the grill on or something. My mind lately. Dratted hormones. See you, Callie.' She gave me a cheery wave and headed off to her own car.

Feeling quite pleased that I seemed to have made a friend, I settled myself in the driver's seat, wrinkling my nose in dismay as I caught sight of my reflection in the rear-view mirror. I hadn't had time to put make-up on, and my hair was all over the place. Plus, I hadn't brought my comb with me, which was typical. Great impression I was going to make on my new tenants.

Ah, well, I wasn't going back to *Howling* Hall just for a comb. Time to go to Rowan Farm and see those kittens.

It was a warm, sunny day, and driving back along the Cotswolds lanes towards Rowan Vale, I thought it was the perfect day to introduce myself to as many of the villagers as I could manage.

Betty was delighted to see me, particularly when I told her the reason for my visit.

'Oh, what a lovely idea. Can't get a better birthday present than a kitten, can you? Come and have a look at them, lovely.'

She ushered me into the farmhouse and through to the "back room" as she called it, where I was soon cooing over the little kittens.

'Oh,' I said, my heart melting despite having had my heart set on a puppy, 'aren't they adorable?'

'They are. Just like their mum,' Betty said, stroking Mitzi's face fondly.

The proud mum was a black and white cat with green eyes. She'd given birth to five kittens: two mostly black with a bit of white on them, two mostly white with a bit of black on them, and one black and white like her.

They were all so cute and friendly, I couldn't resist picking each one of them up for a cuddle.

'Have any of them got homes?' I asked.

'Two of the girls have,' she said. 'They're going to their new homes tomorrow. I've got someone coming round this evening to look at the two boys and the other girl, so I'd choose one now if I were you, or your favourite might be gone if you think about it overnight.'

I had to admit I was drawn to the two boys.

'Tuxedo cats,' Betty said, 'on account of how they look like they're wearing a tux. Gorgeous, aren't they?'

They were, but I was particularly smitten with the bigger one. He had a thick, bushy tail, and was far fluffier than his siblings.

'Takes after his dad, that one,' Betty said.

'You know who his dad is then?'

'Oh,' she said, pursing her lips, 'I know all right, and by the time I'd finished with his owner, I'd made very sure that there wouldn't be any more kittens from *him*. Mind you, I'm going to make sure there won't be any more kittens from her either,' she added, rubbing Mitzi between the ears. 'Five's enough for anyone, isn't it, petal?'

'So, can I have this one then?' I asked hopefully, cradling the little tux kitten in my arms. He stared up at me with bright-blue eyes, and for a moment, he made me think of Brodie.

'Course you can,' she promised. 'Do you want to take him now? He's ready to go.'

'I haven't got anything for him,' I explained. 'And he's a surprise for my daughter's birthday, so would it be okay for you to keep him until the night before?'

'No problem,' she said. 'I'll be sad to part with him to be honest. Wish I could keep them all, but Nick's put his foot down with a firm hand.' She laughed. 'Anyway, good homes are all I ask, and what better home for him than Howling Hall, eh?'

Wow, it really was a nickname! I got to my feet, brushing off the cat hairs. 'Well, thanks so much for showing me the kittens, Betty. How much are they going for, by the way?'

'Forty pounds each, please,' she said. 'Just bring the money when you collect him.'

I bid the kittens and Mitzi a reluctant farewell and followed Betty into the kitchen.

'I understand your tractor's in need of repair,' I said, aiming to demonstrate my concern for my tenants.

She frowned. 'It is. Nick's cleared it with Brodie. He said the estate will loan us the money at the usual rate. Is there a problem?'

'No, of course not. I was just saying.'

'Brodie knows Nick would never ask for money if it wasn't necessary,' she said firmly. 'If you've got any concerns, you should talk to Brodie. He'll steer you right.'

'I don't have any concerns,' I assured her, although suddenly

I realised the fact that Nick and Betty were still going to Brodie for clearance was worrying. Shouldn't they have asked me? Not that I knew the first thing about tractors, but I should at least have been involved in the decision, surely? And Brodie had no right to clear a loan without telling me. It was my estate which, I realised, made me sound awful, but I had to know what was coming out of the funds, didn't I?

Anyway, Betty telling me to talk to Brodie, as if I was incapable of making up my own mind, had annoyed me.

I knew I should say something, but I didn't have the nerve, especially since I'd just reserved one of the kittens. I decided it was time I headed off to Churchside.

'Thanks again, Betty,' I said. 'I'll be back on Friday night to collect the kitten and pay you.' *Though maybe I should ask Brodie if it's okay to do that first.*

'Nice to see you again, Callie. I'll take care of young Tux until you pick him up,' she said, all smiles again now that I'd apparently accepted her advice.

I headed back to my car trying to keep my mind focused on the next job for the day. I was going to visit the Swinging Sixties shops and introduce myself formally to my tenants, and I had to think about that, nothing else.

Even so, Betty's words kept nudging me. I couldn't help wondering if all my tenants felt the same way, and if so, would they ever accept me – even when Brodie and Lawrie were gone?

21

Churchside consisted of a row of six shops and a terraced house, decorated in authentic period style.

Entering the toy shop was just like walking into the past, with old-fashioned Sindy and Barbie dolls and Action Man figures in pristine boxes, toy cars, a train set running in one corner, doll's houses, rocking horses, jigsaw puzzles, old versions of board games like Mousetrap, Cluedo, and Frustration, and even vintage children's books.

Eric, who ran the shop, explained that these items weren't for sale, as replacing them would be hugely difficult. They'd been in the family since he was a boy, and his father ran the shop. However, there was a whole section where books and jigsaws and more modern toys could be purchased by visitors. I was delighted to see some of the jigsaws were scenes of Rowan Vale, the Wyrd Stones, and Harling's Halt, which Eric said had been specially commissioned by the estate.

There was a newsagents with copies of vintage magazines, newspapers, and children's comics on the shelves, as well as jars and trays of sweets that would have been familiar to children at the time.

Next door to that was a boutique, with racks of sixties-style fashions. The assistants were young and looked very trendy – or would have done sixty years ago. There were huge posters on the walls of 1960s icons like Twiggy, Brigitte Bardot, and Audrey Hepburn.

There was also a hairdressing salon, set up just as one would have been in the sixties. The staff all had heavily lacquered beehives and wore mini dresses and told me tourists often requested vintage hairstyles just for fun, although they assured me that they did modern cuts and styles for the villagers and would be happy to do my hair any time I wanted.

Conscious of how untidy it looked, I'd promised I'd book an appointment soon and headed quickly next door to the record shop, where I met the young couple, Lucy and Sam, who ran it. They wore authentic-looking sixties clothes too and had obviously paid a visit to the salon.

I also encountered Millie, their resident ghost.

'I'm very fond of her,' Lucy admitted. 'She was my mum's older sister, but she died tragically young—'

She shut up quickly as a young girl bounced into the shop. The prickling along my shoulders told me that this was Millie, and my heart went out to her. She couldn't have been more than a teenager, and she was so pretty with her blonde hair heavily backcombed and eyelashes so thick and heavy, it was a wonder she could open her eyes. She was wearing a black and white mini dress and flat, knee-high, white boots, and the thought that this vibrant young girl had been taken so soon was heartbreaking.

Millie seemed cheerful enough, though. The first thing she

asked me was if I was a Beatles fan, and when I cautiously replied that I liked their music, she immediately asked me who my favourite Beatle was.

I saw Lucy mouth, 'Paul' at me, and said dutifully, 'Paul McCartney.'

Millie beamed at me. 'Cool! He's just so dreamy, isn't he? I've got posters of him all over my bedroom, and Sam and Lucy buy me all his latest records.'

She ran into the back room as if she'd just decided she couldn't spend another moment of her time not gazing at her idol.

Lucy sighed. 'She still imagines him as a young man with a mop top. We're very selective about the records we play for her. We haven't introduced her to The Frog Chorus. I don't think she's ready for the shock of "We All Stand Together".'

'I see what you mean,' I said, deciding to keep quiet about how much I loved 'We All Stand Together'. 'What happened to her?' I covered my mouth in horror. 'Sorry! Not supposed to ask that, am I?'

To my surprise, Lucy shrugged. 'It's no secret. Gran and Grandad had grounded her, but she wanted to go to a concert her boyfriend had got tickets for. The Beatles played the Birmingham Odeon in October 1964 and there was no way she was going to miss it. The silly little sod climbed out of the bathroom window meaning to shimmy down the drainpipe, but she slipped and fell. Her boyfriend and their two friends had parked just up the road waiting for her, and they saw it happen. Awful.'

'I'm guessing you can't see her, Sam?' I said.

'Nope. Not a blood relative, is she? I never know where she is,' he admitted. 'It used to really freak me out, but I'm used to it now. She won't go near her old home, and who can blame her?

So why not let her live here with us? Not that we could stop her if we tried, naturally.'

'We make her feel like one of the family, because she is,' Lucy said firmly. 'She's got her own room, and we made it as authentic as we could for her. She says it's cooler than the one she had when she was alive, so that's nice. Mum comes to see her as often as she can, though she lives in Scotland now, but they have a catch up when she does. Honestly, Millie feels like my little sister.'

I thought it was amazing that people around here accepted the presence of ghosts so easily. When I thought back to my own fraught childhood, it filled me with awe that no one seemed to find it a curse.

The final shop on Churchside was a vintage fish and chip shop, with pale-green walls and black and white checked flooring. The fish and chips came wrapped in authentic-looking newspaper, although Barbara, one of the staff members, assured me that it wasn't, as that would be illegal, and that it had been specially printed for the shop. Seeing as the newspaper was titled *The Rowan Vale Recorder*, I could believe it. Either way, the fish and chips smelled delicious, and I made a mental note to try them before too long.

The Victorian shops on the green consisted of an old-fashioned sweet shop, which I knew Immi was keen to try, a chemist, a grocer, a butcher, a photographic studio where tourists could have their photos taken and buy their very own sepia portraits to take home, and The Curiosity Shop, which was stuffed full with the most eclectic items ranging from stuffed animals and birds to pocket watches and old books.

As with the Churchside row, there was a house that visitors could walk around, which was decorated and furnished exactly as it would have been in the late nineteenth century. I thought Aubrey would feel right at home here, and supposed he must visit the green regularly.

My final visit for the first day was to the mill complex. I'd already toured the museum on the school trip, but I popped in again to introduce myself properly, before having a cup of tea at Mrs Herron's Teashop and buying a delicious-looking Victoria sponge from Blighty's Bakery.

Arriving home later that afternoon, I was pleased to bump into Brodie. Well, maybe pleased isn't the right word. He was just about to enter the study, and I decided it was the perfect opportunity to tackle him about the loan for the tractor.

'What about it?' he asked, reaching for a ledger off the shelf.

'Well, for one thing, why are we lending them cash for repairs?'

He paused, clutching the ledger to his chest. 'Because they haven't got the money up front,' he explained, as if it was obvious. 'The estate always grants loans to the tenants when it comes to things like that. They pay us back with interest. Just at a much lower rate than any bank. Is there a problem?'

'Yes, as a matter of fact there is,' I said. 'Why did they go to you instead of asking me? And what gave you the right to grant the loan? You're not the owner of the estate. Why wasn't I consulted?'

'Are you serious?' he asked, his eyes wide.

'Oh, don't give me that look! Yeah, I get it. I'm new here. I'm a stupid woman who needs an *Idiot's Guide* to help her understand how things work. That doesn't give you the right to lend money from the estate funds without telling me. Is it even legal?'

He dropped onto the sofa and sighed. 'Callie, did you even read the *Idiot's Guide*?'

I gave him a nervous look. Was that relevant? 'I'm working my way through it,' I said, as confidently as I could. 'Why?'

'Because if you had, you'd know that the estate accountant deals with all matters of finances for the tenants. And right now, at least, I'm still the estate accountant. And I would never do anything illegal. I rather resent you suggesting otherwise.'

My face burned. 'Sorry,' I said. 'It's just – well, it felt as if I was being pushed aside, you know? Betty kept telling me you'd cleared it and to take it up with you, as if you were in charge and I was just some numpty she had to placate.'

He pulled a face. 'Yeah, I can see how that would rankle. I'm sorry. It's not as bad as it sounds. It's just easier for the accountant to deal with all the finances because that's how Grandpa wanted it. I'm sure we could get an amendment written into the contract if you'd prefer. I could contact Mr Eldridge—'

'Heck, no!' I held up my hands in horror. 'You're right. It's best the way it is. I guess I'm just being oversensitive. Sorry again. I honestly didn't mean to accuse you of anything. I know you'd never rip me off or do anything remotely underhanded.'

'I really wouldn't,' he said solemnly.

'So... friends?' I held out my hand and, after a moment's pause, he shook it.

My eyes widened as I felt a jolt of electricity course through my body at his touch. My mouth felt dry as I stared up at him, my heart thudding with a sudden rush of adrenaline.

Brodie swallowed hard. 'Friends,' he said at last.

It seemed like forever before we both blinked, and he dropped my hand. 'Work,' he mumbled, feebly waving the ledger at me.

'Work,' I murmured, and left him to it, wondering what the hell had just happened.

* * *

The next day, I continued my introductions by heading to Harling's Halt, where I found Ronnie and Bill still arguing on the platform. They shut up pretty quickly when they saw me and gave me sheepish looks – no doubt remembering how they'd rushed to complain about me to Lawrie. I assured them there were no hard feelings, and that they were free to continue as they pleased, given that it wasn't bothering anyone.

Unfortunately, at that moment, Percy Swain appeared and informed me in aggrieved tones that it was bothering *him*, and he didn't see why he should have to put up with those two rogues causing a scene every single day when he was trying to run a professional station here, given that there was no longer a stationmaster present.

Percy – nope, I couldn't call him that, he was always going to be Perks to me – had a point, as I tried tactfully to explain to Ronnie and Bill, who reluctantly agreed to shake hands and try harder to stop fighting. Perks looked doubtful and I didn't blame him. I imagined that the moment I left, they'd be at it again, but there wasn't a lot I could do about that.

To mollify the porter, I asked him if he'd be so kind as to take me on a tour of the station and tell me a bit about its history, which he was more than happy to do. By the time I left – having been shown around the Edwardian-style tearooms and given a bag of scones to take home with me, as well as being introduced to the station and tearoom staff – he was clearly quite taken with me, and we parted on extremely good terms, with Perks, bless him, doffing his cap to me quite deferentially.

The final two days of the week flew by as I visited other tenants in their homes, the garage and cinema, and popped into The Quicken Tree, where I chatted to the landlady, Penny, and a couple of her bar staff. I also visited All Souls to chat more to Amelia, who was more than happy to show me around the stunning church.

I tried valiantly to ignore Silas, although it wasn't easy, as he contradicted and criticised Amelia's every word. Amelia, lucky thing, was totally oblivious to his sniping and I wasn't going to burst her bubble. I thought I'd have to have words with Silas at some point, though. He may have been a pious man in life, but in afterlife, his manners left a lot to be desired.

Before I knew it, Friday had rolled around, and as soon as Immi was settled in bed, I headed out to Rowan Farm to collect the kitten.

Betty had him all ready and waiting for me, and as I bundled him into the brand-new cat carrier I'd bought, I was touched to see her in tears as she said her goodbyes.

Lawrie and Brodie were waiting when I got back and made a huge fuss of the kitten.

'What a lovely little chap,' Lawrie said, clearly delighted. 'It will be good to have a pet in the house again. We haven't had one since my old retriever, Harvey, passed.'

'He's so cute,' Brodie agreed, scooping the kitten into his arms. 'Aren't you? Aren't you?'

The kitten rubbed his head against Brodie's chin and clearly thought Brodie wasn't so bad himself.

A kitten with taste.

'I hope he doesn't cry,' I said worriedly. 'I don't want Immi to hear him in the night.'

'He can sleep in my room,' Brodie offered immediately. 'I'm in the east wing so even if he does cry, she won't hear him from there.'

'Are you sure?' I asked, surprised.

'Of course. It's no trouble,' he assured me.

'What about Agnes? What if she complains about the noise?' I asked doubtfully.

'I shan't complain about the noise.'

I spun round, blushing as I realised Agnes, Aubrey, and Florrie were all standing in the kitchen behind me.

'Although,' she added pointedly, 'it would have been nice if you'd asked if we minded you bringing a new animal into our home. Good manners cost nothing.'

'You're quite right,' I said meekly. 'I should have asked. I'm sorry, Agnes.'

She looked momentarily astounded that I'd capitulated so easily but recovered herself quickly. 'Yes, well, as it happens, I used to have a cat called Jessop, and I was very fond of him. It will be nice to have another one around the place.'

The kitten, who had been nestling comfortably in Brodie's arms, stiffened suddenly and hissed in their direction.

'Oh, dear,' I said. 'I think he can see you, or at least sense you. What am I going to do about that?'

'Don't worry,' Aubrey said reassuringly. 'It's the shock, but they get used to it. Harvey was just the same. Do you remember, Lawrie? The day you brought him here as a puppy, he was going berserk every time he saw us, but by the time he passed, we were the best of friends.'

'How come there aren't any animal ghosts here?' I asked, half to myself.

'My grandad had a lovely old cat, but when he died and I asked if 'e'd go to 'eaven, my ma said animals don't have no souls,' Florrie remarked. 'I didn't 'alf cry.'

'What an ill-educated comment,' Agnes snapped. 'It's nonsense, Florence. The woman knew nothing.'

'I believe animals have the purest souls,' said Aubrey hastily. 'I'm quite sure there's a place reserved especially for them in

Heaven, where they are admitted immediately, and that's why there are no animals on our plane.'

'So my soul ain't pure?' demanded Florrie.

We all looked at each other, except for Brodie, who clearly had no idea what was going on and had reverted to stroking the kitten and pretending he didn't care.

'Not at all,' Lawrie said gently. 'It's just, there are different rules for animals. That's all.'

Thankfully, she didn't push the subject. Instead, she said, almost grudgingly, 'He's cute, ain't he? What's 'is name?'

'*His* name, Florence,' Agnes said with a sigh. 'And it's *isn't*, not *ain't*. How many times do I have to tell you?'

'He doesn't have a name yet,' I began, but she said eagerly, 'Can I name 'im then?'

'I'm sorry,' I said. 'He's a present for Immi's birthday tomorrow. She'll name him herself.'

Florrie glared at me then flounced out of the room.

Agnes hurried after her and Aubrey rolled his eyes.

'One simply has to learn that one can't have everything,' he said sadly. 'It's a lesson Florence must be taught, but unfortunately Agnes is reluctant to teach her. So, it's Immi's birthday tomorrow, eh? Is she to have a party?'

'Not really,' I said slowly, thinking I should have organised one.

'Well,' he said, 'I expect it's difficult. She doesn't really know anyone round here, does she?'

But I could have invited Violet, who'd posted a card and present for her. And thinking about it, I could have invited Clara and Jack's boys too. At least Ashton. He was in her class, after all. I could have done *something*.

I was a terrible mother. I'd thought things would get easier once we moved here and I was able to give up my job, but in fact,

I'd been busier than ever, and my head was so full of new things to learn that I hadn't given my own daughter's birthday much headspace at all. If not for Brodie's suggestion, she might not even have had a present from me.

I went to bed that night feeling completely wretched. Something would have to change, and soon.

22

I may have been a terrible mother, but Brodie, Lawrie, and Mia were amazing friends. When Immi and I came downstairs the following morning, we were stunned to find the hallway and dining room decorated with balloons and birthday banners.

Mia informed us that she'd be serving a special birthday tea at four, and that she'd made Immi a cake complete with candles.

They'd even bought her presents, which moved me to tears. They were so kind, and I couldn't believe how much effort they'd all gone to.

Agnes and Aubrey came downstairs to wish her a happy birthday, though there was no sign of Florrie.

Brodie brought the kitten into the dining room, and I handed him to Immi, who promptly burst into tears.

'What's wrong?' I asked worriedly. 'Don't you like him?'

'Oh, Mum!' She buried her face in the kitten's fur so I could barely make out what she was saying. 'He's so gorgeous. Thank you. Thank you!'

Relieved, I laughed as she finally hugged me.

'What are you going to call him?' I asked as she cuddled him to her, forgetting all about her breakfast.

'I really don't know,' she said. 'It has to be just right, so I'll need to think about it.'

Agnes cleared her throat. 'Florence suggested Brian,' she said tentatively.

Immi wrinkled her nose. 'Brian? What kind of name is that for a cat?'

'Apparently, her late grandfather had a cat called Brian, and Florence was very fond of him.'

'Who?' I asked. 'The cat or the grandfather?'

She tutted. 'Both. She was hoping...'

'She's not calling her kitten Brian,' I said firmly.

'No. Well...' Agnes nodded. 'As you wish. He's Immi's present after all.'

'He's just lovely, isn't he?' Immi said happily. 'I can't believe he's mine. I'll miss him so much when I'm at school.'

'Well, you have an entire weekend to spend with him now,' I reminded her. 'Why don't you put him on his bed and eat your breakfast? I think he's pretty overwhelmed with all the fuss and probably needs a nap. He's only a baby, after all.'

Immi did as I'd suggested but spent the entire time she was eating her breakfast giving him loving looks. Tux, meanwhile, curled up on his bed and fell fast asleep immediately.

Mia was as good as her word and prepared a delicious tea for Immi's birthday treat. There were sandwiches with loads of different fillings, sausage rolls, cheese straws, some yummy pastries, and finally a huge birthday cake, complete with eleven candles.

Agnes and Aubrey joined us as we all gathered round and sang happy birthday to her.

'Make a wish!' Aubrey called, as she blew out the candles, and Immi closed her eyes and concentrated.

I wondered what she was wishing for.

Lawrie had earlier retired to the sitting room for forty winks, having missed his usual afternoon nap, and Mia decided to prepare a tray for him since he'd not eaten.

'Shall I take it into him?' Brodie asked but she shook her head.

'It's no trouble,' she said and opened the dining-room door.

'Oh, watch out!' Brodie called. 'The kitten's run into the hallway. Don't stand on him.'

'I won't,' Mia promised, laughing. 'But I'll wait until he's back in here, just to be on the safe side. Oh! What am I like? I've forgotten to pour Lawrie a cup of tea.' She put the tray down and hurried over to the teapot, while Immi and I ventured into the hallway in search of the runaway kitten.

'Come here, kitty,' Immi coaxed as we spotted him at the bottom of the stairs.

'You'll never manage to climb up there,' I told him as I picked him up and stroked his silky ears. 'Although, no doubt in a few weeks, you'll manage it with no difficulties at all.'

'I haven't told Violet about him,' Immi said brightly. 'I should take his photo and send it to her. I wanted to message her later anyway to thank her for the present. Can you hang onto him, Mum, while I get my phone?'

'Of course,' I said.

Agnes and Aubrey joined me.

'We should go and find Florence,' Agnes said. 'She's having a rather difficult time at the moment, and I don't want to leave her on her own too long.'

'She should have come to the tea party,' I said. I mean, I

wasn't keen on Florrie at the best of times, but I didn't like the thought of her sitting upstairs alone while the rest of us enjoyed ourselves. She was only ten, after all.

'I did suggest it,' Aubrey said. 'You know Florence when she's got a bee in her bonnet.'

'Perhaps she's a little envious of Immi's birthday tea party, and I think she's been pining for her grandfather and his cat,' Agnes said sadly. 'It's brought back a lot of memories for her.'

'I'm sorry,' I said. 'I never intended that to happen.'

'No. Well.' Agnes sniffed. 'If you'd told us you were going to bring a kitten to the house, I could perhaps have warned her, but there we are. It's done now.'

'Oh, I say,' Aubrey said reproachfully, 'that's hardly fair, Agnes.'

'Can you deny it, Mr Wyndham?' she demanded.

I sighed. She was back on form then.

Mia came through with the tea tray. 'All set,' she said. 'Oh, you got him then? Good. Can someone just open the sitting-room door please?'

I was just about to do so when I heard the kitten hiss in my arms. He was staring at the stairs, and I looked up, seeing Immi coming down them, scrolling on her mobile phone. Florrie, a look of hatred on her face, was just behind her. Mia gave a startled cry and there was a loud crash as the tray fell to the floor, but I barely registered it as my heart thudded with fear. Florrie had stretched out her arms and shoved Immi hard in the back.

I nearly dropped the kitten with relief as I realised her hands had gone straight through Immi, who continued walking down the stairs, oblivious to what was happening behind her.

'Florence!'

Aubrey and Agnes omitted a shocked cry at the same time,

and Florrie stared down at them for a moment, before turning and running back to her room.

Immi looked up. 'What's the matter?'

'Oh!' I shook my head, hardly able to put into words the dread I'd experienced before I'd remembered that Florrie couldn't physically harm Immi, no matter how much she clearly wanted to.

'Let me do that,' Brodie said, and I looked round, realising Mia was staring in dismay at the tray, which was on the floor beside a broken teacup and tea-soaked sandwiches and cake.

'My fault,' Mia said shakily. 'I must have tripped.'

'No harm done,' he told her. 'It's easily cleaned up. While I do that, why don't you go and make up another tray for Grandpa?'

'I will do,' she said, and hurried into the kitchen to collect a second tray.

I turned to Agnes, shaking with the residue of fear and anger. 'Did you see what she did?'

'She didn't *do* anything,' Agnes said, though I could tell she was upset. 'She knew she couldn't harm Immi. It was just high jinks.'

'High jinks?' I squealed. 'What sort of mentality does she have that she'd even think of doing such a thing?'

'What do you mean, "she couldn't harm" me?' Immi asked suspiciously, shoving her phone in her jeans pocket and taking the kitten from me. 'What happened?'

'Florrie,' I said icily, 'tried to push you down the stairs.'

Agnes tutted impatiently. 'How could she do that? You know perfectly well she can't touch her.'

'The intention was there, though,' I said. 'Stop defending her!'

'I'm afraid Callie has a point, Agnes,' Aubrey said firmly. 'The very fact that Florence thought about it is worrying, particularly given the way she passed.'

'The way she passed?' I asked. 'What do you mean?'

'Mr Wyndham!' Agnes gasped.

'I think after that little display, Callie should know,' he said defiantly. 'The fact is,' he said turning to me, 'Florence was sent here during the war as an evacuee from London. She was rather a handful from the moment she arrived and disobeyed the rules about wearing outdoor shoes in the house. She'd sneaked upstairs in her wellington boots, which were slightly too big for her, and when she ran down the stairs later that day, she tripped and fell. She...'

Agnes's hand flew to her mouth, and I saw the distress in her eyes.

'It's okay,' I said gently. 'You don't have to explain the rest.'

'She's just a little girl,' Agnes whimpered.

'Even so,' Aubrey said, 'we need to have a word with her, as I've told you many times before.'

Agnes pulled her bed-jacket tighter. 'But—'

'I'm sorry,' he told her kindly, 'but this sort of behaviour just isn't on. You must know that, Agnes.'

'I know.' Her voice came out as a whisper – most unlike Agnes. I could see she was genuinely worried and desperately trying to mask her fear, and my heart softened towards her. 'She's jealous, you see. Of Immi. First the kitten, and now all this fuss... Birthday cake and a tea party. I don't think Florence ever had either of those things, or if she did, it was such a long time ago. It's hard for her to see Imogen celebrating her eleventh birthday when she'll never celebrate her own.'

'I understand that, Agnes, I really do,' I said, 'but her behaviour is awful all the time, not just today. It seems to me that

Florrie needs some discipline and routine in her life.' I turned to Aubrey. 'Don't you agree?'

'Well...' He hesitated then sighed. 'Yes, yes I do.'

'Mr Wyndham!'

'Agnes, there's no use denying it. The girl is out of control and running wild. We need to do something.'

'It's those boys she's associating with,' Agnes said. 'I blame them.'

'John and Robert?' I shook my head. 'From what I saw of them, it's Florrie who's in charge there. Maybe it's time we did something about all three of them.'

She frowned. 'What do you mean by that?'

'I think it's time we gave them some routine,' I said. 'How would you feel about them having lessons?'

'Lessons? I already give Florence elocution lessons.'

'I mean proper lessons. School lessons. All of them.'

'I think that sounds very sensible,' Aubrey considered. 'Give them something to do every day as well as educating them. Splendid idea.'

'Florence having lessons would be bad enough,' Agnes said with a sniff. 'What does a girl need to be educated for anyway? But the thought of her spending even more time with those two young ruffians... No, it's out of the question.'

'Well, I think it's a good idea,' I said firmly. 'And if it's the only way we can start to calm her down I think it's our best option.'

'Girls do need to be educated, Mrs Wyndham,' Immi said meekly. 'And I enjoy school. It's fun, and I like learning. Maybe Florrie will too.'

'It's Florence,' Agnes said sharply. 'And things are different now, I'm sure. But in my day—'

'But we're not in your day any more,' I reminded her gently.

'Those children need a routine. I suspect they're bored and having lessons would give them something to focus on.'

'I say,' Aubrey said thoughtfully, 'they could use the old schoolroom upstairs. It's where I had my lessons with the governess.'

'And who would teach them?' Agnes demanded. She turned to me with some satisfaction. 'Didn't think of that, did you?'

'Actually,' I said slowly, 'I might have the very man for the job. Walter Tasker.'

'Walter Tasker!' She snorted. 'Man's a buffoon.'

'Agnes, that's just not true. Educated at Oxford. Highly intelligent chap.' Aubrey nodded at me. 'He taught William Shakespeare, you know.'

'I had heard,' I said, trying to hide my amusement. 'So, what do you think, Agnes? If he was good enough to teach Shakespeare, he's surely good enough to teach Florence.'

Agnes shook her head. 'I refuse to even contemplate it.'

Aubrey put his hand on her arm. 'We must do *something*, Agnes. This is for Florence's sake, remember.'

She shrugged him away. '*I* know what's best for Florence.' She cleared her throat. 'I'm terribly sorry, Imogen. Florence shouldn't have done what she did. I know she couldn't harm you but even so. As your mother rightly said, the intention was there. I shall go upstairs now and have stern words with her, I promise.'

'Thank you,' Immi mumbled.

'However, there is no question of her having lessons with Walter Tasker, let alone spending even more time with those two boys.' Her voice rose to a cry as she turned to me. 'And if you try to enforce this, I shall have words with Lawrie. He'll stop you!'

The door opened and Lawrie peered out. 'What on earth's going on? What's with the raised voices?'

I started to tell him what had happened, but Agnes was far louder and more insistent.

Brodie, who'd been carefully collecting broken china and putting it on the tray, got to his feet.

'From what I can gather, Florrie tried to push Immi down the stairs, and now Callie wants her to have lessons with Walter Tasker.'

'With those two ruffians,' Agnes added with a shriek, as Brodie finished, 'Did I miss anything out?'

'We have to do something about her,' I said. 'Lessons will give her afterlife some structure and routine and she certainly needs it after over eighty years of running wild. And it will be good for John and Robert too.'

'I sort of feel sorry for them all,' Immi admitted. 'It must be rotten being stuck at such a young age, knowing you'll never get to be a grown up. Especially when you haven't got your real mum with you.'

'So do I,' I said, 'but even so, they can't carry on like this, and Florrie can't be allowed to behave the way she does. I think it will be far better for her if she's got something to focus on. Although,' I added thoughtfully, 'I don't know what Walter Tasker will say when I ask him if he'll do it. After all—'

'He did teach Shakespeare, you know,' Brodie and I finished together and burst out laughing.

'Did he really?' Immi asked, wide-eyed. 'I thought you were all joking.'

'Oh, most definitely,' Brodie told her. 'It's been checked and verified, right, Grandpa? The question is, will he lower himself to come here and teach our three little ragamuffins?'

'He won't be coming here to teach anyone,' Lawrie said firmly.

I stared at him. 'What do you mean?'

'I mean, Agnes has said no, and since she's responsible for Florence's welfare, that's the end of the matter,' he said.

Agnes gave me a triumphant smirk and headed up the stairs.

'I disagree most strongly with this,' Aubrey said, jutting out his chin at Lawrie. 'Most strongly. My deepest apologies once again, Callie and Immi.'

With that, he followed his wife, a stony expression on his usually genial face.

Mia came through carrying another tray. 'Oh, look at that mess,' she said. 'I'll be back in a moment with a mop and bucket and a dustpan and brush. Oh, Lawrie! Did I wake you up?'

'This is all wrong,' I told Lawrie. 'You can't let Agnes call the shots like this. How will Florrie's behaviour ever get any better?'

'The subject's closed,' Lawrie said, returning to the sitting room and shutting the door behind him.

'Says who?' I muttered. 'Whose bloody house is this anyway?'

'Just leave it for now,' Brodie said quietly.

'But—'

'I know. Honestly, I do,' he said. 'But not now. Please, Callie.'

'I'd better take him his tea tray,' Mia said. 'I'm so sorry for the mess.'

'Come on, Mum,' Immi said. 'Let's go into the kitchen and I'll make you a cup of tea, eh?'

There was so much I wanted to say but the look on Brodie's face and Mia's anxious expression made me reluctantly agree to Immi's suggestion. I was seething, though. What hold did Agnes have over Lawrie, I wondered? And who was he to insist we all obeyed her? Florrie might be her adoptive daughter, but Immi was my child, and I wasn't going to let that nasty little girl continue to run rings around us all.

Later, I thought as I headed to the kitchen, still carrying the kitten. *I'll have this out with Lawrie later.* Then I frowned as something else nagged at me. A cry of alarm before Mia dropped the tray. Was it my faulty memory or had she been looking up the stairs at the time?

She said she'd tripped but...

I dismissed the thought. I was being stupid. Mia couldn't see ghosts so she couldn't possibly have been startled by the sight of Florence pushing Immi.

Could she?

23

After an eventful weekend, it was almost a relief to get back to work. I spent Monday going slowly and painfully over the *Idiot's Guide* from Brodie, as well as the written notes that Lawrie had prepared for me, which basically listed all the tenants, where they lived, a little bit about their family history, and whether or not they had any family connection to the resident ghosts. There was also a list of all the ghosts he could name, although he'd added a reminder that not all the ghosts on the estate had made themselves personally known to him.

On Tuesday, I ventured out to the Wyrd Stones with Mia. Despite my initial apprehension, it was amazing to see them in person. There was a distinct atmosphere around the area, which was in the very centre of the Harling Estate.

After making our way through thick woodland, The King's Court was the first thing we came to – an almost perfect circle of fourteen stones enclosing a separate group of three in a huge clearing, overlooked by a solitary rowan tree.

'The Queen Stone and her children,' Mia said, and shivered.

'You know the legend then,' I said.

'I do. Such a sad story, isn't it?'

'But just a story,' I reminded her, much as I'd done Lawrie. 'No need to get upset.'

'I can't help it,' she admitted. 'The thought of being separated from your family like that. It always gets to me.'

I looked at her with curiosity. 'What about *your* family, Mia?'

'Mine?' She laughed. 'What's that got to do with it?'

'I'm just asking,' I said. 'I don't really know anything about you, and I'd like to. Your parents, for example. Are they still alive?'

'Oh yes. Fighting fit.'

'Where are they?' I asked her.

She tilted her head, considering. 'What month is it? June? They'll be in Copenhagen. July, it will be Quebec.'

I stared at her. 'Wow! They like to travel then.'

'They love it.'

'And you don't?'

'I used to. Thing is, I've been all over the place with them. By the time I was twenty-five, I was bored and looking to put down roots. I don't think Mum and Dad ever will and let's face it, it was time for me to strike out on my own anyway.'

'So, you ended up in the Cotswolds?'

'I know. Crazy, isn't it? One minute, I was on a gondola in Venice; the next, I was dragging a suitcase to The Quicken Tree, never imagining that my life would change forever.'

'Do you regret it?'

There was a slight pause. 'No. I was ready to settle down and earn my own living. Mum's very protective and wanted me to stay with them, but Dad's a bit more level-headed. He's a financier who made his own way in the world, unlike Mum, and he thought I should at least learn how to make a living, even if I never had to do it, so from my mid-teens, he started teaching me how to do accounts and basic administration tasks.

'Overruled Mum about me learning advanced computer skills as soon as I finished boarding school and sent me to a private college to learn. Paid for me to do an expensive cookery course. That kind of thing. He always insisted I could never have too many strings to my bow. Poor Mum was horrified. She wanted me to be like her and basically do nothing except marry a rich man.'

There was a twinkle of amusement in her eyes, and I sensed that, despite everything, she was fond of her parents.

'You must miss them.'

'Sometimes, but we chat on the phone and I video call them. If they're ever at home, I pop over and see them.'

'Where is home?' I asked.

'Richmond.'

'North Yorkshire?' I asked in surprise.

She smiled. 'London.'

'Oh, of course. You already said you were from London. I'm originally from Yorkshire so I automatically think of *our* Richmond. Is that where you grew up then?'

'Not really. I was at boarding school in Scotland and during the holidays, I was often taken abroad to various glamorous destinations.'

'Sounds idyllic,' I murmured, though deep down, I wasn't too sure it did. It sounded quite unsettled to me. There was a lot to be said for staying at home if you asked me.

'I was very lucky,' she said flatly. Then her eyes sparkled, and she said, 'Sometimes, I'd go to Grandma's for Christmas. I loved that. She lived in Hampstead, and she used to make such a fuss of me. We'd go all out decorating her house for Christmas. It couldn't have been more traditional. I suppose it was to make up for the fact that I was often abroad for the holidays and missed out on British Christmases. She always said that was a terrible shame.'

'She sounds very nice,' I said. 'Very down to earth.'

'She was,' she said wistfully. 'She died five years ago. I wish —' She broke off and shook her head. 'Anyway, that's more than enough about me. We have stones to look at. Shall we visit the barrow next? It's just along that track there.'

I had the definite feeling that the subject of Mia's private life was now firmly closed, so I nodded in agreement. 'Sure. Why not?'

To reach the barrow, we followed a track which threaded its way between the trees and went through a gate to where The Guardians stood, overlooked by another rowan tree. To me at first they were just another bunch of stones. They did, however, look a bit creepier as I got closer to them and realised they looked uncannily like four people huddled together.

The barrow was apparently beneath the stones, and an excavation, decades earlier, had uncovered the bones of twelve people as well as cremated remains.

'What's with the rowan trees?' I asked. 'They're everywhere. Is it true that another name for rowan is quicken tree, and even the pub's named after them?'

'It is. Rowans are one of the nine sacred trees in Druidry, and it was believed that they protected against witches and evil, mainly due to the little pentagrams embedded in the bottom of each red berry. Red is supposed to be the most effective colour of protection too. It has another name – the witch tree. So you see, given the mythology around these stones, it's not surprising rowans were planted everywhere and are held in such high regard around here.'

'Wow,' I said. 'I had no idea.'

'This is the oldest of the three sites,' Mia told me. 'It dates back to early Neolithic times. Probably around five and a half thousand years old.'

'No way.' I shivered. 'That's incredible. So how old is the circle?'

'Late Neolithic,' she said. 'Probably around a thousand years younger than this place. The stones are local. They think they were brought here from this area, long before these trees were planted.'

'Brought here?' I said with a smirk. 'Thought the witch made them from people?'

She laughed and we turned to head back up the track. We passed the stone circle again then followed a well-worn track through dense trees until we found The Penitent King standing all alone, away from his supposed Queen, children, and courtiers, a ring of rowan trees surrounding him.

Despite my earlier lack of sympathy, I couldn't help but feel a pang of sadness for this lonely stone all by itself, surrounded by an iron fence and so many trees. There was no clearing for this stone. It was as if it was being punished. Though bigger than the others, it was rather misshapen and had a forlorn look about it.

Callie, you're being ridiculous. How can a stone look forlorn?

I was so lost in my thoughts that at first, I didn't realise we weren't alone in this part of the woods. Then a prickling started on my shoulders and down my neck and I spun round, my jaw dropping as I saw, standing between two trees in the distance, a distinguished-looking man who, judging by his clothing and North-African appearance, could be none other than Quintus Severus himself.

He was watching us, an impassive look on his face. Mia frowned at me and said, 'What are you looking at?'

'We're being watched,' I told her. 'I have a feeling it's the Roman centurion.'

'Ah,' Mia said. 'I see. Not surprising, I suppose. Lawrie says he's taken it upon himself to patrol the outer reaches of the estate and keep a special eye on the stones. Apparently, they've been vandalised over the centuries, with people chipping bits off them to take home. That's why this old chap's such an odd shape, and why Sir Edward fenced him off.'

'I don't see what good the centurion will be able to do,' I said. 'He can hardly push them away or call the police, can he?' Seeing that Quintus Severus was still watching us, I gave him a feeble wave.

I saw him visibly start and he took a step towards us but then seemed to think better of it. There was a moment's hesitation, then he bowed.

'He's just bowed to me,' I said in amazement. 'What's all that about?'

'You waved to him,' she pointed out. 'He's probably just realised who you are and is showing you respect. After all, you're the new protector of the stones and they mean a lot to him.'

'I am?' I hadn't even thought about that before, and it felt like a huge responsibility. In a weird way, it felt like more of a responsibility than looking after a complete village with all its tenants – alive and dead. I frowned. 'I didn't know Roman soldiers bowed. I thought they saluted. I've seen it in the films.'

'Not sure the films are strictly accurate, though. Besides, Quintus Severus has been around a long, long time. He probably observes the etiquette of the current period.'

'And how would he know what that is?' I asked, curious. 'He doesn't come into the village, and I can't see him having a television set out here, can you?'

Mia shrugged. 'Who knows? There are so many mysteries

around here, it's just another one to add to the list. Is he still watching?'

'No.' My gaze followed the soldier as he marched purposefully through the woods until the trees obscured him from my sight. 'Can't see him now. I suppose he's continuing his inspection. Not much of a life, is it? I mean, not much of an afterlife. Poor fella. Wish I could persuade him to come into the village and mingle a bit. He deserves a break, if you ask me. A Roman soldier. I mean – wow.'

'If he wants to socialise, he knows where to find other ghosts,' she pointed out.

'I suppose so. Just seems a shame.'

'Come on. Let's get back to the Hall,' she said, and I had to agree. I was ready for a nice, cold glass of her homemade lemonade.

As we walked, I thought about Quintus Severus and his lonely life on the edges of the estate, and about Harmony Hill, who was rarely seen and lived goodness knows where. I wondered about the other ghosts who never came to the village and felt sad for them. Why did they stay away? Did they have company? Or were they all as isolated as this Roman soldier?

At least Agnes, Aubrey, and Florence had each other. And they had us. I thought about the ghosts who had no living relatives in the village. Since only Lawrie and I could see them, it couldn't be much fun for them. Did they mingle with each other? Or did they all stick to their own areas, much like the ghosts at the Hall?

It occurred to me that I'd never known Aubrey and Agnes leave the house.

'Oh, they wander the gardens sometimes,' Mia assured me when I voiced my concerns to her. 'Lawrie tells me they like to check on the gardeners and see what's been planted and what's growing. Although,' she admitted, 'I've never heard him mention them leaving the grounds.'

'*Can* they leave the grounds?' I asked doubtfully. 'Are they sort of restricted to certain areas?'

'I shouldn't think so,' she said. 'Florrie goes all over the estate, doesn't she? If she can leave the Hall, I don't see why Aubrey and Agnes shouldn't. As far as we're aware, all the ghosts can come and go as they please, as long as they don't cross the estate boundaries.'

'How strange,' I mused. 'I must ask them why they don't go further afield.'

'It's probably Agnes's doing,' she said knowingly. 'Maybe she doesn't want to mix with the hoi polloi, and what Agnes wants, Agnes gets after all.'

For a moment, she sounded quite bitter, and I stared at her.

'You don't like Agnes?'

She laughed. 'Why wouldn't I like her? I can't see her. I can't hear her. I have no feelings about her one way or the other. I'm just going by what Lawrie has told me, that's all. Now, enough of all this ghost talk. Let's hurry home because I'm gasping for a lemonade.'

24

As it turned out, I didn't ask Agnes and Aubrey why they never left the grounds. At dinner that evening, I'd mentioned to Lawrie about seeing Quintus Severus and the questions it had thrown up for me, and when I told him my thoughts about our housemates never leaving the grounds of Harling Hall, he'd advised me not to discuss it with them.

'It's their business, Callie,' he said. 'Best not to interfere.'

'I wasn't going to interfere,' I said indignantly. 'I'm just curious, that's all.'

'But if you mention it, you could stir up some issues that are best left,' he explained. 'Take it from me; however Agnes and Aubrey choose to live their afterlives is up to them. You've still got a lot to learn about this place and it's best to tread lightly until you're better acquainted with the facts.'

'So, what *are* the facts?' I asked, feeling rather annoyed. I was still peeved that he'd blocked the lessons, so I wasn't in any mood for him to make even more demands.

'It's not for me to say,' he said, clearly uncomfortable.

'But if I can't ask *them*, and *you* won't tell me, how am I supposed to know?'

He sighed. 'You don't have to know everything. Agnes and Aubrey are entitled to a private life. Just leave them to it.'

I couldn't hide my annoyance, and Brodie clearly sensed it. As Lawrie and Immi headed into the sitting room after dinner, he stayed behind to help Mia and me clear the table, something I did regularly, even though Mia insisted she didn't need my help.

'Don't take it personally,' Brodie said as he scraped the leftovers from each plate and stacked them on a tray. 'He's very protective of the ghosts – especially the ones in this house.'

'Especially Agnes,' Mia added primly. As we both looked at her, she said, 'Sorry. None of my business.'

'Don't be silly,' I said. 'You're as entitled to your opinion as anyone else. Why do you say he's especially fond of Agnes?'

She shrugged. 'No reason really. Just the things he says sometimes, and the way he talks about her. I don't know. He always seems to have a soft spot for her, that's all. I don't know why.'

'I do,' Brodie admitted. 'Agnes was the first ghost he can remember seeing when he was tiny. He was born in this house, remember? Agnes apparently spent a lot of time with him when he was a small child. His first memory isn't of his own parents, but of her, sitting by his bedside, telling him stories. She doted on him by all accounts, and he saw her almost like a loving grandmother.'

'Really?' I gasped. 'Agnes?'

'Yes, really.' He grinned. 'Is it so hard to believe? Is she really that bad?'

'Yes,' Mia and I chorused, then looked at each other.

'From what I've heard,' Mia added hastily. 'You're right, though, and it would explain a lot. Lawrie always speaks of her so fondly, and even when she's being stubborn and annoying, he makes excuses for her. Poor Aubrey doesn't stand a chance, really.'

'Well, the fact remains that Grandpa doesn't want Agnes upset, so it's best we just let them get on with things,' Brodie said. 'But that doesn't mean you should see it as an insult, Callie. I'm sure he didn't mean to offend you. He's just protective of her, as I said, and was desperate to ensure you didn't rock the boat in any way.'

Thinking about it, I supposed I had been a bit pushy. After all, Lawrie had lived in this village all his life. He knew the ghosts and what they needed more than I did, and I was probably unwise to think I should just barge in and change things. I didn't really have the right to interfere in the Wyndhams' relationship. Maybe I'd been wrong to push for the children to have lessons too, although I still thought it was a good idea. But if Lawrie said it wasn't...

'I don't want to fall out with him,' I said reluctantly. 'Especially not over Agnes.'

'Well then.' His face brightened. 'Let's forget all this and join them in the sitting room.'

'Yes, do that,' Mia said with feeling. 'Leave me to do my job for once. You're making me feel surplus to requirements, Callie.'

'I seem to be in everyone's way lately,' I said with a sigh.

'Not at all.' She placed the empty gravy jug on the tray beside the stack of plates. 'I do appreciate you offering to help and your concern for my welfare, but I promise you, I'm quite happy with my own routine and I'd rather you joined Lawrie and Immi for the evening. And you were saying you've barely had time to be with Immi lately so make the most of it while you can.'

She had a point so, reluctantly, I left her to finish up in the dining room and headed into the sitting room where Lawrie and my daughter were sitting in opposite armchairs and Immi had the kitten – still nameless – on her lap.

Lawrie turned and beamed at me, our rather heated conversation evidently forgotten. 'I was just saying to Immi,' he said, 'that she really ought to think of a name for this poor little chap. We can't keep calling him Kitty and Tux. Unless, of course, she intends to name him Kitty or Tux.'

'It has to be just right,' Immi insisted. 'I can't just call him any old thing.'

'You've had him for five days now,' I reminded her, settling on the sofa where I was joined by Brodie. 'It can't be that hard to think of a name, surely?'

'How old was I when you thought of *my* name?' she asked slyly.

She had me there. As I'd foolishly once told her, I'd ummed and aahed and dithered pathetically after she'd been born, changing my mind on a daily basis until the deadline for registering her birth was nearly upon me.

At that point, my stepmother's patience snapped, and she wrote all the names I'd been considering on scraps of paper, stuck them in an empty cereal bowl and made me draw one out. I'd drawn out the name Olivia, and she'd insisted Dad drive me to the register office immediately before I could change my mind.

Except, I *had* changed my mind, and when the registrar asked me for the baby's name, I'd blurted out Imogen. So, Imogen she was, and with only twenty-four hours to the deadline too.

'All right,' I said with a sigh. 'You win. Take your time.'

'Hmm,' Brodie said, 'I get the feeling there's a story behind that sudden surrender.'

'Never you mind,' I said darkly. 'Though I've no doubt Immi will fill you in before too long.'

He winked at Immi, who grinned back. Yep, no doubt about it. She'd tell him everything. Although, it was nice to see the two of them getting on so well. He was really good with her. In fact, I had to admit that, just lately, he'd been very easy to live with. He seemed to have accepted that it was time to move on and made his peace with it.

It was odd, but it was I who was struggling to accept it. The thought of Harling Hall without Brodie – and Lawrie of course – was depressing. I'd got used to having them around and enjoyed their company. It just wouldn't be the same without them, even though I knew it was for the best.

'Violet sent me a text earlier,' Immi told me. 'She was asking me loads of questions about this place and how we're getting on. I can't wait for her to visit in the summer holidays. She'll love the kitten.'

My heart sank like a stone. 'I don't think that's such a good idea,' I said, trying to hide how appalled I felt at the notion.

Her face fell. 'But you promised! We've already told her she can come in the summer.'

'I know,' I said uncomfortably. 'But we're still getting used to this place ourselves. Maybe it would be better if she visited later in the year. Maybe after Christmas?'

'Christmas? That's months away!'

'Not really. It will fly by, we're both so busy.'

'Well,' Immi said stubbornly, 'I think you're wrong, but I suppose you get the final say as usual.'

She scooped the kitten up and flounced out of the sitting room.

'So now she's eleven, she starts to act like a moody teenager?'

I asked, throwing up my hands in despair. 'Great. That's all I need.'

'I'll go and talk to her,' Lawrie said, easing himself out of the chair. 'Might coax her back into a good mood with some ice cream.'

'She's just had a dessert,' I pointed out. 'She doesn't need bribing with more food.'

'No, but I really fancy some ice cream,' he said, his eyes twinkling. 'She can watch me eat mine if nothing else.'

He reached for his stick and made his way out of the room, and I gave a heavy sigh.

'Not having a good day, are you?' Brodie said sympathetically.

'Does it show?' I gave him a rueful smile. 'It will be okay. Immi's not one to hold a grudge.'

'Forgive me if I'm speaking out of turn,' he said, 'but I really don't see the big deal about inviting her friend to stay. There's certainly enough room here.'

'She wouldn't like it at the Hall,' I said, although I wasn't convinced that was true. Violet hadn't minded Immi seeing ghosts so I couldn't see her freaking out about this old house, particularly as she'd nagged to go ghost hunting in graveyards. 'She'd find it old and creepy.'

He laughed. 'Oh well, maybe she can bring a tent and pitch it in the grounds.'

'I wouldn't put it past her,' I said glumly. 'And I wouldn't put it past Immi to suggest it to her.'

'What's the problem, really? Don't you like this girl or something? She surely can't be as bad as Florrie!'

'She's not. She's actually a really nice girl,' I said.

'Then...'

'Violet knows that Immi can see ghosts,' I said heavily.

'Well, that's – that's good. Isn't it? I mean, the fact that she still wants to be friends with her is great. Right?'

'Is it? Right now, her mum just thinks Immi had a vivid imagination when she was very young,' I said. 'What if, after Violet comes here and discovers what this village really is, she tells her mum the truth about us? About me!'

'You sound so panicky,' he said gently. 'This is a really big deal to you, isn't it?'

'Of course it is! All I ever wanted was to be normal. It's all Mum ever wanted, too, and I've tried so hard...'

To my horror, I realised tears had escaped my eyes and were sliding down my cheeks. How embarrassing!

'Sorry,' I said, frantically wiping my face. 'Ignore me.'

'Your mum,' Brodie said, 'is she—'

'She died when I was six,' I said, swallowing down my grief. 'Everything changed then.'

'Do you want to talk about it?'

I half laughed, aware that tears were still escaping. 'You wouldn't want to know.'

'Try me.' He headed to the bureau in the corner of the room and took out a box of tissues. 'Here,' he said, handing them to me.

'Thanks.' I wiped my eyes and nose and stuffed a tissue up my sleeve. 'Where do I even start?'

'Tell me about your mum. You and she got on?'

I nodded. 'She was lovely. Except... except she hated that I could see the ghosts. It really freaked her out. I always thought it was an overreaction, but then Dad – God, I hate calling him that, he never deserved the title – was so bloody horrible about it. It was Dad who called it a curse, but Mum agreed with him.'

'I see,' Brodie said slowly. 'So, they made you feel...'

'Like a freak,' I said bitterly. 'Mum made me lie constantly because Dad used to get so angry when I'd talked to a ghost, so in the end, I was paranoid about showing any signs of communicating with them. I used to ignore them. Close my eyes to them. Cover my ears when they tried talking to me. Then Mum died and it was just me and him and things got so much worse. You know,' I said bitterly, 'for the first time, I'd have given anything to be able to see a ghost. I used to wait for her – for Mum. But she never came. And then, gradually, they all stopped coming and... Well, I think I just forgot about them. That I could ever see them. Or I blocked it all out. This place,' I said, 'reawakened something. Not just the memories, but the curse itself.'

'I wish you'd stop thinking of it as a curse,' he said earnestly. 'It's an amazing gift. That's how Immi sees it too.'

'How do you know?' I asked. 'Have you been talking to her about it?'

'A bit,' he said. 'She's good at telling me when Agnes, Aubrey, and Florence are around and filling me in on what they're doing or saying. Aubrey and I have been able to have brief conversations, thanks to Immi being our go-between. It's kind of nice.'

I wasn't sure I liked that idea. I'd been hoping Immi would be more interested in living people now she was at school, and I didn't want Brodie encouraging her to spend time with the ghosts.

'I had no idea,' I murmured. Then again, how would I? I hadn't been around much for her lately, had I? 'Why didn't your grandfather do that for you?' I asked as the thought suddenly occurred to me.

'He never offered, and I never liked to ask. He was always so busy when I was younger, and by the time he started to slow down, the pattern had been set, I suppose. The estate took up such a lot of his time, and I didn't want to be a bother or get in the way.'

I nibbled my thumbnail. I could well understand how running the estate would take up Lawrie's time, but to the exclusion of his grandson? Brodie must have been left alone quite a lot of the time. I didn't want that to happen to Immi.

'It's different for you,' he said, as if he knew what I was thinking. 'Immi can see the ghosts too. She can be part of it. I never could. I wish I could be, though. That's what I mean when I say it isn't a curse. It's a gift, and I can't believe your parents made you feel that way.'

He waited while I tore another tissue from the box and dabbed at the fresh tears.

'Are you okay? Do you want to leave it?' he asked.

'No, it's all right. Now that I've started, I just want to pour it all out. I'm so bloody angry!'

He nodded. 'Anger's good. Get it all off your chest. I'm here to listen. So, after your mum died, you lived with your dad?'

'Huh!' I gave a bitter laugh. 'You must be joking. He couldn't pack me off quickly enough. I spent my childhood being passed from one of his relatives to another, and none of them were that eager to have me. It was only because of the benefits they could claim that they took me in at all.'

'Didn't – didn't your mum have any relatives you could go to?'

'No. Mum was an only child, and her mum – my gran – died before I was born. Gran was adopted and had no brothers or sisters or even any aunts or uncles. I don't know anything about my grandad's side at all. All I had were my dad's relatives, and they were as lousy as he was. Then he moved to Leicestershire and remarried, and I was sent to live with *them*. I was fifteen. He was a bit better while *she* was around, but she got fed up when I had Immi. Didn't want a baby in the house. It was us or her, so obviously he chose her.'

Brodie rubbed his eyes with his forefinger and thumb, as if he couldn't quite believe what he was hearing. 'Bloody hell, Callie. I'm so sorry.'

I shrugged. 'It's okay. Social services got involved and they got us a flat. When Immi was old enough to go to nursery, I started working – barmaid, waitress, checkout girl, school dinner lady. You name it, I did it. I got help with childcare and then, when Immi started school, she made friends with Violet and her mum offered to mind her until I got home from work and during the school holidays. I signed on with the care agency and I've been there ever since. I was lucky.'

'Yeah,' Brodie murmured. 'Really lucky.'

'Don't feel sorry for me!' I said, alarmed. 'I'm not some helpless victim. I did all right. I did all right by Immi too.'

'More than all right, Callie. I think you're amazing.'

I hardly knew how to react to the way he was looking at me. The warmth in those blue eyes of his had made me go all funny inside, and that was something I wasn't expecting.

'I'm sorry too,' I said. 'That you can't see the ghosts, I mean. It must be awful for you when you've grown up in a household where talking to ghosts is nothing unusual. I don't know. We've both struggled because we're not normal in our families, haven't we? Shame we can't swap places.'

'It would be so much better if we could both see them,' he said. 'I really wouldn't want you to lose your gift. And it *is* a gift, Callie. I hope one day you'll come to fully accept that.'

'It's getting easier,' I admitted. 'Being here in this village where everyone takes it for granted that ghosts exist and that I can see them all – well, it's stopped me feeling like such an oddity. But the fear never leaves. The feeling of being rejected. Abandoned. I don't want Immi to go through that with Violet. Right now, they're friends, but if she tells her mum...'

'It's odd,' he mused. 'You and Immi both having this gift. I wonder where it comes from?'

'My gran,' I said. 'I remember Mum telling me once, when I was very young. I can't remember all the details, but she said Gran could see ghosts, too, and that she had an awful life because of it, and she didn't want the same for me. Well, look what happened. She died and I was left with *him*. And you say it's not a curse?'

'I understand why you'd feel that way.' Brodie reached out and lightly stroked the side of my face with his forefinger. 'But you're special, Callie. So is Immi. Just remember, there's nothing wrong with either of you, and you have nothing to be ashamed of, so don't ever let *anyone* make you feel that way again.'

His blue eyes were warm with understanding, and I wondered how I'd ever considered him to be an arse. God, he was gorgeous! I could sit here gazing at him forever, him stroking my face and...

'Pub quiz,' I said as the thought occurred to me.

He blinked, dropping his hand. 'Sorry?'

'Clara says there's a pub quiz on Thursday nights at The Quicken Tree. She's invited me along tomorrow. Do you – I mean, do you ever go?' I asked hopefully, just about stopping short of inviting him.

He looked a bit awkward. 'Not really. I'm usually busy. I've got a lot on tomorrow evening.'

Of course he had. My heart sank as I realised he was making excuses and I'd been carried away by his kindness, seeing things that just weren't there, probably because his was the only attention I'd had from any man in years. I'd forgotten that they could be nice without wanting anything in return.

Anyway, what on earth was I doing? He would be leaving soon. At the end of June, Lawrie had said. That was only a couple of weeks away. There was no point in me going all gooey over Brodie Davenport.

I jumped up and he leaned away, startled by my sudden movement.

'I'm just going to pop upstairs and go through the *Idiot's Guide* again...'

'Oh.' Clearly taken aback by my change in attitude, he said, 'Okay. Look, Callie, if you need to talk at any time—'

'Thanks,' I said. 'I'm fine now, honestly.'

I swept into the hallway without looking back and practically galloped upstairs, wincing as I heard Agnes calling, 'Has no one ever told you that you should walk sedately up the stairs, Callie? You're not a Labrador.'

Thank goodness Brodie couldn't hear her.

Though it didn't matter in the slightest what he thought.

It mustn't ever matter.

25

'Can't I come with you?' Immi asked, in an annoyingly whiny voice that wasn't like her at all.

I twisted the lipstick down and put the cap back in place before giving myself one last look in the mirror.

I barely recognised myself with make-up on, my hair neatly washed, dried and brushed. Not to mention the fact that I was wearing a skirt and a rather nice shirt. Who, I asked myself in wonder, was this woman who looked passably attractive for a change?

'Mum!'

'Sorry.' I blinked and turned to Immi, feeling another rush of guilt. She was sitting on my bed, kitten in her arms, watching me with an undisguised plea in her eyes. 'You know you can't, sweetheart. It's a pub quiz. You're not allowed in there. You're far too young.'

'Bet I could answer more questions than you,' she said sulkily.

'You probably could,' I admitted. 'It doesn't alter the fact that eleven-year-olds aren't allowed in the bar of The Quicken Tree. I'm sorry.'

'But we're allowed in the restaurant part,' she pointed out.

'And I won't be in the restaurant part. I'll be in the bar where the quiz is being held. What part of that aren't you getting?' I sighed, seeing the resentment in her eyes. 'I'm really sorry. Look, how about I take you there for your tea tomorrow night? We can spend the whole evening together if you like. I'll even take you to the cinema after we've eaten.'

She gave me a dubious look. 'What's on?'

I bit my lip. 'Er, *Mrs Miniver*.'

'Who?'

'It's a wartime film. But,' I added hastily as I saw the disgust in her face, 'it's not about battles. It's about a family and how their lives change during the war, and how it impacts the community they live in... It might be useful for your school project.'

'Don't you think I've seen enough about the flipping war?' she groaned. 'What have I done to deserve this?'

I realised I wasn't selling it to her. 'Well, it's an excellent film,' I finished.

'I'd rather watch *Percy Jackson*,' she said coldly.

'You've seen *Percy Jackson*.'

'I'd like to see it again.'

'We haven't got *Percy Jackson*.'

'It's probably on Netflix. When are we getting Netflix?'

'Soon. Hopefully. I'm sure we'll find something else to watch,' I soothed.

'Well, anything will be better than Mrs Vinegar,' she said, pouting.

'*Mrs Miniver* and... oh, never mind. Look, Mia's going to sit with you while I'm gone, and I want you to promise you'll be in bed by nine. School in the morning, remember?'

'As if I could forget.'

'I'll be back before you know it,' I promised her, feeling a pang of guilt as I saw the disappointment in her face.

'Don't do me any favours.'

She shuffled off the bed and went to her own room, cradling the kitten in her arms.

Mia popped her head round the door. 'That went well.'

'You heard?' I sighed. 'I feel so terrible about it. She's right, isn't she? I've hardly spent any time with her at all since we moved here, and I shouldn't be going out tonight.'

'You deserve a night off,' she said. 'Okay, you haven't spent much time with Immi, but you've been busy getting to know the estate, poring over Brodie's *Idiot's Guide* and Lawrie's endless notes, as well as the accounts and other admin. If you're not careful, you'll end up just like Brodie.'

'Brodie?' I asked, startled. 'What do you mean?'

'You know what they say about all work and no play,' she said. 'It makes Brodie a dull boy and Callie a dull girl.'

'Brodie's been working?' I asked, surprised. 'At night, I mean?'

She raised an eyebrow. 'You didn't know?' She whistled. 'Wow, Brodie's always working. If he's not doing odd jobs for the tenants, he's organising repairs or pricing things up or working on the accounts or updating the website. He's busy every day and every evening. What did you think he was doing, holed up in that study all the time?'

I had to admit, I hadn't realised he was in the study all the time. I rarely used it myself and never thought to check if anyone else was. I was busy during the day and hadn't given much thought to where Brodie was, and in the evening, knowing

Lawrie was in bed by eight, I tended to retire to the sitting room in the west wing, struggling with the *Idiot's Guide* while Immi watched television or did her homework.

'I had no idea,' I said feebly. Wow, Brodie never ceased to surprise me.

'This last couple of weeks, he's also been making a list of all the jobs he does so that Mr Eldridge can find someone to take over when he's gone. Though it's looking as if you're going to need at least two people to take Brodie's place. I doubt many accountants would be up for doing all the other stuff he does.'

'I thought he was making excuses,' I admitted, remembering the bitter disappointment I'd experienced and tried to dismiss when he'd declined my hinted-at invitation to the pub quiz.

'Excuses? For what?'

I shook my head, a little embarrassed. 'Yesterday, I sort of asked him if he'd come to the pub quiz with me and he said he was too busy. I thought...'

'That he was fobbing you off.' Mia grinned. 'So, you wanted him to accompany you, eh? Interesting.'

'Just as a friend,' I protested hotly. 'Nothing more than that.'

She clasped her chest dramatically. 'I thought *I* was your friend, yet you didn't ask me? I'm wounded.'

'Only because you'd already offered to mind Immi,' I said quickly. 'I'm really sorry, Mia. I never—'

I broke off as she burst out laughing. 'Don't worry, sweetie, I'm only teasing. I can think of many ways I'd like to spend an evening but sitting in a pub answering questions about songs from the 1970s and South American football players, while grown men swill beer and women moan about their hot flushes, really isn't one of them.'

'Have you ever been to a pub quiz?' I asked doubtfully.

'Not in person, but I saw one once on a television drama. It was truly appalling. It's an experience I'll happily pass on, thanks very much.'

'You will let me know if she's any trouble?' I asked quietly, jerking my thumb in the vague direction of Immi's bedroom.

She smiled. 'She'll be fine. Once you've gone, she'll be all sweetness and light again. I've baked cookies and I've brought a game for us to play.'

'Immi hates games,' I said.

'She likes this one,' she told me confidently. 'We've played it before. It's a bit naughty.'

I stared at her. 'She's eleven!'

'I said a bit naughty, not frighteningly filthy!' She shook her head. 'Stop worrying and have a bit of faith. Go and enjoy yourself before I change my mind, and you're condemned to spend the evening sitting here watching your daughter sulk.'

'Okay, okay, I'm going.' I managed a smile. 'Thanks, Mia. I'm really grateful.'

'My pleasure. Now scat!'

* * *

The room at The Quicken Tree where the quiz was taking place was heaving, which came as quite a surprise to me. Clara had told me that the bar was closed to tourists on Thursday evenings, though they were welcome in the restaurant, so I'd expected to find the room almost empty, not jammed to the rafters with locals. Evidently, the pub quiz was popular.

Clara and Jack were sitting at a table in the far corner beside a few other people who, it turned out, were the other members of The Travelling Boffins – the pub quiz team consisting of various bus and train staff.

They all made me very welcome, and Jack got me a drink while Clara explained about the other teams.

'Over there, they're The Smart Cookies – they work at the Victory Tearooms, Mrs Herron's Teashop, and the Blighty Bakery. Then at that table in the other corner are The Rowan Brainiacs. They work—'

'On the farm,' I finished for her, recognising the two 'land girls', the two 'prisoners of war', and Nick and Betty.

'That's right. Now, you see that team nearest the bar? They're The Clever Clogs. They work in the Victorian shops.'

'I recognise one or two of them,' I told her. 'And that's Lucy and Sam – though it's funny to see them in modern clothing – so I presume that table's occupied by the Swinging Sixties staff?'

'Yep. The Bright Sparks. And the final team, sitting there looking so smug and sure of themselves, is The Mill Crew. Cos they work in the Mill Museum they think they know everything, but they don't.' She raised her voice and said, 'Pretty sure they cheat.'

There was a whoop of laughter, and a red-faced man shouted out, 'You wish what, Clara?'

At least the insults and accusations that followed and which eventually involved every single team in the pub seemed to be nothing more than harmless banter, with no real malice involved. I began to relax and even started to look forward to the evening at last, where up until that point, I'd been too nervous to enjoy myself.

After all, I was their new boss, and I wasn't sure how they'd react to me socialising with them. I remembered Betty's suspicion when I'd mentioned the tractor, and I didn't want to be faced with hostile expressions and mutterings that I should defer to Brodie or Lawrie whenever I ventured to answer a question.

Not that I expected to answer many questions. General knowledge wasn't my strong point. I wasn't sure what was.

As the landlady, Penny, tested the microphone and urged us to have our pens and paper at the ready, Clara nudged me, a wide grin on her face.

'Ooh, look who's just walked in!'

My gaze flickered to the door and my heart leapt unexpectedly as I saw Brodie looking around.

'What's he doing here?' I murmured. 'He said he was too busy.'

'He never comes to the quiz,' she told me. 'We've asked him loads of times, but he's always said he's got too much on.' She eyed me thoughtfully. 'Yet here you are. And here he is. Funny that.'

My stomach lurched with something that, if I hadn't known better, I'd have sworn was excitement.

'Don't be daft. He probably just finished work earlier than he expected,' I said.

'Hmm. Keep telling yourself that. Aren't you going to invite him to join us?'

Brodie's eyes met mine and a smile lit up his face, which was immediately dampened as Betty called, 'Brodie! Smashing to see you, love. Come and join us. We could use your brain power.'

'Oh yes! Come on, Brodie. This lot's useless,' Nick laughed, waving him over.

Brodie gave me a regretful look then headed over to sit with the rest of The Rowan Brainiacs, and I turned back to Clara with a shrug, determined not to let on how disappointed I felt.

'Better luck next time,' she whispered, grinning. 'You two need to arrive together in future, then there'll be no more separation.'

'We're not... I mean, it's not—'

She patted my arm. 'Course it's not, love. I wouldn't dream of suggesting it was.'

'Right,' called Penny, 'are we ready?'

'Settle down now,' someone called, and I glanced round, noting a jolly-looking man standing behind the bar, beaming at his customers, who took no notice of him.

'First question,' Penny said.

'Here we go,' Clara muttered. She winked at me. 'Now you're about to find out how woeful our general knowledge really is.'

'Well, don't look to me for help,' I said. 'I'm useless.'

'Now she tells us,' Jack groaned.

I gave him an apologetic smile, my gaze flickering over to the table where Brodie sat among The Rowan Brainiacs. He was sitting between Betty and Rissa, and I felt a sudden pang of jealousy as I saw him saying something to the younger woman and watched her laugh in response then slip her arm through his, for all the world as if they were a couple.

'On what date,' Penny said, 'did Apollo 11 land on the moon?'

'Apollo 11,' the barman called. 'On the moon.' He chortled. 'A likely story.'

'1969,' Jack whispered as one of our teammates tapped the table with his pen.

'Think they're gonna want more than that,' the other man – a bus driver called Ken – said gloomily.

'And I don't just want the year,' Penny added, as if she'd heard us.

'Not just the year,' the barman boomed. 'And I'll bet not one of you gets it. I know it. I'll never forget it and I don't even believe it happened. The things they tell you. Honestly!'

'Who on earth is he?' I asked, frowning.

'Hmm? Who?' Clara was barely paying attention. She leaned towards Ken and said, 'I'm almost sure it was in July, you know.'

'It *was* in July,' he confirmed. 'Question is, what date in July?'

'20th July 1969,' the barman said merrily. 'And who, I wonder, came up with that bright idea, eh? Biggest hoax ever, I reckon.'

I stared at him then glanced around. No one was listening. No seemed remotely interested that this person had just given away the answer to the question.

Light dawned.

'20 July,' I whispered, leaning across the table.

'Really? You're sure?' asked Andy, one of the bus conductors, or 'clippies' as they were known in their roles.

I nodded. 'Sure.'

'Wow,' Clara said admiringly. 'Get you!'

'I can't take credit for that, I'm afraid,' I said regretfully. 'Look, I'm really sorry. I've just got to...'

'Ghost?'

'Yeah, sorry.'

She smiled. 'No worries. I'll look after your bag.'

I eased my way between the tables and headed to the bar, where I plonked my glass on the counter and faced the startled barman.

'Good evening.'

'Blimey,' he said, clearly taken aback. 'You can see me. You must be the new owner.'

'I am indeed, and yes, I can see you,' I told him. 'More to the point, I can hear you, which means you just gave me the answer to the first question. Thank you very much.'

'Oh, heck.' He sighed. 'Well, if I were you, I'd keep that quiet. I can tell you the rest of the answers if you like. I can see her notes from here.'

'That,' I said sternly, 'would be cheating. I've withdrawn from the team, just in case. So, who are you? You weren't here when I called at the pub before.'

'I was changing a barrel,' he said. 'Well,' he added, 'I was supervising someone else changing a barrel. Well, strictly speaking, I was just watching, but you know... I was proper upset when I heard them all talking about your visit and I realised I'd missed you. I'm Isaac Grace,' he said. 'Landlord of this fine establishment since 1685.' He nodded at Penny. 'Whatever it says above the door. Callie, isn't it?'

'That's right.' I held out my hand for him to shake, then realising what I was doing I hastily dropped it. 'Callie Chase.'

'Callie Chase. Isaac Grace. Grace and Chase. We were made for each other.' He gave me a wide grin, revealing several gaps where teeth should be. 'So, what are you doing here then?'

I frowned. 'Well, I *was* taking part in the pub quiz, but with you calling out the answers, I feel honour-bound to withdraw, so I guess I'm just having a drink and people watching.'

'Same,' he said, propping his chin in his hand as he leaned on the counter. 'Well, not the drink part, obviously, but people watching. You could call it my thing. I'm a student of human nature, and by heck, I've seen it all in here.'

'I should imagine you have,' I said, smiling. 'I'd love to know more about it. The pub, I mean.' I gazed around, admiring the thick, oak beams, the inglenook fireplace, the latticed windows, and the polished, wooden bar. 'It's so lovely and clearly very popular.'

'Always was,' he said proudly. 'Finest coaching inn in these parts, you know. Our stables were second to none. We had a coach house, and ostlers to care for the 'osses, and the people who stayed here all complimented us on our facilities.' He sighed. 'Course, the buildings have all been converted into blooming holiday accommodation now. Got tourists lounging around where the 'osses once did their business.' He chortled again. 'If they only knew.'

'I'd like to know more,' I said, genuinely interested. 'I'll bet you've got so many stories you could share.'

His eyebrows shot up. 'Are you serious?'

'Of course. Why wouldn't I be?'

I blushed heavily as Brodie arrived at my side. He smiled.

'Hi,' I said. 'Thought you were too busy to attend the quiz?'

'I changed my mind,' he told me. 'After all, I'm going to be leaving here soon so I thought I should make the most of the place before it's too late.'

Of course. Nothing to do with me, whatever Clara wanted to think. I'd suspected as much of course, but it still stung a little. 'Friend of yours?' I asked, a little frostily, as I nodded towards Rissa, who was looking daggers at me.

'Hmm.' Was it my imagination or did he look awkward suddenly? 'They all are. Sorry if this is a ridiculous question,' he said, 'but who are you talking to?'

My face scorched. I'd completely forgotten that I was standing in full view of the entire bar. I'd been so engrossed in my conversation with Isaac Grace that it hadn't entered my mind that the locals had probably been watching me converse with thin air.

I risked a glance around, relieved to see that, although a couple of people were watching me with curiosity, most – including Penny – were just carrying on with their business. I supposed everyone knew I could see ghosts, and since ghosts were fairly commonplace in Rowan Vale, it was probably no big deal to them. I still couldn't quite believe that.

'I'm talking to a former landlord of the pub,' I told Brodie. 'His name's Isaac Grace.' I turned back to Isaac. 'Are you the only ghost in The Quicken Tree?'

He nodded gloomily. 'That I am, and no one can see me in

here which is a bit boring. It's proper brightened my evening having you to talk to.'

'Isaac Grace?' Brodie frowned. 'Name doesn't ring a bell.'

It didn't with me either, although I had a sudden memory of seeing a figure outside The Quicken Tree in the model village that could well have been the jovial landlord.

'Grandpa's never mentioned him,' Brodie added.

'Well,' Isaac said, shaking his head, 'he wouldn't, would he? I'm irrelevant to him.'

'I'm sorry?' I said. 'Irrelevant in what way?'

'Sir Lawrence Davenport,' Isaac said heavily, 'has never entered this pub in all his years as head of the estate. Can you believe that? Hates the place, and there's no wonder I suppose, given what happened here, but that's hardly my fault, is it?'

'What happened here?' I said, puzzled. 'What *did* happen here?'

He hesitated. 'He hasn't told you? Ah, well, not for me to say, that's for sure. But look, I've got rights too. Visits other ghosts in their place of work and habitation, but me! No chance. Discrimination, I call it. And that one,' he added, nodding in Brodie's direction, 'isn't much better. I know he can't see us ghosts, but he can see Penny all right, and the rest of the staff, and he never comes in here for a drink or anything. I think it's a disgrace. He should be supporting local businesses. Suppose he drinks in The Royal Oak in Kingsford Wold,' he added with a disparaging sniff.

'I don't think he drinks anywhere,' I said carefully, mindful of Brodie listening closely beside me. 'He's far too busy for that.'

'Are you talking about me?' Brodie asked.

'Sorry,' I said. 'Isaac was just saying that you rarely come in here for a drink.'

'*Never* comes in here for a drink,' Isaac corrected me. 'I said "never". Like his grandfather.'

'Do you ever go up to Harling Hall?' I asked him. 'Only, I've never seen any of the ghosts anywhere in the grounds, let alone in the house.'

Isaac looked deeply shocked. 'Certainly not! It just isn't done.'

'Why not?'

'Because... because... it just isn't! Besides, we've never been invited,' he added.

'Do you need an invitation?'

'My dear young lady, of course we need an invitation! Sir Edward would have had a fit if we'd all turned up unannounced, and Sir Lawrence wouldn't like it either, I'm sure.'

'Well,' I said, feeling a sudden spark of mischief, 'it's my house now, isn't it? So what if I invite you?'

Beside me, Brodie straightened. 'Are you inviting a ghost to the Hall?' he asked.

'What if I am?'

'Well...' He hesitated. 'I don't know. I'm not sure Grandpa would like it.'

'Why not, though?' I asked. 'Why has he never done it before, anyway?'

'To be honest,' Brodie admitted, 'I've never asked him. It just didn't occur to me. Maybe it never occurred to him either.'

'Or maybe,' I said darkly, 'it's because his precious Agnes would disapprove.'

Behind the bar, Isaac tutted. 'Oh, her. I remember her. Proper dragon. Not seen her for years, now you mention it. Yeah, she'd definitely not approve if I turned up at the Hall uninvited.'

'She wouldn't, would she?' I said, giving him a sly grin.

'Callie, what are you doing?' Brodie asked suspiciously. 'It sounds to me like you're inviting this Isaac Grace fella to the Hall just to annoy Agnes?'

'Not just Isaac Grace,' I said, barely able to hide my amusement. I turned back to Isaac. 'Could you spread the word? I'd like all the ghosts to come to the Hall tomorrow afternoon after lunch. I'll give you a tour of the Hall if you like?'

'Callie!' Brodie gasped.

Isaac scratched his chin. 'I could,' he said slowly, 'but what for? What's the point? Just to annoy that old harridan in the big house?'

'Not just for that,' I said, although I couldn't deny it would be a bonus. 'I want to meet them all – well, as many as I can anyway. And more than that, I want to find out exactly what they'd like from me as new owner of the estate.'

Brodie nudged me. 'What on earth are you talking about? Just carry on doing what Grandpa's been doing and you'll be fine.'

'But I'm not your grandpa,' I said. 'Isaac's just told me that Lawrie's never visited the pub since he inherited the estate, and he's quite put out about it. I want to know if any of the other ghosts have grievances, and if so, what I can do to put things right for them.'

Isaac beamed at me. 'Well, aren't you a star?' he said.

'I'm not so sure about this, Callie,' Brodie said nervously.

'I'll spread the word,' Isaac boomed. 'We'll be round at yours tomorrow afternoon, so you'd better warn the old bat.'

'Callie...'

'Too late,' I murmured, as Isaac disappeared into another room, perhaps already on his way to invite my guests.

Brodie sighed. 'I suppose I'd better warn Grandpa.'

'Never mind your grandpa,' I said sheepishly, already wondering if I'd made a huge mistake. 'I think someone had better warn Agnes.'

26

Perhaps I should have realised that the next day was Friday the thirteenth. If I had, maybe I'd have thought twice about inviting a whole lot of ghosts to Harling Hall for the first time. It seemed I'd also invited trouble as Lawrie was clearly appalled.

'What on earth were you thinking?' he demanded. 'The ghosts have their own homes. Why do you have to bring them here?'

'Why shouldn't I?' I asked defiantly, even though I was already doubting the wisdom of my actions. Agnes had been horrified when I'd told her that there was to be a meeting at the Hall and had shrieked at me that I had no right to invite all those strangers to her home.

'They're only strangers because you don't mix with them,' I pointed out. 'If you'd go into the village, you'd get to know them, and then you'd probably invite them over here yourself. I'm doing you a favour.'

'How dare you presume to tell me how to live my afterlife?' she cried. 'Mr Wyndham, tell her!'

Aubrey sighed. 'You really should have run this past us,

Callie,' he said. 'I appreciate that this is now your house, and of course you're free to do as you wish, but manners dictate that you consult with us. We do live here too, after all.'

'But don't you want to get to know the rest of the ghosts?' I asked. 'It must get boring, stuck in these grounds all the time. You never leave, do you? Why not?'

Aubrey cast a nervous look at Agnes, who practically snarled at me. 'That's none of your business, young lady. I'm going to have words with Lawrie about this. Lawrie!'

She marched out of the room and Aubrey shook his head. 'Now you've done it. Bad form, Callie. I really expected better of you.'

He followed Agnes downstairs, and I stood still, wondering what to do next. I'd fully expected Agnes to be a pain in the butt about this, but I'd honestly thought Aubrey would be all for it. He was far more sociable than his wife after all, and I thought the company would do him good. Apparently, I was wrong.

Lawrie wasted no time in telling me so when I headed into the sitting room, and was fully on Agnes's side, which came as no surprise. I got quite annoyed in the end, and even though I'd had my doubts when I woke up that morning, I pushed them away, determined that I was going to do things my way from now on.

I held up my hands to silence the Wyndhams and Lawrie, who were all chipping in with their grievances.

'Look,' I said firmly, 'it's done now. The ghosts will be here soon and it's just one meeting. You might be surprised. You might enjoy it.'

'I certainly won't,' Agnes said, 'because I won't be in attendance, and neither will Mr Wyndham, will you?'

Aubrey cleared his throat. 'Ahem. No. No I won't.'

'And nor,' she continued, 'shall Florence. I shall make certain of that. So you can have your wretched meeting without us, and if any of those other ghosts dare to venture upstairs, I shall not be responsible for my actions.'

I sighed. 'I sort of promised them a tour of the Hall.'

'Well, you can sort of un-promise it then, can't you,' she warned, before flouncing out of the room, Aubrey trailing dutifully behind her.

Lawrie sighed. 'I really can't think what you're up to,' he said. 'There are ways of doing things, Callie.'

'Clearly,' I said, 'but don't you think they're a bit elitist? I can't believe you've never invited them to the Hall before, and why do they need an invitation anyway? We go to their homes uninvited all the time. I'm sorry but I think your ways are wrong.'

'Not just mine. I've merely continued the traditions. As I said, there are ways of doing things…'

'You mean, whatever Agnes wants?' I asked.

He gave me a stern look. 'That's not it at all,' he said.

'Isn't it? Well anyway, it's done now, so we're just going to have to get on with it,' I said.

'On your own head be it,' he muttered. 'I'll be in my room.'

Brodie had business in the village, so he wasn't around, but Mia offered to make me a coffee and bring it into the dining room when the meeting began. She'd already helped me out earlier, smoothing Immi's ruffled feathers after my daughter had discovered that the meeting was taking place while she was at school.

'But you could have held it on the Saturday when I was at home,' she'd protested. 'I could have been there. I wanted to meet them all too!'

'I don't know how this is going to go,' I explained. 'I've not met them all, and there could be some difficult ghosts. I don't want you getting mixed up in any arguments.'

'But I need to learn,' she wailed. 'One day, I'll be the one looking after them. They're my responsibility too!'

'Hopefully, not for a very long time,' I said firmly. 'Get yourself to school and put all this out of your mind.'

'I might as well have moved in with Violet,' she snapped, grabbing her bag. 'And I'd rather Mia took me to school if it's all the same to you.'

I opened my mouth to argue but Mia held up her hand. 'That's fine. I need to call at the shops anyway.'

She squeezed my shoulder as Immi pushed past me.

'She'll be okay,' she murmured. 'Concentrate on what's ahead of you for now.'

Just one more thing I'd got wrong, I thought wretchedly as I peered out of the window waiting for the first of the ghosts to arrive. I seemed to be permanently in Immi's bad books these days, and now I'd alienated Lawrie and Aubrey.

I opened the window and leaned out, aware of a commotion at the end of the drive. I could hear some shouting and jeers. What on earth was going on?

I hurried downstairs and opened the front door, in time to see a stream of ghostly visitors heading my way.

'What's all the shouting?' I asked Isaac as he beamed a greeting at me.

He rolled his eyes. 'That blooming Reverend Alexander,' he said. 'Warning us to stay away from this house of fornication.'

I giggled. 'Fornication?'

'Oh yes. He's refusing to enter the property but he's happy to stand just outside warning us all that we're about to enter a den of iniquity.'

'Who knew?' I directed him to the dining room and told him to make himself at home while I waited to greet the rest of my guests.

I knew some of them by sight, of course, but others were new to me. There was Walter Tasker, bowing low upon seeing me and gracing me with some literary prose which, no doubt, was by William Shakespeare, though inspired by Walter, naturally.

I was quite surprised to see Millie practically skipping down the drive, looking all excited. I'd have thought she'd have found the record shop far more interesting, but she informed me she'd wanted to see inside the big house for years, and that her mum would be beside herself if she could see her now.

I groaned inwardly upon seeing Bill and Ronnie marching towards me, too busy arguing to even notice me standing on the step until I ordered them to halt and cease talking. I made them swear that they'd refrain from arguing during the meeting and, reluctantly, they agreed.

Perks, who was just behind them, told me I was wasting my time but thanked me profusely for the invitation and said he couldn't get over being invited to the big house, and what an honour it was, and how his wife would never have believed it.

My eyes widened as a young couple headed down the drive, gazing around them in awe. They were probably in their mid to late twenties, but it was their clothing that made me look twice.

The young man was dressed in a most flamboyant fashion, and I'd have thought he was from the eighteenth or nineteenth century if not for the make-up he was obviously wearing.

Was that guyliner? Seriously? Not to mention the stripes of blusher and eyeshadow.

I remembered the old music programmes I'd seen on the television from the eighties. The New Romantics. Adam and the Ants. He was wearing a Hussars jacket just like that.

The young woman on the other hand looked comparatively scruffy. She was wearing dark-grey, high-waisted trousers that came to just above her ankles, a white T-shirt, and red braces, along with heavy ankle boots, a black belt, and a big, floppy, red bow in rather wild hair that looked as if it had been moussed or sprayed to within an inch of its life. I frowned as a memory stirred.

'Bananarama!' I murmured suddenly as I realised why she looked so familiar. It seemed these two ghosts were from the eighties and had modelled themselves on major pop stars of the era.

As we all settled in the dining room, Mia brought me a coffee and wished me luck before closing the door.

'Right,' I said, looking round at them all. 'Is that everyone? Are we expecting anyone else?'

I'd been quite shocked when I realised there weren't enough spaces around the dining room table, and Mia and I had had to bring in extra chairs from the ballroom.

They all looked at each other and shrugged.

There was no sign of Quintus Severus, though I hadn't really expected to see him. I wasn't surprised that there was no appearance from the Hollywood actress who Immi had met either, although I was disappointed. I'd have loved to meet her.

'Before we begin,' I said, 'do any of you know where Harmony Hill is staying?'

There were a few murmurings, and some people shifted on their seats, but no one offered any information. Either they didn't know, or they weren't saying. Fair enough.

'All right,' I said. 'First of all, I'd like to welcome you to Harling Hall. My name's Callie Chase, and if you don't know I'm the new owner of the Harling Estate. If it's all right with you, I'd really like to know who you all are, so can we go round the room and introduce ourselves, please?'

There was an awkward silence until Isaac Grace, bless him, said cheerfully, 'Well come on, everyone, don't be shy. We've waited a long time for this. I'm Isaac Grace and I'm the landlord of The Quicken Tree.'

'You *were* the landlord,' Bill said helpfully.

To his credit, Isaac's smile didn't falter. 'I *am* the landlord,' he said firmly. 'I never left. Never relinquished the role. There you go.'

'But you can't even serve the customers,' Ronnie pointed out. 'I'd say you've lost the pub by default.'

'Good grief,' cried Perks, 'do you two have to argue with everyone? I thought it was just each other you picked a fight with, but here you go again.'

He turned to me. 'I knew it was a mistake to invite those two,' he said. 'No respect, Callie. Not even for you.'

'I did warn you,' I told Bill and Ronnie sternly. 'One more cross word and you're out.'

'We'll behave,' Ronnie said meekly.

'You'd better,' Perks said. 'I'm Percy Swain and I was the station porter at Harling's Halt. I still keep an eye on things and try to ensure the current station staff are doing their jobs properly.'

Ronnie and Bill grinned and nudged each other, but seeing my beady eyes on them, they sat up straight and introduced themselves politely.

One by one, each ghost gave me their name and the role they'd played in the village. The New Romantic's name was Danny. He was twenty-nine and had worked in IT in Gloucester, which made me think maybe he hadn't died in the 1980s after all. The Bananarama girl lookalike was twenty-five-year-old Brooke, who'd been a receptionist at the same company where Danny worked.

Millie revealed that she'd been a waitress in Mrs Herron's

Teashop when she died, aged just seventeen, earning a warm smile from none other than Mrs Herron herself.

Polly Herron, a curvy brunette with green eyes, was probably in her thirties. She was wearing a printed dress in a familiar style from the 1940s.

To my surprise, she said she'd been the manager of Deakin's Teashop.

'Deakin's? I thought you were the manager of Mrs Herron's Teashop?' After all, it made sense, didn't it?

There was some audible murmuring around the table and Mrs Herron shrugged.

'Same place, lovey. Back then it was Deakin's Teashop. It was only named Mrs Herron's Teashop afterwards...'

There were some uneasy stares aimed in my direction, and I realised they were wondering if I was about to ask her about her demise. I wasn't daft enough to go there.

'Lovely to meet you,' I told her warmly. 'All of you,' I added, glancing around at them all. 'And now that we've all been introduced, perhaps I should explain why I've invited you all here. This is, of course, all new to me, but I want us to start off on the right foot. I know there's been a certain way of doing things here and I appreciate that, but perhaps with my arrival, it's a good opportunity to look at what's working for you and what isn't.'

They all looked at each other.

'What do you mean, working for us?' Millie asked blankly.

'Well,' I said awkwardly, 'is there anything you have concerns about? Anything you'd like to change?'

'Like what?' asked Walter.

'I don't know. You tell me.' I gave a nervous laugh.

'But things never change here,' Ronnie told me. 'Leastways, not in all the time *we've* been stuck here.'

'Well maybe,' Isaac said firmly, 'it's time they did. I'll tell you what, it was a smashing surprise yesterday when Callie here came into the pub and talked to me. I'm so used to being on my own behind that bar with no one to chat to. When was the last time Lawrie popped his head round the door, eh? I can't even remember, that's how long it was.'

'Well, you can hardly blame him for that,' Walter said. 'The poor boy was traumatised. After everything that happened...'

'What *did* happen?' I asked, my curiosity getting the better of me.

'It's not for us to tell you that,' Walter said pompously.

'I know!' Millie squealed in delight. She waved her hand in the air, ignoring the looks she was getting from some of the older ghosts. 'I was fifteen at the time and my mum and her mates talked about nothing else. Lawrie's mum died, and it turned out that she'd been carrying on with some bloke from Much Melton. He turned up at her funeral and told everyone it was true love, and he had every right to be there, and demanded to go to the wake, but then Sir Edward lost his temper and told him he was kidding himself because he was just one in a long line, and if all Charlotte's lovers had turned up for the funeral, there'd be no room for the family.'

'Oh my word,' I breathed. 'How awful.'

'It was, cos Lawrie had no idea what his mum had been up to, and he was devastated. And worse than that, the landlord at The Quicken Tree had known all about it and let her get up to her shenanigans in his best room. He told everyone she kept him in business. The village was agog, wasn't it?'

She looked cheerfully around at everyone, only to be met with stony silence.

'I never knew all that,' Danny said at last. 'Imagine.'

'My Auntie Pearl used to clean here in this house,' Millie continued, unabashed, 'and she told us that Lawrie was heartbroken and blamed his dad for neglecting his wife, and he went to see Johnnie, who was landlord at the time and gave him merry hell for letting her use the room at the pub, and Johnnie told him that he'd gone to Sir Edward the first time she tried to book it and tipped him off, and Sir Edward had said to take her money and spare him the details. So there you have it.'

'Well,' Brooke said with a shrug, 'I suppose it *was* the swinging sixties at the time.'

'Not here,' Walter said, shocked. 'Such behaviour was never encouraged in Rowan Vale; I can assure you of that.'

'I suppose that's what Silas meant about this being a den of iniquity,' I said, amazed.

'That man!' Polly Herron said crossly. 'You heard him then? Yelling at us as we arrived?'

'I did,' I admitted. 'It's a long time to still be going on about it.'

'He's not talking about the livings,' Bill said with a smirk.

'What?' I stared at him, not entirely sure if he was joking. 'You mean, ghosts?' I frowned, confused. 'Not wishing to be intrusive, but *can* ghosts fornicate?'

'Chance would be a fine thing,' Brooke muttered.

'Of course we can,' Ronnie said. 'Leastways, if we had anyone to fornicate with.' He nudged Bill. 'Bet you wish your Lily was still here, don't you? I know I do.'

Bill glared at him, and I gave them both a warning look.

'It was just a joke,' Ronnie said, holding up his hands. 'Didn't mean nothing by it. But to answer your question, yeah, ghosts can do it, all right. I mean, we're all on the same plane, aren't we? Anyway, the problem is them toffs upstairs,' he said, jerking his thumb in the direction of the ceiling. 'They're what's given old Silas a bee in his bonnet. Well, them and women vicars. And tourists. But mainly them two.'

'Enough of that,' Perks said immediately. 'Show some respect.'

'I'm only telling her what Silas has been telling us forever,' Bill said indignantly. He turned to me, a smirk on his lips. 'It's that Agnes Ashcroft and Aubrey Wyndham.'

I eyed him doubtfully. 'What about them?'

He and Ronnie looked at each other, for once in complete agreement, judging by the grins on their faces. 'They're the ones that are fornicating,' Bill burst out as he and Ronnie dissolved into laughter.

I couldn't believe what I'd just heard. 'Are you having me on?'

Perks looked at them in disgust. 'It's not for us to judge our betters,' he said. 'Fancy you talking like that, and in the King's uniform too.'

'I'm sorry,' I said, holding up my hand, 'but are you honestly telling me that Silas is talking about Agnes and Aubrey when he calls this place a den of iniquity?'

What on earth did they get up to? No, strike that. I really didn't want to know.

'Well,' Isaac said with a shrug, 'isn't it obvious? They're living here as man and wife.'

'But,' I said hesitantly, 'they *are* man and wife, aren't they? That's how they were introduced to me anyway.'

Although, hadn't I always thought it didn't make sense, given the timescale?

'Of course they're not,' Ronnie said scornfully. 'She snuffed it years before him. A year before he was even born as a matter of fact. When he, er, passed over, they got together, and they've been telling everyone they're man and wife ever since. Even adopted that kiddie, didn't they?'

Walter shuddered. 'Oh, that girl! What a rude little beast she is too.'

'You're not wrong there,' Millie said with feeling. 'One of these days, I'll boot her up the backside, you see if I don't. Cheeky little blighter she is.'

'Something,' Perks agreed, 'should be done about her.'

'She's ventured as far as the railway station?' I asked incredulously, thinking Agnes would have a fit if she knew.

'Not yet, no,' he admitted. 'But I don't live at the railway station, see? I've got my own little cottage in the village, and she keeps pestering me there.'

'You have your own cottage?' I asked, surprised.

'Well... not strictly mine. I sort of share it. But it was mine first, so there you go,' he added defiantly.

I was about to ask if the other occupants of the cottage were aware of his presence, but he'd got the bit between his teeth about Florrie. 'She brings them two boys with her, too, you know. Little ragamuffins that they are.'

There was a loud sigh from a man who looked to be in his forties. He'd introduced himself as Peter and told me he was a baker who'd passed on in 1790.

'Poor little wretches,' he said.

'Poor little wretches?' Perks asked. 'Nothing but trouble the lot of them.'

'It's not them so much,' Millie said. 'It's her. That Florrie. She's the ringleader. Gets them to do whatever she wants.'

'It's my fault,' Peter groaned. 'I keep trying to tell them but they're not having it.'

'What's your fault?' I asked, surprised.

'They're scared of me,' he said, 'and because they're scared of me, they stick too closely to that girl. I'm sure she's telling them a lot of nonsense, you know.'

'And why would they be scared of you?' I asked him, my suspicions aroused.

'It's a long story,' he said, shifting uncomfortably. 'Let's just say we passed on the same day.'

My mouth fell open. So, John and Robert had died in 1790? Poor little mites. And how had Florrie managed to get her claws into them so thoroughly? What exactly was she telling them? And why were they so scared of this Peter that they stuck to Florrie anyway? Since it clearly had something to do with his death, I could hardly ask him, which was frustrating.

'The trouble with Florrie,' I said, 'and probably Robert and John, too, is that there's no structure or discipline in their lives.'

'Hear, hear,' Perks said, nodding furiously.

I thought about my earlier suggestion to the Wyndhams, and to Lawrie, about making the children have lessons. They'd shouted me down and I'd let them, but now I wasn't so sure that I hadn't given in too easily.

'What they need is some routine,' I said.

'What they need is the cane,' Millie told me. 'Some of the lads at school got it regularly and it didn't do them any harm. What about it, Walter? Got your old school cane?'

'What they need is conscription,' Bill said gloomily. 'Being in the army's enough to make anyone behave.'

'Fat lot of good it did you,' Perks said.

'I'm not about to make them join the army,' I said, 'even if that were possible. But what I did think might be useful is sending them to school. Or at least, getting someone to give them lessons.'

Walter nodded furiously. 'Education is the key,' he said. 'Put those children into school and ensure their minds are turned to loftier pursuits. They'd soon lose interest in their current foolish pastimes. Excellent idea, Mistress Chase.'

'It's Callie,' I told him, 'and I'm so glad you think so, Walter, because I was hoping you'd be the one to teach them.'

His face fell as several of the ghosts chortled in glee.

'Me? Oh no, no! I couldn't possibly.'

'Yes, you could. Who else would be better?' I asked, deciding a little flattery was in order. 'With your experience and wisdom, there's no one else who could possibly do the job. I need you, Walter. The children need you. Please say you'll step up for them.'

'But... but they're ruffians,' he protested.

'Diamonds in the rough,' I said. 'With a little polishing from you, I'm sure they could be transformed. Of course,' I added slyly, 'if you think you're not up to the job... I expect you're right. I mean, your teaching practice will be hopelessly out of date by now.'

He looked most indignant. 'Excuse me? I have kept up to date with all events of the last four hundred years and I spend a lot of my time continuing to educate myself. Sir Lawrence,' he added pompously, 'values my gifts and has provided me with many books and newspapers over the years, which he has read to me on a regular basis. I am more than capable of teaching three young children, thank you kindly.'

'But that's even better,' I cried. 'Imagine if one of the three turns out to be another Shakespeare, all thanks to you!'

Millie snorted and even Isaac frowned as if he thought I was pushing it.

'It's hardly likely,' Walter said, though there was an obvious wavering in his voice.

'Did you ever expect young William to grow up to be the greatest poet and playwright this country has ever produced?' I asked him.

'Of course not! Well, not really.' He thought about it. 'He did have a raw talent, of course, but it took my nurturing and guidance to bring that talent to the surface.'

'Exactly! And look what he became, all thanks to you,' I said, pointing dramatically up at the ceiling as if gesturing to the stars. 'What if Florrie or John or Robert are gifted poets, or playwrights, or scholars? All that potential could be lying there, dormant within them, because, unlike Shakespeare, they've got no way to bring it to the surface. They need someone like you, Walter. Someone with his own remarkable gift of seeing talent where others see only... ragamuffins. Ruffians.'

I turned slowly to look at him and saw him gazing into the middle distance, clearly imagining the glorious success he could make of his potential new pupils. I held my breath, wondering if he'd let himself be persuaded.

'Well...' he said slowly. 'I suppose...'

'Oh, thank you, Walter!' I said immediately, rewarding him with my brightest smile. 'This whole village will be in your debt when you've finally tamed these children and turned them into model citizens, with who knows what gifts they can share with us all.'

Isaac shook his head, as Ronnie muttered, 'Mug.'

Walter, though, had bought it and was now beaming at me. 'My dear Mistress Chase, it will be an honour. When would you like me to start?'

27

Monday morning brought two arguments. The first was with Immi, who was furious that, once again, she was missing out on something she considered to be exciting.

'It's only Mr Tasker teaching the children,' I said.

'Exactly! I wanted to meet him, and I wanted to meet John and Robert! Why didn't you organise the lessons for the weekend so I could have been here?' she demanded.

'You've got enough to do with your own schooling,' I said. The last thing I wanted was for her to make friends with John and Robert too. She needed to start hanging out with the kids from her class. Living, breathing kids. 'Why don't you invite Ashton over for tea?'

'Oh!' She gave a snort of impatience and flounced out of the room, not even finishing her cornflakes.

The second argument was with Lawrie, who didn't take the news about the lessons very well at all.

'It's out of the question,' he said. 'You'll have to send Walter away again. What were you thinking going against my wishes like that? Not to mention overruling Agnes. She's Florence's mother and has every right to refuse schooling if—'

'For one thing,' I said, 'that's not how it works. Nowadays, children must be educated, whether the parents like it or not. They don't have to go to school, but they must receive an education, and it's my duty to make sure the children of this village get theirs. For another,' I added as he opened his mouth to speak, 'Agnes isn't Florrie's mother. She claims to have adopted her but as far as I'm aware, there are no adoption agencies in the afterlife, so what gives her the right to decide what happens to Florrie anyway?'

'Callie!'

'No, I'm sorry, Lawrie. If you'd heard the other ghosts last night, you'd realise how much of a disruption Florrie is to this village. Not to mention the terrible influence she's having on John and Robert.' I shook my head. 'Do you ever actually listen to the other ghosts? Or is it all about Agnes with you?'

'I can't believe you've just said that to me,' he snapped. 'You've been here five minutes, and you already think you know better than I do about everything.'

'It's not that at all,' I said huffily, 'but the way you boss everyone about just to keep that woman happy... Telling me I can't ask Aubrey and Agnes why they never leave these grounds, for example. Although,' I added smugly, 'I think I've figured that out.'

He paled. 'What do you mean?'

'It's obvious, isn't it? Silas was here at the gates last night, warning the others not to come into this den of iniquity. Apparently, he's furious that Agnes and Aubrey are living in sin. They're not legally married, are they? And that's no doubt why Agnes won't go into the village. She'd hardly want Silas yelling that across the street, would she?'

'Oh, for goodness' sake. That man. He knows nothing.'

'Or maybe you just don't know as much as you think. I'm sorry, Lawrie, I don't want us to fall out about this but I just don't get it. Why do you always put Agnes ahead of everyone else? Those kids...' I took a deep breath, remembering my own struggles at school, 'they deserve an education. The chance to learn. It's important.'

'Well,' Lawrie said abruptly, 'you've obviously made your mind up. Clearly you have no further need of my services, so the sooner I leave here, the better.'

He turned and walked away, leaning heavily on his stick, and I felt sick to my stomach. I really hadn't wanted an argument, but he'd been so dismissive of my attempts to help the kids that my anger had risen until I couldn't help but dig my heels in. He was far too old to be arguing like that and I should have known better. Even if I was right.

'You're proper mean.'

I jumped, hearing a voice behind me, and turned to find Florrie glaring at me, her arms folded.

'Fancy talking to Lawrie like that. Agnes'll 'ave your guts for garters.'

'Oh, be quiet, Florrie,' I said, hardly in the mood for her antics today.

'I'm not going to any stupid classes,' she informed me. 'And there's no way John and Robert will go either. Stupid lessons. Who needs 'em? You'll never find those lads without me and I'm not gonna help you. You might as well tell that stupid teacher to go 'ome cos he's wasting 'is time.'

I rubbed my forehead, suddenly feeling so tired, I could happily go back to bed and sleep for the rest of the day.

'You're probably right,' I said.

She surveyed me through narrowed eyes. 'Eh?'

'You're probably right,' I repeated. 'He probably would be wasting his time. Your favourite word, judging by your recent outburst, is stupid, and maybe that's the problem. Maybe you're too stupid to learn anything, and maybe I'm stupid for thinking you were capable.'

'I'm not stupid,' she said angrily. 'I got nine out of ten in my last spelling test, so stick that in your pipe and smoke it.'

'That was a long time ago,' I reminded her. 'You've probably forgotten it all now. Intelligence needs nurturing and it's been so long since you tried to learn anything, I doubt very much you're capable any longer. I should imagine even John and Robert would be brighter than you. After all, they'd be starting completely from scratch, which is always easier than having to relearn things.'

'Is it?' she asked, clearly surprised.

I shouldn't think so for a minute.

'Of course it is. Everyone knows that. Well, most people.'

'I'll bet I could learn anything faster than those two,' she said scornfully. 'You're daft if you think I couldn't.'

'Well,' I said with a shrug, 'we'll never know, will we? Which is lucky for you, I should think. I'll go and find Walter. Tell him not to bother.'

'Scared, are you?' she demanded as I turned away.

I stopped, a smile hovering on my lips. 'Scared? Of what?' I changed my expression to one of disinterest and turned back to her.

'Of losing the bet.'

'I wasn't aware I'd made any bet.'

'I said I'd bet you I could learn anything faster than those two,' she reminded me. 'Are you too chicken to take the bet?'

I pretended to consider it. 'What do I get if you lose?' I asked.

'I won't lose,' she said confidently. 'But if I do, which I won't, but if I do – what would you want?'

'Hmm. How about you agree to do lessons with Walter for the rest of this year, even if you're not very good at them?'

She shrugged. 'I'll be good at them. Easy peasy. Now, what are you going to give *me* when *I* win the bet?'

'Well,' I said, 'what would you like me to give you?'

She tilted her head to the side, thinking about it. Then a slow smile spread across her face. 'You make that girl of yours call her kitten Brian.'

I laughed. 'I can't do that!'

'Okay. So you *are* scared then?'

How had she managed to turn this around so successfully? Now I was the one on the backfoot. How could I promise that Immi would name her kitten Brian? He wasn't my kitten to name, and I couldn't force her to call him that. Could I? Lord knows I was in her bad books already without adding something else to her long list of reasons to be angry at me.

But if I took the bet, Florence would take her lessons, and John and Robert would join her, and we might actually have a chance of taming the three of them and giving them a better afterlife. I sent a silent apology to Immi and nodded.

'Okay. You're on.'

She grinned. 'She's gonna hate you,' she said gleefully.

'No she won't, because you'll lose the bet,' I said, with far more confidence than I felt.

'We'll see,' she said happily. 'I'll go and fetch John and Robert, shall I? Then you'll find out how smart I am and how stupid they are.'

'Go ahead,' I told her. 'Don't be long, though, because Walter will be here very soon.'

'I won't be!'

As she ran through the front door, I heard a movement behind me and spun round to see Mia pushing open the kitchen door, a look of admiration on her face.

'Oh, well done!'

'You heard that?'

'Some of it, and you played it brilliantly.' She laughed. 'Though I wouldn't like to be in your shoes when Immi finds out what you've agreed to.'

I sighed. 'I know. I'm just hoping it doesn't come to that. Have you seen Lawrie?'

'No. Why?'

'We had a bit of an argument. I shouldn't have said what I said to him.'

'What did you say to him?' she asked worriedly.

'I basically accused him of only caring about pleasing Agnes and not giving a fig what happened to the rest of the ghosts,' I said with a sigh.

'Well...'

'You agree?' I asked, my eyebrows shooting up in surprise.

'I wouldn't put it quite like that,' she said, 'but there's no doubt in my mind that her happiness comes before any of the other ghosts' and I don't think that's fair. Maybe it's time he realised that, and maybe you telling him so will give him pause for thought.'

'I could have phrased it a bit more kindly, though,' I said sadly. 'And I really don't know what Brodie's going to say when he hears I've been arguing with his grandpa. You know how much he adores him.'

'Maybe he does, but he's not completely blind to him either,' she assured me. 'Perhaps it's time things were shaken up around here, and I have a feeling you're just the woman for the job.'

28

Florrie was, surprisingly, as good as her word and arrived back at the Hall with a clearly terrified John and Robert trailing behind her.

'Stop being babies,' she told them sternly, probably seeing, as did I, the trembling of Robert's lip and John's visible shaking. She gave me a smug look. 'Told you I'd get 'em, didn't I? Is 'e 'ere yet? The teacher bloke?'

'Not yet but—'

I broke off as someone boomed, 'Knock, knock.' Then Walter stepped awkwardly through the front door and bowed low.

'Forgive my intrusion. I did knock.'

Florrie rolled her eyes. 'We've got a right one 'ere,' she told the boys, who were staring at Walter in disbelief.

'Children, children,' Walter said. 'I am so very happy to meet you all properly at last. My name is Walter Tasker, but you may address me as Master. Now—'

'What on earth is this?'

I groaned inwardly as Agnes came marching down the stairs, an expression of fury on her face.

'What does it look like?' I asked her. 'Mr Tasker is here to teach the children.'

'Teach the children?' She gave the boys a look of disdain. 'And by whose permission is Mr Tasker here?'

'Mine,' I said firmly.

'And what does Lawrie have to say about that? I think you'll find he won't allow it,' she told me.

'I think you'll find Lawrie and I have already had this conversation, and he's realised that what happens under this roof is up to me now, not him. I say the children are to have lessons and have lessons they shall.'

Agnes's mouth opened and closed in shock. Was it wishful thinking or did Florrie sneak me a look of admiration?

'Florence, you don't have to do this,' Agnes said urgently, placing her hand on the little girl's shoulder. 'She can't make you.'

To my surprise, Florrie shrugged off her hand. 'I want to do it,' she said. 'Me and the boys are gonna learn stuff and get clever. I'm gonna get cleverer than they will, obviously, and then I'll win my bet with 'er,' she added, nodding at me.

Agnes frowned. 'A wager? I don't approve of gambling.'

'Too late,' Florrie said with a grin. She turned to Walter. 'Are we gonna get started or what?'

'Certainly,' he replied, clearly surprised by her enthusiasm.

Agnes gave a gasp of dismay and hurried back up the stairs, no doubt to tell Aubrey that the world had gone mad and that he needed to say something quickly.

'Apparently there's an old schoolroom upstairs,' I said. 'Aub — Mr Wyndham suggested it would make a good place for you to teach the children. Although I'm not exactly sure—'

'I know where it is,' Florrie said. 'It's in the east wing. I'll show you, Mister.'

'Master,' Walter said. 'Lead the way, young lady.'

The old schoolroom was, according to Florrie, almost slap-bang in the middle of the landing, halfway between the Wyndhams' suite of rooms, and the Davenports'. I half expected Lawrie to come charging out, all guns blazing, but his door remained closed, as did the Wyndhams'. Maybe they were all together somewhere, plotting my downfall. They must all have despised me. I hadn't felt this miserable since I'd arrived here, and it wasn't a great feeling. Even so, I knew it was for the best. These kids needed structure and an education.

I removed the dust sheets that covered the little desks and apologised for not thinking to get the room ready earlier as I coughed and sneezed, dust whirling around me in clouds.

Walter shrugged. 'It hardly matters to us,' he pointed out, and I realised that, after all, dust was hardly likely to be an irritant to them. 'The question is, do you have any books?'

Oh blimey, I really hadn't thought this through. 'I'm guessing there are lots of books somewhere,' I said feebly.

Florrie grinned. 'Not much cop at being the boss, are you?'

'There's the library in the village,' John said meekly. 'They've got lots of books. I go there sometimes when it's dark in winter and it's all lit up inside. I sit with the people and look at the pictures in their books. It's nice in there.'

'Really?' I smiled at him. That boded well for his future. At least he liked being around books and associated them with something good.

'We don't need no village library,' Florrie said scornfully. 'Got one 'ere in this 'ouse. Mind you, don't think they've got no picture books and them two can't read.'

'Can't read?' Walter asked. 'At all?'

John and Robert shook their heads and Walter sighed. 'This

is going to be more of a challenge than I thought. Mistress Chase—'

'Callie.'

'Mistress Chase. We need better organisation than this. I'm going to have to teach John and Robert how to read before we can progress any further, whereas Florence here can already read and will be moving at a different pace. We have no books. And, pray tell, who is going to turn the pages when requested?'

I frowned. 'Turn the pages? Oh...'

That hadn't occurred to me either. Of course, ghosts couldn't physically touch books. I'd have to be with them in the schoolroom, turning pages every time Walter demanded it. Perhaps unfolding maps. Writing things on the blackboard... It wasn't going to work.

'I never thought about this,' I admitted. 'It's a logistical nightmare. I'd have to find someone to be in the room with you throughout your lessons. I simply haven't got the time to be here myself.'

'But it would have to be someone who could see and hear us,' he pointed out. 'How else would they know when we need a page turning?'

'Do you have any relatives in the village?' I asked glumly. 'Anyone who can see you?'

He shook his head.

'None of us 'as,' Florrie said. 'Looks like we're stuck, don't it?'

'I'll think of something,' I said determinedly. 'I'm not giving up just yet.'

'Very well,' Walter said. 'In the meantime, I think I'll spend our first day talking to these children and finding out what they already know and what's likely to interest them. All shall be well.'

'You fink?' Florrie asked doubtfully. 'I fink we're sunk before we start.'

'Nonsense,' Walter told her. '"Doubt is a thief that often makes us fear to tread where we might have won."'

Florrie gave him a blank look. 'Eh?'

'It's a quote by William Shakespeare, one of my former pupils. It's based on something very similar to what I said to him myself,' he said, nodding furiously. 'Doubt can stop us from even trying, but we must have courage and confidence! We shall prevail, children. We shall prevail.'

I left them to it and headed downstairs, deep in thought. I couldn't possibly spend every day with Walter and the children, but who else would be able to turn pages for them? And where was I going to get the books anyway? What was he even going to teach them, given the different times they'd all lived in and the differences in their abilities?

Mia was at a dental appointment in Much Melton and Brodie was, apparently, in the study, interviewing applicants for a tenancy for a cottage that had been standing vacant for some months and was not to be disturbed. He'd asked me if I wanted to sit in on the interview, and I probably should have done, but I'd been too busy thinking about the meeting and wondering how Lawrie and Agnes were going to take the news of Walter's imminent arrival, so I'd passed.

I was all alone without an ally to call upon.

I made myself a coffee and sat at the kitchen table feeling depressed beyond words.

'Well, you look happy. Not.'

My heart leapt as Brodie entered the kitchen. *Relief*, I told myself firmly. *Just relief*.

'You're finished? How did the interviewing go?'

He flicked the kettle on and reached for a mug. 'Not too bad.

I've narrowed it down to two possible tenants. They're coming back with references for a second interview, but I think you should be with me for that, don't you?'

'I'm sure you can handle it,' I said glumly, reaching for my coffee.

'That's not the point, Callie,' he said. 'I won't be here much longer and you're going to have to take over all this stuff. You need to know what sort of thing you should be asking for future interviews.'

'I can't think of anything worse,' I said flatly.

'Oh wow! That's a great attitude for the new owner of the Harling Estate.' He made himself an instant coffee and sat down opposite me. 'What's wrong? Has something happened?'

'Where do I even start?'

He raised an eyebrow. 'At the beginning?'

With a sigh, I decided he might as well know what a complete idiot I'd been, arranging lessons without realising what it would involve or all the obstacles that made it an impossible situation. Hesitantly, I also confided in him that I'd argued with Lawrie, and that I hadn't been particularly gentle with him.

I expected him to get very angry with me about that, knowing how much he loved his grandpa, but to my surprise, he merely sipped his coffee and shrugged.

'Aren't you furious with me?' I asked. 'Did you not hear what I said to him?'

'You have a point,' he said mildly. 'This is your house now and you make the decisions. But it's what I've been trying to tell you with this interview business. You must take responsibility. It's all well and good telling Grandpa that you're in charge, but that means actually *being* in charge and doing things you don't want to do. Like interviewing prospective tenants.'

'Or turning the pages of books for that lot upstairs,' I said, nodding up at the ceiling.

'Exactly.'

'He's just been so obstinate lately,' I said. 'Lawrie, I mean. He seemed so friendly and amiable at first but now he just keeps digging his heels in and criticising everything.'

'Maybe he's struggling with the idea of leaving,' Brodie mused. 'Now that it's getting closer and more real, he's probably panicking a bit. This place has been his entire life.'

'But I never forced him to go!' I cried. 'That's all his doing. He'd be welcome to stay here. I wish he would. I wish you both would.'

'Do you?' he asked, surprised.

'Of course I do. I'm not ready to run this place alone; we all know it. And you two know so much about it...' I sighed. 'Stubborn as a mule.'

'Hmm.'

'What do you mean, hmm?' I asked suspiciously.

'I mean, he's not the only stubborn one, is he?'

'Hey, he's not always right, you know. I mean, look how he kicked off about me inviting the ghosts over. How mean was that? Just because Agnes didn't like it!'

'Okay,' Brodie said, 'but have you looked at it from her point of view?'

'Meaning?'

'Well, think about it. What if Grandpa had invited the entire village to the Hall and told them they were welcome here any time and didn't need an invitation. How would you feel about that? Living people, just like you and I, coming and going whenever they felt like it. In your home.'

I did think about it, and I realised I didn't like it. The villagers I'd met had been nice people, and I'd really bonded with some of them, but would I want them to have the run of this place? This was mine and Immi's home and it was nice to be able to shut the door and have a sanctuary away from outside problems.

Yet I'd been expecting Agnes and Aubrey to welcome an entire village of ghosts to the Hall without even asking them how they felt about it.

'Oh heck,' I said. 'When you put it like that... I've been a bit of a twerp, haven't I?'

He grinned. 'A bit.'

'I'll apologise,' I said heavily. 'To Lawrie, to Agnes and Aubrey. And I'll talk to the other ghosts. I still think meetings are a good idea, but maybe taking them on a tour of the Hall wasn't.'

'At least you kept them away from the east wing,' he said. 'That's something.'

'Even so... I'll find somewhere else to meet them, and also find a way they can get in touch with me when they need me, rather than coming here.'

'There you go. One problem solved.'

'Maybe,' I said gloomily, 'but it doesn't solve the school problem, does it? Honestly, bloody ghosts!'

He reached out and laid his hand on my arm, making me shiver inside. 'How are you feeling about your ability to see them now? Do you still see it as a curse?'

'Not a great time to ask me that,' I said with a wry grin. 'Given the morning I've had.'

'But generally. Being here, has it changed anything for you?'

His blue eyes melted my heart as he gazed at me with clear compassion. There was the faintest trace of stubble on his chin, and I found myself thinking how soft and deeply kissable his lips looked.

Even as the thought entered my head, Brodie's expression changed: his gaze intensifying, his mouth opening slightly.

My heart thudded as I leaned ever so slightly closer to him, aware that he was mirroring my actions. I caught the faint tang of his aftershave and closed my eyes in delicious anticipation. He was going to kiss me. Or I was going to kiss him. I knew it was inevitable, and that I'd been wanting this to happen for what felt like forever.

The scream shattered the moment, and I pulled away from Brodie before leaping to my feet. I felt dazed, and not entirely sure what had just happened.

'I'm sorry, Callie.' Brodie looked horrified. 'I thought... obviously, I misread the signals. I didn't mean—'

'It's not you,' I assured him. 'Hell, I promise, it's *not* you. Someone screamed.'

I ran into the hall, wondering who on earth had screamed so loudly and why.

Evidently, the Wyndhams had wondered the same, as Aubrey and Agnes were hurrying down the stairs, Lawrie not far behind them.

John and Robert were a few steps from the bottom, hiding behind Florence. Walter stood at the base of the staircase, talking to Peter, the baker who'd claimed the boys feared him.

'What on earth is all this commotion?' Agnes demanded.

'I need to speak to the lads,' Peter said. He turned to me, a plea in his eyes. 'They need to understand.'

'Stop him, Florrie!' John begged.

Robert gave an ear-splitting wail. 'Make him go away,' he cried, his little voice making my heart break for him.

'It's okay,' I said. 'He's not going to hurt you, I promise.'

'But it's Pillory Pete!' John cried. 'He's after us. He's going to make us pay!'

'Pay for what?' I asked, confused.

'For killing him!'

There was a shocked silence before Agnes shrieked, 'You see! This is who you've brought into our home, girl. Murderers! And they've been associating with Florence. Oh, Mr Wyndham! Do something!'

Aubrey seized Peter by the shoulder. 'Look here, my good man, you simply can't—'

'Not to him!' Agnes cried. 'To these two young reprobates! We must lock them up somewhere.' She frowned. 'How *can* we lock them up, Mr Wyndham?'

'No one's locking anyone up,' I said firmly, as John and Robert cowered behind a defiant-looking Florrie. 'There's clearly been some sort of misunderstanding here. Peter, what are you doing here anyway?'

'I heard the lads were having their lesson today with Walter, so I thought it was the perfect opportunity to finally get to speak to them. I've been trying for centuries but they keep running away.'

'He's going to kill us,' Robert sobbed.

'Bit late for that,' Florrie pointed out. 'Mind you, I reckon he's going to torture you. Run!'

She stepped aside, allowing the boys to hurtle down the remaining stairs, but they were no match for Aubrey, who grabbed them both.

'Not so fast, young fellow-me-lads. We're going to get to the bottom of this.'

Florrie gave a cry of outrage and aimed a sharp kick at Aubrey's leg. 'Let 'em go!'

There was no one more surprised than Florrie when Agnes seized her by the arms and shook her. 'How dare you kick your father like that? Where's your respect? Behave yourself, girl, at once!'

Florrie could barely speak; she was clearly so stunned by

Agnes's actions. I knew how she felt. I'd never have imagined Agnes would turn on her precious Florence like that.

'What on earth's going on?' Mia asked from somewhere behind me.

'I have no idea,' Brodie said wearily. 'Evidently, someone screamed and now there seems to be some sort of altercation happening. How did it go at the dentist's?'

'A small fortune spent for the privilege of being told my teeth are fine. Honestly, never a dull moment here, is there?'

'Peter, perhaps you can explain to the boys what you've been wanting to tell them for so long,' I suggested, after casting apologetic looks at Brodie and Mia, who must find all this completely baffling.

'Certainly,' Peter said. He crouched down, rather endearingly, and spoke kindly to John and Robert. 'You think I blame you for my death, don't you? Well, I'm here to tell you that I don't. You weren't the ones who killed me. Do you understand? I know who did that. I'm so sorry you got scared and ran, and so sorry for what happened to you. It was a terrible day all round. Can we please be friends now?'

John's and Robert's eyes were like saucers.

'We chucked the stone,' Robert whispered.

I couldn't help myself. 'What stone?' I asked. As they all turned to look at me, I held up my hands. 'Yeah, I know. I'm not supposed to ask. But none of this is making sense to me right now, and I'd love to know why these two are so scared of you.'

'Because we killed him,' John said. 'We killed Pillory Pete.'

'What *is* a pillory?' I asked, confused.

'A method of punishment,' Peter said with a sigh. 'A wooden structure on the village green, where they push your head and your hands through holes in the wood and lock you in position so people can throw stuff at you.'

'You mean stocks?'

'Stocks? I wish! At least with stocks, only your feet are trapped. No, it was the pillory for me. I suppose it was my fault. I had a drop or two of ale when I should have been in church.' He leaned forward and murmured, 'But honestly, those sermons! They were enough to make anyone drink. If you think the Reverend Alexander is bad, you should have met the Reverend Samuels. Anyway,' he added in a more conversational tone, 'the locals took great delight in throwing missiles at me. Rotten vegetables, that sort of thing. Even stale bread which I thought was a bit of a liberty, given I'd probably baked it.'

John and Robert looked at each other.

'We didn't mean no harm,' John said, trembling.

'And you did no harm,' Peter assured him. 'At least, the stone you threw might have stung a little, but it didn't kill me. No,' he said, his eyes narrowing, 'it was the rock that did that. The blooming great rock that was hurled at me by none other than my loving wife.'

'Your wife?'

'Oh yes. I saw the look in her eyes as she threw it. She meant to harm me, though I doubt she meant to kill me. She considered me an embarrassment. She was a pious woman, believe it or not, who hung on the reverend's every word. I think she thought I'd disgraced her in the eyes of the village and, more importantly, in the eyes of God.'

'So, your wife killed you? Not John and Robert?' I checked, seeing the look of astonishment on both boys' faces.

'That's right. And she got away with it, too, in all the confusion, as no one could be sure who'd actually thrown the rock.'

'But what happened to the boys?' I asked, regretting my question immediately as Robert covered his eyes.

'They panicked,' Peter said softly. 'Ran out into the road and got mowed down by a horse and cart. Bless them. I tried to reach them when it happened, when I saw them leave their bodies, but they were in such a state with themselves, and when they saw me running towards them, they took flight. They've been hiding from me ever since.'

'Harmony did say you didn't blame us,' John said reluctantly, 'but we didn't believe her.'

'Harmony?' I gasped. 'You know where Harmony is?'

John's mouth clamped shut.

'Not supposed to talk about them,' Robert admitted. 'They're ever so good to us. Look after us, like.'

'*They* take care of you?' I asked, astonished. 'Who's *they*?'

'Robert!' John burst out. 'What are you *doing*?'

'It's okay,' I promised them. 'I'm not going to ask any more questions. I'm just glad someone looks out for you. I've been worried about you, and about her. So, if Harmony already told you Peter wasn't about to hurt you, why were you still running?'

Robert and John exchanged glances, then looked at Florrie.

'*She* said she heard him talking to some of the others, and he's promised to torture us when he gets hold of us because it's our fault he's trapped here.'

'Florrie, you didn't!' I said.

Agnes shook her head. 'Tell me this isn't true, Florence.'

'It's that Pillory Pete what's lying,' Florrie cried. 'He's gonna make them pay for what they did. I 'eard him say so.'

Aubrey took hold of her hand and bobbed down in front of her. 'Now, Florence,' he said sternly, 'no good comes of lying. You must tell the absolute truth, and somehow, I fear that, so far, you've failed to do that.'

Florrie's brows knitted together. 'I 'ate you! You're all liars!' she cried, breaking away from Aubrey and running out of the Hall.

'If it helps,' Walter told the boys, 'I know Peter here quite well, and I truly believe he only wants to be friends with you. He certainly doesn't blame you for what happened to him.'

'Of course I don't,' Peter said gently. 'It's my wife who did it, like I said, and to be honest, I don't even blame her any longer. I mean, it was so long ago. What does it even matter now?'

'So, you're not going to torture us?' Robert asked hopefully.

'Of course not.' Peter ruffled the boys' hair. 'What sort of fella do you think I am, eh? Didn't I used to give you the odd crust of bread when it was fresh out of the oven, and you were hungry? Don't you remember that?'

John tilted his head to one side. 'Oh, yeah, so you did,' he said in astonishment. 'I'd forgotten.'

'So had I,' Robert admitted. 'You made ever such nice bread. It stopped my belly from rumbling for a bit.'

'Well then, there you are,' I said. 'Peter's just a nice man who used to give you bread. Not an angry person who wants to torture you. Is that all settled now?'

'Peter,' Walter suggested, 'why don't you come upstairs and view our schoolroom? I'm sure the boys would love to show you where they're going to be having their lessons.'

'Don't mind if I do,' Peter said. 'If that's all right with you boys?'

John and Robert exchanged looks then nodded. The four of them headed happily up the stairs, passing Lawrie on the way and greeting him with respect.

Agnes sank onto the bottom step and put her head in her hands. 'I'm exhausted.'

Aubrey sat beside her. 'It's been quite a day,' he agreed. 'But you must see now, Agnes, that Callie is quite right about Florence. Something needs to be done, and lessons are just the start of it. Discipline and routine. That's what she needs. I'm very grateful to you, Callie, and if there's anything we can do to help with the children's lessons, we'll be only too glad to do so.'

'Really?' I asked. 'Well, that's... that's very kind of you, Aubrey.'

Agnes sighed. 'Quite right. I'm sorry, Callie. I didn't want to accept that we'd failed Florence so spectacularly, but Mr Wyndham is correct. We must do something about her behaviour. When I think about the terror in those poor boys' eyes...' She shook her head in despair. 'I'm very glad you over-ruled us in this matter. The lessons are a good idea. You have my full support.'

'Has someone gone after Florrie?' Mia asked me.

'Er, no, not yet,' I said.

'I'll go.' Aubrey got to his feet, but Agnes pulled him back down.

'She'll be back,' she said. 'And when she does come back, I shall see to it that she apologises to you. Kicking you in the leg and yelling at you like that! I won't have her talking to you with such a lack of respect, Mr Wyndham. I simply won't.'

Aubrey's expression softened and I could see the pleasure in his eyes that she was defending him against her precious Florence.

'Well, er, thank you, my dear.' He patted her hand gently and I thought, married or not, these two were clearly terribly fond of each other, and if the Reverend Alexander could see them together at this moment, surely even he couldn't disapprove?

My gaze met Lawrie's, and he stared at me for a long moment, before turning and heading back up the stairs.

I sighed. It seemed I still had some bridges to mend there. And how exactly was I going to do that?

29

It was the following evening when the things that had been nagging away at me finally slotted into place. When they did, I couldn't imagine how I hadn't noticed them before.

I was sitting in my living room, idly watching an old episode of *Midsomer Murders* while dipping into a packet of chocolate digestives when, for some inexplicable reason, my thoughts slid to various recent scenarios involving Mia and I sat up straight, excitement bubbling away in me. How had I been so blind?

The next morning, I sought her out. She was in the kitchen, passing on my instructions to one of the cleaning ladies, so it was bad timing really, as Angela gave me a filthy look and said, 'The schoolroom? Are you serious?'

Walter had decreed that lessons would commence properly the following week and had gently suggested that I get my act together in the meantime, finding books and a way for the children to actually read them.

I still hadn't figured out a way for that to happen, but I was determined that at least the schoolroom would look better, so I'd decided to ask the cleaners to give the room a good scrubbing and vacuum it over, and that I'd hang up posters and maps and even bring in fresh flowers to brighten the room up, particularly as Aubrey had told me that the ghosts' sense of smell was stronger than it had been even in life.

'If you wouldn't mind,' I said meekly.

'But no one uses the schoolroom,' she said. 'Have you spoken to Lawrie about this?'

I bit down my impatience. 'As a matter of fact, the schoolroom will be in use in future, and as for Lawrie – it's nothing to do with him, is it? I'm in charge now, and I'd greatly appreciate it if you'd do as I asked, Angela.'

I wanted to be polite, naturally, but I had to let everyone know, in no uncertain terms, that they couldn't keep bringing up Lawrie whenever they disagreed with me. The fact was, Lawrie would be gone very soon, and I had to have exerted my authority by then. I couldn't afford to faff about any longer.

Angela gave me a dark look but nodded. 'As you like.'

She scuttled out of the kitchen and Mia grinned at me. 'Well done. Coffee?'

While I was in an assertive mood, I pulled out a chair and sat down. 'Maybe later. Right now, I want you to sit too. You and I have to talk.'

'Sounds ominous,' she said, slipping into the chair beside me. 'What have I done wrong?'

'It's not what you've done wrong,' I told her. 'It's more what you've done that you really shouldn't have done.'

She frowned. 'Isn't that the same thing?'

'No,' I said. 'It's not. This is about things you've said that make no sense – unless they totally do.'

She burst out laughing. 'Callie, that's as clear as mud! What on earth are you talking about?'

'Okay.' I held up one hand and began counting my fingers.

'One. Florence goes to push Immi down the stairs. You let out a cry of alarm and drop the tray. You say you tripped.'

She paled. 'I did. I already apologised for that.'

I held up a second finger. 'Two. And this only dawned on me last night, which I can't believe. You knew exactly what I'd agreed to when I made that bet with Florence. But I'm almost 100 per cent certain that I didn't mention what the wager was. It was Florrie who talked about the kitten, so how did you know? And thirdly, when all that kerfuffle was going on with Pillory Pete on Monday, you asked if anyone had gone after Florrie. How did you even know Florrie had left? No one had told you that.' I held up the three fingers in triumph, 'One, two, three. There might even be more, but that's what I remember. So how do you explain that, eh?'

Mia swallowed. 'I... I—'

'You can see the ghosts, can't you?' I asked. 'Why did you keep quiet? You could have taken over the entire estate if you'd let Lawrie know.' I frowned. 'I'm presuming he *doesn't* know?'

'No! I mean, no, I can't see ghosts. Well, not all of them.' She sighed. 'I can see Florrie, that's all.'

'Florrie? But how? I thought people could only see the ghosts they were related to. Oh...' I stared at her, seeing the stricken expression in her eyes. 'You're related to Florrie? How?'

'Okay, but you mustn't say anything, right? Promise?'

'If that's what you want. But Mia, why on earth are you keeping it quiet? Does Florrie not even know? How are you related to her?'

She ran a hand through her dark hair, her expression troubled. 'She's my great-aunt,' she explained. 'My grandma was her little sister. When she died, five years ago, I decided I'd find out what happened to Florrie. I wished I'd done it earlier, when Grandma was alive, really. She was always curious about the place Florrie was sent to during the war, but never came here to see for herself. She said she thought it would be too painful, you see. All the memories tied up here.'

'So you came to Rowan Vale, why? Were you hoping to see Florrie?'

'Good grief, no! I had no idea about the ghosts or anything like that. I certainly wasn't expecting to see her. I booked into the pub and then went up to the Hall where I met Lawrie. I was hoping he wouldn't mind me having a bit of a look around the grounds, that's all. I never expected him to be so helpful. He invited me in. Showed me the records there are of when the Hall was home to evacuees. Even pointed out her photo.' She shook her head. 'Looking back, it was obvious there was something odd about it. The photos weren't even labelled with the children's individual names, so how did Lawrie know which one was Florrie? I suppose, at first, I just thought he was being kind. Fobbing me off with any old photo, but then I took out the photo Grandma had given me of her, and I realised he'd picked the right child. It seemed incredible.'

'And then what happened?' I asked, caught up in the story.

'I was about to go back to the pub. I thanked Lawrie and he opened the living-room door, and then this, this child came running down the stairs.' She shook her head. 'Little plaits flying, those ridiculous wellington boots, that thin little cotton dress and knitted cardigan... She was Florrie. I knew it immediately.'

'Bloody hell, Mia. I can't imagine how much of a shock that was! What did she say to you?' I didn't like to imagine, knowing Florrie.

'She didn't even notice me. She went skipping down the hall and through the front door. The closed front door. I practically fell back into the living room, babbling away to Lawrie about seeing things.'

'What did Lawrie say?'

'He poured me a stiff drink then called for Agnes and Aubrey. I had no idea who they were and obviously couldn't see them, but it was apparent that he was having some sort of conversation with someone. Quite a heated conversation. I barely took any of it in. I just gulped down the brandy and helped myself to another.' She laughed. 'What a day that was!'

'So how did it end up with you living here and keeping it quiet that you can see Florrie?' I narrowed my eyes. 'She doesn't know, does she?'

'No. It was down to Agnes,' she admitted. 'Apparently, she was quite distressed that someone from Florrie's past had turned up. She was afraid that it would bring back terrible memories for Florrie and begged Lawrie to send me away. Well, I wasn't about to do that. In fact, once the shock started to wear off and I realised what had happened, I started asking questions. Lots of questions. Agnes didn't like it one bit, but Lawrie was very understanding.'

She raised an eyebrow. 'You must think this is all crazy, but at the time, it seemed to make sense. Lawrie got Agnes to agree to my staying here, on condition that I never let onto Florrie that I could see her. In return, he gave me a home and a job so that I could be around her, get to know her. To be honest, I think it was only ever intended to be temporary, but I settled in here and got to like it. I got to like Lawrie. I loved the job and the village. And I—' she hesitated, then added, 'I love Florrie. I know she can be a little madam, but I do see a lot of Grandma in her, and she's not always so bolshy, you know. When it's just her and she's not playing up... There's a lot more to her than you'd think.'

'What do you mean, when it's just her?'

She gave me a sad smile. 'She comes to see me. She doesn't realise I can see or hear her of course, but she often follows me into the kitchen and sits at the table while I cook. She's said some very complimentary things about my cooking! Oh, the times I've wished I could feed her up. She's really taken to the kitten too.' She nodded over to the blanket in the corner where Kitty/Tux was sleeping. 'He doesn't even hiss at her any longer. He's so used to her. When Immi's at school, Florrie spends so much time here with him. She talks to him. She tells him things.' She paused and I was astonished to see her wipe away a tear. 'She's a good girl at heart. She's just lost her way a bit. I think she's lonely, even though she's got Agnes and Aubrey.'

'But it might make all the difference to her if she knew you were related to her,' I said, feeling quite dazed that I'd missed the signs which, thinking about it now, were so obvious. 'Surely it's up to you whether you tell her, not Lawrie? And certainly not Agnes.' As a thought struck me, I said hesitantly, 'Does Brodie know about all this?'

'I don't think so. I've never mentioned it to him, and he's never brought up the subject, which I think he would if he knew. And you know what those two are like,' she said. 'They can be very persuasive. Agnes can wrap Lawrie round her little finger, and if she doesn't want me to talk to Florrie then he's not going to allow it.'

'But what if you ignored them both and talked to her anyway? How could they stop you?'

She nibbled her thumbnail. 'I thought of that, but what if Lawrie had sacked me and sent me away? I'd never get to see her again. At least this way, I do have contact with her, even if she doesn't realise it.'

'You know what,' I said, feeling my anger resurface. 'This just about takes the biscuit. Those two! They're really getting on my nerves. I'm going to have a word with Lawrie about this.'

'No, don't, Callie!' Mia urged. 'Don't rock the boat. I don't want any bad feeling between us.'

'Lawrie will be gone very soon,' I pointed out. 'He can't sack you or send you away. You work for me now, and I say you can talk to Florrie all you like. This has to stop. This entire estate doesn't revolve around Agnes and her demands and I'm going to make damn sure he knows it.'

30

There was no sign of Lawrie in the house, though it was quite possible he'd gone for a wander around the grounds, or even into the village. Mia pleaded with me not to have another argument with him, as it wasn't worth falling out with him again after we'd only just made up.

I supposed she had a point. Before I'd learned the truth about Mia, I'd apologised profusely to Lawrie, Agnes and Aubrey yesterday, explaining that I'd realised that inviting all the ghosts to the Hall without even asking if it was okay had been completely out of order, and that I would take steps to ensure another meeting place would be found in future.

Agnes had been surprisingly generous in accepting my apology, and Lawrie had looked very relieved, as if he'd hated arguing with me and was more than happy to put past grievances behind us.

To Mia's relief I decided, therefore, to give myself a chance to calm down, so I spent the morning in the library at the Hall, looking for books that might prove suitable for young children and realising that, as old and sombre as they were, they weren't even suitable for me. I decided the local library might be a better option and wondered how to go about getting library memberships for three dead people.

I gave up and wandered back towards the living room just as Brodie arrived home, his arms full of papers.

'What's all that?' I asked curiously.

'More details of jobs,' he explained briefly.

'What sort of jobs?'

He didn't meet my gaze. 'Accountancy mostly. It's what I'm trained for, after all.'

'Accountancy? You mean, those are details of jobs *you're* thinking of applying for?'

He nodded. 'Time's ticking on. I need to find employment. These are all in Devon. That's where the house is that Dad's bought for us to live in when we leave here.'

I realised I hadn't given much thought to where Brodie and Lawrie would end up. I hadn't wanted to think about it really, but this was bringing it home to me that in a week's time, I'd be alone in this place without Lawrie to interfere. Or advise. And without Brodie to do the million and one things Brodie did around here. Or just be Brodie.

I swallowed. 'Devon? That's... that's nice for you. Bit far away, though.'

'Not as far as Oz,' he said briefly. 'Which was Dad's first suggestion. Anyway, what have you been doing today?'

'Do you really want to know?'

'I wouldn't ask otherwise, would I?'

'You'd better come into the living room,' I said. 'You might need a brandy for this.'

When I'd told him the truth about Mia and Florrie, and how Agnes and Lawrie had manipulated the situation, he agreed that a brandy was just the job.

'Oh wow,' he said, putting down his now empty glass. 'I can't believe Grandpa kept this quiet from me. And Mia! How did she manage to fool even Florrie?'

'She was so scared they'd sack her that she did exactly as they asked,' I said grimly.

'Mia doesn't strike me as the scared sort,' he mused. 'Not easily bullied, either.'

'But she loves Florrie,' I pointed out. 'She doesn't want to lose her, and until now, Lawrie and Agnes held all the power.'

'What are you going to do about it?' he asked.

'Tell them both to back off, and that it's up to Mia if she wants Florrie to know who she is. What else?'

'So, another row with Grandpa then? Haven't you just made it up with him?'

'I don't want to,' I admitted. 'But the situation here is ridiculous. This thing between him and Agnes is crazy. He lets her get away with anything and it's not fair. Florrie has every right to know about her family.'

'I completely agree,' he said.

'You do?'

'Of course. Florrie's lost everything. She may have died back in 1941 but she's still a ten-year-old child at heart. A ten-year-old child who was sent away from her family to live among strangers in an area she was totally unfamiliar with. I'm sure she'd love to know that her sister never forgot about her, or that her great-niece is right here in this house because of her.'

'Exactly!' I said, so glad he understood.

'But I don't think arguing with Grandpa is the way to approach this,' he cautioned. 'You've got to be smarter than that. He's never going to cross Agnes. What you must understand, is that she was by his side from him being a baby. When his own parents weren't around for him, she was. He genuinely does view her as family, and he loves her. And believe it or not, she loves him.'

'Then they should both understand how important family is,' I said. 'How come it's all right for them to cling to each other, but they expect Florrie and Mia to stay separated and alone?'

'It's hypocritical,' he acknowledged, 'but if you go in there like a bull in a china shop, you're going to get nowhere. All you'll do is make Grandpa dig his heels in even deeper. No, it's Agnes you need to tackle.'

'Agnes? She'll never give in,' I said. 'You haven't met her but believe me, she's as stubborn as they come.'

'From what I've heard of her, though, she's got a gentle side. A caring side. And she did give in about the lessons when she realised what was best for Florence. Whatever you think of her, you can't deny that she loves that girl. You need to talk to her, mother to mother. Make her see how unfair she's being but at the same time acknowledge her fears and let her know you understand where she's coming from. Tell her you'll help her figure out where they all go from here. Make her feel that you're on her side but that she needs to put Florence first in all this.'

'Hmm.' I sipped my own brandy and nodded. 'You might be onto something. I'll give that a go. Honestly, how can she be so blind as to how unhappy her own daughter is?'

Brodie crossed the room and refilled his glass. 'Ah. While we're on that subject...'

My eyes widened. 'Meaning what?'

He sat next to me on the sofa, brandy glass in hand. 'Far be it from me to tell you how to raise your own daughter, but you *have* noticed how unhappy Immi is lately?'

'I've noticed how *grumpy* she is lately,' I said with feeling. I swilled the brandy round in my glass. '*Is* she unhappy? Has she said as much?'

'I think,' he said carefully, 'that she's feeling a little neglected. The estate does take up so much of your time, and I've explained to her that it's all so much harder while you're settling in and finding your feet here, and that things will get better. She's not convinced.'

'She's talked to you about it?' I asked, astonished and not a little hurt. 'Why you? Why not me?'

'She's tried to talk to you, Callie,' he said patiently. 'Unfortunately, you're not listening to her.'

'Meaning what? I always listen to her!'

'Okay, well you're not hearing her then.'

'I have no idea what you're talking about,' I said sullenly.

'She wants to be involved more in the estate. I know, I know.' He held up his hand as I opened my mouth to protest. 'There are things that she can't understand that are far too grown up for her, and I get that. I think she does too. But she's not asking to hire and fire people, or learn the accounts, or deal with repairs. She wants to meet the ghosts properly, and she wants to be part of that community. She feels very aggrieved that you won't let her.'

I bit my lip, aware that I'd done my best to keep her away from the ghosts. I knew she had to see the ones that lived in the Hall, but I'd figured that was more than enough. It was why I'd arranged the meeting with the other ghosts and the lessons with Walter for times when I knew she'd be in school, safely out of their way.

'I'm just trying to protect her,' I murmured. 'Give her a normal life.'

'Have you any idea how much she hates the word *normal*?' Brodie shook his head. 'Callie, this *is* normal for her and for you. When are you going to realise that? She has a gift. Let her use it.

Let her be part of this community or she'll grow up very resentful of you, and you wouldn't want that, would you?'

I gulped down the remaining brandy thinking about it.

'I'm sorry,' he said at last. 'I know she's your child and it's none of my business how you raise her. I just don't like to see her so unhappy, and I'd hate for you two to drift apart when it wouldn't take much to bring you so much closer together.' He paused. 'She misses you, you know. You don't spend nearly enough time in each other's company. And I promise, that's the last thing I'll say on the subject. It's up to you now.'

We sat in silence for a few moments.

'Are you okay?' he asked at last.

'Just thinking how good you are with kids,' I admitted. 'For a man.'

He laughed. 'Wow, how sexist is that! Thank you, I think, although plenty of men are good with kids.'

'Not in my experience,' I told him. 'You know about my dad. As for Immi's father...'

His fingers tightened around the brandy glass.

'You've never mentioned him before,' he said, trying and failing to sound casual.

'Why would I? He was the worst. Total jerk.'

'Does he see Immi at all?'

I laughed. 'He's never even met her! And you know, she never asks about him. Not once. And I've never mentioned him to her either. What a terrible situation, eh?'

'So, you broke up before Immi was born then?' he asked. 'Sorry, you don't have to tell me. It's none of my business.'

I hesitated, not sure whether I was brave enough to say what was on my mind. But heck, I was a new woman, wasn't I? I was learning fast that the only way to get anywhere was to be more assertive. Keeping quiet and saying nothing had got me nowhere after all.

'Given that we almost kissed the other day, I think it *is* your business. Well, a bit.'

His eyes widened. 'Are we really going there?'

I sighed. 'It wouldn't make much sense, would it? I mean, with you leaving so soon.'

He stared into his glass for a moment. 'It wouldn't. No.'

We both looked a bit awkward, then Brodie cleared his throat and said, 'So, Immi's father?'

Back to earth with a bump. I'd hoped we could have floated around in hope for a bit, but Brodie was obviously determined to ground us. Even though it made sense, I felt a pang of loss for something I'd never really had.

'Immi's father. Right.' I took a deep breath, preparing myself to relive memories I'd buried for years. 'We were only together for six months. I was nineteen. He was twenty-five. I'm ashamed to say I was completely smitten with him, which is ridiculous because all the signs were there that he was a loser. I'd caught him out lying a few times, and I can't honestly say I trusted him. But he was ever so good looking and lots of girls fancied him, and I'd never been the object of anyone's envy before, so it was nice to have people who'd always looked down on me looking up to me for a change.'

'Not really a good reason to stay with a liar,' he said.

'Absolutely not, but I was young and daft, and...' I sighed. 'I wanted to have a boyfriend and be normal.'

'Ah,' he said, nodding. '*Normal*. Obviously.'

'Besides, he was an escape from home. He took me out, got me out from under their feet. I know it doesn't seem much now, but at the time... Anyway, when I told him I was pregnant, he seemed okay with it at first,' I said, my face burning as I remembered how gullible I'd been. 'But then he told me it wasn't working for him and that he wouldn't be seeing me again. I didn't believe him, but then he just vanished from my life. No sign of him at all. He'd never been on social media – said he thought it was boring – and his number had been disconnected. I was devastated, and Dad and Judy – my stepmother – thought I'd done something stupid to put him off me. They said he was a nice lad and trust me to ruin things.'

'But you can't think it was your fault?' Brodie asked disbelievingly. 'He just ghosted you? Sorry, bad choice of word, but you know what I mean.'

'I did at first,' I said grimly. 'Then, when I was about six months pregnant, there was a knock on the door and there was some woman standing there. She was pregnant too. Put us back-to-back and we'd have looked like a pair of bookends. Turns out she was his wife, and that was their second baby. He already had a two-year-old daughter.'

'Oh, Callie!' Brodie sounded horrified. 'I'm so sorry.'

'Don't be sorry for *me*,' I said defiantly. 'Be sorry for *her*. She burst into tears and admitted this was the third affair he'd had in as many years. She begged me to leave him alone and give them a chance to be happy. Can you imagine? I said to her, "Bloody hell, my name's Callie, not Jolene!" As if it was all my fault when I didn't even know he was married... I dread to think what number he's up to now.'

'My God, I can't believe men like him actually exist.' Brodie's tone was one of disgust. 'I feel I should apologise on behalf of every decent man on the planet.'

I laughed. 'Yeah, well, now you know.'

'And Immi knows nothing about this?'

'Nothing. She's never asked, and I've never brought it up.

How would I tell her what a jerk her father was? She's clearly not interested and that's fine by me.'

'But what if she does ask one day?'

'Then,' I said heavily, 'I'll tell her the truth. I'll have no choice. I'm not going to lie to her. Can't say I'm looking forward to that day, though.'

'Has... has there been anyone else since?'

'Boyfriends, you mean?' I shook my head. 'Nope. Just me and Immi. The thing is, I messed up so badly. Look at the man I chose to be her father! I don't ever want to let her down again and while she's so young, it's hard to trust another man. I mean, how do you know?'

'You can't really,' he said. 'But you shouldn't let that put you off trying. I get it, I really do. You want to protect Immi. But you've got to allow love into your life, Callie. Or at least the possibility of it.'

'Have *you*?' I asked. 'You must have had a few relationships in your time.' He must have done. Looking like that, how could he not?

He shrugged. 'Of course. Well, I've dated. I'm not sure I've had many actual relationships.'

'Anything serious?'

'Not on my part, which I realise makes me sound as bad as Immi's father, but I don't mean it that way. Most of the women I dated were as casual about it as I was and that was fine, but there was one... I never led her on or gave her any reason to believe we had a real future, but she got... obsessed with me. Started dropping heavy hints about a wedding, showing me engagement rings online, that kind of thing. I had to end it with her, and I tried to do it as gently as possible, but it took her a while to get over it.'

'I see. Do you still see her? Is she local?'

He hesitated. 'She works at the farm. It's Rissa.'

'The girl who was cosying up to you at the pub quiz?' I remembered the jealousy I'd experienced as I'd watched them laughing together.

There was a faint tinge of pink on his cheeks. 'There's nothing between us now, I swear! We're just friends, that's all.'

'Well,' I said after a moment's thought, 'I'm glad to hear it.'

His eyes softened. 'Are you?'

'I suppose I am, yes. And I believe you. I know you're nothing like Immi's father.'

Brodie stroked my hair, and I suppressed a shiver as he murmured, 'He must have been an idiot, using someone as lovely as you like that.'

Fighting to stay in control, I said flippantly, 'Is that a cheesy chat-up line?'

'My very best,' he admitted. 'Failed the test?'

'I'm afraid so.'

'Ouch. So, I guess that's us done and dusted?'

'I wasn't aware there was an "us",' I told him. 'And didn't we just agree that it would be a bad idea, given you'll be leaving soon?'

'We did,' he said heavily. 'Which is a shame.'

'Yeah, it is, but we have to be sensible.'

'But,' he said slowly, 'it must have meant something, mustn't it? That we almost kissed.'

'The thing is, *almost* doesn't really cut it,' I said. 'I *almost* got a job in a posh department store once, but then I didn't. I don't think I can put that on my CV, can I?'

'So, what do you suggest?'

I couldn't go there. I just couldn't.

When I didn't reply, he said, 'Maybe we could finish what we started. Just to put a full stop after it.' He leaned closer and put his arms around me and I stiffened.

'Sorry,' he said, letting go immediately. 'I didn't mean—'

'Oh, Brodie!' I cried, exasperated.

'What?' He sounded confused and no wonder.

'I just... Why do you have to be so polite and considerate all the time?'

'Because it's the decent thing to do, and it's the way you deserve to be treated.'

I took his hand in mine, unable to resist any longer. 'This is such a bad idea.'

'Because it would be stupid to start something when we're about to say goodbye, wouldn't it?'

'It really would,' I agreed, trying not to shiver as his fingers gently caressed my face.

'Callie? May I kiss you?'

There was no way I could make myself say no. I merely nodded, closed my eyes, and waited for the inevitable.

There was a moment that seemed to last forever when I wondered if he'd changed his mind, then his lips gently met mine, and a tingle shot through me as he cupped my face in his hands and the kiss slowly deepened and intensified. It was the very opposite of being near the ghosts. Instead of ice and death, Brodie's kiss spread warmth through my body, as if he was bringing me back to life. The memory of every bad thing that had ever happened to me turned to dust in one shining, golden moment. If it had brought me to this point in time, with this man, it had been worth it.

And yet...

Even though I wanted him desperately, and even though part of me hoped he'd never let me go, the fear was breaking through again. Brodie was leaving. This could go nowhere, and if I let myself fall any deeper, the pain when he went would be unbearable. Maybe it was already too late, but I had to protect myself somehow.

I pulled away with a sob and jumped up. 'I can't,' I said. 'I can't do this. I'm sorry.'

'Callie?' he asked anxiously.

There was hurt in his eyes, but I couldn't help him. I had to look out for myself and for Immi. I'd let her down so badly before she was even born. I simply couldn't allow that to happen again.

31

The problem with living in Harling Hall was that you never knew when you were being spied on. I'd have understood it if it had been a ghost watching us, but when I wrenched open the door after making a bolt for it, it was Bonnie, one of the cleaners, I collided with. She was standing there with a tray of cleaning products in one hand and a knowing look on her face.

I galloped upstairs, my face burning with embarrassment, and my heart breaking.

I think it's fair to say that Brodie and I avoided each other for the rest of the day until, after dinner, we managed to muster our courage and had a murmured conversation in the dining room after the others had left, in which we agreed that it was best to leave things as they were and accept that it had been a pleasant interlude but there was nowhere for it to go.

We were both adults, after all. It had been a kiss. That was all.

That night in bed, I had a long think about what Brodie had said. Well, I had a long think about Brodie in general, but even though the memory of our kiss was enough to keep me awake for hours, I did also remember what he'd told me about Immi, and I can't deny it stung.

Bad enough that she'd confided in him about how frustrated she was feeling, but it was even worse when I realised he was right. She'd been telling me for ages that she wanted to see more of the ghosts and that she felt left out of everything. I'd just refused to listen because it suited me to keep her away from them.

If I wasn't careful, I was going to push her away for good. The prospect of putting a barrier between me and Immi was unbearable. I had to fix this. I had to accept that ghosts were, ironically, part of her life and that trying to keep her away from them was only going to ruin our relationship.

Knowing I also had to do something about the Agnes, Mia, and Florrie situation, as well as find a way forward with the lessons, it was a wonder I got any sleep at all that night, and honestly, I don't think I got much.

I know when I woke up the following morning, I felt exhausted, but somehow my subconscious had decided to take one problem at a time, starting with Immi, who had to be my priority. I thought, maybe by helping her, I could solve at least some of the problems with Walter and the children too.

I went in search of 'Master' that very day. I'd learned that he lived above the sweet shop on the green, sharing the flat with Mr and Mrs Chesterton, who ran the shop and knew perfectly well that Walter occupied one of their spare bedrooms but, as with so many of the other tenants in this village, were perfectly happy about the situation since they couldn't see him and he had no impact on their lives.

I supposed they were in a similar situation to Brodie and – for the first time ever – I felt a pang of sympathy for those without the ability to see ghosts. It was an unfamiliar feeling and startled me. I couldn't imagine what it must be like to share a home with someone you couldn't see or hear, and thought Brodie and the people like him were missing out on a lot.

Walter was delighted to see me and welcomed me into the living room, after Mrs Chesterton had happily ushered me through the shop and up the stairs, as if having visitors to her resident ghost was an everyday occurrence.

'To what do I owe the pleasure, Mistress Chase?' he enquired cordially. 'Have you come up with a solution to our problem?'

'Partly,' I said. 'Walter, would you mind if we started lessons on Saturday instead of Monday? And how would you feel about having a little helper?'

He settled himself on the sofa and considered the matter. 'Which little helper would that be?'

I quickly explained my plan and he nodded enthusiastically. 'An excellent idea! The subject matter should be comforting for Florence and yet exciting enough for two young boys.'

'Are you familiar with that time period yourself, Walter?' I asked worriedly. I didn't want him to feel left out, after all.

He smiled. 'I think you forget that I've been around a long time. I lived through that period, as did my three young pupils. Well, not lived exactly, but you understand what I mean. I was here when the villagers could talk of nothing else. I saw the impact it had on life right here in Rowan Vale. I listened to the wireless with the gentleman who ran the sweet shop back then. Ah, how well I remember the emotions it invoked.'

He struck a dramatic pose, and I braced myself for another Shakespearean quote. He didn't disappoint.

'"Sound trumpets! Let our bloody colours wave! And either victory, or else a grave."' He beamed at me. 'Henry VI, part three.'

'Really? Wonderful,' I told him. 'So, you're happy to go ahead with that then?'

'Absolutely. I shall be at the Hall on Saturday morning. You can rely on me, Mistress Chase.'

'Callie,' I reminded him.

He smiled. 'Good day to you, Mistress Chase.'

I sighed. 'Good day, Walter.'

* * *

Having sorted that out with Walter, it was time to tackle Immi. Luckily, Clara's children were absent from school that day, having succumbed to what appeared to be a nasty stomach bug, so I was able to collect her alone. Well, obviously it wasn't lucky for the Milsom kids, or for poor Clara and Jack, who were apparently also suffering, but you know what I mean.

Moments after the school bell sounded, Immi strolled into the car park, clutching her bag, looking deep in thought. I popped my head out of the window and called her name, and she slid into the passenger seat, dumped her bag on the floor and fastened her seatbelt.

A few minutes later, we were heading to the other side of the village.

Immi frowned. 'This isn't the way home. Where are we going?'

'You'll see,' I said, smiling.

I'd booked us a table at The Royal Oak, determined that Immi and I were going to have a long chat away from anyone who knew us and, hopefully, away from ghosts.

Fat chance. As we took our seats, I felt a familiar icy sensation running along my shoulders and down my arms. I glanced at Immi, and she grinned.

'Even here.'

'Well,' I conceded, 'it *is* an old pub. Perhaps I was naïve to think there'd be no ghosts here.'

Her eyes scanned the room. 'Two,' she said. 'Nope, make that three.'

'I should have taken you to The Quicken Tree,' I said. 'At least there's only one ghost there.'

Immi picked up the menu. 'Who's that? Oh, sorry, none of my business.'

I sighed inwardly, sensing her resentment from across the table. 'His name's Isaac Grace,' I told her, 'and you'll see him for yourself very soon.'

She lowered the menu cautiously. 'I will? How come?'

'I've decided that the next meeting of the ghosts will be an evening meeting, and you're invited.'

The smile on her face made any doubts I'd had fly away. 'Seriously?'

'Seriously. You're right, Immi. You need to meet them all. This is your village as much as mine and I was wrong to stop you from mixing with the ghosts. I'm sorry.'

'Oh, Mum! Thank you!'

'And there's another thing I wanted to ask you,' I said. 'I've spoken to Walter about the kids' lessons. We've decided that they should do a class project to start them off.' I grinned at her. 'Guess what on?'

She gave me a blank look for a moment then burst out laughing. 'Not the Second World War? Oh, those poor kids! I've been doing a project on that for what feels like forever.'

'Exactly,' I said. 'So you'd be a wonderful help to Walter.'

Her eyes widened. 'What?'

'I've asked him to do some of the lessons at weekends until your school holidays start. We'd really like it if you could assist him. You know such a lot about the war, thanks to the projects you've had to do recently, and obviously, Walter can't turn the pages of books or write on the blackboard. You could.'

Immi considered the matter. 'There are loads of books on the war in the village library,' she told me. 'I could borrow some and read bits out to the boys, because they can't read yet, can they? Ooh!' Her eyes lit up. 'We could take them to the cinema. Show them that film you were banging on about! Imagine how excited they'd be.'

'Great idea,' I said warmly. 'Maybe we could take them to the library, too?'

'I'm sure Florrie would get involved,' she said. 'After all, it's her era, isn't it?'

'That's what we're hoping,' I told her. 'And boys are always interested in war, aren't they? Anyway, if we can get Florrie onside, they'll follow her lead.'

She nodded. 'We'll make it work. Somehow.'

'You're happy to help then?' I asked.

'Mum, you've no idea! I can't wait to get started.'

32

Immi reported back to me on Saturday evening that the first lesson had gone very well. John and Robert had been quite excited to learn about a war, and Florrie had grudgingly said that she supposed it was okay, if a bit boring.

Immi had cannily pointed out to her that she'd have an unfair advantage over the boys, as she'd been alive during part of the war rather than observing it from a distance as the boys had done, and Florrie had smirked, as realisation no doubt dawned that she was more than halfway to winning her bet already.

I'd had to tell my daughter the truth about the wager I'd made with Florrie and what the girl had asked for if she won.

'Brian?' Immi cuddled the kitten to her chest and shook her head. 'I'm not calling him Brian!'

'Well,' I pointed out, 'you still haven't got a name for him and if you're not careful, he's going to think he's called Kitty. So why not Brian?'

'But it's not a cat's name,' she protested.

'Neither is Kitty. No self-respecting adult male cat is going to want to answer to that,' I said. 'It would be like calling an adult human Baby or Bubba. Humiliating. You should think about his feelings in all this.'

She gave me one of her stares. 'That's emotional blackmail,' she said. 'Just because you made a bet about something you had no right to, don't try to twist it now. I'm not calling him Brian and that's that, so you'd better hope Florrie loses her bet or she's going to explode.'

'Even if she loses,' I mused, 'she's agreed to have lessons until Christmas, so either way, she's going to be in that schoolroom. And maybe, after a while, she'll start to enjoy them for their own sake. Who knows?'

I'd arranged with the manager of the cinema for a private viewing of *Mrs Miniver* the following evening, something which had excited even Florrie. Agnes had been rather worried about her watching one of those "new-fangled cinefilms" and had demanded assurances that there were no scenes of gratuitous violence and no bad language.

'In *Mrs Miniver*?' I'd laughed. 'I promise.'

Although, there were scenes of air raids, and… Still, I reasoned, Florrie was from wartime London. I was pretty sure *Mrs Miniver* would seem tame to her after what she'd experienced.

Walter seemed as excited as the children as we settled ourselves in the front row of the cinema and waited expectantly for the film to begin. Immi and I had passed on the rather watery orange squash offered by an usherette. For one thing, it wouldn't have been fair when the others couldn't have any. For another, ugh!

I wondered if it would be worth mentioning to the manager that he'd probably get a lot more customers if he offered coffee, Coke, nachos, and popcorn but decided I wasn't quite brave enough yet.

I soon forgot all about that when the film began and I was swept away by the story of the Miniver family and their friends and neighbours in a pretty, English village. I risked a glance at the others and saw Walter's rapt expression. John's and Robert's eyes were like saucers when the escaped Nazi pilot made his appearance, and even Immi was clearly absorbed in the story.

Florrie was sitting with her feet up on the seat, her arms wrapped around her knees, and her chin tucked into her chest. I couldn't see the expression on her face but the fact that she was so still was reassuring. She must be enjoying the film too.

It was during the flower-show scene that things changed. Lady Beldon had just announced that the winning rose was The Mrs Miniver, grown by Mr Ballard, when the air raid sirens began. As the villagers began to run for cover, Florrie leapt from her seat and ran out of the cinema.

John and Robert jumped up to follow her, but I told them to stay put.

'Immi and I will go after her,' I said. 'Walter, will you stay with the boys please? Don't worry,' I reassured them, 'she'll be fine. We'll look after her.'

Florrie, however, was nowhere to be seen when we left the cinema.

'Where do you think she'll be?' Immi asked.

'She can't have got too far. Wait! Did you hear that?'

There was the unmistakable sound of a sniff and then what sounded suspiciously like someone crying. Immi and I looked at each other.

'She's crying?' Immi mouthed, clearly shocked.

I felt sick. I should have considered that the traumatic scenes in the film would be too much for a little girl who might well have lived through them. Florrie could have PTSD for all I knew. What had I been thinking?

The truth was, I hadn't been thinking, I thought grimly. I'd been an idiot, so focused on making a success of these lessons that I'd totally forgotten this little girl had feelings and memories. Agnes would never forgive me for this, and I didn't blame her.

'Mum,' Immi whispered and motioned to me to follow her. We found Florrie curled up behind the gatepost of a nearby cottage. Immi pushed open the gate and crouched down beside her while I stayed where I was, leaning on the gate. I glanced around but, luckily, the area was deserted. Many of the tourists had gone home, or back to their holiday accommodation. With many of the attractions closed at this time of the evening, most people were over at the other side of the village in The Quicken Tree.

'Florrie,' I told her, 'I'm so sorry. I never meant to frighten you.'

Florrie sniffed again and wiped her nose on her cardigan sleeve. 'I ain't frightened,' she said gruffly.

'If you're not frightened,' Immi said, 'why did you run away?'

'I was bored,' Florrie said belligerently. 'Never seen such a borin' film, that's all.'

'Oh.' Immi sat beside her and folded her arms. 'I thought it was really good. I never expected to like it. When Mum suggested it, I thought it sounded a bit rubbish, but it wasn't. Especially with me doing my projects on the war. Brought it all home to me. What it must have been like.'

Florrie snorted with laughter. 'Are you kidding? It weren't nuffink like that! All them posh people with their fancy 'ouses and boats and servants. Weren't like that for us. We lived in a tiny little 'ouse with an outside lavvy and a tin bath. And my mum didn't read us *Alice in Wonderland* when the air raids came. She was too busy trying to keep blooming Janet quiet and make the boys stay put. And Dad weren't there either cos 'e was away fighting.' She shrugged. 'Till 'e wasn't.'

'Did your dad die in the war?' Immi asked, wide-eyed.

'Got taken prisoner just before Mum sent me away. He'd been fighting in Greece or sumfink and got sent to some camp in Australia.'

'I think you might mean Austria,' I suggested gently.

She shrugged. 'Maybe. Mum said it was typical of 'im to get out of the fighting and she'd bet 'e was living the life of Riley while she was struggling to feed four kids on 'er own.'

I wondered if Florrie's mother had tried to make light of the situation, reassuring the children that their father was fine. I hoped that was the case anyway.

'It's only natural the film brought back bad memories,' I told her. 'I'm so sorry, Florrie. I should have thought. You must have heard those sirens yourself so many times.'

'It weren't that.' She rubbed her eyes and sighed. 'It weren't the bombs and that. It was—' She broke off and tilted her head to look at me. 'You'll think I'm soft.'

'I promise I won't,' I said. I pushed open the gate and sat down so she was between Immi and me. 'You can tell us anything, Florrie.'

'It was... the people,' she said at last. 'Being together like that. When they all gathered together and went into that cellar. I just thought, why couldn't it 'ave been like that for us? Why did we 'ave to be split up like that?'

'You had a little sister, didn't you?' Immi asked.

'Yeah. Janet. She was just a baby. Always crying. Got on my nerves, to be honest,' she said. 'And of course, she took up all Mum's time. It was all about Janet. She forgot all about me when *she* came along.'

'Was it just you two girls and your mum then?' I asked, realising that all these years later, Florrie was still clearly resentful of her sister.

'No. When I was a kid,' she said, as if she'd reached a great age by the time she passed, 'there was me and Dad, Mum, Francis and 'Enry. They're my brothers. It was all right then. We were 'appy. But then the war started, and Dad went away, and Janet came along not long after and it all started to go wrong. Mum wanted to send us away. She said London weren't safe no more. She asked Uncle Vic if he'd take us. 'E had a farm, you see, in Essex, and she thought that would be best.'

'So how come you ended up here?' Immi asked.

'Uncle Vic didn't want me. Said girls were no use on a farm. He took 'Enry and Francis cos they were boys and older than me and could earn their keep. That's when Mum agreed to send me to this place,' she added bitterly. 'All on my own. Well, there were other kids, like, but none I really knew or cared about. I just wanted to stay with Mum. I didn't care about the bombs. I wasn't scared,' she added defiantly. 'I'd have took care of 'er if she'd let me. But no. I was packed off to 'Arling 'All and then look what 'appened! Never saw any of them again.'

Immi's eyes filled with tears. 'I'm sorry,' she said. 'It must have been awful for you.'

'As a matter of fact, it were,' Florrie agreed. 'And now I'm stuck 'ere forever while my family are all together. Well, *were* all together.' She sighed. 'I suppose they're long gone now. Bet they forgot all about me. Bet it was all about Janet. Bet when Dad and the lads came 'ome, she was all they bovvered wiv.'

I thought about Mia. Florrie was clearly under the impression that she'd been forgotten, but Janet *hadn't* forgotten. Janet had been too young to remember her big sister, yet she'd spoken about her so much to her granddaughter that Mia had come to the Cotswolds in search of her story. Florrie's family must have kept her memory alive for Janet. She'd not been forgotten at all.

Florrie needed to know that. Whatever Agnes thought. However much it upset her and Lawrie. Florrie had a right to know, and Mia had the right to tell her.

'Come on,' I said to Florrie, 'let's go home. I'm sure Agnes will be glad to see you.'

'You won't tell 'er, will you?' Florrie said anxiously. 'I don't want 'er to think I've gone daft. She'll only stop me going out again and I don't want 'er to. She might even make me give up the lessons.'

'Don't you want to give them up?' Immi asked, sounding surprised.

Florrie got to her feet and shrugged. 'Not really. They're all right. For now, anyway. At least it's sumfink to do, right?'

'Let's see if the film's finished,' I said. 'Then we can all walk home together.'

I'd carefully avoided promising her that I wouldn't tell Agnes what had happened because the fact was, I'd have had to break that promise.

It was time to ruffle more feathers.

33

Brodie was in the study. I tapped on the door and entered the room without waiting for a reply. A quick glance at the desk told me he was filling in more job applications. He gave me a rueful smile and reminded me that this was my house, and I didn't have to knock.

When I didn't contradict him as I usually did, he pushed the papers away and leaned towards me as I sat facing him from the other side of the desk.

'Okay, what's wrong?' he asked. 'I know that look. What catastrophe's occurred now?'

Briefly, I told him about our cinema trip and how Florrie had reacted to the film.

'Poor little thing,' he said when I finished. 'Where is she now?'

'Immi's invited her to her room,' I said. 'They're bonding over the kitten.'

He raised an eyebrow. 'That's promising.'

I nodded. 'If you'd just seen her, Brodie. If you'd heard her. Mia told me she wasn't as bad as everyone thought, and I can see that for myself now. Mia's right. She's lost. She feels abandoned. It's horrible, especially when I know I can take some of that pain away from her.'

'You mean, let Mia tell her the truth?'

I nodded. 'Exactly.'

'But you know what Grandpa said. Agnes—'

'This isn't about Agnes,' I told him. 'And I'm sorry but it isn't about Lawrie either. This is about a little girl who was separated from her family and died believing they didn't care about her. She deserves to know that's not true.'

'You're really going to do this then?' Brodie tapped his pen on the desk, a worried expression on his face. 'You're going to tackle Agnes?'

'You think I'm wrong?'

He considered for a moment then shook his head. 'No. I'd do the same in your position. One thing, though, Callie. Remember what I said before. Mother to mother. Don't go charging in there all guns blazing. You need to get Agnes onside, and once that's done, Grandpa won't stand in your way.'

I nodded. 'Okay. Wish me luck.'

'Want me to come with you?'

'There wouldn't be much point, would there? You can't see or hear her.'

'But I can hold your hand. Moral support,' he added hastily.

I managed a smile. 'Thanks, Brodie. I'll do this myself. You get on with...' I nodded at the applications, my heart sinking as I realised any one of those could result in him receiving an offer of a job. 'With those,' I finished lamely.

I found Aubrey first and he enquired how the cinema trip went and where Florrie had got to.

When I told him she and Immi were playing with the kitten, his face lit up.

'Really? A breakthrough at last! Splendid. Agnes will be... Er, she'll be pleased, I'm sure.'

'Where is Agnes?' I asked him. 'I'd really like to talk to her.'

His brow furrowed. 'Is everything all right?'

I hesitated. I'd planned to talk to Agnes alone, but thinking about it, that wouldn't be fair. It seemed to me that Aubrey had been pushed out of too many decisions in this house, and he was, after all, as much Florrie's father as Agnes was her mother.

'Actually, Aubrey, no it isn't. I wonder if I could have a word with you. With both of you.'

'Of course. Of course.' He looked deeply worried but was ever the gentleman. 'I believe she's in the schoolroom.'

'The schoolroom?'

He cleared his throat. 'She, er, wanted to see what sort of things Florence is learning.'

Of course she did. Still, I was the same with Immi so I couldn't blame her for that. Aubrey led me to the schoolroom, where Agnes was sitting at one of the desks studying what Immi had written on the blackboard.

'Mr Wyndham, I was just— oh! Callie!' She looked rather discomfited to see me. 'I was just, er, looking at Immi's handiwork,' she said, waving a hand at the board. 'Very good. Beautiful handwriting. Not easy to write on that thing, I should imagine.'

'Agnes, dear, Callie has something she'd like to talk to us both about,' Aubrey said, sitting beside her.

'If this is about Florence's behaviour, I don't want to hear it,' Agnes said firmly. 'The lessons have only just started. If Walter Tasker can't deal with her then—'

'I *do* need to talk to you about Florence,' I said. 'And about Mia.'

Agnes's hand flew to her chest. 'What... what about Mia?'

Aubrey frowned. 'Yes, what about Mia?'

He looked completely baffled. It suddenly dawned on me that he was in the dark about the agreement Agnes and Lawrie had made with Mia. Poor Aubrey.

'Do you want to tell him or shall I?' I asked her.

'Tell me what?' Aubrey turned to Agnes. 'Tell me what?'

'I did it for the best, Mr Wyndham,' she spluttered. 'And Lawrie agreed with me. Oh, yes, he did! We both thought it would only upset her, and she'd already been through so much.'

'My dear, what on earth are you talking about?' he asked.

Agnes, though, seemed unable to speak. She gave me a beseeching look, and I realised she simply couldn't find the words to tell Aubrey the truth.

'Okay. I'll tell you,' I said. 'Mia is Florrie's great-niece. The granddaughter of Florrie's baby sister, Janet.'

Aubrey's mouth dropped open.

'I'm sorry but it's true. Mia came here after Janet died five years ago, looking for information on Florrie. Lawrie was very helpful at first, but when Mia spotted Florrie running down the hallway, things got a bit complicated. Right, Agnes?'

He shook his head, dazed. 'Is this true?' he asked her.

'Lawrie told me what had happened,' Agnes said shakily. 'He said Mia wanted to meet Florence. I told him it was out of the question. The past is the past! Well,' she demanded suddenly, 'isn't it? Why rake it up again? You know how Florence feels about Janet. She wouldn't want to meet any descendant of hers anyway.'

'That's not our decision to make, Agnes,' Aubrey said firmly. 'It's Florence's.'

'But Mr Wyndham,' she pleaded, 'think about it! We've given her a good afterlife here. We've been mother and father to her. We've taken care of her for a lot longer than those people did. What good would it do to remind Florence of her past? Of those people? Of that dreadful time? I did what I did for the best. For Florence's sake.'

'Except it's not for the best,' I said gently. 'Not for Florence.'

'What would you know about it?' she demanded. 'You don't know her like I do!'

'Maybe you don't know her as well as you think you do,' I said. 'I had a chat with Florence earlier this evening. It was quite an eye-opener.'

As kindly as I could manage, I told them exactly what Florrie had told Immi and me as she'd crouched by that gate, a pathetic little figure so determined not to cry in front of us or show us how deeply hurt she truly was.

'I... I didn't know,' Agnes whispered. 'She never said. Never gave any indication. I didn't know, Mr Wyndham, I swear it.'

'Perhaps so,' he said, 'but the fact is, we know now. So, what are we going to do about it, eh?'

'But if Mia tells her the truth, if Florence finds out they're related...' Agnes stifled a sob. 'She'll leave us, Mr Wyndham. You do understand that? She'll see Mia as her family, and she'll forget all about us.'

'She can hardly leave,' I pointed out. 'Harling Hall will always be her home, no matter what.'

'But it won't be the same,' Agnes pleaded. 'She'll look to Mia as a mother figure. She'll turn to her for comfort and love. I'll be... no one.'

Aubrey lifted his chin determinedly, though I saw the doubt and anxiety in his eyes. 'Nevertheless, we must do the right thing. Florence has a right to the truth. We must be brave, Agnes. It's the only decent and honourable course of action.' He nodded at me. 'You may tell Mia that she's free to discuss the matter with Florence.'

As Agnes gave a strangled sob, he sighed. 'If you'd only told me from the beginning,' he chided her gently.

'Do you hate me, Mr Wyndham?' she asked in a pathetic voice that didn't sound like Agnes at all.

His eyes widened for a moment, then he clasped her hand tightly. 'Never. I could never hate you, my dear. Why on earth would you think such a thing?'

I left them to it. Something told me they had a lot to talk about, and besides, I had to find Mia.

34

FLORRIE

Florrie wasn't entirely sure what to make of it when that Callie woman told her she was needed in the kitchen. Not that she needed coaxing into the kitchen. Far from it. It was probably her favourite place in the entire house, what with them nice smells coming from the range all the time, and Mia singing softly to herself in quite a decent voice. Nice songs an' all. Songs Florrie remembered her mum singing to her when she was back home.

Even so, choosing to go and sit in the kitchen was entirely different to being summoned there.

'What 'ave I done now?' she asked suspiciously as Callie ushered her down the hall.

'You haven't done anything,' Callie assured her. 'We're just going to have a little talk, that's all.'

Florrie sighed, expecting another lecture. Oh well, Immi had promised that she could go back and play with the kitten later, so that was something to look forward to. She could sit still for a few minutes while Callie moaned about whatever it was she was going to moan about and that would be that.

To her surprise, Mia was sitting at the table. Callie pulled out a chair and indicated to Florrie to sit down next to her, while Callie herself sat at the other side of her. I'm a Florrie sandwich, she thought, to cheer herself up and quell the sudden fear that had made her tummy go all funny.

'What's going on?' she asked, determined not to show how nervous she was feeling, because what was there to be nervous about, really? Callie couldn't grab hold of her. She could escape any time she wanted. And Mia probably didn't even know she was there. Nothing to worry about at all.

'Florrie,' Callie said gently. 'I have some news for you, and it might come as a bit of a shock.'

Florrie's eyes narrowed. 'Oh yeah? What's that then?'

Callie's eyes met Mia's. Mia coughed, then, in a hesitant voice, she said, 'Hello, Florrie.'

Florrie grinned. Party tricks or summat! They'd got it planned between them.

'What is it? A joke?' She winked at Callie. 'Very good.'

'It's no joke, Florrie,' Mia said quietly. 'I can see you. I can hear you. I always could.'

Florrie jumped to her feet and stared at Mia in horror. 'You never can! You're fibbing!'

'I'm really not fibbing,' Mia said, leaving Florrie in no doubt that the woman could hear her.

'What is this? What's going on?' she demanded. 'Who else can see me?'

'It's just me,' Mia assured her. 'Please, sit down, Florrie. There's no need to be afraid.'

'I don't get it,' Florrie said, taking her seat and eyeing Mia suspiciously. 'Are you like 'er then?' She jerked her thumb towards Callie. 'Can you see us all? Since when?'

Mia shook her head. 'I can't see any other ghosts. Only you.

And the reason for that is, I'm related to you. I'm your great-niece, Florrie. You're my great-aunt.'

Florrie stared at her. 'What you on about? 'Ow can I be your great-aunt? You're way older than I am! Oh...'

Her face crumpled as she tried to make sense of what she was hearing. 'Who?' she asked at last, her voice barely a whisper. 'Who's your mum and dad?'

'My mum's name isn't important at the moment. It's my grandma's name you'll recognise. She was called Janet.'

Florrie couldn't take it in. She pictured that squawking, annoying baby, who'd been the bane of her life. That was how Janet had remained in her thoughts and memories. A baby. Now Mia was telling her that Janet was a granny. *Had* been a granny. *Was* called Janet, Mia had said. Not *is*.

She felt a sudden and unexpected grief.

'Janet's passed over?'

'Five years ago,' Mia told her kindly. 'That's when I came here, looking to find out about you. You see, my grandma never forgot about you. She so wanted to know more about you, but she was always too afraid to come here. Afraid of the emotions it would stir.'

'Janet never knew me,' Florrie said cautiously. 'Not really. She was just a baby.'

'But she grew up hearing all about you. You were so loved, Florrie,' Mia told her tearfully, 'and so missed.'

Florrie swallowed. 'I was?'

'Of course. Your mother never got over your loss. And your dad – he was broken. They lost so much in the war, you see. The family never recovered, and my grandma grew up in a terribly sad household.'

'She did? Why? What else happened?'

Mia hesitated and looked at Callie.

'Do you really want to know, Florrie?' Callie asked her. 'We can do this another time, if you like. It's a lot to take in.'

'I want to know it all now!' Florrie begged. 'Please.'

Mia nodded. 'As you wish. Well, your brothers, Henry and Francis, enlisted in 1943. I'm sorry to say that Henry was killed that same year, and Francis died in early 1945.'

'My brothers?' Florrie's hand flew to her mouth. 'I thought – I mean, I always pictured them all together after the war. 'Aving a good time without me. But all this time they were dead and gone! Mum! My poor mum. How did she ever get over that?'

'She didn't. Not really. Three children lost. You can imagine her grief.'

Florrie thought about her poor mum without her three eldest children. She couldn't imagine it. What had she done without Florrie, Francis and Henry to look after? They'd been her life.

'She had Janet, though,' she said at last. 'I expect they were glad of 'er. I expect she was their little princess, what with being all they 'ad left.'

Mia shook her head. 'It wasn't like that. You see, when your father came home from the war, he was a different person. The day he arrived home, Janet was playing in the street. He picked her up and cuddled her, but she screamed blue murder. She was four years old, and she'd never seen him before. She had no idea he was her father. It set the pattern, unfortunately. He tried, but she wasn't you. He simply didn't take to her.'

Florrie gasped. 'But that ain't fair! She couldn't 'elp it if she didn't know who 'e was!'

'No, but you must understand that your father had been a prisoner of war for a long time. He'd suffered a great deal. More than you or I could ever imagine. He was changed. When he came home, he struggled to adapt to civilian life. He and your mother were never the same. They were both mired in grief, and Janet grew up in a very sad and oppressive atmosphere.'

Florrie couldn't take it in. She'd imagined Janet being spoilt rotten, but it sounded awful.

'What 'appened to Janet?' she asked eventually.

Mia's face brightened. 'She did very well for herself. Something amazing happened to her. She was talent-spotted by a modelling agent and given a contract. It was the 1960s and Janet became a big name.' She glanced at Callie. 'Have you heard of The Wisp?'

Callie's face brightened so Florrie assumed she had.

'What's a wisp?' she asked curiously.

'Wasn't she one of the supermodels of the sixties? I saw a programme about them once. Twiggy, The Shrimp, and The Wisp. I can't remember...' Callie's voice trailed off. 'Oh. It was a tribute programme because one of them had passed away.'

Mia nodded. 'Five years ago. My grandma.'

'I'm so sorry,' Callie said. 'Hey, wait a minute! I saw her photo in the boutique down Churchside! There was a big display of sixties' icons, and she was one of them!'

'That's right,' Mia said, smiling. 'I'll take you to see her photo if you like, Florrie.'

'Blimey,' Florrie said. 'So, she was famous? And her photo was there all the time? I've probably seen it. Just never took no notice.'

'She made a fortune,' Mia told her. 'That's how my mum got such great opportunities to travel, and how she came to marry my dad. They met at a party in Cannes, and they have a fabulous life. But if not for Grandma's hard work, Mum would never have moved in those circles, and she'd never have met my dad.'

Florrie wasn't entirely sure what they were talking about, but she got the gist. Janet had done well for herself. Well, good for her.

'What about Mum and Dad?' she asked. 'What happened to them?'

'Your dad passed in 1973,' Mia told her. 'Your mum six years later. Grandma had bought them a lovely house by then, though. They had a few happy years together in the countryside at the end. She did her best for them, Florrie.'

Florrie nodded, thoughts running wild as she tried to picture the sort of life Janet must have had. She couldn't understand all this talk of shrimps and twigs, and had no idea what a supermodel was, but she grasped the fact that Janet had had a tough childhood. Fancy Dad not taking to her! He'd been so good with Florrie, but Janet had missed out on all that. All them years, growing up with a mum and dad who didn't really care about you cos they were too lost in grief for their other kids. It didn't bear thinking about really.

'Why didn't you tell me before?' she asked as the thought occurred to her. 'You've bin 'ere ages. Why are you only telling me now?'

Mia looked at Callie and Florrie had a feeling there was something they were both reluctant to tell her.

'Go on,' she said. 'I've got a right to know, ain't I?'

'All right,' Callie said. 'I suppose you do. But I want you to try to look at it from Agnes's point of view, okay?'

'What do you mean by that?' Florrie asked suspiciously.

Mia shook her head. 'Oh! I wish I could hold your hand or give you a hug or something! Look, Florrie, the fact is, Agnes didn't want you to know about me. She and Lawrie asked me not to let on to you that I could see you.'

Florrie gasped. 'Agnes did? But why? Why would she do that to me?'

'Because,' Callie said gently, 'as odd as it sounds, she loves you. She was afraid that seeing a member of your family would bring back horrible memories for you. Unsettle you again.'

'And,' Mia added, 'she was afraid you wouldn't want her any more. That she and Aubrey would be pushed aside.'

'Why would she think that?' Florrie asked, confused.

'Maybe,' Callie said gently, 'she's not entirely sure how you feel about them.'

Florrie pursed her lips. 'She should've told me,' she said.

'I know. But it's done now. She did the right thing in the end,' Mia reminded her. 'Are you okay? I know this must be really upsetting for you.'

Florrie got to her feet.

'I'm all right,' she said. 'It's a lot. Too much really. I'll 'ave a good think about it all later.' She gave Mia a brief smile. 'I'm glad, though. I'm glad we're family. I always liked you. I'll bet your cooking tastes smashing.'

Mia smiled. 'I cook a lot of things just for you, because I know you like the smells.'

'You never do!' Florrie grinned. 'Well, would you believe it?' The smile slid from her face, and she said quietly, 'Do you mind if I go now? I want... I want to go.'

Mia and Callie assured her that she was free to go and that if she needed them, she knew where to find them.

Florrie left them behind and headed slowly into the hallway, deep in thought. She could hardly believe what had just happened. She'd been so envious of her siblings – of Henry and Francis, who'd been accepted by Uncle Vic while she'd been rejected. And of Janet. Precious Baby Janet who took up so much of her mum's time and energy. Yet Henry and Francis hadn't made it through the war, and Janet hadn't received all the love and attention she should have. Not like her. Her mum and dad had loved her.

And then...

She stood at the bottom of the stairs, remembering. Remembering that day when she'd tumbled down them. Remembering the confusion, the sheer panic when she'd seen herself lying there, crumpled and broken. The memory of it still made her shudder. How she'd screamed! And no one heard her. No one saw her. A terrified little girl who didn't understand what had happened to her.

But then a man had come running down the stairs. He'd put his arms around her. He'd held her tightly to him and murmured soothing words to her as he'd carried her back to the landing, where a woman had been waiting for them. They'd stroked her hair and told her everything was going to be all right. They'd taken her to a room and laid her on a sofa and told her she didn't have to be afraid; they would look after her. Always.

And they had.

She looked up. Agnes and Aubrey were standing at the top of the stairs. They were holding hands, and she could see their anxious expressions from here. All that love they'd given her, ever since the day she'd fallen down these very stairs. All the hugs and comfort. All the tenderness and understanding.

She'd envied Janet, but now she saw that she'd been the lucky one, and she wouldn't exchange places with Janet for all the tea in China.

With a sob, she ran up the stairs, as fast as her slightly-too-big wellies would allow, and threw herself into the waiting arms of her mum and dad.

Because they *were* her mum and dad. And she thought the blinkin' world of 'em.

35

The hall was full of boxes and the cleaners weren't happy about it.

'Trip hazard, that's what they are,' Angela grumbled. 'You ought to be careful cos if any of us have a fall, you'll be sued. Cost you a packet, that will.'

'I don't know why you're having a go at me,' I said indignantly. 'They're not my boxes. They're Lawrie's and Brodie's, remember?'

'Ah, but it's your house,' Angela said craftily. 'You're the boss. The buck stops with you.'

'Oh, you've finally realised that, have you?' I folded my arms. 'Amazing how you accept that fact when it suits you.'

Angela laughed. 'Oh, we accepted you ages ago, lovey. Don't expect us to start fawning over you now, though. That's not our style.'

'I wouldn't dream of it,' I said. Seeing the twinkle in her eyes, I laughed too. 'I'll speak to Brodie. See if we can move these boxes into another room until the removal van comes.'

She gave me a sideways look. 'He's definitely going then?

Thought maybe he'd changed his mind. That he'd decided there were reasons to stay here after all.'

My face burned. Bloody Bonnie and her big mouth! 'It's all arranged. He's got a house in Devon waiting for him and... and three interviews lined up.'

'All systems go then,' she said. 'Ah, well. It'll be a shame when they leave. I'll miss the pair of them. Won't be the same round here without the Davenports. No offence, lovey.'

'None taken.'

I headed into the study, all too aware that I agreed entirely with Angela. It wouldn't be the same without the Davenports. Not at all.

I'd been taken aback when Brodie told me about the interviews the previous evening at dinner.

'Three of them,' he'd said. 'Great, eh? Surely even I will manage to get a job from one of them.'

'I'm sure you'll be offered all three,' I'd said. 'They'd be lucky to have you.'

'Ha. Yeah.' He'd sounded offhand. Not as thrilled as I'd expected. Then again, I supposed leaving Rowan Vale was going to be such a wrench that even landing a new job and having a new home in beautiful Devon wasn't going to make up for it.

I couldn't deny that his news had hit me like a punch in the stomach. This was real. He was actually going. I'd known it was coming of course, but it had always been at some point in the future. One day. Later.

But now we were at the end of June and there was no more putting it off. Lawrie and Brodie had packed up their personal possessions and booked a removal van.

'Just a self-drive transit,' Brodie had explained. 'It's not like we've got furniture to take with us or anything. I can load it myself.'

'I'll help,' I'd said, then cursed inwardly. It sounded like I couldn't wait to see him off the premises. 'If you like,' I'd added lamely.

He bit his lip, considering. 'I'll manage,' he'd said in the end and the subject was closed.

Feeling wretched, I picked up the letter I'd received that morning from Mr Eldridge. An old-fashioned solicitor, he liked to put things in writing and post them, rather than ping me an email like anyone else under retirement age. The letter had informed me that he'd interviewed suitable candidates for the position of estate accountant and that he'd shortlisted five of them. He felt I needed to sit in on the final interviews, since I would be working closely with the person I eventually employed.

I didn't see why. I'd had almost nothing to do with the accounts since I arrived here. Brodie dealt with all that, and he understood that figures and spreadsheets just weren't my thing. What if the new accountant didn't get that? What if he or she kept pestering me about it all?

'Penny for them?'

I looked up, my heart fluttering as it always did when Brodie entered the room.

'Not worth a penny,' I told him glumly. 'It's this letter from Mr Eldridge. Here, read it.'

He sat down opposite me, and I handed the letter to him. After a moment he said, 'Well, that's a good thing, isn't it? You need a new accountant.'

'But I don't want to be involved in any of that stuff!' I protested. My heart thudded at the thought of what I might be expected to do in future. I wasn't up to this. I couldn't manage without Brodie. I waved a bundle of papers around, increasingly agitated. 'See, he's sent me CVs to look at! What do I care about any of this?'

'It's your job, Callie,' he said quietly. 'The estate is your responsibility.'

'Lawrie doesn't deal with any of it,' I pointed out.

'Well, no, but he's got...' His voice trailed off.

Yeah. He's got you.

'It's not just the accounts either,' I said, increasingly panicked. 'What about all the other stuff you do around the estate?'

'You don't have to worry. There are people who work in the village that can take over the things I did.'

'Then why did you do them?' I asked resentfully. 'You do realise you've made yourself indispensable? Everyone looks to you for advice. Do you have any idea how many times I've heard, "Have you run this past Brodie?" or "Oh, it's all sorted. Check with Brodie. He'll tell you." It's so frustrating!'

'I had no idea I was such a pain in the arse,' he said, grinning.

'Well, why did you anyway?' I asked. 'Make yourself indispensable? You'd already got the job of estate accountant. Surely that's enough for anyone? Why do all that extra stuff when you could have passed it to other people?'

'Honestly?'

'Honestly.'

'Okay.' He sighed. 'I suppose, if you must know, I was trying to prove myself to everyone.'

I frowned. 'Why?'

'Think about it,' he said heavily. 'When it became obvious Dad didn't have the gift, it was all reliant on me. Everyone hoped I'd inherited it. But then it was clear I hadn't, and we all knew what that meant. Grandpa was devastated and I felt like I'd let everyone down. Let him down most of all.' He ran a hand through his hair. 'And not just him. The entire estate. All the villagers. All the ghosts I can't even see. They wanted some continuity and security, but I couldn't offer them that. I felt terrible, and so ashamed.'

'Why on earth would you be ashamed?' I gasped. 'It's not your fault. It's just one of those things.'

'Like seeing ghosts is in your world. You know what it's like when you're different. Except, in my family, *not* being able to see ghosts is a problem, whereas in yours, it's the other way around. I felt as if I needed to prove my worth in some other way, and the only thing I could think of was to make myself indispensable. I wanted – I needed – people to rely on me. To say, "That Brodie, he might not have the gift, but we'd be lost without him". Oh, I know! I know it's stupid. And as it turns out it was incredibly selfish of me, too, because now people do rely on me and I'm leaving. And all this will fall on your shoulders. And I'm sorry.'

He looked so miserable that I couldn't help myself. I reached for his hand and squeezed it.

'While we're being honest, there's something I should probably have told you and Lawrie before I took over this place.'

He raised an eyebrow. 'Oh? What's that?'

I took a deep breath, my pulse racing as I prepared to humiliate myself in front of him. 'The fact is... I'm dyslexic,' I said hurriedly.

There was silence for a moment then Brodie said, 'Ah!'

'What do you mean, *ah*?' I asked indignantly.

'Nothing bad,' he assured me. 'Just it's starting to make sense now. Why you needed an *Idiot's Guide*, and why you're so reluctant to do anything that involves any kind of reading and writing. You should have told us, Callie. Why didn't you?'

'Well, why do you think?' I cried. 'It's humiliating. I struggle to read and write. I mean, I can do it, but it takes me ages, it's a real effort and I sometimes get it all mixed up. I feel so stupid. I'm ashamed.'

He studied me then said slowly, '"Why on earth would you be ashamed? It's not your fault. It's just one of those things."'

'Ooh,' I said, narrowing my eyes. 'Throwing my own words back at me. Sneaky.'

He smiled. 'Couldn't resist. But it's true. You have no reason to be ashamed. I wish you'd told me earlier, Callie. I could have been much more of a help to you than I have been.'

'You've done enough. Besides, I couldn't face telling you. If you knew how much I struggled at school... As if seeing ghosts wasn't enough for my dad, having a daughter he considered stupid just about put the tin lid on it for him. No wonder he despises me.'

'He's a moron,' Brodie said fiercely. 'He never deserved a wonderful daughter like you. If anyone's a failure, it's him. I think you're amazing!' He shook his head. 'And now I'm adding to your troubles by leaving you in the lurch. I'm so sorry.'

'It's okay.' I was so relieved at how well he'd taken it that I could afford to be generous. 'Like you said, there are other people who can take over some of your jobs. I'll have a think about it. I'm sure I can ask around and figure something out.'

It took all my willpower not to hurl myself across the desk and beg him to unpack those boxes, cancel the van and tell Mr Eldridge to stuff his CVs where the sun didn't shine.

Don't leave me to do all this! I'm going to mess it up! Stop being so stubborn and stay!

But I didn't. He'd made his choice. He already knew I wanted him to stay. I couldn't have made it any clearer really. I just wasn't important enough to him.

'How are things going with the lessons?' he asked at last, after we'd sat in silence for what felt like forever.

I managed a smile. 'Really well. Immi and I went to the library the other day and got some early reading books for John and Robert. Immi's teaching them how to read and she's so patient with them. Walter's very impressed with her.'

'I understand why those lessons were so important to you now. And Florence? How's she doing?'

'Still plays up now and then when she's bored,' I said, 'but she told Immi she's enjoying the classes so I'm not too worried. It's funny, the two girls are getting on famously, and when you think how much Florrie hated her not so long ago! Even Agnes has warmed to Immi, especially after she announced the new name for her kitten.'

He laughed. 'Ah yes. Brian. Who'd have thought it?'

'She decided it wasn't a big deal, given everything Florrie's been through, and that Brian quite suited him after all.'

'She's a good kid,' he said softly.

'Yeah,' I agreed. 'She is.'

I wished he wouldn't look at me that way. He was making me go all squirmy inside, and the fact that he and Immi got on so well only made all this more difficult. Where was I ever going to find someone like Brodie again?

Well, I wasn't, was I? I already knew that. He was one in a million.

And he was leaving me.

* * *

Lawrie had been increasingly quiet over the last few days, hardly saying anything at mealtimes and retiring to his room earlier and earlier, but it seemed today, he hadn't bothered to leave the room at all, and both Mia and Brodie were concerned.

'I offered to take him a tray up,' Mia said as she served

dessert, 'but he wasn't interested. Mug of Ovaltine. That's all he wanted. I'm so worried about him.'

'Maybe I should go up and try to coax him into eating,' Brodie said anxiously.

'Or maybe,' I said heavily, '*I* should. There are things we need to talk about anyway. I need to put this right.'

Brodie and Mia exchanged glances.

'Are you sure?' Brodie asked.

I wasn't sure at all, but I had to do something. Lawrie and I had started off so well and, despite everything, I still really liked and admired him. I hated the way things had deteriorated between us.

When I tapped gently at his door a few moments later, it was Agnes who called me to come in. She was sitting on his bed, watching fondly as he sipped his Ovaltine. I wondered how many times that scene had played out in the past.

'I shall leave you to it, Lawrie,' she said, nodding at me as she glided past, giving me a look of sympathy that quite unnerved me.

He looked older than ever, and so tired. Like Mia, I felt terribly worried about him. He was getting on, after all, and this stress couldn't be doing him good. Lawrie looked so depressed, and as I was at least partly responsible for this, I had to fix it.

'What can I do for you, Callie?' he asked wearily as I pulled up a chair and sat close to the bed.

'We missed you at dinner,' I told him. 'Aren't you feeling well?'

'What I'm feeling,' he said, putting his mug on the bedside table, 'is my age. I think it's finally caught up with me. I suppose it was inevitable.'

'Rubbish, you've got lots of years left in you yet.'

He lifted his eyebrows, and I shifted uncomfortably. 'Lawrie, is this because of me? I know I've upset you and I'm truly sorry. I never meant to, really I didn't.'

He held up his hand. 'You've done nothing wrong, Callie. This situation was never going to be easy for any of us. I'm amazed how well you've coped with the changes. Far better than I have, it seems. You know, I've been sitting here thinking about the way I've behaved over the last few weeks, and I've concluded that I've been a foolish old man.'

'Don't say that,' I said. 'It's not true.'

'Well, I've certainly behaved like one,' he said. 'Even Agnes has just given me a bit of a lecture, and if Agnes thinks I've been silly, who am I to argue?'

I laughed. 'Well, no one's perfect. Even Agnes.'

'She speaks very highly of you, Callie,' he said, suddenly serious. 'She was so afraid that you'd destroy her relationship with Florence, but in fact, it's stronger than ever. You were right. Florence did need to hear the truth. I was wrong to prevent Mia from telling it to her. I behaved badly and I'm deeply sorry. I shall be apologising to both Florence and Mia forthwith.'

'I'm just glad it worked out,' I told him. 'For my sake as much as anything. Agnes would have made my life a misery if it hadn't.'

'You haven't seen the best of Agnes. She's a good woman with a big heart. You wait and see.'

'Well,' I said, 'Aubrey must see something in her, mustn't he? And Florrie clearly loves her – even if it took her a while to realise it.'

His eyes twinkled. 'Agnes says she tried to get Florence to call them Mama and Papa, but the child wasn't having it. They've compromised on Mother and Poppa. Agnes wanted her to call Aubrey Father, but she stubbornly insisted she preferred Poppa, and Aubrey is absolutely delighted.' He sighed with pleasure. 'It does my heart good to see them so happy.'

'She's doing very well in her lessons, too,' I told him. 'As are John and Robert. Immi's teaching them to read when she can. She's been helping at the weekend but when the summer holidays start, she'll be there every day. Not my idea,' I added hastily, in case he thought I was a proper tyrant. 'It's all her. She's happy to help them and Walter really appreciates having someone to turn the pages of the books and write on the blackboard for him.'

'Something else I tried to veto,' he said regretfully. 'I was wrong about that too, wasn't I? You said what Florence needed was routine and discipline and you were clearly right.'

'I was only partly right,' I said. 'She didn't just need those. She needed lots of love and comfort too. The lessons are doing her good, but I think realising how loved she was all along – by her own family and by Agnes and Aubrey – has made all the difference.'

'That's a good point. Either way, if I'd had my way, Florence would have missed out. Stupid old man that I am. I'm very glad that the children are having lessons. I'm sure it will do them all the world of good. John and Robert must be so much happier now this business with Peter has been sorted out.'

'I think Peter's pretty relieved, too,' I said. 'Or should I say, Pillory Pete.'

'Pillory Pete!' He chuckled. 'I don't know. Those children! You know, I might pop along to the one of the lessons and see how they're all doing. What do you think?'

'I think that would be a great idea,' I said. 'I'm sure Walter would be over the moon to have you there so he can show off his excellent teaching.'

'I'm sure he would. I wonder what quote he'll throw at me to

Kindred Spirits at Harling Hall

demonstrate his pleasure?' he mused. 'Maybe I will then. I'm running out of time, after all.'

'I wish you'd change your mind and stay,' I said. 'I really don't want you to go.'

'You don't need me here, Callie,' he said. 'You've proved yourself a worthy successor to the Davenports. It's your time now and you're going to be brilliant. You already are brilliant. I'm so glad you walked into the Hall that day to complain about Bill and Ronnie.'

'And Florrie,' I reminded him. 'You can't forget her.'

'Never. I'll never forget her.' He gazed wistfully out of the window. 'I'll never forget any of them.'

I reached for his hand. 'Lawrie...'

'Now, Callie,' he said briskly. 'About Brodie.'

My face began to burn, and I dropped my hand. 'What about him?'

'I understand that your relationship has, er, warmed up shall we say?'

How on earth did he know that?

'Has he said something?'

He smiled. 'Brodie? He would never be so indiscreet.'

'Then how...?' I scowled. 'Ah. Bonnie.'

'Indeed. I have eyes and ears everywhere, Callie. Never forget it.' He chuckled which made me feel a bit better. At least he wasn't outraged or devastated.

'It's nothing,' I said. 'Honestly. It was a kiss. Just a silly kiss. But we both know the score. It can't work and that's that.'

'Can't it?' He frowned. 'Why not?'

'You know why not! Brodie's going away with you. He's got job interviews in bloody Devon. Hardly seems like he's planning a long-term future with me, does it?'

'Have you asked him to stay?'

'Well... No. There'd be no point,' I said hurriedly. 'He'd never leave you and you won't stay, so that's that.'

'We're not joined at the hip,' he told me sternly. 'Perhaps if you'd just ask him, he'd surprise you.'

I shook my head. 'He wouldn't stay if you were going. He's devoted to you. You either both stay, or you both go. Simple as that.'

'Are you trying emotional blackmail, Callie?'

'Not at all. I'm just stating the facts as I see them,' I said glumly. 'I like Brodie a lot. And to be honest, I think he really likes me too. But he *loves* you, and that's the difference. We're both grown-ups and we can deal with this. Don't worry about it.'

'Brodie might be a professional man,' he said, 'but he's also a gentle, sensitive soul. When he gives his heart, it will be for good. You know, you two could be good for each other. A team. I... I never told you about my parents, did I?'

I blushed, wondering if I should inform him that Millie hadn't been so discreet. I decided honesty wasn't always the best possibility. 'No. What about them?'

'This is very difficult for me. My father was devoted to this estate. It was everything to him. I suppose, looking back, it must have been quite lonely for my mother. She – well, let's just say she found solace elsewhere. It was a dreadful shock when I found out the truth about their marriage, yet how could I blame her? My father certainly didn't. In fact, it seemed that as long as he was free to continue focusing on the estate, he didn't really care.'

He shook his head sadly. 'I always swore I would never be so blind. So selfish. When I married Jacqueline – Brodie's grandmother – I thought I would be the perfect husband. Everything my father wasn't. Looking back, it's hard for me to see when that changed, and to admit that I ended up just as selfish and obsessed as my father.'

'You mean, Jacqueline…'

'Oh no! No, she would never betray me that way. She loved me dearly, and I loved her. But she must have felt so alone so much of the time, and that was my fault. I only saw the truth after she died, more than a decade ago now, and I have so many regrets. You and Brodie wouldn't have that problem. You both know and love this estate and neither one of you would feel neglected.' He gave me a hopeful look. 'You know, if you spoke to him, if you asked him to stay, I'm sure he would. Maybe he's just waiting for you to ask.'

But Brodie already knew I wanted him to stay. What more could I do? Issue a written invitation? Lawrie had it all wrong. Brodie hadn't given me his heart at all, let alone for good.

'It was just a kiss, Lawrie,' I repeated, not quite meeting his gaze. 'Nothing to get so upset about. Now, are you going to come downstairs for breakfast tomorrow, or do I have to sit by your bedside nagging you at every meal from now on?'

He smiled. 'I'll be there,' he promised.

I got up to leave and he reached for my hand. 'I'm glad we're friends again, Callie.'

Somehow, I managed to swallow down the lump in my throat. 'Always, Lawrie.'

36

Later that evening, Brodie very kindly helped me go through the CVs that Mr Eldridge had sent.

It had been an emotional day as he'd brought down the last of the boxes from upstairs and announced that everything was now packed and ready to go, other than a few remaining clothes that he'd need before leaving.

I'd barely eaten a thing at dinner and had escaped to the study to hide how upset I was feeling, giving the CVs as an excuse, so it had been a bit of a shock when Brodie followed me and offered to help. I had to pretend to be interested in the qualifications and previous jobs of five total strangers, which wasn't easy when all I wanted to do was gaze at this man and plead with him to stay.

'He'd be my choice,' he told me, jabbing his finger at one of the papers, clearly oblivious to my yearning looks. 'Well qualified and he has experience working for a country house estate, which means he'll probably understand the ins and outs of this place better than most.'

'Ghosts and all?' I asked. 'Just how am I supposed to explain all that to him?'

'I shouldn't think there'd be any need,' he said. 'Look, he only lives in Cirencester, which is probably partly why Mr Eldridge considers him so suitable. He wouldn't need to stay in the village if things cropped up and he needed to speak to you in person. He'd be dealing with the financial side of things, that's all. No need for him to know about the other side of this place.'

'I suppose not. I'll give it some thought.'

'I think he's probably the best of the bunch, although she sounds pretty good, too,' he added, showing me another CV. 'If it were me, I'd be looking closely at these two. If they perform well in the interview, obviously.'

'And if I click with them,' I said.

'Click with them?'

'You know. I have to get on with them. They have to "get" me.'

'Do they? It's a business arrangement, that's all.'

'Oh, Brodie! I can't hire someone I don't feel I could be friends with. Not that I'd be friends with them probably, but the potential has to be there.'

'Really?' He sounded baffled. 'Good job you didn't have to interview me then. That first day we met, I hardly made a good impression, did I?'

'No, you didn't.' I smiled, remembering how I'd considered him to be a complete arse. 'But I did think you were gorgeous.'

His eyebrows shot up. 'You did?'

'Yeah...' I shrugged. 'Don't get too carried away. I decided good looks didn't make up for how miserable and rude you were.'

'I was *very* miserable and rude,' he agreed.

'I guess you had good reason.'

'I guess. Even so.'

We were both quiet for a moment then he said, 'I've just been in to see Grandpa. I'm glad you two have sorted things out.'

'Me too. Did he tell you he's going to sit in on the kids' lessons tomorrow while you're...'

While you're picking up the van that's going to take you away from me.

'He did.' He gave me a wry grin. 'Walter will be deeply honoured, I'm sure.'

'Oh, I'm sure I'll hear all about it.'

'You know, while we're on the subject of lessons,' he said cautiously, 'I've had a few thoughts about that myself.'

'Oh? Such as?'

'Well, I was thinking that some of the other ghosts might be able to help teach the kids,' he said. 'Think about it. Who knows more about the war than Mrs Herron? Then there's the Great War, which I'm sure Ronnie and Bill will be happy to talk about.'

I pulled a face. 'You haven't met Ronnie and Bill. It would turn into a punch-up with those two.'

He laughed. 'Well, anyway... Then there's Aubrey. He could tell them all about life in Victorian times, and Agnes could talk about the Georgian and Regency period.'

'And Silas Alexander could give them religious instruction,' I said with a giggle.

His face fell. 'You think it's a stupid idea?'

'Not at all. I think it sounds amazing. Not the Silas bit,' I added hastily. 'I was also wondering if some of the adult ghosts might like to have lessons too. Why not? Lots of adults go to evening classes, so why not ghosts? And maybe some of them would like to learn to read. I'm sure some of the older ones never got the chance when they were alive.'

'Great idea,' he said. 'Of course, you and Immi would be in big demand, turning pages and so on.'

'But some of the ghosts have relatives who can see them,' I pointed out. 'Like Mia, for example. If we can co-ordinate it, we might be able to get them to help each other. You know, I really want them to have more to do. I was thinking of asking about special showings of their favourite films at the cinema. And maybe holding a tea dance for them somewhere in the village once a week? Just something where they can all get together and enjoy themselves,' I said, thinking of Harmony and Quintus and the other ghosts who must live such lonely afterlives. 'Do you think they'd be interested?'

'You can only ask, but I think most of them would love it,' he said, his eyes shining.

'And not just for the ghosts,' I added. 'Maybe we could arrange a social gathering in the village for the tenants too. Or maybe they'd like to come along to the tea dance or the film showings?'

'Great ideas,' he said. 'Can I venture something, too?'

'Of course.'

'The model village,' he said. 'I honestly think it's wasted shut away at Honeywell House like that.'

'So do I!' I cried. 'I'd love to see it open to the public. The villagers and the tourists would love it. I wonder if I should have a word with Jack and Clara? There must be some way we can come to an arrangement, so visitors don't encroach on their privacy. Maybe Jack would sell it to the estate?'

'Or maybe he and Clara could run it themselves? Extra income for them, after all.'

'We could surely make another entrance to the model village, so they didn't have to go through the courtyard,' I mused.

'And Jack could make models of the newer ghosts,' Brodie said eagerly. 'So no one feels left out. I'm sure he'd be up for that. We could help them financially to get it off the ground if that's what they want to do.' The sparkle left his eyes suddenly. 'I mean, *you* could. I'm sure you'll make a success of this, Callie. I really am.'

The excitement that had been fizzing away in the pit of my stomach dissolved, leaving me flat and suddenly depressed. I collected up the papers and shoved them in the top drawer of the desk.

'All done?' he asked, all brisk and businesslike again.

'Yeah. I think I'll look at them again tomorrow. Your last day here,' I said, as if either of us needed reminding.

'I know.'

'I'll... I'll miss you, Brodie,' I said quietly.

He gazed across the desk at me, those bright-blue eyes looking rather sad and wistful. 'I'll miss you too.'

Then why are you leaving me?

I waited, wondering if he was going to kiss me again, but he didn't. Instead, he got to his feet, rather wearily, and said, 'It's been a long day. I think I'll get an early night. Lots to do tomorrow.'

'Oh yes, me too. Lots to do, I mean. Well, goodnight.'

'Goodnight, Callie.'

* * *

Two hours later, I was still wide awake and lying in bed in the darkness, staring up at the ceiling, my mind whirling with thoughts and ideas.

Everything Brodie had suggested sounded amazing to me, and as he'd told me his ideas, they'd sparked new ones of my own. This place had so much potential – not just to increase revenue, but to make life (and afterlife) better for the residents. I wanted to bring them together. I never wanted any of them to feel alone or lonely again.

But I couldn't do this by myself, and I didn't want to. The more I thought about it, the more I realised that if I let Brodie leave, *I* was the one who was going to be lonely. Life without him in it would be too miserable to contemplate. Seeing his smile every day had kept me going through my most difficult times here, and the thought of saying goodbye to him broke my heart.

I'd been lying when I'd told Lawrie that my relationship with Brodie amounted to nothing more than a kiss. It was so much more than that, and I'd never be able to live with myself if I didn't tell him so.

I sat up and flicked on the bedside lamp, my stomach churning with nerves. But what if I told him how I felt, and he didn't want to know? What if he left anyway? How would I deal with that?

After all, he had a lovely house in Devon waiting for him. I'd seen the photos, and it looked stunning. And then he had those interviews lined up. Mia had told me only that afternoon that they were with excellent companies, and she was sure they'd snap Brodie up. What could I offer him in exchange for that?

And then a thought entered my head, and I pulled up the duvet, snuggling under it as I allowed the thought to grow. Of course! It was perfect. He couldn't possibly say no to that.

Feeling a new hope, I flicked off the bedside lamp and settled down to sleep. It was going to be okay after all.

* * *

The following morning, I went in search of Brodie. I found him in the garden at the back of the house, cutting some roses for Mia who wanted to display them in the hallway. I could have waited for him to return to the house, but with so many people coming and going already, and Walter due to arrive very soon with the boys, I thought the peace and quiet of the garden would be the perfect place to put the proposition to him.

'They're lovely,' I told him, nodding at the perfect, pale-pink blooms in his hands.

'Aren't they? I thought I'd offer to cut them for Mia. Take my mind off things. I'm picking up the van in an hour.'

'I know,' I said. 'But does it have to be that way?'

'What do you mean?' He snipped off another rose before turning to face me.

'Brodie,' I said. 'I don't want you to leave. Please change your mind.'

Was it my imagination or did his face light up? There was a definite hint of a smile on his lips, and a sudden sparkle in those gorgeous, blue eyes.

'Callie, I don't know what to say,' he told me.

'But you must surely have realised that I didn't want you to go?' I said, surprised.

'I... I hoped... but you never said, and I'd already made my feelings clear, and I didn't know what else...'

'Then you'll stay?' I beamed at him. 'Please just say it.'

He seemed lost for words, though I thought it was in a good way. He certainly seemed to be happier than he'd been a few moments ago anyway. Time to nudge him over the edge and seal the deal.

'I can't lose you,' I said firmly. 'This place can't lose you.' I waved my arm around, as if taking in the entirety of the estate in one swoop. 'And that's why I've come up with an offer I don't think you'll be able to refuse. Brodie, will you...'

I closed my eyes. *Be brave. Be brave.*

'Brodie, will you be my estate manager?'

I opened one eye and peered at him. He was still smiling but now it wasn't quite reaching his eyes. I saw him swallow.

'Estate manager?'

'Yes! You're far too good to just be the accountant, and besides, you work way too hard. I was thinking about all the ideas you'd had last night, and it occurred to me that this would be the perfect solution. We could still hire one of Mr Eldridge's accountants, to take the load off your shoulders, and you could concentrate on the business side of the estate. Obviously, the accountant would be answerable to you, not me, and I'd give you a pay rise. What do you say?'

He shook his head. 'I... I don't know *what* to say.'

My heart thudded. He couldn't possibly turn this down, could he? Surely even that pretty house in Devon wasn't enough to compete with such a good job offer?

'Last night,' I said, 'when we were coming up with ideas for the estate, we agreed on everything. We bounced off each other, didn't we? You can't deny we made a good team. Can you?'

'No,' he said. 'I don't deny that.'

'Well then! Oh, come on, Brodie! I need you. Please stay. I can't do this without you.'

Brodie stared down at the roses in his hands. I noticed his finger was bleeding.

'The thorn,' I said. 'Didn't you feel it prick you?'

'No... No, I didn't.'

He sounded numb, as if nothing was making sense to him. All my hope and optimism began to drain away as if someone had pulled the plug on my plans for the future. Our future.

It wasn't enough. Even the prospect of promotion and more money – it wasn't enough to make him stay with me. But then, how could it be? He would never stay here without Lawrie. I'd been such an idiot.

'It doesn't matter,' I said dully. 'I can see you're not interested.'

Brodie shoved the secateurs in his pocket and carefully bundled the roses together. 'It's all sorted,' he said. 'Like I said, I'm picking up the van in an hour. By tomorrow afternoon, I'll be in Devon. I've got my first job interview on Monday, so...'

'Yeah. Of course. Well, it was worth a shot,' I said, 'but don't worry about it. Maybe Mr Eldridge can help me find an estate manager. I'm sure they're not *that* hard to come by.'

Trying desperately not to reveal how hurt I was, I spun away and headed back to the house. That would teach me to wear my heart on my sleeve, I thought bitterly. Well, lesson learned. Never again.

37

The following morning dawned bright and sunny, which I thought deeply unfair. Surely it should have been pouring with rain? If nothing else, it would have ensured that Brodie Davenport got soaked while he loaded up his bloody van.

There was a tap on the door and Mia popped her head round, her eyes widening as she saw me standing fully dressed by the window.

'Immi says you're not coming down for breakfast. I thought you must be ill, but you look okay to me.'

'I'm not ill,' I said. 'Just felt like having coffee in my room if that's okay.'

She pushed open the door and walked in.

'Come in, why don't you?' I grumbled, turning back to stare out of the window at the drive where, in approximately one hour, Brodie would be loading up the rental van with all his and Lawrie's belongings.

'You've got to come downstairs,' she said, sounding shocked. 'It's Lawrie's and Brodie's last day! Our last chance to have breakfast all together. Even the Wyndhams are sitting at the table with us. Agnes is in floods. Poor Aubrey's doing his best stiff-upper-lip routine, but you can bet he's almost as devastated as she is.'

'How do you know?' I asked automatically before realising. 'Oh, of course, Florrie's told you.'

'Yes. She's rather upset too. As am I.'

I turned round, feeling suddenly ashamed. Mia was clearly sad about the Davenports leaving and here she was, trying to cajole me into having breakfast downstairs when she should have been spending every precious moment with them.

'I'm sorry,' I said. 'I suppose I'll come down then. Are you having breakfast with us for a change?'

'Yes. You know, I only preferred eating in the kitchen because Florrie often joined me there,' she said, nudging me. 'She liked the smell of my cooking, and I liked her sitting close by, even though she wasn't aware I could see her.'

'That makes sense,' I said. 'All that time, you could have been in the dining room with us, though, instead of eating alone. The things we do for love, eh?' I could hardly keep the bitterness from my voice.

'Callie is there something wrong?' she asked anxiously. 'You're not yourself today.' She hesitated, then put her arm around me. 'It's Brodie, isn't it? Has something happened between you?'

'Why should this be about Brodie?' I demanded.

She raised her eyebrows. 'I'm not blind,' she said. 'I hold my hands up. I hoped something would happen between you, and yes, I heard all about it from Bonnie. Fevered kisses and all that stuff. She swears she could hear you two sizzling from the other side of that door.'

'Bloody Bonnie!' I said furiously. 'Is there anyone she hasn't told?'

'I'm sure there are a few people she hasn't met yet,' she said with a giggle. 'Oh Callie, don't look like that! If you want Brodie to stay, why don't you just ask him?'

'Oh, what a brilliant idea!' I gave her a wide, fake smile. 'Why didn't I think of that?'

'You mean, you've already asked him? And he said *no*?' she said incredulously. 'I don't believe it.'

'Believe it or not, he turned me down flat. Something about the house in Devon and his job interviews.'

She shook her head. 'That doesn't make sense. He wouldn't put those things above you.'

'You mean the estate,' I said. 'And he has.'

'I mean you! Oh, Callie.' She sounded almost impatient. 'Surely you know how he feels about you? As if I needed Bonnie to tell me what was happening between you! Those puppy-dog looks he gives you would be almost laughable if they weren't so sweet.'

'You're very much mistaken,' I told her. 'All that's between me and Brodie is a silly kiss. Anyway, I couldn't compete with Lawrie. In the end, I'm a very poor second. And that's okay,' I added hastily. 'Lawrie's his grandfather and he loves him. I get that.'

'But he loves you too,' she said earnestly. 'You have to trust me on this. I simply don't understand why he's turned you down when all he wanted—'

She broke off and I stared at her.

'When all he wanted was what?'

'Nothing,' she said. 'Look, let's go downstairs and have breakfast. It will be getting cold.'

'I'll be down in a minute,' I said. When she gave me a doubtful look, I added, 'Promise.'

She nodded and, rather reluctantly, left the room.

I heard some mumbling and then there was another knock.

'I should just instal a revolving door,' I said crossly, then blushed as Lawrie walked in, leaning heavily on his stick. 'Sorry.'

'That's quite all right,' he said. 'I'm sorry to disturb you but I wanted to have a word with you in private.'

'Okay,' I said, surprised. 'Please, sit down.' I pulled up a chair for him and dropped onto the edge of the bed. 'What can I do for you?'

'Well,' he said, carefully easing himself onto the chair, 'this is rather awkward and somewhat embarrassing. I'm here to ask you a favour, my dear. And to eat humble pie.'

'Ooh, that sounds intriguing.' I smiled. 'What could be so embarrassing?'

Lawrie rubbed his eyes. 'You know, of course, that I sat in on Walter's lesson yesterday?'

'So I heard. How did it go?'

He beamed at me. 'Marvellous. Of course, Walter did show off a little, with me being there, but I expected that. However, I can't deny that he's a good teacher. He was thrilled when I offered to turn the pages for him, and later, while he did some arithmetic with Florence, I gave John and Robert a reading lesson. They're so enjoying it, Callie! You should see their little faces.'

'Immi told me the same thing,' I said. 'She's sitting with them this afternoon after...'

'After we've gone,' he said.

I nodded. Everything came back to that, didn't it? Every conversation. Every thought. Brodie leaving. And Lawrie, too, of course.

'That's what I wanted to speak to you about,' he said slowly. 'I'm... I'm rather embarrassed to ask this of you, Callie, but I was wondering if it would be possible... That is, would you consider... Oh dear.'

'Just say it, Lawrie,' I said gently. 'Whatever it is, if I can help you, I will.'

He nodded and I saw tears gleaming in his eyes. 'I've been such a fool,' he burst out. 'A stubborn, proud fool. Callie, the fact is, I don't want to leave the estate. I love it here, and the thing is, I've finally realised that perhaps there is a place here for me after all. Helping Walter.'

He held up his hand, silencing me before I could speak. 'I promise you, I wouldn't interfere in your work. You are in charge now, Callie, and I fully accept that. But Walter needs me. The children need me. I would have a purpose. A reason to be here. And I realise now that's all I needed. I couldn't stay here doing nothing, my dear. But being in the classroom...'

His voice trailed off and he gave me a pleading look.

'Oh, Lawrie,' I said joyfully, 'I couldn't be happier! Of course you can stay. We'd all love you to stay!' My heart leapt as I realised what this meant. 'Both of you. You and Brodie.'

He shook his head sadly. 'Not Brodie, my dear. I'm afraid his mind is quite made up on this. I spoke to him earlier, you see. Told him how I felt and asked if he would stay with me, but he's not going to change his mind. I must admit, I'm surprised. He loves this place as much as I do. And I'll confess, I'd hoped you and he... Ah, well, none of my business, and as you said, it was just a kiss.'

My heart sank like a stone as I stared at him. Brodie had turned down the chance to stay, even knowing his grandpa wasn't going to leave with him?

So, it *was* the job and the house in Devon? I couldn't even compete with those? Even with everything I'd offered him? Wow, that said it all. How had I got things so wrong?

'I'm sorry to hear that,' I said, swallowing down the lump of grief in my throat. 'Still, it's wonderful that you're going to stay. I'm sure Agnes will be even more delighted than the rest of us.'

'I'm sure she will,' he said, getting to his feet. 'Thank you so much for being so understanding, Callie. Now, shall we go downstairs for breakfast and break the good news to everyone?'

'Of course.'

I stood, too, but turned quickly as I heard the slamming of a door. Looking out of the window, I saw Brodie loading the first of the boxes into the van, watched by a bemused Agnes and Florrie.

Agnes lifted her gaze and stared directly at me, shaking her head slightly. What had I done now? Well, quite frankly I was past caring if I'd offended her.

Nothing really mattered now.

38

For the next hour, Brodie hurried in and out of the house, carrying his belongings to the van before taking Lawrie's things back upstairs for him.

The mood around the breakfast table had lightened immeasurably when Lawrie had revealed he'd decided to stay. Agnes had promptly burst into tears which had caused Florrie to put her arms around her and say, 'There, there, Mother. No need to cry, is there? This is good news, ain't it?'

'*Isn't* it, Florence,' Agnes wailed, patting her arm. 'And yes, my darling, it's very good news.'

'Splendid,' Aubrey agreed. 'Absolutely splendid. Now we just need young Brodie to change his mind and that will be job done.'

'Ah,' Lawrie said sadly, 'I wish it were that easy. For some reason, Brodie seems determined to start over in Devon. It's quite bewildering. I can't imagine why he's still so intent on leaving.'

'Hmm. I think he's barmy, what with 'er offering 'im a new job an' all,' Florrie said, nodding in my direction.

'How on earth did you...' I stared at her in horror. 'Were you spying on me?'

'A new job?' Lawrie asked, surprised. 'What new job is this?'

'Estate manager,' Immi told him.

I gaped at her. 'How did *you* know?'

'Florrie told me,' she said with a shrug.

'And me,' Mia admitted.

'Ahem, and me,' Aubrey said with a sigh. 'I must say, it's bad form to spy on other people, and I have told Florence that, but in this case, she was only doing it because she wants him to stay. We all want him to stay.' He gave me a knowing look. 'Don't we?'

'Well,' I said, feeling about six inches tall, 'now you know. I offered him the job and he didn't want it. Turned me down flat. So now that's sorted... If you'll excuse me.'

I pushed away the mug of cold coffee – the third I'd had that morning while I lingered in the dining room, staying well out of Brodie's way – and ran upstairs, just managing to time my exit so he was outside as I careered through the hallway.

I flung myself on the bed and dug the heels of my hands into my eyes. I would *not* cry. I refused point blank to waste any tears on someone who didn't care about me.

'A good cry might do you good.'

I yelped and sat up, realising Agnes had entered my room and plonked herself on the chair Lawrie had recently vacated.

'Good grief,' I said. 'I might as well take the bloody door off the hinges the way everyone just comes and goes in here.'

She shrugged. 'It wouldn't make any difference to me one way or the other.'

'No,' I said with a sigh. 'I don't suppose it would.'

'Callie, I'm very sorry that Florence was eavesdropping on your conversation with Brodie,' she said sheepishly. 'She shouldn't have done that, as Mr Wyndham rightly pointed out. However, in a way, I'm rather glad she did.'

'Are you? I thought you were a stickler for manners.'

'I am, naturally. But if she hadn't listened, I perhaps wouldn't have understood what's going on, and why young Brodie is so determined to leave.'

I swung my legs off the side of the bed and eyed her dolefully. 'It doesn't take a genius to work it out, does it? He's not interested.'

'Interested?'

I gulped. 'In this place, I mean. In being estate manager. I mean, what more could I have offered him? I thought he loved this estate. I thought being in charge would be everything he'd dreamed of. It seems an accountancy job and a house in Devon mean more. Who knew?'

'Well now you're just being silly,' Agnes said.

'Pardon?'

'You must know that this was never about the house or the estate or any job. This was about you. It always was.'

'You've completely lost me,' I said. 'Unless you mean he'd rather take a job in Devon than stay here with me, in which case thanks, but I'd already figured that out for myself.'

She rolled her eyes. 'You know, the thing I regret more than anything is that I didn't let Mia tell Florence who she really was. Since our little girl found out the truth, she's been so much happier. It's been delightful to see how much lighter she seems. She smiles so much more. She calls me Mother, you know.'

'I know,' I said, trying to smile. 'And she calls Aubrey Poppa.'

Agnes coughed. 'Yes, well, I'm hoping I can cajole her into calling him Father at some point. I mean, really, what sort of word is Poppa? Papa maybe, but Poppa? And yet Mr Wyndham seems quite taken with it so what do I know?' She sighed heavily.

'Anyway, the point is, perhaps we could have had all this happiness so much earlier if I'd just allowed Mia to speak out. But I didn't. And do you know why I didn't?'

'Because you were scared Florrie wouldn't love you as much, and would want to be with Mia more than you,' I said.

Her eyebrows shot up. 'Oh yes, of course, you already know that because I told you.'

'It didn't take much figuring out, to be honest,' I said.

'Oh really? Well, aren't you the clever one? What a pity you can't be as perceptive when it comes to your own life.'

'Agnes,' I said wearily, 'if you've got something to say just say it.'

'You and I are a lot alike,' she said.

My eyebrows shot up even higher than hers had. 'I don't think we are,' I said.

'Don't you? You know little about my life, Callie, but we were both let down by people who should have loved us, and it's left both of us feeling a little bruised and – dare I say it – afraid. I think you, like me, believe yourself unworthy of love, and that if someone better were to come along, those we love would abandon us without a second thought. Am I wrong?'

She wasn't, though it pained me to admit it. '*Okay*,' I said slowly. 'And?'

'My fears made me cling to those I love even tighter. I couldn't bear the thought of Florence turning to Mia, so I refused to give them the opportunity to get to know each other. Instead, I schemed with Lawrie to keep them apart, so I could hold tight to my daughter. By doing so, I made her very unhappy and hurt Mia in the process. I regret that deeply.'

'I know,' I said. 'But it all worked out in the end.'

'You, on the other hand,' she said, nodding vigorously, 'express your fear by pushing people away. Rather than clinging to them too tightly, you act as if they don't really matter to you at all. No wonder young Brodie is so confused.'

'Confused? Agnes, I couldn't have made it any clearer,' I protested.

'Nonsense! Florence told me word for word what occurred between you in the rose garden,' she said. 'You offered him a job, Callie. A job!'

'A very good job! A promotion!'

'Anyone can offer him a job. Can't you see that? You made it very plain to him that you need him. That the estate needs him.'

'And so we do,' I said.

'Yes, but did you make it clear that you also *want* him? That you *love* him? That the reason you want him to stay isn't because you need an estate manager? That it's because he means everything to you, and you can't bear the thought of him walking away.'

'But... but surely...'

Oh. Sweet. Lord.

'Hmm. That's what I thought. There's your explanation, Callie. Brodie doesn't feel wanted. He feels needed but not as a loving partner. As a business partner. If you want him to stay, you need to tell him how you really feel. No more hedging your bets. No more trying to protect that heart of yours. You're a lucky woman. Yours is still beating. Now go and make the most of it!'

'Agnes,' I said, 'I wish I could kiss you.'

She wrinkled her nose. 'The very idea!'

But there was a hint of a smile on her face as I shot out of the bedroom door, fingers tightly crossed for my own happy ever after.

39

Brodie jumped out of the van and slammed the door shut. The sound of it made me wince. It seemed so final. A full stop on the story of us.

Except it couldn't be, could it? Right now, there wasn't really an *us* at all, and I so wanted there to be. If only I could be brave enough.

He turned round and saw me standing on the front steps. He immediately adopted an impassive look, blocking any chance I might have had of judging how he was really feeling. It was almost enough to make me give up before I'd started. That and the fear churning inside me.

What if, no matter what I said, it made no difference?

What if, even after I'd poured my heart out, he said he was leaving?

What if he'd been toying with me, just like Immi's dad?

What if he didn't care about me at all, just like my own?

I stared at him, stricken with terror. My throat felt so tight that I wasn't sure I could say anything, let alone tell him how I felt.

My expression clearly alarmed him, because the impassive look vanished to be replaced by genuine concern.

'Callie? What is it? What's happened?' He hurried towards me, his hand reaching for mine.

I forced down the terror and somehow, my voice managed to squeeze its way past the lump in my throat.

'Do you care?'

He stopped, looking confused. 'What sort of question's that? Of course I care.'

'But do you, though?' I persisted. 'Do you really?'

His eyes narrowed and he put both hands on my shoulders. 'I'm not entirely sure what you're asking me here, but you look bloody terrified, so I'll ask you again, what's happened?'

'What's happened?' I gave a half-laugh. '*What's happened*? What do you think's happened? You're leaving me! That's what's happened!'

He stepped back and tilted my face so I was forced to meet his gaze. 'You've got to have more faith in yourself,' he said roughly. 'I've told you, Mr Eldridge will help you. He's got some good candidates lined up and—'

'Brodie,' I said brokenly, tears welling in my eyes, 'you're not listening to me. I didn't say you're leaving the estate. I said you're leaving *me*!'

For a moment, there was silence as my words finally penetrated his brain. Then there was a weird sound, which I think came from him, and he took my face between his hands, the look in his eyes almost making me crumble with longing.

'Callie... you mean it?'

'Of course I bloody mean it! How could you... how could you even think...'

'But you offered me a job! You said you needed me to be your estate manager.'

'Well of course I did. I do. But how could you not know what I really meant? How could you not understand the code?'

'What bloody code?' he asked, baffled.

'The code that meant, "Here's an offer of a job but really what I'm asking is if you care enough about me to stay with me because I think I'm falling in love with you!"'

'How was I supposed to know that?'

'Well, *I* don't know,' I said, pulling far enough away from him to give him a light thump on the arm. 'But you should have done, okay? Instead, all I got was you banging on about your new house in Devon and your sodding job interviews.'

His eyes were wet with tears, but he was smiling. 'Well, how could you not know what I really meant? Didn't you understand the code? I was really saying, "I can't stay around here if all you want me for is to work on the estate, because it will kill me to be here and not be with you. Because I think I'm falling in love with you too."'

I gazed up at him. 'You do?'

'Oh, Callie,' he said with a sigh. 'Didn't you get all the hints I've been dropping like bricks for the last few weeks?'

'I'm a very insecure person,' I admitted. 'I couldn't quite believe it all meant what I hoped it meant. I so wanted you to stay with me, but I thought – I thought, if I wrapped up the question in a job offer and a pay rise, it might be enough to convince you to stay.'

'I didn't need a job offer. I don't need a fancy title or a pay rise. Hell, I'd rather walk away from this estate and even from Grandpa than stay here knowing you didn't see any future for us. All you had to do was tell me, but you kept pushing me away.'

'But you didn't make it clear enough,' I said. 'I can't read signals unless they're loud, flashing, red ones. I never believe I'm good enough so how was I supposed to know you thought I was?'

He mulled that over for a moment. 'You're right,' he said at last. 'I should have realised.' He stroked my hair and sighed. 'Well, will you please start believing in yourself now? You *are* good enough. You're *more* than good enough. You're bloody incredible, and I really want to get to know you so much better and give us a real chance.'

'Well,' I said, 'that's lovely, but you *will* still take the estate manager's position, won't you?'

He laughed. 'If you insist. But you're right. We'll have to hire another accountant because I don't intend to work every evening. I'm going to have far better things to do with my time.'

The thought of what those things might be made me go all tingly inside. Even so, there was one thing I had to make clear.

'Brodie,' I said hesitantly, 'there's not just you and me in this relationship. Immi. She's never had a father figure in her life because you know what her real father did to her. He abandoned her before she was even born. I can't... I can't risk that again.'

He kissed the top of my head. 'I promise you, Callie, I will never hurt you or Immi. You know I think she's a great kid, and we get on so well already. Hopefully, she'll be okay with all this, but of course we'll tell her together. Or you can tell her. Whatever you think best.'

'We must tell her first. About us, I mean. We'll have to tell everyone that you've changed your mind about going to Devon, but we can't say anything about us until Immi knows. Deal?'

'Of course. I'll follow your lead. All I want is for us to be happy. Believe me?'

The look in those blue eyes was intense and genuine.

I smiled. 'I believe you.'

'Good.'

He glanced round at the van and sighed. 'I guess that means I'd better unpack all my stuff again.'

'I guess it does.'

'Honestly, the amount of time I've wasted this week, packing my stuff, packing Grandpa's stuff...'

'I can imagine.'

'Then *unpacking* Grandpa's stuff. Then loading up the van.'

'Hours and hours.'

'And now I've got to unload it all again and rearrange the drop-off and let Dad know we won't be moving to Devon, and cancel the interviews and phone Mr Eldridge—'

'Brodie?'

'Yes, Callie?'

'Will you just shut up and kiss me?'

There was a sudden intake of breath, then he moved closer.

'Yes, Callie.'

He put his arms around me, and the softness of his mouth on mine melted away the last of my doubts and fears, leaving only joy, and the excitement of a future filled with new possibilities.

You can never really be sure of anything in this life, but sometimes, you have to be brave if you want something badly enough. My heart was telling me that all I wanted right now was the chance to start a whole new journey with Brodie and see where it took us.

With obvious reluctance, he finally pulled away from me. 'Should we go and tell everyone the good news?'

'In a minute,' I said, wondering if he could hear my heart as it thudded in my chest. 'But not just yet. Do you think – if it's not too much trouble – that you could possibly kiss me again?'

His eyes sparkled as he cradled my face in his hands.

'It would be my pleasure,' he assured me. 'In fact, I can't think of anything I'd like more.'

And so he did.

* * *

Immi gently closed the upstairs window and turned to her friend, who was eyeing her knowingly.

'Told you, Imms,' Florrie said. 'I knew we'd get the best view from up 'ere, and that we'd 'ear it all.'

'We shouldn't really have eavesdropped,' Immi admitted. 'Mum's warned me about that before.'

'Oh,' Florrie said airily, 'I get told that all the time. I take no notice. 'Ow else are we supposed to know what's going on around 'ere? No one tells us kids anything.'

'That's true.' Immi stroked Brian as she leaned against the wall, deep in thought.

'So, it looks like your mum's got 'erself a boyfriend then,' Florrie said cautiously.

'Hmm.'

'Are you okay with that?'

Immi thought about it. 'It's going to be a bit weird. It's always been just me and Mum till now.'

'Aw, you can't go wrong with Brodes,' Florrie told her. "E's one of the good ones, ain't 'e? You don't 'ave to worry about your mum cos 'e'll look after 'er.'

'I know,' Immi said, smiling. 'I like Brodie, and I've known for ages that Mum likes him too. I don't know why they took so long to tell each other. I mean, look at that! His van's packed. Talk about cutting it fine.'

'That's grown-ups for you,' Florrie said with a sigh. 'Proper daft they are sometimes. Although,' she added warmly, 'they're all right really. I s'ppose we're lucky. We've both got family what loves us. Can't complain.'

Immi grinned. 'Tell you what, do you fancy going to the shops down Churchside to see that poster of your sister?'

Florrie's eyes lit up. 'Our Janet? Ooh, yeah! That'd be great.'

'We'll have to sneak out,' Immi said, 'or Mum and Brodie might collar me to give me the big news, and I don't think I'm ready to act all surprised just yet.' She giggled. 'I'll have to practice. You can help me.'

They crept quietly down the stairs, Florrie taking as much care as Immi not to be seen or heard. They both knew Agnes had ears like radar sets when it came to her daughter.

Luckily, no one was in the hallway, though judging from the loud cry of delight from Lawrie that came from the sitting room as Immi carefully pulled open the front door, they were all far too busy celebrating the fact that Brodie had changed his mind about leaving.

They fairly ran down the drive, laughing in delight as they made it out of the gates and onto the pavement outside.

'Did I ever tell you,' Florrie asked as they headed in the direction of Churchside, 'about the murder we 'ad in this village?'

Immi gaped at her. 'Are you joking?'

'Ooh, no! You ain't 'eard? Well, a proper to-do it was, and it caused such a kerfuffle. Mother nearly 'ad a stroke and Poppa had to calm 'er down by promising to make Sir Edward keep the doors locked at all times. Like that would make a difference! What was she scared of anyway? Not like they could've killed 'er an' all, is it?'

'But who was murdered?' Immi asked, her eyes like saucers.

Florrie grinned. 'Let me tell you all about it.'

They headed along the pavement, chatting animatedly as

they went. And if anyone saw Immi deep in conversation with an invisible companion, no one thought anything about it. It was that sort of village, after all.

They were just two little girls. A bit cheeky, prone to eavesdropping, far keener to discuss the grisly details of a murder than they should have been.

And very much loved.

ACKNOWLEDGEMENTS

Thank you so much for reading *Kindred Spirits at Harling Hall*. I hope you enjoyed our first visit to Rowan Vale! None of this would be possible without my readers, and I'm so grateful to each and every one of you for making my dream to be a full-time writer possible.

I may have done the writing, but this book has a whole team behind it, working hard to make sure the story is the best it can be. Thank you to the wonderful Team Boldwood! I'm still pinching myself that I get to be part of this incredible team. I wonder when I'll fully believe it?

Special thanks must go to my editor, Francesca Best, who really understood what I was trying to do and not only let me write this book, but came up with some brilliant suggestions to make it so much better. Thanks also to copy editor, Debra Newhouse, who spotted so much that needed changing, tightening up, or clarifying, and did an amazing job. Thank you to my proofreader Emily Reader for her hard work, and for catching my remaining mistakes, and to the talented Rachel Lawston for the wonderful cover. And thank you to all the behind-the-scenes people like Jenna, Wendy, Ben, and others whose names I'm still learning. It's a big team!

I must also mention Nia Beynon, who took my submission and kindly passed my work onto Francesca. I'm so grateful she did. And, of course, Boldwood's founder and CEO, Amanda Ridout, without whom none of this would be happening!

Being part of Boldwood Books has special significance to me, as four of my Write Romantics friends are also Boldwood writers: Jessica Redland, Jo Bartlett, Helen Rolfe, and Alexandra Weston. It's a real pleasure to have so many friends with the same publisher, and thank you to them all for keeping my secret for so long!

I'm so lucky to have so many supportive writing friends – far too many to name really, and also there's the fear that I'd miss someone out and unintentionally offend them. I hope they know who they are and how much I value them. But I will give a special mention to these two: my good friend, Eliza J Scott, who is always so understanding and the perfect companion to chat writing with – especially over one of our favourite cheese scones; and Helen Phifer, my partner in witchiness! Helen and I have recently started our own Witchy Wednesday Book Chat podcast, and although I've known her for years, it's been an absolute pleasure getting to see her every fortnight – even if it's only on a screen.

Thanks and hugs to my best friend, Jessica Redland. I seriously doubt that I'd be part of Boldwood without her help and encouragement, because I don't think I'd have had the nerve to even try. She has a way of inspiring me and making me believe in myself, and who could ask for more than that?

Finally, a big thank you to The Husband, who hides in the background but is always there for me, cheering me on, commiserating with me when things don't go so well, celebrating when they do, keeping me supplied with an endless stream of coffee as I write, driving me to locations I need to see, and even agreeing to holiday in areas I want to investigate for my books. He is an absolute star and my own hero.

All these wonderful people in my life! How lucky am I?

ABOUT THE AUTHOR

Sharon Booth is the author of feel-good stories set in charming, quirky locations, and now writes cosy romances with a magical twist for Boldwood. She lives with her husband in East Yorkshire, England.

Sign up to Sharon Booth's mailing list for news, competitions and updates on future books.

Visit Sharon's website: www.sharonboothwriter.com

Follow Sharon on social media:

- facebook.com/sharonboothwriter
- instagram.com/sharonboothwriter
- youtube.com/@sharonboothwriter
- bookbub.com/authors/sharon-booth
- pinterest.com/sharonboothwriter

BECOME A MEMBER OF

THE SHELF CARE CLUB

The home of Boldwood's book club reads.

Find uplifting reads, sunny escapes, cosy romances, family dramas and more!

Sign up to the newsletter
https://bit.ly/theshelfcareclub

Boldwood

Boldwood Books is an award-winning fiction publishing company seeking out the best stories from around the world.

Find out more at www.boldwoodbooks.com

Join our reader community for brilliant books, competitions and offers!

Follow us
@BoldwoodBooks
@TheBoldBookClub

Sign up to our weekly deals newsletter

https://bit.ly/BoldwoodBNewsletter

Printed in Great Britain
by Amazon